E. F. BENSON

Map and Lucia

PENGUIN CLASSICS

Published by the Penguin Group
Penguin Books Ltd, 80 Strand, London WC2R ORL, England
Penguin Group (USA) Inc., 375 Hudson Street, New York, New York 10014, USA
Penguin Group (Canada), 90 Eglinton Avenue East, Suite 700, Toronto, Ontario, Canada M4P 2Y3
(a division of Pearson Penguin Canada Inc.)
Penguin Ireland, 25 St Stephen's Green, Dublin 2, Ireland (a division of Penguin Books Ltd)
Penguin Group (Australia), 250 Camberwell Road, Camberwell, Victoria 3124, Australia
(a division of Pearson Australia Group Pty Ltd)
Penguin Books India Pvt Ltd, 11 Community Centre, Panchsheel Park, New Delhi – 110 017, India
Penguin Group (NZ), 67 Apollo Drive, Rosedale, North Shore 0632, New Zealand
(a division of Pearson New Zealand Ltd)
Penguin Books (South Africa) (Pty) Ltd, 24 Sturdee Avenue,
Rosebank, Johannesburg 2196, South Africa

Penguin Books Ltd, Registered Offices: 80 Strand, London WC2R ORL, England

www.penguin.com

First published by Hodder and Stoughton 1935
Published by William Heinemann 1967
Published by Penguin Books 1970
Published in Penguin Classics 2004

I

This edition produced for The Book People Ltd,
Hall Wood Avenue, Haydock, St Helens, WA11 9UL

Copyright © E. F. Benson, 1935
Introduction © Philip Hensher, 2004
All rights reserved

ISBN: 978-1-956-13280-0

www.greenpenguin.co.uk

Penguin Books is committed to a sustainable future
for our business, our readers and our planet.
The book in your hands is made from paper
certified by the Forest Stewardship Council.

£3-20

PENGUIN BOOKS

Mapp and Lucia

Edward Frederic Benson was born in 1867 at Wellington College, where his father Edward White Benson (later Archbishop of Canterbury) was headmaster. He was educated at Marlborough and King's College Cambridge. His main interests were classics and archaeology and from 1892 to 1895 he studied and worked at the British School of Archaeology in Athens. In 1893 his first novel *Dodo* had considerable success, and there followed a stream of novels and biographies, including his famous social comedies, the *Lucia* series, cult books since they were first published in the 1920s. Mayor of Rye from 1934 to 1937, E. F. Benson was awarded the OBE and made an Honorary Fellow of Magdalene College, Cambridge. He died in 1940, having published over 100 books.

Philip Hensher was born in 1965 in London, where he now lives. He is the author of five novels, including *Kitchen Venom* (1996, Penguin 1997), which won the Somerset Maugham Award, *The Mulberry Empire* (2002) which was shortlisted for the W. H. Smith Literary Award, and *The Fit* (2004) as well as a collection of short stories, *The Bedroom of the Mister's Wife* (1999) and the libretto to Thomas Ades's opera, *Powder Her Face*. He is a regular critic and columnist for the *Spectator*, the *Independent* and the *Mail on Sunday*.

*Cordially dedicated to the
Marquess of Carisbrooke*

Mapp and Lucia

Introduction

It is a sad comment on the English nation, no doubt, that it persists in regarding many narratives of humiliation, shame and cruelty as delightful and amusing entertainments, suitable to be given to children. Most English light comedies tell tales as heartbreaking as *Madam Butterfly*. The two wasted lives of Jeeves and Wooster might be deeply moving: the brain of a Keynes condemned to an existence steaming spats, shackled to a man terrified of anyone resembling a grown-up. You can imagine what Gogol would have done with that. How horrible and poignant the Pooters might seem in a rational light, living out their days under the total contempt of everyone they ever meet, including their own family. If you thought about the cast of *Vile Bodies*, *Love in a Cold Climate* or even *The Pickwick Papers* as if they were real people living real lives, you would probably break down in tears of pity. Alas, however, we don't. They are deplorably funny books.

E. F. Benson's rather remarkable achievement is to have written a series of books which hardly contain one single generous or kind action, with a cast of characters with hardly one single redeeming quality between them, which are basically stories about revenge, spite and ruthless ambition; books, however, whose unrelentingly

3

negative view of human nature and delight in the most refined cruelty results in an atmosphere of sunny cheerfulness and exuberant amusement. Orwell said that you couldn't explain to a foreigner why the Jeeves and Wooster books are not indictments of an outdated feudalism. Similarly, when the characters in *Mapp and Lucia* take some elaborate revenge, or are horribly humiliated in their turn, as all of them sooner or later are, it would be difficult to say quite why your laughter is untinged with pity, or, still stranger, why even at their worst-behaved, his characters never stop being lovable.

The pleasure of *Mapp and Lucia* is summed up, surely, in Alice Roosevelt's *bon mot*: 'If you have nothing good to say about anybody,' she is supposed to have said, 'come and sit right by me.' This sordid and unforgiving tale of unfulfilled bourgeois life in the English provinces portrays characters of quite monstrous selfishness and cruelty, devoted to humiliating each other in public, telling lies and compensating in heartbreaking ways for the frustrations and narrowness of their lives. Lucia herself is monstrously selfish, snobbish, ruthless, wildly affected, prone to absurd fads and vain.

Considering that nobody in *Mapp and Lucia* has anything at all to do all day long, they exist in a condition of extraordinary haste. They 'hurry home'; they 'bustle back'; they 'slant across the street . . . making a beeline . . .'; they 'dart' and 'scuttle' and 'scamper'. What is all this hurry in aid of? Why, to carry the latest despatches from the war. 'War' may seem a strong word, but it seems quite reasonable to the inhabitants of Tilling; fey Georgie gloriously says at one moment 'I feel like the fourth of August, 1914.' Novels establish their own scale of drama; when Jane Austen's Emma tells Miss Bates on Box Hill how boring she is, it has roughly the same catastrophic quality as the battle of Waterloo in *Vanity Fair*. And we, too, believe in the life-and-death struggle for power in a small country town, fought over games of bridge and tea parties.

It is a war between Miss Elizabeth Mapp, a long-time resident of Tilling, and a newcomer, Mrs Emmeline Lucas, or Lucia. Miss Mapp, before Lucia's arrival, was the undoubted queen of local society. Mean, bossy and pinching in her household arrangements, her tyrannical position over Tilling is more tenuous than she knows, resting on nagging and the undisputed primacy of her house. When Lucia arrives, renting the house for the summer, it is very quickly clear that here is someone who can run rings around poor Mapp. Subsequently, Mapp may win minor skirmishes in the vicious social struggle: Lucia, unfailingly, wins every major battle, and yet Mapp limps on from humiliation to humiliation.

Lucia, really, is not much less ghastly than Mapp. She is an unspeakable snob, an egotist and a bully, uses her thin smatterings of music, literature and foreign languages entirely for the purposes of showing off, and almost entirely without a sense of humour. Nevertheless, she wins every battle with Mapp, and we always hope that Quaint Irene will be proved right when she predicts that 'that old witch will get what for'. 'As usual,' Georgie reflects at one point, 'Lucia had come out on top.' What she does have, in inexhaustible amounts, is energy, which is always immensely attractive – 'lovable energy', as the padre has it in his premature obsequies, or 'full of pep and pop and vim', as someone else puts it. Mapp is mean-minded and frequently vindictive; Lucia's ambitions are exercised on a much larger scale, and she never stoops to revenge, is always sickeningly magnanimous. In the end, we love her because she is a radiator, where Mapp is a drain. She is one of those characters, like Jane Austen's Mrs Elton – another addict of Italian – whom everyone secretly loves for their energy.

Although Lucia's superiority over Mapp is somehow sealed by her being a widow rather than a spinster, it's one of E. F. Benson's most brilliant strokes to make it clear that she has absolutely no interest in sex. After all, you have to have sex with someone else; and Lucia hardly notices whether anyone else is even in the room. Similarly, what would be the point of Lucia learning Italian properly? She doesn't have much interest in holding a conversation with anyone else even in English.

Quite how Lucia contrives such overwhelming victories over Mapp is an interesting question, and it's worth looking at her first major triumph to see how she does it. In chapter five, Mapp's habit of snooping around her rented house is foiled by a clasp on the front door, and in the subsequent conversation, protesting about Lucia holding a vast fête in her garden, is comprehensively routed. How does Lucia do it? The reason is, surely, that Mapp fails to pick her battles. There is no reason on earth for her to sneak into her house, and once she has broken the clasp, Lucia can bring off the following rather brilliant coup:

'The fête itself, dear one' [Mapp] said, 'is what I must speak about. I cannot possibly permit it to take place in my garden . . . And how do I know that they will not steal upstairs and filch what they can find?'

'"There will be no admission to the rooms in the house," [Lucia] said. "I will lock all the doors, and I am sure that nobody in Tilling will be so ill bred as to attempt to force them open."'

Mapp, surely, has a point in not wanting a general fête to be held in her house by her tenant, but she has allowed Lucia to bring off a showy double, complimenting the good manners of the town and insulting her directly. Within a page or two, Lucia is transforming her opponent's position until she is made to feel that she has suggested that the fête should include a menagerie of wild animals, and is proposing to tell Lucia who she may or may not invite round for tea. The splendid stroke is that, immediately afterwards, Mapp goes round to take it out on poor Diva, as a bullied child goes home and kicks the dog, and starts using Lucia's exact ripostes on her, where they make no sense whatsoever. The reason Lucia always wins is that she picks her battles very carefully, and waits until exactly the right moment. Over the fête, the affair of the returned pictures, or the stolen recipe for Lobster a la Riseholme, she carefully preserves the appearance of great magnanimity, and then ruthlessly strikes. Mapp, on the other hand, is always being assaulted by her own mean-minded chickens, coming home to roost; always having to force down her own revolting marrow jam over tea.

Mapp and Lucia are only part of it, of course, and they are surrounded by an enchanting cast of one-note grotesques, their wavering and periodically disloyal troops. Glorious as they are, most of them only do one thing; Mr Wyse is always bowing, Susan is forever coming up the road in the Rolls in her sable, the padre is always speaking in a sort of Scotch and his wife never says anything, merely squeaks. (To be strictly accurate, she does very occasionally say something, but only ever as reported speech, as if she can't quite be heard). Even Georgie, the Major and Quaint Irene, who are a little more varied in their habits, run along very clear grooves, doing pretty well exactly the same thing from one end of the novel to the other. They may surprise each other – 'No!' is their favourite exclamation – but they don't surprise us, and we know that at any moment, Georgie is doing his needlework, Quaint Irene is painting some naked models while a six-foot maid brings in the refreshments, and the Major is calling 'Quai-hai!'. All change is quite superficial, and order is very soon restored.

Rationally, it ought to grow dull, but it doesn't; one could watch Mr Wyse bowing for ever. The enchantment of the unchanging simplicity is in the way it seems almost to reduce us to children, for whom grown-ups, once glimpsed, have their characters defined forever. I remember, for instance, when I was very young, being shouted at by a neighbour of my grandmother's for bouncing a ball off his car; a month later, he came round for a cup of tea when we happened to be there, and I was astonished that, in fact, he didn't shout at everybody all the time. The sunny quality of the novel, surely, is down to the unchanging simplicity of the characters. Just as Waugh said about P. G. Wodehouse, when nothing ever changes and nothing ever will, there is a sense of a lost paradise. Benson's Tilling, Wodehouse's Blandings Castle, even the Grossmiths's suburban villa have a little touch of the Garden of Eden, where monstrous behaviour is safely contained by our knowledge that nothing here will ever really alter.

The language is demonically intense throughout: 'innumerable crises might still arise, volcanoes smoked, thunder-clouds threated, there were hostile and malignant forces to be thwarted'; the town 'boiled and seethed with excitements'; a character is 'an early bird feeding on the worms of affliction'. People cry out, scream, shudder, rush, mount 'counter-attacks' and 'manoeuvres', plan 'campaigns' in their 'Napoleonic brains,' are 'rent with pangs of jealousy'. Sometimes, it sounds as extreme as Mrs Radcliffe. But we always know that these are not real dangers, and indeed the source of much enjoyment, however extreme the language; at one crisis, we are told that 'the tension next day grew very pleasant'. And when a real danger arises, and Mapp and Lucia's lives are threatened, there is no real horror there either, because we know that they will be safe, and in the end have an interesting experience. To put it like that makes Benson sound trivial, but there is an insight about *Mapp and Lucia*, as well as charm and amusement; these people, entering with such passion and intensity into the smallest details of their lives, find themselves very well equipped to deal with any situation when it arises. Of course Lucia behaved very well when swept out to sea: someone who could wrest the role of Queen Elizabeth from Daisy Quantock against all odds could, if required, have led a cavalry charge.

E. F. Benson was an extraordinary member of an extraordinary family. His father was a very prominent figure in late-Victorian England, both as headmaster of Wellington College and subsequently as Archbishop of

Canterbury. Somehow, this respectable man produced a ripely eccentric brood of six children. All except the eldest, who died young, were prolific authors; none married; and all, it is plausibly thought, were homosexual or lesbian. Benson was a specifically late-Victorian type, the sportsman as aesthete; some of his novels indulge themselves in Wagnerian *sehnsucht* on the subject of cricket matches, and he represented England at figure-skating competitions in his youth. He lived much of his life in Rye, in Sussex, in Henry James's old house, immortalizing it as Tilling in the Mapp and Lucia books and serving three times as its mayor. The town returned, and continues to return its devotion; a casual visitor to the town, even now, may easily leave with the impression that its more literary residents are prouder of Benson than of Henry James.

Benson was a prolific writer, and despite his image as a Edwardian gentleman-of-letters, was an efficient professional, turning out biographies, novels, plays and more miscellaneous offerings in large numbers. Though the Mapp and Lucia novels are his best-known works now, his admirable and ingenious ghost stories are still read, and probably rank in merit only slightly behind those of M. R. James in that delightful Edwardian genre. Further investigation of the vast Benson oeuvre always turns up something with a powerful period atmosphere, if not often a great work of literature. He is very much the sort of writer in whose name people found societies and put on fancy dress; and once or twice, such as in *Mapp and Lucia*, his facility looks very much like true inspiration.

They are essentially Edwardian books in tone and

confidence, though published long afterwards; occasional later fads turn up, such as sunbathing, Quaint Irene's cocktails, and bridge, but the whole atmosphere comes from the long Edwardian summer. It still seems immensely daring, in a subsequent book in the series, for Lucia to take to bicycling; a fad, surely, of the 1890s rather than the 1930s. The spectre of the Great War is nowhere felt – it is amazing that Georgie even knows about August 1914. In reality, men like Georgie were destroyed by shell-shock; women like Mapp were robbed of any chance of marriage; and men very like the Major sent men very much like Cadman the chauffeur to their deaths. Edwardian light literature, on the other hand, revelled and delighted in malice, cruelty, and sheer horror. The ghost stories of M. R. James, the short stories of Saki, the macabre rhymes of Harry Graham lightly evoke horror and beastliness, secure from any real possibility of harm. *Mapp and Lucia*, too, loves malice, and sees it in the end as harmless, contained and even enjoyable. It is the last breath of the Edwardian; the last moment, perhaps, when it seemed as if nothing could ever come to harm.

Philip Hensher, 2004

I

Though it was nearly a year since her husband's death, Emmeline Lucas (universally known to her friends as Lucia) still wore the deepest and most uncompromising mourning. Black certainly suited her very well, but that had nothing to do with this continued use of it, whatever anybody said. Pepino and she had been the most devoted couple for over twenty-five years, and her grief at his loss was heart-felt: she missed him constantly and keenly. But months ago now, she, with her very vital and active personality, had felt a most natural craving to immerse herself again in all those thrilling interests which made life at this Elizabethan village of Riseholme so exciting a business, and she had not yet been able to make up her mind to take the plunge she longed for. Though she had not made a luxury out of the tokens of grief, she had perhaps made, ever so slightly, a stunt of them.

For instance. There was that bookshop on the green, 'Ye Signe of ye Daffodille', under the imprint of which Pepino had published his severely limited edition of *Fugitive Lyrics* and *Pensieri Persi*. A full six months after his death Lucia had been walking past it with Georgie Pillson, and had seen in the window a book she would have liked to purchase. But next to it, on the shelf, was the thin volume of Pepino's *Pensieri Persi*, and, frankly, it had been rather stuntish of her to falter on the threshold and, with eyes that were doing their best to swim, to say to Georgie:

'I can't quite face going in, Georgie. Weak of me, I know, but there it is. Will you please just pop in, caro, and ask them to send me *Beethoven's Days of Boyhood*? I will stroll on.'

So Georgie had pressed her hand and done this errand for her, and of course he had repeated this pathetic little incident to others. Tasteful embroideries had been tacked on to it, and it was soon known all over Riseholme that poor Lucia had gone into 'Ye Signe of ye Daffodille' to buy the book about Beethoven's boyhood, and had been so sadly affected by the sight of Pepino's poems in their rough brown linen cover with dark green tape to tie them up with (although she constantly saw the same volume in her own house), that she had quite broken down. Some said that sal volatile had been administered.

Similarly, she had never been able to bring herself to have a game of golf, or to resume her Dante-readings, and having thus established the impression that her life had been completely smashed up it had been hard to decide that on Tuesday or Wednesday next she would begin to glue it together again. In consequence she had remained in as many pieces as before. Like a sensible woman she was very careful of her physical health, and since this stunt of mourning made it impossible for her to play golf or take brisk walks, she sent for a very illuminating little book, called *An Ideal System of Callisthenics for those no longer Young*, and in a secluded glade of her garden she exposed as much of herself as was proper to the invigorating action of the sun, when there was any, and had long bouts of skipping, and kicked, and jerked, and swayed her trunk, gracefully and vigorously, in accordance with the instructions laid down. The effect was most satisfactory, and at the very, very back of her mind she conceived it possible that some day she might conduct callisthenic classes for those ladies of Riseholme who were no longer young.

Then there was the greater matter of the Elizabethan fête to be held in August next, when Riseholme would be swarming with tourists. The idea of it had been entirely Lucia's, and there had been several meetings of the fête-Committee (of which, naturally, she was President) before Pepino's death. She had planned the great scene in it: this was to be Queen Elizabeth's visit to the *Golden Hind*, when, on the completion of Francis Drake's circumnavigation of the world, Her Majesty went to dine with him on board his ship at Deptford and knighted him. The *Golden Hind* was to be moored in the pond on the village green; or, more accurately, a platform on piles was to be built there, in the shape of a ship's deck, with masts and rudder and cannons and bulwarks, and banners and ancients, particularly ancients. The pond would be an admirable stage, for rows of benches would be put up all round it, and everybody would see beautifully. The Queen's procession with trumpeters and men-at-arms and ladies of the Court was planned to start from the Hurst, which was Lucia's house, and make its glittering and melodious way across the green to Deptford to the sound of madrigals and medieval marches. Lucia would impersonate the Queen, Pepino following her as Raleigh, and Georgie would be Francis Drake. But at an early stage of these incubations Pepino had died, and Lucia had involved herself in this inextricable widowhood. Since then the reins of government had fallen into Daisy Quantock's podgy little hands, and she, in this as in all other matters, had come to consider herself quite the Queen of Riseholme, until Lucia could get a move on again and teach her better.

One morning in June, some seven weeks before the date fixed for the fête, Mrs Quantock telephoned from her house a hundred yards away to say that she particularly wanted to see Lucia, if she might pop over for a little talk. Lucia had heard nothing lately about the preparations for the fête, for the last time that it had been mentioned in her presence, she had gulped and sat with her hand over her eyes for a moment overcome with the memory of how gaily she had planned it. But she knew that the preparations for it must by this time be well in hand, and now she instantly guessed that it was on this subject that Daisy wanted to see her. She had premonitions of that kind sometimes, and she was sure that this was one of them. Probably Daisy wanted to address a moving appeal to her that, for the sake of Riseholme generally, she should make this fête the occasion of her emerging from her hermetic widowhood. The idea recommended itself to Lucia, for before the date fixed for it, she would have been a widow for over a year, and she reflected that her dear Pepino would never have wished her to make this permanent suttee of herself: also there was the prestige of Riseholme to be considered. Besides, she was really itching to get back into the saddle again, and depose Daisy from her awkward,

clumsy seat there, and this would be an admirable opportunity. So, as was usual now with her, she first sighed into the
telephone, said rather faintly that she would be delighted to see
dear Daisy, and then sighed again. Daisy, very stupidly, hoped
she had not got a cough, and was reassured on that point.

Lucia gave a few moments' thought as to whether she would
be found at the piano, playing the funeral march from Beethoven's Sonata in A flat which she now knew by heart, or be
sitting out in Perdita's garden, reading Pepino's poems. She decided on the latter, and putting on a shady straw hat with a
crêpe bow on it, and taking a copy of the poems from the shelf,
hurried out into Perdita's garden. She also carried with her a
copy of today's *Times*, which she had not yet read.

Perdita's garden requires a few words of explanation. It was a
charming little square plot in front of the timbered façade of
the Hurst, surrounded by yew hedges and intersected with
paths of crazy pavement, carefully smothered in stone-crop,
which led to the Elizabethan sundial from Wardour Street in
the centre. It was gay in spring with those flowers (and no
others) on which Perdita doted. There were 'violets dim', and
primroses and daffodils, which came before the swallow dared
and took the winds (usually of April) with beauty. But now in
June the swallow had dared long ago, and when spring and the
daffodils were over, Lucia always allowed Perdita's garden a
wider, though still strictly Shakespearean scope. There was eg-
lantine (Penzance briar) in full flower now, and honeysuckle
and gillyflowers and plenty of pansies for thoughts, and yards
of rue (more than usual this year), and so Perdita's garden was
gay all the summer.

Here then, this morning, Lucia seated herself by the sundial,
all in black, on a stone bench on which was carved the motto
'Come thou north wind, and blow thou south, that my garden
spices may flow forth'. Sitting there with Pepino's poems and
The Times she obscured about one-third of this text, and fat
little Daisy would obscure the rest. . . . It was rather annoying
that the tapes which tied the covers of Pepino's poems had got
into a hard knot, which she was quite unable to unravel, for she
had meant that Daisy should come up, unheard by her, in her

absorption, and find her reading Pepino's lyric called 'Lone-liness'. But she could not untie the tapes, and as soon as she heard Daisy's footsteps she became lost in reverie with the book lying shut on her lap, and the famous far-away look in her eyes.

It was a very hot morning. Daisy, like many middle-aged women who enjoy perfect health, was always practising some medical regime of a hygienic nature, and just now she was a devoted slave to the eliminative processes of the body. The pores of the skin were the most important of these agencies, and, after her drill of physical jerks by the open window of her bedroom, she had trotted in all this heat across the green to keep up the elimination. She mopped and panted for a little.

'Made quite a new woman of me,' she said. 'You should try it, dear Lucia. But so good of you to see me, and I'll come to the point at once. The Elizabethan fête, you know. You see it won't be till August. Can't we persuade you, as they say, to come amongst us again? We all want you: such a fillip you'd give it.'

Lucia made no doubt that this request implied the hope that she might be induced to take the part of Queen Elizabeth, and under the spell of the exuberant sunshine that poured in upon Perdita's garden, she felt the thrill and the pulse of life bound in her veins. The fête would be an admirable occasion for entering the arena of activities again, and, as Daisy had hinted (delicately for Daisy), more than a year of her widowhood would have elapsed by August. It was self-sacrificing, too, of Daisy to have suggested this herself, for she knew that according to present arrangements Daisy was to take the part of the Virgin Queen, and Georgie had told her weeks ago (when the subject of the fête had been last alluded to) that she was already busy pricking her fingers by sewing a ruff to go round her fat little neck, and that she had bought a most sumptuous string of Woolworth pearls. Perhaps dear Daisy had realized what a very ridiculous figure she would present as Queen, and was anxious for the sake of the fête to retire from so laughable a rôle. But, however that might be, it was nice of her to volunteer abdication.

Lucia felt that it was only proper that Daisy should press her a little. She was being asked to sacrifice her personal feelings which so recoiled from publicity, and for the sake of Riseholme to rescue the fête from being a farce. She was most eager to do so, and a very little pressing would be sufficient. So she sighed again, she stroked the cover of Pepino's poems, but she spoke quite briskly.

'Dear Daisy,' she said, 'I don't think I could face it. I cannot imagine myself coming out of my house in silks and jewels to take my place in the procession without my Pepino. He was to have been Raleigh, you remember, and to have walked immediately behind me. The welcome, the shouting, the rejoicing, the madrigals, the Morris-dances and me with my poor desolate heart! But perhaps I ought to make an effort. My dear Pepino, I know, would have wished me to. You think so, too, and I have always respected the soundness of your judgement.'

A slight change came over Daisy's round red face. Lucia was getting on rather too fast and too far.

'My dear, none of us ever thought of asking you to be Queen Elizabeth,' she said. 'We are not so unsympathetic, for of course that would be far too great a strain on you. You must not think of it. All that I was going to suggest was that you might take the part of Drake's wife. She only comes forward just for a moment, and makes her curtsey to me – I mean to the Queen – and then walks backwards again into the chorus of ladies-in-waiting and halberdiers and things.'

Lucia's beady eyes dwelt for a moment on Daisy's rather anxious face with a glance of singular disdain. What a fool poor Daisy was to think that she, Lucia, could possibly consent to take any subordinate part in tableaux or processions or anything else at Riseholme where she had been Queen so long! She had decided in her own mind that with a very little judicious pressing she would take the part of the Queen, and thus make her superb entry into Riseholme life again, but all the pressure in the world would not induce her to impersonate anyone else, unless she could double it with the Queen. Was there ever anything so tactless as Daisy's tact . . . ?

She gave a wintry smile, and stroked the cover of Pepino's poems again.

'Sweet of you to suggest it, dear,' she said, 'but indeed it would be quite too much for me. I was wrong to entertain the idea even for a moment. Naturally I shall take the greatest, the *very* greatest interest in it all, and I am sure you will understand if I do not even feel equal to coming to it, and read about it instead in the *Worcestershire Herald.*'

She paused. Perhaps it would be more in keeping with her empty heart to say nothing more about the fête. On the other hand, she felt a devouring curiosity to know how they were getting on. She sighed.

'I must begin to interest myself in things again,' she said. 'So tell me about it all, Daisy, if you would like to.'

Daisy was much relieved to know that even the part of Drake's wife was too much for Lucia. She was safe now from any risk of having the far more arduous part of the Queen snatched from her.

'All going splendidly,' she said. 'Revels on the Green to open with, and madrigals and Morris-dances. Then comes the scene on the *Golden Hind* which was entirely your idea. We've only elaborated it a little. There will be a fire on the poop of the ship, or is it the prow?'

'It depends, dear, which end of the ship you mean,' said Lucia.

'The behind part, the stern. Poop, is it? Well, there will be a fire on the poop for cooking. Quite safe, they say, if the logs are laid on a sheet of iron. Over the fire we shall have an Elizabethan spit, and roast a sheep on it.'

'I wouldn't,' said Lucia, feeling the glamour of these schemes glowing in her. 'Half of it will be cinders and the rest blood.'

'No, dear,' said Daisy. 'It will really be roasted first at the Ambermere Arms, and then just hung over the fire on the *Golden Hind.*'

'Oh, yes: just to get a little kippered in the smoke,' said Lucia.

'Not to matter. Of course I shan't really eat any, because I never touch meat of any sort now: I shall only pretend to. But there'll be the scene of cooking going on for the Queen's dinner on the deck of the *Golden Hind*, just to fill up, while the Queen's procession is forming. Oh, I wonder if you would let us start the procession from your house rather than mine. The route would be so much more in the open: everyone will see it better. I would come across to dress, if you would let me, half an hour before.'

Lucia of course knew perfectly well that Daisy was to be the Queen, but she wanted to make her say so.

'Certainly start from here,' said Lucia. 'I am only too happy to help. And dress here yourself. Let me see: what are you going to be?'

'They've all insisted that I should be Queen Elizabeth,' said Daisy hurriedly. 'Where had we got to? Oh yes: as the procession is forming, the cooking will be going on. Songs of course, a chorus of cooks. Then the procession will cross the Green to the *Golden Hind*, then dinner, and then I knight Drake. Such a lovely sword. Then Elizabethan games, running, jumping, wrestling and so on. We thought of baiting a bear, one out of some menagerie that could be trusted not to get angry, but we've given that up. If it didn't get angry, it wouldn't be baited, and if it did get angry it would be awful.'

'Very prudent,' said Lucia.

'Then I steal away into the Ambermere Arms which is quite close, and change into a riding-dress. There'll be a white palfrey at the door, the one that draws the milk-cart. Oh, I forgot. While I'm dressing, before the palfrey comes round, a rider gallops in from Plymouth on a horse covered with soap-suds to say that the Spanish Armada has been sighted. I think we must have a megaphone for that, or no one will hear. So I come out, and mount my palfrey, and make my speech to my troops at Tilbury. A large board, you know, with Tilbury written up on it like a station. That's quite in the Shakespearean style. I shall have to learn it all by heart, and just have Raleigh standing by the palfrey with a copy of my speech to prompt me if I forget.'

The old familiar glamour glowed brighter and brighter to Lucia as Daisy spoke. She wondered if she had made a mistake in not accepting the ludicrous part of Drake's wife, just in order to get a footing in these affairs again and attend committees, and, gradually ousting Daisy from her supremacy, take the part of the Queen herself. She felt that she must think it all over, and settle whether, in so advanced a stage of the proceedings, it could be done. At present, till she had made up her mind, it was wiser, in order to rouse no suspicions, to pretend that these things were all very remote. She would take a faint though kindly interest in them, as if some elderly person was watching children at play, and smiling pensively at their pretty gambols. But as for watching the fête when the date arrived, that was unthinkable. She would either be Queen Elizabeth herself, or not be at Riseholme at all. That was that.

'Well, you have got your work cut out for you, dear Daisy,' she said, giving a surreptitious tug at the knotted tape of Pepino's poems. 'What fun you will have, and, dear me, how far away it all seems!'

Daisy wrenched her mind away from the thought of the fête.

'It won't always, dear,' she said, making a sympathetic little dab at Lucia's wrist. 'Your joy in life will revive again. I see you've got Pepino's poems there. Won't you read me one?'

Lucia responded to this gesture with another dab.

'Do you remember the last one he wrote?' she said. 'He called it "Loneliness". I was away in London at the time. Beginning:

"The spavined storm-clouds limp down the ruinous sky,
    While I sit alone.
Thick through the acid air the dumb leaves fly ..."

But I won't read it you now. Another time.'

Daisy gave one more sympathetic poke at her wrist, and rose to go.

'Must be off,' she said. 'Won't you come round and dine quietly tonight?'

'I can't, many thanks. Georgie is dining with me. Any news in Riseholme this morning?'

Daisy reflected for a moment.

'Oh, yes,' she said. 'Mrs Arbuthnot's got a wonderful new apparatus. Not an ear-trumpet at all. She just bites on a small leather pad, and hears everything perfectly. Then she takes it out of her mouth and answers you, and puts it back again to listen.'

'No!' said Lucia excitedly. 'All wet?'

'Quite dry. Just between her teeth. No wetter anyhow than a pen you put in your mouth, I assure you.'

Daisy hurried away to do some more exercises and drink pints and pints of hot water before lunch. She felt that she had emerged safely from a situation which might easily have become menacing, for without question Lucia, in spite of her sighs and her wistful stroking of the covers of Pepino's poems, and her great crêpe bow, was beginning to show signs of her old animation. She had given Daisy a glance or two from that beady eye which had the qualities of a gimlet about it, she had shown eager interest in such topics as the roasting of the sheep and Mrs Arbuthnot's gadget, which a few weeks ago would not have aroused the slightest response from her stricken mind, and it was lucky, Daisy thought, that Lucia had given her the definite assurance that even the part of Drake's wife in the fête would be too much for her. For goodness only knew, when once Lucia settled to be on the mend, how swift her recuperation might be, or what mental horse-power in the way of schemings and domination she might not develop after this fallow period of quiescence. There was a new atmosphere about her today: she was like some spring morning when, though winds might still be chilly and the sun still of tepid and watery beams, the air was pregnant with the imminent birth of new life. But evidently she meant to take no hand in the fête, which at present completely filled Daisy's horizon. 'She may do what she likes afterwards,' thought Daisy, breaking into a trot, 'but I will be Queen Elizabeth.'

Her house, with its mulberry-tree in front and its garden at the back, stood next to Georgie Pillson's on the edge of the Green, and as she passed through it and out on to the lawn behind, she heard from the other side of the paling that tap-tap of croquet-mallet and ball which now almost without cessation punctuated the hours of any fine morning. Georgie had developed a craze for solitary croquet: he spent half the day practising all by himself, to the great neglect of his water-colour painting and his piano-playing. He seemed indeed, apart from croquet, to be losing his zest for life; he took none of his old interest in the thrilling topics of Riseholme. He had not been a bit excited at Daisy's description of Mrs Arbuthnot's new apparatus, and the prospect of impersonating Francis Drake at the forthcoming fête aroused only the most tepid enthusiasm in him. A book of Elizabethan costumes, full of sumptuous coloured plates, had roused him for a while from his lethargy, and he had chosen a white satin tunic with puffed sleeves slashed with crimson, and a cloak of rose-coloured silk, on the reproduction of which his peerless parlour-maid Foljambe was at work, but he didn't seem to have any keenness about him. Of course he had had some rather cruel blows of Fate to contend against lately: Miss Olga Bracely the *prima donna* to whom he had been so devoted had left Riseholme a month ago for a year's operatic tour in the United States and Australia, and that was a desolate bereavement for him, while Lucia's determination not to do any of all those things which she had once enjoyed so much had deprived him of all the duets they used to play together. Moreover, it was believed in Riseholme (though only whispered at present) that Foljambe, that paragon of parlour-maids, in whom the smoothness and comfort of his domestic life was centred, was walking out with Cadman, Lucia's chauffeur. It might not mean anything, but if it did, if Foljambe and he intended to get married and Foljambe left Georgie, and if Georgie had got wind of this, then indeed there would be good cause for that lack of zest, that air of gloom and apprehension which was now so often noticeable in him. All these causes, the blows Fate had already rained on him, and the anxiety concerning this possible catastrophe in the future, probably contributed to the eclipsed condition of his energies.

Daisy sat down on a garden-bench, and began to do a little deep-breathing, which was a relic of the days when she had studied Yoga. It was important to concentrate (otherwise the deep-breathing did no good at all), or rather to attain a complete blankness of mind and exclude from it all mundane interests which were Maya, or illusion. But this morning she found it difficult: regiments of topics grew up like mushrooms. Now she congratulated herself on having made certain that Lucia was not intending to butt into the fête, now she began to have doubts – these were disconcerting mushrooms – as to whether that was so certain, for Lucia was much brisker today than she had been since Pepino's death, and if that continued, her re-awakened interest in life would surely seek for some outlet. Then the thought of her own speech to her troops at Tilbury began to leak into her mind: would she ever get it so thoroughly by heart that she could feel sure that no attack of nervousness or movement on the part of her palfrey would put it out of her head? Above all there was that disturbing tap-tap going on from Georgie's garden, and however much she tried to attain blank-ness of mind, she found herself listening for the next tap. . . . It was no use and she got up.

'Georgie, are you there?' she called out.

'Yes,' came his voice, trembling with excitement. 'Wait a minute. I've gone through nine hoops and – Oh, how tarsome, I missed quite an easy one. What is it? I rather wish you hadn't called me just then.'

Georgie was tall, and he could look over the paling. Daisy pulled her chair up to it, and mounted on it, so that they could converse with level heads.

'So sorry, Georgie,' she said, 'I didn't know you were making such a break. Fancy! Nine! I wanted to tell you I've been to see Lucia.'

'Is that all? I knew that because I saw you,' said Georgie. 'I was polishing my bibelots in the drawing-room. And you sat in Perdita's garden.'

'And there's a change,' continued Daisy, who had kept her mouth open, in order to go on again as soon as Georgie stopped. 'She's better. Distinctly. More interested, and not so faint and die-away. Sarcastic about the roast sheep for instance.'

'What? Did she talk about the fête again?' asked Georgie. 'That is an improvement.'

'That was what I went to talk about. I asked her if she wouldn't make an effort to be Drake's wife. But she said it would be too great a strain.'

'My dear, you didn't ask her to be Drake's wife?' said Georgie

24

incredulously. 'You might as well have asked her to be a confused noise within. What can you have been thinking of?'

'Anyhow, she said she couldn't be anything at all,' said Daisy. 'I have her word for that. But if she is recovering, and I'm sure she is, her head will be full of plans again. I'm not quite happy about it.'

'What you mean is that you're afraid she may want to be the Queen,' observed Georgie acutely.

'I won't give it up,' said Daisy very firmly, not troubling to confirm so obvious an interpretation. 'I've had all the trouble of it, and very nearly learnt the speech to the troops, and made my ruff and bought a rope of pearls. It wouldn't be fair, Georgie. So don't encourage her, will you? I know you're dining with her tonight.'

'No, I won't encourage her,' said he. 'But you know what Lucia is, when she's in working order. If she wants a thing, she gets it somehow. It happens. That's all you can say about it.'

'Well, this one shan't happen,' said Daisy, dismounting from her basket-chair which was beginning to sag. 'It would be too mean. And I wish you would come across now and let us practise that scene where I knight you. We must get it very slick.'

'Not this morning,' said Georgie. 'I know my bit: I've only got to kneel down. You can practise on the end of a sofa. Besides, if Lucia is really waking up, I shall take some duets across this evening, and I must have a go at some of them. I've not touched my piano for weeks. And my shoulder's sore where you knighted me so hard the other day. Quite a bruise.'

Daisy suddenly remembered something more.

'And Lucia repeated me several lines out of one of Pepino's last poems,' she said. 'She couldn't possibly have done that a month ago without breaking down. And I believe she would have read one to me when I asked her to, but I'm pretty sure she couldn't undo one of those tapes that the book is tied up with. A hard knot. She was picking at it . . .'

'Oh, she must be better,' said he. 'Ever so much.'

So Georgie went in to practise some of the old duets in case Lucia felt equal to evoking the memories of happier days at the piano, and Daisy hit the end of her sofa some half-dozen times with her umbrella bidding it rise Sir Francis Drake. She still wondered if Lucia had some foul scheme in her head, but though there had ticked by some minutes, directly after their talk in Perdita's garden, which might have proved exceedingly dangerous to her own chance of being the Queen, these, by the time that she was knighting the sofa, had passed. For Lucia, still meditating whether she should not lay plots for ousting Daisy, had, in default of getting that knotted tape undone, turned to her unread *Times*, and scanned its columns with a rather absent eye. There was no news that could interest anybody, and her glance wandered up and down the lists of situations vacant and wanted, of the sailings of steamers, and finally of houses to be let for summer months. There was a picture of one with a plain pleasant Queen Anne front looking on to a cobbled street. It was highly attractive, and below it she read that Miss Mapp sought a tenant for her house in Tilling, called Mallards, for the months of August and September. Seven bedrooms, four sitting-rooms h. & c., and an old-world garden. At that precise psycho-logical moment Daisy's prospects of being Queen Elizabeth became vastly rosier, for this house to let started an idea in Lucia's mind which instantly took precedence of other schemes. She must talk to Georgie about it this evening: till then it should simmer. Surely also the name of Miss Mapp aroused faint echoes of memory in her mind: she seemed to remember a large woman with a wide smile who had stayed at the Ambermere Arms a few years ago, and had been very agreeable but slightly superior. Georgie would probably remember her. ... But the sun had become extremely powerful, and Lucia picked up her *Times* and her book of poems and went indoors to the cool lattice-paned parlour where her piano stood. By it was a book-case with volumes of bound-up music, and she drew from it one which contained the duets over which Georgie and she used to be so gay and so industrious. These were Mozart quartettes ar-ranged for four hands, delicious, rippling airs: it was months since she had touched them, or since the music-room had re-sounded to anything but the most sombre and pensive strains. Now she opened the book and put it on the music-rest. 'Uno, due, tre,' she said to herself and began practising the treble part which was the more amusing to play.

Georgie saw the difference in her at once when he arrived for dinner that evening. She was sitting outside in Perdita's garden and for the first time hailed him as of old in brilliant Italian.

'Buona sera, caro,' she said. 'Come sta?'

'Molto bene,' he answered, 'and what a caldo day. I've brought a little music across with me in case you felt inclined. Mozartino.'

'What a good idea! We will have un po' di musica afterwards, but I've got tanto, tanto to talk to you about. Come in: dinner will be ready. Any news?'

'Let me think,' he said. 'No I don't think there's much. I've got rather a bruised shoulder where Daisy knighted me the other day – '

'Dear Daisy!' said Lucia. 'A little heavy-handed sometimes, don't you find? Not a light touch. She was in here this morning talking about the fête. She urged me to take part in it. What part do you think she suggested, Georgie? You'll never guess.'

'I never should have, if she hadn't told me,' he said. 'The most ludicrous thing I ever heard.'

Lucia sighed.

'I'm afraid not much more ludicrous than her being Queen Elizabeth,' she said. 'Daisy on a palfrey addressing her troops! Georgie dear, think of it! It sounds like that rather vulgar game called "Consequences". Daisy, I am afraid, has got tipsy with excitement at the thought of being a queen. She is running amok, and she will make a deplorable exhibition of herself, and Riseholme will become the laughing-stock of all those American tourists who come here in August to see our lovely Elizabethan village. The village will be all right, but what of Elizabeth? Tacete un momenta, Georgie. Le domestiche.'

Georgie's Italian was rusty after so much disuse, but he managed to translate this sentence to himself, and unerringly inferred that Lucia did not want to pursue the subject while Grosvenor, the parlour-maid and her colleague were in the room.

'Sicuro,' he said, and made haste to help himself to his fish. The domestiche thereupon left the room again, to be summoned back by the stroke of a silver bell in the shape of a pomander which nestled among pepper and mustard-pots beside Lucia. Almost before the door had closed on their exit, Lucia began to speak again.

'Of course after poor Daisy's suggestion I shall take no part myself in this fête,' she said; 'and even if she besought me on her knees to play Queen Elizabeth, I could not dream of doing so. She cannot deprive me of what I may call a proper pride, and since she has thought good to offer me the rôle of Drake's wife, who, she hastened to explain, only came on for one moment and curtsied to her, and then retired into the ranks of men-at-arms and ladies-in-waiting again, my sense of dignity, of which I have still some small fragments left, would naturally prevent me from taking any part in the performance, even at the end of a barge-pole. But I am sorry for Daisy, since she knows her own deficiencies so little, and I shall mourn for Riseholme if the poor thing makes such a mess of the whole affair as she most indubitably will if she is left to organize it herself. That's all.'

It appeared, however, that there was a little more, for Lucia quickly finished her fish, and continued at once.

'So after what she said to me this morning, I cannot myself offer to help her, but if you like to do so, Georgie, you can tell her – not from me, mind, but from your own impression – that you think I should be perfectly willing to coach her and make the best I can of her as the embodiment of great Queen Bess. Something might be done with her. She is short, but so was the Queen. She has rather bad teeth, but that doesn't matter, for the Queen had the same. Again she is not quite a lady, but the Queen also had a marked strain of vulgarity and bourgeoisie. There was a coarse fibre in the Tudors, as I have always maintained. All this, dear Georgie, is to the good. If dear Daisy will only not try to look tall, and if she will smile a good deal, and behave naturally these are advantages, real advantages. But in spite of them Daisy will merely make herself and Riseholme silly if she does not manage to get hold of some semblance of dignity and queenship. Little gestures, little turnings of the head, little graciousnesses; all that acting means. I thought it out in those dear old days when we began to plan it, and, as I say, I shall be happy to give poor Daisy all the hints I can, if she will come and ask me to do so. But mind, Georgie, the suggestion must not come from me. You are at liberty to say that you think I possibly might help her, but nothing more than that. Capite?'

This Italian word, not understanded of the people, came rather late, for already Lucia had struck the bell, as, unconsciously, she was emphasizing her generous proposal, and Grosvenor and her satellite had been in the room quite a long time. Concealment from le domestiche was therefore no longer possible. In fact both Georgie and Lucia had forgotten about the domestiche altogether.

'That's most kind of you, Lucia,' said Georgie. 'But you know what Daisy is. As obstinate as – '

'As a palfrey,' interrupted Lucia.

'Yes, quite. Certainly I'll tell her what you say, or rather suggest what you might say if she asked you to coach her, but I don't believe it will be any use. The whole fête has become an awful bore. There are six weeks yet before it's held, and she wants to practise knighting me every day, and has processions up and down her garden, and she gets all the tradesmen in the place to walk before her as halberdiers and sea-captains, when they ought to be attending to their businesses and chopping meat and milking cows. Everyone's sick of it. I wish you would take it over, and be Queen yourself. Oh, I forgot, I promised Daisy I wouldn't encourage you. Dear me, how awful!'

Lucia laughed, positively laughed. This was an enormous improvement on the pensive smiles.

'Not awful at all, Georgino mio,' she said. 'I can well imagine poor Daisy's feverish fear that I should try to save her from being ridiculous. She loves being ridiculous, dear thing; it's a complex with her – that wonderful new book of Freud's which I must read – and subconsciously she pines to be ridiculous on as large a scale as possible. But as for my taking it over, that's quite out of the question. To begin with, I don't suppose I shall be here. Twelfth of August isn't it? Grouse-shooting opens in Scotland and bear-baiting at Riseholme.'

'No, that was given up,' said Georgie. 'I opposed it throughout on the Committee. I said that even if we could get a bear at all, it wouldn't be baited if it didn't get angry – '

Lucia interrupted.

'And that if it did get angry it would be awful,' she put in.

'Yes. How did you know I said that?' asked Georgie. 'Rather neat, wasn't it?'

'Very neat indeed, caro,' said she. 'I knew you said it because Daisy told me she had said it herself.'

'What a cheat!' said Georgie indignantly.

Lucia looked at him wistfully.

'Ah, you mustn't think hardly of poor dear Daisy,' she said. 'Cheat is too strong a word. Just a little envious, perhaps, of bright clever things that other people say, not being very quick herself.'

'Anyhow, I shall tell her that I know she has bagged my joke,' said he.

'My dear, not worth while. You'll make quantities of others. Also trivial, Georgie, not worth noticing. Beneath you.'

Lucia leaned forward with her elbows on the table, quite in the old braced way, instead of drooping.

'But we've got far more important things to talk about than Daisy's little pilferings,' she said. 'Where shall I begin?'

'From the beginning,' said Georgie greedily. He had not felt so keen about the affairs of daily life since Lucia had buried herself in her bereavement.

'Well, the real beginning was this morning,' she said, 'when I saw something in *The Times*.'

'More than I did,' said Georgie. 'Was it about Riseholme or the fête? Daisy said she was going to write a letter to *The Times* about it?'

'I must have missed that,' said Lucia, 'unless by any chance they didn't put it in. No, not about the fête, nor about Riseholme. Very much not about Riseholme. Georgie, do you remember a woman who stayed at the Ambermere Arms one summer called Miss Mapp?'

Georgie concentrated.

'I remember the name, because she was rather globular, like a map of the world,' he said. 'Oh, wait a moment: something's coming back to me. Large, with a great smile. Teeth.'

'Yes, that's the one,' cried Lucia. 'There's telepathy going on, Georgie. We're suggesting to each other. ... Rather like a hyaena, a handsome hyaena. Not hungry now but might be.'

'Yes. And talked about a place called Tilling, where she had a Queen Anne house. We rather despised her for that. Oh, yes, and she came to a garden-party of mine. And I know when it was, too. It was that summer when you invented saying "Au reservoir" instead of "Au revoir". We all said it for about a week and then got tired of it. Miss Mapp came here just about then, because she picked it up at my garden-party. She stopped quite to the end, eating quantities of red-currant fool, and saying that she had inherited a recipe from her grandmother which she would send me. She did, too, and my cook said it was rubbish. Yes: it was the au reservoir year, because she said au reservoir to everyone as they left, and told me she would take it back to Tilling. That's the one. Why?'

'Georgie, your memory's marvellous,' said Lucia. 'Now about the advertisement I saw in *The Times*. Miss Mapp is letting her Queen Anne house called Mallards, h. & c. and old-world garden, for August and September. I want you to drive over with me tomorrow and see it. I think that very likely, if it's at all what I hope, I shall take it.'

'No!' cried Georgie. 'Why of course I'll drive there with you tomorrow. What fun! But it will be too awful if you go away for two months. What shall I do? First there's Olga not coming back for a year, and now you're thinking of going away, and there'll be nothing left for me except my croquet and being Drake.'

Lucia gave him one of those glances behind which lurked so much purpose, which no doubt would be disclosed at the proper time. The bees were astir once more in the hive, and presently they would stream out for swarmings or stingings or honey-harvesting. ... It was delightful to see her looking like that again.

'Georgie, I want change,' she said, 'and though I'm much

touched at the idea of your missing me, I think I must have it. I want to get roused up again and shaken and made to tick. Change of air, change of scene, change of people. I don't suppose anyone alive has been more immersed than I in the spacious days of Elizabeth, or more devoted to Shakespearean tradition and environment – perhaps I ought to except Sir Sidney Lee, isn't it? – than I, but I want for the present anyhow to get away from it, especially when poor Daisy is intending to make this deplorable public parody of all that I have held sacred so long.'

Lucia swallowed three or four strawberries as if they had been pills and took a gulp of water.

'I don't think I could bear to be here for all the rehearsals,' she said; 'to look out from the rue and honeysuckle of my sweet garden and see her on her palfrey addressing her lieges of Riseholme, and making them walk in procession in front of her. It did occur to me this morning that I might intervene, take the part of the Queen myself, and make a pageant such as I had planned in those happy days, which would have done honour to the great age and credit to Riseholme, but it would spoil the dream of Daisy's life, and one must be kind. I wash my hands of it all, though of course I shall allow her to dress here, and the procession to start from my house. She wanted that, and she shall have it, but of course she must state on the programmes that the procession starts from Mrs Philip Lucas's house. It would be too much that the visitors, if there are any, should think that my beautiful Hurst belongs to Daisy. And, as I said, I shall be happy to coach her, and see if I can do anything with her. But I won't be here for the fête, and I must be somewhere and that's why I'm thinking of Tilling.'

They had moved into the music-room where the bust of Shakespeare stood among its vases of flowers, and the picture of Lucia by Tancred Sigismund, looking like a chessboard with some arms and legs and eyes sticking out of it, hung on the wall. There were Georgie's sketches there, and the piano was open, and *Beethoven's Days of Boyhood* was lying on the table with the paper-knife stuck between its leaves, and there was animation about the room once more.

Lucia seated herself in the chair that might so easily have come from Anne Hathaway's cottage, though there was no particular reason for supposing that it did.

'Georgie, I am beginning to feel alive again,' she said. 'Do you remember what wonderful Alfred says in *Maud*? "My life hath crept so long on a broken wing." That's what my life has been doing, but now I'm not going to creep any more. And just for the time, as I say, I'm "off" the age of Elizabeth, partly poor Daisy's fault, no doubt. But there were other ages, Georgie, the age of Pericles, for instance. Fancy sitting at Socrates' feet or Plato's, and hearing them talk while the sun set over Salamis or Pentelicus. I must rub up my Greek, Georgie. I used to know a little Greek at one time, and if I ever manage any tableaux again, we must have the death of Agamemnon. And then there's the age of Anne. What a wonderful time, Pope and Addison! So civilized, so cultivated. Their routs and their tea-parties and rapes of the lock. With all the greatness and splendour of the Elizabethan age, there must have been a certain coarseness and crudity about them. No one reveres it more than I, but it is a mistake to remain in the same waters too long. There comes a tide in the affairs of men, which, if you don't nip it in the bud, leads on to boredom.'

'My dear, is that yours?' said Georgie. 'And absolutely impromptu like that! You're too brilliant.'

It was not quite impromptu, for Lucia had thought of it in her bath. But it would be meticulous to explain that.

'Wicked of me, I'm afraid,' she said. 'But it expresses my feelings just now. I do want a change, and my happening to see this notice of Miss Mapp's in *The Times* seems a very remarkable coincidence. Almost as if it was sent: what they call a leading. Anyhow, you and I will drive over to Tilling tomorrow and see it. Let us make a jaunt of it, Georgie, for it's a long way, and stay the night at an inn there. Then we shall have plenty of time to see the place.'

This was rather a daring project, and Georgie was not quite sure if it was proper. But he knew himself well enough to be certain that no passionate impulse of his would cause Lucia to regret that she had made so intimate a proposal.

'That'll be the greatest fun,' he said. 'I shall take my painting things. I haven't sketched for weeks.'

'Cattivo ragazzo!' said Lucia. 'What have you been doing with yourself?'

'Nothing. There's been no one to play the piano with, and no one, who knows, to show my sketches to. Hours of croquet, just killing the time, Being Drake. How that fête bores me!'

'Oo poor thing!' said Lucia, using again the baby talk in which she and Georgie used so often to indulge. 'But me's back again now, and me will scold oo vewy vewy much if oo does not do your lessons.'

'And me vewy glad to be scolded again,' said Georgie. 'Me idle boy! Dear me, how nice it all is!' he exclaimed enthusiastically.

The clock on the old oak dresser struck ten, and Lucia jumped up.

'Georgie, ten o'clock already,' she cried. 'How time has flown. Now I'll write out a telegram to be sent to Miss Mapp first thing tomorrow to say we'll get to Tilling in the afternoon, to see her house, and then 'ickle musica. There was a Mozart duet we used to play. We might wrestle with it again.'

She opened the book that stood on the piano. Luckily that was the very one Georgie had been practising this morning. (So too had Lucia.)

'That will be lovely,' he said. 'But you mustn't scold me if I play vewy badly. Months since I looked at it.'

'Me too,' said Lucia. 'Here we are! Shall I take the treble? It's a little easier for my poor fingers. Now: Uno, due, tre! Off we go!'

2

They arrived at Tilling in the middle of the afternoon, entering it from the long level road that ran across the reclaimed marsh-land to the west. Blue was the sky overhead, complete with larks and small white clouds; the town lay basking in the hot

June sunshine, and its narrow streets abounded in red-brick houses with tiled roofs, that shouted Queen Anne and George I in Lucia's enraptured ears, and made Georgie's fingers itch for his sketching-tools.

'Dear Georgie, perfectly enchanting!' exclaimed Lucia. 'I declare I feel at home already. Look, there's another lovely house. We must just drive to the end of this street, and then we'll inquire where Mallards is. The people, too, I like their looks. Faces full of interest. It's as if they expected us.'

The car had stopped to allow a dray to turn into the High Street from a steep cobbled way leading to the top of the hill. On the pavement at the corner was standing quite a group of Tillingites: there was a clergyman, there was a little proud bustling woman dressed in a purple frock covered with pink roses which looked as if they were made of chintz, there was a large military-looking man with a couple of golf-clubs in his hand, and there was a hatless girl with hair closely cropped, dressed in a fisherman's jersey and knickerbockers, who spat very neatly in the roadway.

'We must ask where the house is,' said Lucia, leaning out of the window of her Rolls-Royce. 'I wonder if you would be so good as to tell me – '

The clergyman sprang forward.

'It'll be Miss Mapp's house you're seeking,' he said in a broad Scotch accent. 'Straight up the street, to yon corner, and it's richt there is Mistress Mapp's house.'

The odd-looking girl gave a short hoot of laughter, and they all stared at Lucia. The car turned with difficulty and danced slowly up the steep narrow street.

'Georgie, he told me where it was before I asked,' said Lucia. 'It must be known in Tilling that I was coming. What a strange accent that clergyman had! A little tipsy, do you think, or only Scotch? The others too! All most interesting and unusual. Gracious, here's an enormous car coming down. Can we pass, do you think?'

By means of both cars driving on to the pavement on each side of the cobbled roadway, the passage was effected, and Lucia caught sight of a large woman inside the other, who in spite of the heat of the day wore a magnificent sable cloak. A small man with a monocle sat eclipsed by her side. Then, with glimpses of more red-brick houses to right and left, the car stopped at the top of the street opposite a very dignified door. Straight in front where the street turned at a right angle, a room with a large bow-window faced them; this, though slightly separate from the house, seemed to belong to it. Georgie thought he saw a woman's face peering out between half-drawn curtains, but it whisked itself away.

'Georgie, a dream,' whispered Lucia, as they stood on the doorstep waiting for their ring to be answered. 'That wonderful chimney, do you see, all crooked. The church, the cobbles, the grass and dandelions growing in between them. ... Oh, is Miss Mapp in? Mrs Lucas. She expects me.'

They had hardly stepped inside, when Miss Mapp came hurrying in from a door in the direction of the bow-window where Georgie had thought he had seen a face peeping out.

'Dear Mrs Lucas,' she said. 'No need for introductions, which makes it all so happy, for how well I remember you at Riseholme, your lovely Riseholme. And Mr Pillson! Your wonderful garden-party! All so vivid still. Red-letter days! Fancy your having driven all this way to see my little cottage! Tea at once, Withers, please. In the garden-room. Such a long drive, but what a heavenly day for it. I got your telegram at breakfast-time this morning. I could have clapped my hands for joy at the thought of possibly having such a tenant as Mrs Lucas of Riseholme. But let us have a cup of tea first. Your chauffeur? Of course he will have his tea here, too. Withers: Mrs Lucas's chauffeur. Mind you take care of him.'

Miss Mapp took Lucia's cloak from her, and still keeping up an effortless flow of hospitable monologue, led them through a small panelled parlour which opened on to the garden. A flight of eight steps with a canopy of wistaria overhead led to the garden-room.

'My little plot,' said Miss Mapp. 'Very modest, as you see, three-quarters of an acre at the most, but well screened. My flower-beds: sweet roses, tortoise-shell butterflies. Rather a nice clematis. My Little Eden I call it, so small, but so well beloved.'

already, and it wou
the house for twelve
fifteen. Moreover, M
Georgie had seen he
car, so that a few ad
of no significance to
astic about the house
to ask fifteen, for she
say something tireson
when she got safe aw
to be a refusal. But i
about the house when
the price. And not a p
Pipstow, the house-age
said definitely that sh
That was Miss Mapp's
Pipstow. Meantime she
water-colours on the wa

'Little daubs of my
should be known. 'I sh
dear Mr Pillson, if you l
artist you are yourself.
You like the one of my l
that beautiful phrase.) H
isn't quite so bad as the
it's so important, isn't it,
it too. Cream, Mrs Lucas!
berries for us from my li
And Major Benjy was cha
you passed him.'

'Yes, a clergyman,' sai
your house. In fact he se
before I said so, didn't he,

'Dear Padre!' said Miss M
Scotch, though he came fr
player when he can spare
Kenneth Bartlett. Was ther
like a mouse? It would be hi

'Enchanting!' said Lucia, looking round the garden before mounting the steps up to the garden-room door. There was a very green and well-kept lawn, set in bright flower-beds. A trellis at one end separated it from a kitchen-garden beyond, and round the rest ran high brick walls, over which peered the roofs of other houses. In one of these walls was cut a curved archway with a della Robbia head above it.

'Shall we just pop across the lawn,' said Miss Mapp, pointing to this, 'and peep in there while Withers brings our tea? Just to stretch the – the limbs, Mrs Lucas, after your long drive. There's a wee little plot beyond there which is quite a pet of mine. And here's sweet Puss-Cat come to welcome my friends. Lamb! Love-bird!'

Love-bird's welcome was to dab rather crossly at the caressing hand which its mistress extended, and to trot away to ambush itself beneath some fine hollyhocks, where it regarded them with singular disfavour.

'My little secret garden,' continued Miss Mapp as they came to the archway. 'When I am in here and shut the door, I mustn't be disturbed for anything less than a telegram. A rule of the house: I am very strict about it. The tower of the church keeping watch, as I always say, over my little nook, and taking care of me. Otherwise not overlooked at all. A little paved walk round it, you see, flower-beds, a pocket-handkerchief of a lawn, and in the middle a pillar with a bust of good Queen Anne. Picked it up in a shop here for a song. One of my lucky days.'

'Oh Georgie, isn't it too sweet?' cried Lucia. 'Un giardino segreto. Molto bello!'

Miss Mapp gave a little purr of ecstasy.

'How lovely to be able to talk Italian like that,' she said. 'So pleased you like my little . . . giardino segreto, was it? Now shall we have our tea, for I'm sure you want refreshment, and see the house afterwards? Or would you prefer a little whisky and soda, Mr Pillson? I shan't be shocked. Major Benjy – I should say Major Flint – often prefers a small whisky and soda to tea on a hot day after his game of golf, when he pops in to see me and tell me all about it.'

The intense interest in humankind, so strenuously cultivated

at Riseholme, obl...
the secret garden. ...

'I wonder if it w...
Street,' she said. '...
clubs.'

'How you hit h...
miringly. 'That car...
no doubt by the st...
to the links) for a r...
far too hot to play...
naughty and played...
India. Hindustanee...
"quai-hai" when he...
diaries, which we al...
is next to mine dov...
impetuous bridge-pla...
bridge of course, Mrs...
players.'

They had strolled...
where Withers was...
window was shaded...
which, unseen, Miss N...
her gardener was idli...
to the street one curt...
near it, bookcases hal...
many water-colour ske...
estic origin. Their subje...
of the front of Miss Ma...
another of the crooke...
tower looking over the...

Though she continue...
shower of flattering and...
tention was wrestling w...
when it came to the del...
her house, she should as...
tioned in her advertisem...
told the local house-agen...
was clearly more than...

'No, not thin, at all,' said Lucia thoroughly interested. 'Quite the other way round: in fact round. A purple coat and a shirt covered with pink roses that looked as if they were made of chintz.'

Miss Mapp nearly choked over her first sip of tea, but just saved herself.

'I declare I'm quite frightened of you, Mrs Lucas,' she said. 'What an eye you've got. Dear Diva Plaistow, whom we're all devoted to. Christened Godiva! Such a handicap! And they *were* chintz roses, which she cut out of an old pair of curtains and tacked them on. She's full of absurd delicious fancies like that. Keeps us all in fits of laughter. Anyone else?'

'Yes, a girl with no hat and an Eton crop. She was dressed in a fisherman's jersey and knickerbockers.'

Miss Mapp looked pensive.

'Quaint Irene,' she said. 'Irene Coles. Just a touch of unconventionality, which sometimes is very refreshing, but can be rather embarrassing. Devoted to her art. She paints strange pictures, men and women with no clothes on. One has to be careful to knock when one goes to see quaint Irene in her studio. But a great original.'

'And then when we turned up out of the High Street,' said Georgie eagerly, 'we met another Rolls-Royce. I was afraid we shouldn't be able to pass it.'

'So was I,' said Miss Mapp unintentionally betraying the fact that she had been watching from the garden-room. 'That car is always up and down this street here.'

'A large woman in it,' said Lucia. 'Wrapped in sables on this broiling day. A little man beside her.'

'Mr and Mrs Wyse,' said Miss Mapp. 'Lately married. She was Mrs Poppit, M.B.E. Very worthy, and such a crashing snob.'

As soon as tea was over and the inhabitants of Tilling thus plucked and roasted, the tour of the house was made. There were charming little panelled parlours with big windows letting in a flood of air and sunshine and vases of fresh flowers on the tables. There was a broad staircase with shallow treads, and every moment Lucia became more and more enamoured of the plain well-shaped rooms. It all looked so white and comfortable, and, for one wanting a change, so different from the Hurst with its small latticed windows, its steep irregular stairs, its single steps, up or down, at the threshold of every room. People of the age of Anne seemed to have a much better idea of domestic convenience, and Lucia's Italian exclamations grew gratifyingly frequent. Into Miss Mapp's own bedroom she went alone with the owner, leaving Georgie on the landing outside, for delicacy would not permit his looking on the scene where Miss Mapp nightly disrobed herself, and the bed where she nightly disposed herself. Besides, it would be easier for Lucia to ask that important point-blank question of terms, and for herself to answer it if they were alone.

'I'm charmed with the house,' said Lucia. 'And what exactly, how much I mean, for a period of two months – '

'Fifteen guineas a week,' said Miss Mapp without pause. 'That would include the use of my piano. A sweet instrument by Blumenfelt.'

'I will take it for August and September,' said Lucia.

'And I'm sure I hope you'll be as pleased with it,' said Miss Mapp, 'as I'm sure I shall be with my tenant.'

A bright idea struck her, and she smiled more widely than ever.

'That would not include, of course, the wages of my gardener, such a nice steady man,' she said, 'or garden-produce. Flowers for the house by all means, but not fruit or vegetables.'

At that moment Lucia, blinded by passion for Mallards, Tilling and the Tillingites, would have willingly agreed to pay the water-rate as well. If Miss Mapp had guessed that, she would certainly have named this unusual condition.

Miss Mapp, as requested by Lucia, had engaged rooms for her and Georgie at a pleasant hostelry near by, called the Trader's Arms, and she accompanied them there with Lucia's car following, like an empty carriage at a funeral, to see that all was ready for them. There must have been some misunderstanding of the message, for Georgie found that a double bedroom had been provided for them. Luckily Lucia had lingered outside with Miss Mapp, looking at the view over the marsh, and

Georgie with embarrassed blushes explained at the bureau that this would not do at all, and the palms of his hands got cold and wet until the mistake was erased and remedied. Then Miss Mapp left them and they went out to wander about the town. But Mallards was the magnet for Lucia's enamoured eye, and presently they stole back towards it. Many houses apparently were to be let furnished in Tilling just now, and Georgie too grew infected with the desire to have one. Riseholme would be very dismal without Lucia, for the moment the fête was over he felt sure than an appalling reaction after the excitement would settle on it: he might even miss being knighted. He had sketched everything sketchable, there would be nobody to play duets with, and the whole place would stagnate again until Lucia's return, just as it had stagnated during her impenetrable widowhood. Whereas here there were innumerable subjects for his brush, and Lucia would be installed in Mallards with a Blumenfelt in the garden-room, and, as was already obvious, a maelstrom of activities whirling in her brain. Major Benjy interested her, so did quaint Irene and the Padre, all the group, in fact, which had seen them drive up with such pre-knowledge, so it seemed, of their destination.

The wall of Miss Mapp's garden, now known to them from inside, ran up to where they now stood, regarding the front of Mallards, and Georgie suddenly observed that just beside them was the sweetest little gabled cottage with the board announcing that it was to be let furnished.

'Look, Lucia,' he said. 'How perfectly fascinating! If it wasn't for that blasted fête, I believe I should be tempted to take it, if I could get it for the couple of months when you are here.'

Lucia had been waiting just for that. She was intending to hint something of the sort before long unless he did, and had made up her mind to stand treat for a bottle of champagne at dinner, so that when they strolled about again afterwards, as she was quite determined to do, Georgie, adventurous with wine, might find the light of the late sunset glowing on Georgian fronts in the town and on the levels of the surrounding country, quite irresistible. But how wise to have waited, so that Georgie should make the suggestion himself.

'My dear, what a delicious idea!' she said. 'Are you really thinking of it? Heavenly for me to have a friend here instead of being planted among strangers. And certainly it is a darling little house. It doesn't seem to be occupied, no smoke from any of the chimneys. I think we might really peep in through the windows and get some idea of what it's like.'

They had to stand on tiptoe to do this, but by shading their eyes from the westerly sun they could get a very decent idea of the interior.

'This must be the dining-room,' said Georgie, peering in.

'A lovely open fire-place,' said Lucia. 'So cosy.'

They moved on sideways like crabs.

'A little hall,' said Lucia. 'Pretty staircase going up out of it.'

More crab-like movements.

'The sitting-room,' said Georgie. 'Quite charming, and if you press your nose close you can see out of the other window into a tiny garden beyond. The wooden paling must be that of your kitchen-garden.'

They stepped back into the street to get a better idea of the topography, and at this moment Miss Mapp looked out of the bow-window of her garden-room and saw them there. She was as intensely interested in this as they in the house.

'And three bedrooms I should think upstairs,' said Lucia, 'and two attics above. Heaps.'

'I shall go and see the agent tomorrow morning,' said Georgie. 'I can imagine myself being very comfortable there!'

They strolled off into the disused graveyard round the church. Lucia turned to have one more look at the front of Mallards, and Miss Mapp made a low swift curtsey, remaining down so that she disappeared completely.

'About that old fête,' said Georgie, 'I don't want to throw Daisy over, because she'll never get another Drake.'

'But you can go down there for the week,' said Lucia who had thought it all out, 'and come back as soon as it's over. You know how to be knighted by now. You needn't go to all those endless rehearsals. Georgie, look at that wonderful clock on the church.'

'Lovely,' said Georgie absently. 'I told Daisy I simply would not be knighted every day. I shall have no shoulder left.'

'And I think that must be the town hall,' said Lucia. 'Quite right about not being knighted so often. What a perfect sketch you could do of that.'

'Heaps of room for us all in the cottage,' said Georgie. 'I hope there's a servants' sitting-room.'

'They'll be in and out of Mallards all day,' said Lucia. 'A lovely servants' hall there.'

'If I can get it, I will,' said Georgie. 'I shall try to let my house at Riseholme, though I shall take my bibelots away. I've often had applications for it in other years. I hope Foljambe will like Tilling. She will make me miserable if she doesn't. Tepid water, fluff on my clothes.'

It was time to get back to their inn to unpack, but Georgie longed for one more look at his cottage, and Lucia for one at Mallards. Just as they turned the corner that brought them in sight of these there was thrust out of the window of Miss Mapp's garden-room a hand that waved a white handkerchief. It might have been samite.

'Georgie, what can that be?' whispered Lucia. 'It must be a signal of some sort. Or was it Miss Mapp waving us good night?'

'Not very likely,' said he. 'Let's wait one second.'

He had hardly spoken when Miss Coles, followed by the breathless Mrs Plaistow hurried up the three steps leading to the front door of Mallards and entered.

'Diva and quaint Irene,' said Lucia. 'It must have been a signal.'

'It might be a coincidence,' said Georgie. To which puerile suggestion Lucia felt it was not worth while to reply.

Of course it was a signal and one long prearranged, for it was a matter of the deepest concern to several householders in Tilling, whether Miss Mapp found a tenant for Mallards, and she had promised Diva and quaint Irene to wave a handkerchief from the window of the garden-room at six o'clock precisely, by which hour it was reasonable to suppose that her visitors would have left her. These two ladies, who would be prowling about the street below, on the look out, would then hasten to hear the best or the worst.

Their interest in the business was vivid, for if Miss Mapp succeeded in letting Mallards, she had promised to take Diva's house, Wasters, for two months at eight guineas a week (the house being much smaller) and Diva would take Irene's house, Taormina (smaller still), at five guineas a week, and Irene would take a four-roomed labourer's cottage (unnamed) just outside the town at two guineas a week, and the labourer, who with his family would be harvesting in August and hop-picking in September, would live in some sort of shanty and pay no rent at all. Thus from top to bottom of this ladder of lessors and lessees they all scored, for they all received more than they paid, and all would enjoy the benefit of a change without the worry and expense of travel and hotels. Each of these ladies would wake in the morning in an unfamiliar room, would sit in unaccustomed chairs, read each other's books (and possibly letters), look at each other's pictures, imbibe all the stimulus of new surroundings, without the wrench of leaving Tilling at all. No true Tillingite was ever really happy away from her town; foreigners were very queer untrustworthy people, and if you did not like the food it was impossible to engage another cook for an hotel of which you were not the proprietor. Annually in the summer this sort of ladder of house-letting was set up in Tilling and was justly popular. But it all depended on a successful letting of Mallards, for if Elizabeth Mapp did not let Mallards, she would not take Diva's Wasters nor Diva Irene's Taormina.

Diva and Irene therefore hurried to the garden-room where they would hear their fate; Irene forging on ahead with that long masculine stride that easily kept pace with Major Benjy's, the short-legged Diva with that twinkle of feet that was like the scudding of a thrush over the lawn.

'Well, Mapp, what luck?' asked Irene.

Miss Mapp waited till Diva had shot in.

'I think I shall tease you both,' said she playfully with her widest smile.

'Oh, hurry up,' said Irene. 'I know perfectly well from your face that you've let it. Otherwise it would be all screwed up.'

Miss Mapp, though there was no question about her being the social queen of Tilling, sometimes felt that there were ugly Bolshevistic symptoms in the air, when quaint Irene spoke to her like that. And Irene had a dreadful gift of mimicry, which was a very low weapon, but formidable. It was always wise to be polite to mimics.

'Patience, a little patience, dear,' said Miss Mapp soothingly. 'If you know I've let it, why wait?'

'Because I should like a cocktail,' said Irene. 'If you'll just send for one, you can go on teasing.'

'Well, I've let it for August and September,' said Miss Mapp, preferring to abandon her teasing than give Irene a cocktail. 'And I'm lucky in my tenant. I never met a sweeter woman than dear Mrs Lucas.'

'Thank God,' said Diva, drawing up her chair to the still uncleared table. 'Give me a cup of tea, Elizabeth. I could eat nothing till I knew.'

'How much did you stick her for it?' asked Irene.

'Beg your pardon, dear?' asked Miss Mapp, who could not be expected to understand such a vulgar expression.

'What price did you screw her up to? What's she got to pay you?' said Irene impatiently. 'Damage: dibs.'

'She instantly closed with the price I suggested,' said Miss Mapp. 'I'm not sure, quaint one, that anything beyond that is what might be called your business.'

'I disagree about that,' said the quaint one. 'There ought to be a sliding-scale. If you've made her pay through the nose, Diva ought to make you pay through the nose for her house, and I ought to make her pay through the nose for mine. Equality, Fraternity, Nosality.'

Miss Mapp bubbled with disarming laughter and rang the bell for Irene's cocktail, which might stop her pursuing this subject, for the sliding-scale of twelve, eight and five guineas a week had been the basis of previous calculations. Yet if Lucia so willingly consented to pay more, surely that was nobody's affair but that of the high contracting parties. Irene, soothed by the prospect of her cocktail, pursued the dangerous topic no further, but sat down at Miss Mapp's piano and picked out God Save the King, with one uncertain finger. Her cocktail arrived just as she finished it.

'Thank you, dear,' said Miss Mapp. 'Sweet music.'

'Cheerio!' said Irene. 'Are you charging Lucas anything extra for use of a fine old instrument?'

Miss Mapp was goaded into a direct and emphatic reply.

'No, darling, I am not,' she said, 'as you are so interested in matters that don't concern you.'

'Well, well, no offence meant,' said Irene. 'Thanks for the cocktail. Look in tomorrow between twelve and one at my studio, if you want to see far the greater part of a well-made man. I'll be off now to cook my supper. Au reservoir.'

Miss Mapp finished the few strawberries that Diva had spared and sighed.

'Our dear Irene has a very coarse side to her nature, Diva,' she said. 'No harm in her, but just common. Sad! Such a contrast to dear Mrs Lucas. So refined: scraps of Italian beautifully pronounced. And so delighted with everything.'

'Ought we to call on her?' asked Diva. 'Widow's mourning, you know.'

Miss Mapp considered this. One plan would be that she should take Lucia under her wing (provided she was willing to go there), another to let it be known in Tilling (if she wasn't) that she did not want to be called upon. That would set Tilling's back up, for if there was one thing it hated it was anything that (in spite of widows' weeds) might be interpreted into superiority. Though Lucia would only be two months in Tilling, Miss Mapp did not want her to be too popular on her own account, independently. She wanted . . . she wanted to have Lucia in her pocket, to take her by the hand and show her to Tilling, but to be in control. It all had to be thought out.

'I'll find out when she comes,' she said. 'I'll ask her, for indeed I feel quite an old friend already.'

'And who's the man?' asked Diva.

'Dear Mr Georgie Pillson. He entertained me so charmingly when I was at Riseholme for a night or two some years ago. They are staying at the Trader's Arms, and off again tomorrow.'

'What? Staying there together?' asked Diva.

Miss Mapp turned her head slightly aside as if to avoid some faint unpleasant smell.

'Diva dear,' she said. 'Old friends as we are, I should be sorry to have a mind like yours. Horrid. You've been reading too many novels. If widows' weeds are not a sufficient protection against such innuendoes, a baby-girl in its christening robe wouldn't be safe.'

'Gracious me, I made no innuendo,' said the astonished Diva. 'I only meant it was rather a daring thing to do. So it is. Anything more came from your mind, Elizabeth, not mine. I merely ask you not to put it on to me, and then say I'm horrid.'

Miss Mapp smiled her widest.

'Of course I accept your apology, dear Diva,' she said. 'Fully, without back-thought of any kind.'

'But I haven't apologized and I won't,' cried Diva. 'It's for you to do that.'

To those not acquainted with the usage of the ladies of Tilling, such bitter plain-speaking might seem to denote a serious friction between old friends. But neither Elizabeth nor Diva had any such feeling: they would both have been highly surprised if an impartial listener had imagined anything so absurd. Such breezes, even if they grew far stronger than this, were no more than bracing airs that disposed to energy, or exercises to keep the mind fit. No malice.

'Another cup of tea, dear?' said Miss Mapp earnestly.

That was so like her, thought Diva: that was Elizabeth all over. When logic and good feeling alike had produced an irresistible case against her, she swept it all away, and asked you if you would have some more cold tea or cold mutton, or whatever it was.

Diva gave up. She knew she was no match for her and had more tea.

'About our own affairs then,' she said, 'if that's all settled – '

'Yes, dear: so sweetly so harmoniously,' said Elizabeth.

Diva swallowed a regurgitation of resentment, and went on as if she had not been interrupted.

' – Mrs Lucas takes possession on the first of August,' she said. 'That's to say, you would like to get into Wasters that day.'

'Early that day, Diva, if you can manage it,' said Elizabeth, 'as I want to give my servants time to clean and tidy up. I would pop across in the morning, and my servants follow later. All so easy to manage.'

'Then there's another thing,' said Diva. 'Garden-produce. You're leaving yours, I suppose.'

Miss Mapp gave a little trill of laughter.

'I shan't be digging up all my potatoes and stripping the beans and the fruit-trees,' she said. 'And I thought – correct me if I am wrong – that my eight guineas a week for your little house included garden-produce, which is all that really concerns you and me. I think we agreed as to that.'

Miss Mapp leant forward with an air of imparting luscious secret information, as that was settled.

'Diva: something thrilling,' she said. 'I happened to be glancing out of my window just by chance a few minutes before I waved to you, and there were Mrs Lucas and Mr Pillson peering, positively peering into the windows of Mallards Cottage. I couldn't help wondering if Mr Pillson is thinking of taking it. They seemed to be so absorbed in it. It is to let, for Isabel Poppit has taken that little brown bungalow with no proper plumbing out by the golf-links.'

'Thrilling!' said Diva. 'There's a door in the paling between that little back-yard at Mallards Cottage and your garden. They could unlock it – '

She stopped, for this was a development of the trend of ideas for which neither of them had apologized.

'But even if Mr Pillson is thinking of taking it, what next, Elizabeth?' she asked.

Miss Mapp bent to kiss the roses in that beautiful vase of flowers which she had cut this morning in preparation for Lucia's visit.

'Nothing particular, dear,' she said. 'Just one of my mad-cap notions. You and I might take Mallards Cottage between us, if it appealed to you. Sweet Isabel is only asking four guineas a week for it. If Mr Pillson happens – it's only a speculation – to want it, we might ask, say, six. So cheap at six.'

Diva rose.

'Shan't touch it,' she said. 'What if Mr Pillson doesn't want it? A pure speculation.'

'Perhaps it would be rather risky,' said Miss Mapp. 'And now I come to think of it, possibly, possibly rather stealing a march – don't they call it – on my friends.'

'Oh, decidedly,' said Diva. 'No "possibly possibly" about it.'

Miss Mapp winced for a moment under this smart rap, and changed the subject.

'I shall have little more than a month, then, in my dear house,' she said, 'before I'm turned out of it. I must make the most of it, and have a quantity of little gaieties for you all.'

Georgie and Lucia had another long stroll through the town after their dinner. The great celestial signs behaved admirably; it was as if the spirit of Tilling had arranged that sun, moon and stars alike should put forth their utmost arts of advertisement on its behalf, for scarcely had the fires of sunset ceased to blaze on its red walls and roofs and to incarnadine the thin skeins of mist that hung over the marsh, than a large punctual moon arose in the east and executed the most wonderful nocturnes in black and silver.

They found a great grey Norman tower keeping watch seaward, an Edwardian gate with drum towers looking out landward: they found a belvedere platform built out on a steep slope to the east of the town, and the odour of the flowering hawthorns that grew there was wafted to them as they gazed at a lighthouse winking in the distance. In another street there stood Elizabethan cottages of brick and timber, very picturesque, but of no interest to those who were at home in Riseholme. Then there were human interests as well: quaint Irene was sitting, while the sunset flamed, on a camp-stool in the middle of a street, hatless and trousered, painting a most remarkable picture, apparently of the Day of Judgement, for the whole world was enveloped in fire. Just as they passed her her easel fell down, and in a loud angry voice she said, 'Damn the beastly thing.' Then they saw Diva scuttling along the High Street carrying a bird-cage. She called up to an open window very lamentably, 'Oh, Dr Dobbie, please! My canary's had a fit!' From another window, also open and unblinded, positively inviting scrutiny, there came a baritone voice singing 'Will ye no come back again?' and there, sure enough, was the Padre from Birmingham, with the little grey mouse tinkling on the piano. They could not tear themselves away (indeed there was quite a lot of people listening) till the song was over, and then they stole up the street, at the head of which stood Mallards, and from the house just below it came a muffled cry of 'Quai-hai', and Lucia's lips formed the syllables 'Major Benjy. At his diaries.' They tiptoed on past Mallards itself, for the garden-room window was open wide, and so past Mallards Cottage, till they were out of sight.

'Georgie, entrancing,' said Lucia. 'They're all being themselves, and all so human and busy – '

'If I don't get Mallards Cottage,' said Georgie, 'I shall die.'

'But you must. You shall. Now it's time to go to bed, though I could wander about for ever. We must be up early in order to get to the house-agent's as soon as it's open. Woggles and Pickstick, isn't it?'

'Now you've confused me,' said Georgie. 'Rather like it, but not quite.'

They went upstairs to bed: their rooms were next each other, with a communicating door. There was a bolt on Georgie's side of it, and he went swiftly across to this and fastened it. Even as he did so, he heard a key quietly turned from the other side of it. He undressed with the stealth of a burglar prowling about a house, for somehow it was shy work that he and Lucia should be going to bed so close to each other; he brushed his teeth with infinite precaution and bent low over the basin to eject (spitting would be too noisy a word) the water with which he had rinsed his mouth, for it would never do to let a sound of these intimate manoeuvres penetrate next door. When half-undressed he remembered that the house-agents' name was Woolgar and Pipstow, and he longed to tap at Lucia's door and proclaim it, but the silence of the grave reigned next door, and perhaps Lucia was asleep already. Or was she, too, being as stealthy as he? Whichever it was (particularly if it was the last) he must not let a betrayal of his presence reach her.

He got into bed and clicked out his light. That could be done quite boldly: she might hear that, for it only betokened that all was over. Then, in spite of this long day in the open air, which should have conduced to drowsiness, he felt terribly wide-awake, for the subject which had intermittently occupied his mind, shadowing it with dim apprehension, ever since Pepino's death, presented itself in the most garish colours. For years, by a pretty Riseholme fantasy, it had always been supposed that he was the implacably Platonic but devout lover of Lucia: some-how that interesting fiction had grown up, and Lucia had cer-tainly abetted it as well as himself. She had let it be supposed that he was, and that she accepted this chaste fervour. But now that her year of widowhood was nearly over, there loomed in front of Georgie the awful fact that very soon there could be no earthly reason why he should not claim his reward for these years of devotion and exchange his passionate celibacy for an even more passionate matrimony. It was an unnerving thought that he might have the right before the summer was over, to tap at some door of communication like that which he had so care-fully bolted (and she locked) and say, 'May I come in, darling?' He felt that the words would freeze on his tongue before he could utter them.

Did Lucia expect him to ask to marry her? There was the crux and his imagination proceeded to crucify him upon it. They had posed for years as cherishing for each other a stainless devotion, but what if, with her, it had been no pose at all, but a dreadful reality? Had he been encouraging her to hope, by coming down to stay at this hotel in this very compromising manner? In his ghastly midnight musing, it seemed terribly likely. He had been very rash to come, and all this afternoon he had been pursuing his foolhardy career. He had said that life wasn't worth living if he could not get hold of Mallards Cottage, which was less than a stone's throw (even he could throw a stone as far as that) from the house she was to inhabit alone. Really it looked as if it was the proximity to her that made the Cottage so desirable. If she only knew how embarrassing her proximity had been just now when he prepared himself for bed! ...

And Lucia always got what she wanted. There was a force about her he supposed (so different from poor Daisy's violent yappings and scufflings), which caused things to happen in the way she wished. He had fallen in with all her plans with a zest which it was only reasonable she should interpret favourably: only an hour or two ago he had solemnly affirmed that he must take Mallards Cottage, and the thing already was as good as done, for they were to breakfast tomorrow morning at eight, in order to be at the house-agent's (Woggle and Pipsqueak, was it? He had forgotten again), as soon as it opened. Things happened like that for her: she got what she wanted. 'But never, never,' thought Georgie, 'shall she get me. I couldn't possibly marry her, and I won't. I want to live quietly and do my sewing and my sketching, and see lots of Lucia, and play any amount of duets with her, but not marry her. Pray God, she doesn't want me to!'

Lucia was lying awake, too, next door, and if either of them could have known what the other was thinking about, they would both instantly have fallen into a refreshing sleep, instead of tossing and turning as they were doing. She, too, knew that for years she and Georgie had let it be taken for granted that they were mutually devoted, and had both about equally encouraged that impression. There had been an interlude, it is true, when that wonderful Olga Bracely had shone (like evening stars singing) over Riseholme, but she was to be absent from England for a year; besides she was married, and even if she had not been would certainly not have married Georgie. 'So we needn't consider Olga,' thought Lucia. 'It's all about Georgie and me. Dear Georgie: he was so terribly glad when I began to be myself again, and how he jumped at the plan of coming to Tilling and spending the night here! And how he froze on to the idea of taking Mallards Cottage as soon as he knew I had got Mallards! I'm afraid I've been encouraging him to hope. He knows that my year of widowhood is almost over, and on the very eve of its accomplishment, I take him off on this solitary expedition with me. Dear me: it looks as if I was positively asking for it. How perfectly horrible!'

Though it was quite dark, Lucia felt herself blushing.

'What on earth am I to do?' continued these disconcerting reflections. 'If he asks me to marry him, I must certainly refuse, for I couldn't do so: quite impossible. And then when I say no, he has every right to turn on me, and say I've been leading him on. I've been taking moonlight walks with him, I'm at this moment staying alone with him in an hotel. Oh dear! Oh dear!'

Lucia sat up in bed and listened. She longed to hear sounds of snoring from the next room, for that would show that the thought of the fulfilment of his long devotion was not keeping him awake, but there was no sound of any kind.

'I must do something about it tomorrow,' she said to herself, 'for if I allow things to go on like this, these two months here with him will be one series of agitating apprehensions. I must make it quite clear that I won't before he asks me. I can't bear to think of hurting Georgie, but it will hurt him less if I show him beforehand he's got no chance. Something about the beauty of a friendship untroubled with passion. Something about the tranquillity that comes with age. . . . There's that eternal old church clock striking three. Surely it must be fast.'

Lucia lay down again: at last she was getting sleepy.

'Mallards,' she said to herself. 'Quaint Irene . . . Woffles and . . . Georgie will know. Certainly Tilling is fascinating. . . . Intriguing, too . . . characters of strong individuality to be dealt with. . . . A great variety, but I think I can manage them. . . . And what about Miss Mapp? . . . Those wide grins. . . . We shall see about that . . .'

Lucia awoke herself from a doze by giving a loud snore, and for one agonized moment thought it was Georgie, whom she had hoped to hear snoring, in alarming proximity to herself. That nightmare-spasm was quickly over, and she recognized that it was she that had done it. After all her trouble in not letting a sound of any sort penetrate through that door!

Georgie heard it. He was getting sleepy, too, in spite of his uneasy musings, but he was just wide awake enough to realize where that noise had come from.

'And if she snores as well . . .' he thought, and dozed off.

3

It was hardly nine o'clock in the morning when they set out for the house-agent's, and the upper circles of Tilling were not yet fully astir. But there was a town-crier in a blue frock-coat ringing a bell in the High Street and proclaiming that the water-supply would be cut off that day from twelve noon till three in the afternoon. It was difficult to get to the house-agent's, for the street where it was situated was being extensively excavated and they had chosen the wrong side of the road, and though they saw it opposite them when half-way down the street, a long detour must be made to reach it.

'But so characteristic, so charming,' said Lucia. 'Naturally there is a town-crier in Tilling, and naturally the streets are up. Do not be so impatient, Georgie. Ah, we can cross here.'

There was a further period of suspense.

'The occupier of Mallards Cottage,' said Mr Woolgar (or it might have been Mr Pipstow), 'is wanting to let for three months, July, August and September. I'm not so sure that she would entertain – '

'Then will you please ring her up,' interrupted Georgie, 'and say you've had a firm offer for two months.'

Mr Woolgar turned round a crank like that used for starting rather old-fashioned motor-cars, and when a bell rang, he gave a number, and got into communication with the brown bungalow without proper plumbing.

'Very sorry, sir,' he said, 'but Miss Poppit has gone out for her sun-bath among the sand-dunes. She usually takes about three hours if fine.'

'But we're leaving again this morning,' said Georgie. 'Can't her servant, or whoever it is, search the sand-dunes and ask her?'

'I'll inquire, sir,' said Mr Woolgar sympathetically. 'But there are about two miles of sand-dunes, and she may be anywhere.'

'Please inquire,' said Georgie.

There was an awful period, during which Mr Woolgar kept on saying 'Quite,' 'Just so,' 'I see,' 'Yes, dear,' with the most tedious monotony, in answer to unintelligible quacking noises from the other end.

'Quite impossible, I'm afraid,' he said at length. 'Miss Poppit only keeps one servant, and she's got to look after the house. Besides, Miss Poppit likes – likes to be private when she's enjoying the sun.'

'But how tarsome,' said Georgie. 'What am I to do?'

'Well, sir, there's Miss Poppit's mother you might get hold of. She is Mrs Wyse now. Lately married. A beautiful wedding. The house you want is her property.'

'I know,' broke in Lucia. 'Sables and a Rolls-Royce. Mr Wyse has a monocle.'

'Ah, if you know the lady, madam, that will be all right, and I can give you her address. Starling Cottage, Porpoise Street. I will write it down for you.'

'Georgie, Porpoise Street!' whispered Lucia in an entranced aside. 'Com' e bello e molto characteristuoso!'

While this was being done, Diva suddenly blew in, beginning to speak before she was wholly inside the office. A short tempestuous interlude ensued.

' – morning, Mr Woolgar,' said Diva, 'and I've let Wasters, so you can cross it off your books; such a fine morning.'

'Indeed, madam,' said Mr Woolgar. 'Very satisfactory. And I hope your dear little canary is better.'

'Still alive and in less pain, thank you, pip,' said Diva, and plunged through the excavations outside sooner than waste time in going round.

Mr Woolgar apparently understood that 'pip' was not a salutation but a disease of canaries, and did not say 'So long' or 'Pip pip'. Calm returned again.

'I'll ring up Mrs Wyse to say you will call, madam,' he said. 'Let me see: what name? It has escaped me for the moment.'

As he had never known it, it was difficult to see how it could have escaped.

'Mrs Lucas and Mr Pillson,' said Lucia. 'Where is Porpoise Street?'

'Two minutes' walk from here, madam. As if you were going up to Mallards, but first turning to the right just short of it.'

'Many thanks,' said Lucia, 'I know Mallards.'

'The best house in Tilling, madam,' said Mr Woolgar, 'if you were wanting something larger than Mallards Cottage. It is on our books, too.'

The pride of proprietorship tempted Lucia for a moment to say 'I've got it already,' but she refrained. The complications which might have ensued, had she asked the price of it, were endless ...

'A great many houses to let in Tilling,' she said.

'Yes, madam, a rare lot of letting goes on about this time of year,' said Mr Woolgar, 'but they're all snapped up very quickly. Many ladies in Tilling like a little change in the summer.'

It was impossible (since time was so precious, and Georgie so feverishly apprehensive, after this warning, that somebody else would secure Mallards Cottage before him, although the owner was safe in the sand-dunes for the present) to walk round the excavations in the street, and like Diva they made an intrepid short cut among gas-pipes and water mains and braziers and bricks to the other side. A sad splash of mud hurled itself against Georgie's fawn-coloured trousers as he stepped in a puddle, which was very tarsome, but it was useless to attempt to brush it off till it was dry. As they went up the now familiar street towards Mallards they saw quaint Irene leaning out of the upper window of a small house, trying to take down a board that hung outside it which advertised that this house, too, was to let: the fact of her removing it seemed to indicate that from this moment it was to let no longer. Just as they passed, the board, which was painted in the most amazing colours, slipped from her hand and crashed on to the pavement, narrowly missing Diva who simultaneously popped out of the front door. It broke into splinters at her feet, and she gave a shrill cry of dismay. Then perceiving Irene she called up, 'No harm done, dear,' and Irene, in a voice of fury cried, 'No harm? My beautiful board's broken to smithereens. Why didn't you catch it, silly?'

A snort of infinite contempt was the only proper reply, and Diva trundled swiftly away into the High Street again.

'But it's like a game of general post, Georgie,' said Lucia excitedly, 'and we're playing too. Are they all letting their houses to each other? Is that it?'

'I don't care whom they're letting them too,' said Georgie, 'so long as I get Mallards Cottage. Look at this tarsome mud on my trousers, and I daren't try to brush it off. What will Mrs Wyse think? Here's Porpoise Street anyhow, and there's Starling Cottage. Elizabethan again.'

The door was of old oak, without a handle, but with a bobbin in the strictest style, and there was a thickly patinated green bronze chain hanging close by, which Georgie rightly guessed to be the bell-pull, and so he pulled it. A bronze bell, which he had not perceived, hanging close to his head, thereupon broke into a clamour that might have been heard not only in the house but all over Tilling, and startled him terribly. Then bobbins and gadgets were manipulated from within and they were shown into a room in which two very diverse tastes were clearly exhibited. Oak beams crossed the ceiling, oak beams made a crisscross on the walls: there was a large open fireplace of grey Dutch bricks, and on each side of the grate an ingle-nook with a section of another oak beam to sit down upon. The windows were latticed and had antique levers for their control: there was a refectory table and a spice-chest and some pewter mugs and a Bible-box and a coffin-stool. All this was one taste, and then came in another, for the room was full of beautiful objects of a very different sort. The refectory table was covered with photographs in silver frames: one was of a man in uniform and many decorations signed 'Cecco Faraglione', another of a lady in Court dress with a quantity of plumes on her head signed 'Amelia Faraglione'. Another was the King of Italy, another of a man in a frock-coat signed 'Wyse'. In front of these, rather prominent, was an open purple morocco box in which reposed the riband and cross of a Member of the Order of the British Empire. There was a cabinet of china in one corner with a malachite vase above it: there was an 'occasional' table with a marble mosaic top: there was a satinwood piano draped with a piece of embroidery: a palm-tree, a green velvet sofa over the end of which lay a sable coat, and all these things spoke of post-Elizabethan refinements.

Long before Lucia had time to admire them all, there came a jingling from a door over which hung a curtain of reeds and beads, and Mrs Wyse entered.

'So sorry to keep you waiting, Mrs Lucas,' she said, 'but they thought I was in the garden, and I was in my boudoir all the time. And you must excuse my deshabille, just my shopping-frock. And Mr Pillson, isn't it? So pleased. Pray be seated.'

She heaved the sable-coat off the end of the sofa on to the window-seat.

'We've just been to see the house-agent,' said Georgie in a great hurry, as he turned his muddied leg away from the light, 'and he told us that you might help me.'

'Most happy I am sure, if I can. Pray tell me,' said Mrs Wyse, in apparent unconsciousness of what she could possibly help him about.

'Mallards Cottage,' said Georgie. 'There seems to be no chance of getting hold of Miss Poppit and we've got to leave before she comes back from her sun-bath. I so much want to take it for August and September.'

Mrs Wyse made a little cooing sound.

'Dear Isabel!' she said. 'My daughter. Out in the sand-dunes all morning! What if a tramp came along? I say to her. But no use: she calls it the Browning Society, and she must not miss a meeting. So quick and clever! Browning, not the poet but the action of the sun.'

'Most amusing!' said Georgie. 'With regard to Mallards Cottage – '

'The little house is mine, as no doubt Mr Woolgar told you,' said Mrs Wyse, forgetting she had been in complete ignorance of these manoeuvres, 'but you must certainly come and see over it, before anything is settled. . . . Ah, here is Mr Wyse. Algernon: Mrs Lucas and Mr Pillson. Mr Pillson wants to take Mallards Cottage.'

Lucia thought she had never seen anyone so perfectly correct and polite as Mr Wyse. He gave little bows and smiles to each as he spoke to them, and that in no condescending manner, nor yet cringingly, but as one consorting with his high-bred equals.

'From your beautiful Riseholme, I understand,' he said to Lucia (bowing to Riseholme as well). 'And we are all encouraging ourselves to hope that for two months at the least the charm of our picturesque – do you not find it so? – little Tilling will give Susan and myself the inestimable pleasure of being your neighbours. We shall look forward to August with keen anticipation. Remind me, dear Susan, to tell Amelia what is in store for us.' He bowed to August, Susan and Amelia and continued – 'And now I hear that Mr Pillson' (he bowed to Georgie and observed the drying spot of mud) 'is "after" as they say, after Mallards Cottage. This will indeed be a summer for Tilling.'

Georgie, during this pretty speech which Mr Wyse delivered in the most finished manner, was taking notes of his costume and appearance. His clean-shaven face, with abundant grey hair brushed back from his forehead was that of an actor who has seen his best days, but who has given command performances at Windsor. He wore a brown velveteen coat, a Byronic collar and a tie strictured with a cameo-ring, he wore brown knickerbockers and stockings to match, he wore neat golfing shoes. He looked as if he might be going to play golf, but somehow it didn't seem likely . . .

Georgie and Lucia made polite deprecating murmurs.

'I was telling Mr Pillson he must certainly see over it first,' said Mrs Wyse. 'There are the keys of the cottage in my boudoir, if you'll kindly fetch them, Algernon. And the Royce is at the door, I see, so if Mrs Lucas will allow us, we will all drive up there together, and show her and Mr Pillson what there is.'

While Algernon was gone, Mrs Wyse picked up the photograph signed Amelia Faraglione.

'You recognize, no doubt, the family likeness,' she said to Lucia. 'My husband's sister Amelia who married the Conte di Faraglione, of the old Neapolitan nobility. That is he.'

'Charming,' said Lucia. 'And so like Mr Wyse. And that Order? What is that?'

Mrs Wyse hastily shut the morocco box.

'So like servants to leave that about,' she said. 'But they seem proud of it. Graciously bestowed upon me. Member of the British Empire. Ah, here is Algernon with the keys. I was showing Mrs Lucas, dear, the photograph of Amelia. She recognized the likeness at once. Now let us all pack in. A warm morning, is it not? I don't think I shall need my furs.'

The total distance to be traversed was not more than a hundred yards, but Porpoise Street was very steep, and the cobbles which must be crossed very unpleasant to walk on, so Mrs Wyse explained. They had to wait some little while at the corner, twenty yards away from where they started, for a van was coming down the street from the direction of Mallards, and the Royce could not possibly pass it, and then they came under fire of the windows of Miss Mapp's garden-room. As usual at this hour she was sitting there with the morning paper in her hand in which she could immerse herself if anybody passed whom she did not wish to see, but was otherwise intent on the movements of the street.

Diva Plaistow had looked in with the news that she had seen Lucia and Georgie at the house-agent's, and that her canary still lived. Miss Mapp professed her delight to hear about the canary, but was secretly distrustful of whether Diva had seen the visitors or not. Diva was so imaginative; to have seen a man and a woman who were strangers was quite enough to make her believe she had seen Them. Then the Royce heaved into sight round the corner below, and Miss Mapp became much excited.

'I think, Diva,' she said, 'that this is Mrs Lucas's beautiful car coming. Probably she is going to call on me about something she wants to know. If you sit at the piano you will see her as she gets out. Then we shall know whether you really –'

The car came slowly up, barked loudly and instead of stopping at the front door of Mallards, turned up the street in the direction of Mallards Cottage. Simultaneously Miss Mapp caught sight of that odious chauffeur of Mrs Wyse's. She could not see more than people's knees in the car itself (that was the one disadvantage of the garden-room window being so high above the street), but there were several pairs of them.

'No, it's only Susan's great lumbering bus,' she said, 'filling up the street as usual. Probably she has found out that Mrs Lucas is staying at the Trader's Arms, and has gone to leave cards. Such a woman to shove herself in where she's not wanted I never saw. Luckily I told Mrs Lucas what a dreadful snob she was.'

'A disappointment to you, dear, when you thought Mrs Lucas was coming to call,' said Diva. 'But I did see them this morning at Woolgar's and it's no use saying I didn't!'

Miss Mapp uttered a shrill cry.

'Diva, they've stopped at Mallards Cottage. They're getting out. Susan first – so like her – and . . . it's Them. She's got hold of them somehow. . . . There's Mr Wyse with the keys, bowing. . . . They're going in . . . I was right, then, when I saw them peering in through the windows yesterday. Mr Pillson's come to see the house, and the Wyses have got hold of them. You may wager they know by now about the Count and Countess Far-adiddleone, and the Order of the British Empire. I really didn't think Mrs Lucas would be so easily taken in. However, it's no business of mine.'

There could not have been a better reason for Miss Mapp being violently interested in all that happened. Then an idea struck her and the agitated creases in her face faded out.

'Let us pop in to Mallards Cottage, Diva, while they are still there,' she said. 'I should hate to think that Mrs Lucas should get her ideas of the society she will meet in Tilling from poor common Susan. Probably they would like a little lunch before their long drive back to Riseholme.'

The inspection of the cottage had taken very little time. The main point in Georgie's mind was that Foljambe should be pleased, and there was an excellent bedroom for Foljambe, where she could sit when unoccupied. The rooms that concerned him had been viewed through the windows from the street the evening before. Consequently Miss Mapp had hardly had time to put on her garden hat, and trip up the street with Diva, when the inspecting party came out.

'Sweet Susan!' she said. 'I saw your car go by. . . . Dear Mrs Lucas, good morning, I just popped across – this is Mrs Plaistow

– to see if you would not come and have an early lunch with me before you drive back to your lovely Riseholme. Any time would suit me, for I never have any breakfast. Twelve, half past twelve? A little something?'

'So kind of you,' said Lucia, 'but Mrs Wyse has just asked us to lunch with her.'

'I see,' said Miss Mapp, grinning frightfully. 'Such a pity. I had hoped – but there it is.'

Clearly it was incumbent on sweet Susan to ask her to join them at this early lunch, but sweet Susan showed no signs of doing anything of the sort. Off went Lucia and Georgie to the Trader's Arms to pack their belongings and leave the rest of the morning free, and the Wyses, after vainly trying to persuade them to drive there in the Royce, got into it themselves and backed down the street till it could turn in the slightly wider space opposite Miss Mapp's garden-room. This took a long time, and she was not able to get to her own front door till the manoeuvre was executed, for as often as she tried to get round the front of the car it took a short run forward, and it threatened to squash her flat against the wall of her own room if she tried to squeeze round behind it.

But there were topics to gloat over which consoled her for this act of social piracy on the part of the Wyses. It was a noble stroke to have let Mallards for fifteen guineas a week without garden-produce, and an equally brilliant act to have got Diva's house for eight with garden-produce, for Diva had some remarkably fine plum-trees, the fruit of which would be ripe during her tenancy, not to mention apples: Miss Mapp foresaw a kitchen-cupboard the doors of which could not close because of the jam-pots within. Such reflections made a happy mental background as she hurried out into the town, for there were businesses to be transacted without delay. She first went to the house-agent's and had rather a job to convince Mr Woolgar that the letting of Mallards was due to her own advertisement in *The Times*, and that therefore she owed no commission to his firm, but her logic proved irresistible. Heated but refreshed by that encounter, she paid a visit to her greengrocer and made a pleasant arrangement for the sale of the produce of her own kitchen-garden at Mallards during the months of August and September. This errand brought her to the east end of the High Street, and there was Georgie already established on the belvedere busy sketching the Land-gate, before he went to breakfast (as those Wyses always called lunch) in Porpoise Street. Miss Mapp did not yet know whether he had taken Mallards Cottage or not, and that must be instantly ascertained.

She leaned on the railing close beside him, and moved a little, rustled a little, till he looked up.

'Oh, Mr Pillson, how ashamed of myself I am!' she said. 'But I couldn't help taking a peep at your lovely little sketch. So rude of me: just like an inquisitive stranger in the street. Never meant to interrupt you, but to steal away again when I'd had my peep. Every moment's precious to you, I know, as you're off this afternoon after your early lunch. But I must ask you whether your hotel was comfortable. I should be miserable if I thought that I had recommended it, and that you didn't like it.'

'Very comfortable indeed, thank you,' said Georgie.

Miss Mapp sidled up to the bench where he sat.

'I will just perch here for a moment before I flit off again,' she said, 'if you'll promise not to take any notice of me, but go on with your picky, as if I was not here. How well you've got the perspective! I always sit here for two or three minutes every morning to feast my eyes on the beauty of the outlook. What a pity you can't stay longer here! You've only had a glimpse of our sweet Tilling.'

Georgie held up his drawing.

'Have I got the perspective right, do you think?' he said. 'Isn't it tarsome when you mean to make a road go downhill and it will go up instead?'

'No fear of that with you!' ejaculated Miss Mapp. 'If I was a little bolder I should ask you to send your drawing to our Art Society here. We have a little exhibition every summer. Could I persuade you?'

'I'm afraid I shan't be able to finish it this morning,' said Georgie.

'No chance then of your coming back?' she asked.

'In August, I hope,' said he, 'for I've taken Mallards Cottage for two months.'

'Oh, Mr Pillson, that is good news!' cried Miss Mapp. 'Lovely! All August and September. Fancy!'

'I've got to be away for a week in August,' said Georgie, 'as we've got an Elizabethan fête at Riseholme. I'm Francis Drake.'

That was a trove for Miss Mapp and must be published at once. She prepared to flit off.

'Oh how wonderful!' she said. 'Dear me, I can quite see you. The *Golden Hind*! Spanish treasure! All the pomp and majesty. I wonder if I could manage to pop down to see it. But I won't interrupt you any more. So pleased to think it's only au reservoir and not good-bye.'

She walked up the street again, bursting with her budget of news. Only the Wyses could possibly know that Georgie had taken Mallards Cottage, and nobody that he was going to impersonate Francis Drake. . . . There was the Padre talking to Major Benjy, no doubt on his way to the steam-tram, and there were Diva and Irene a little farther on.

'Good morning, Padre: good morning, Major Benjy,' said she.

'Good morrow, Mistress Mapp,' said the Padre. 'An' hoo's the time o' day wi' ye? 'Tis said you've a fair tenant for yon Mallards.'

Miss Mapp fired off her news in a broadside.

'Indeed, I have, Padre,' she said. 'And there's Mallards Cottage, too, about which you won't have heard. Mr Pillson has taken that, though he won't be here all the time as he's playing Francis Drake in a fête at Riseholme for a week.'

Major Benjy was not in a very good temper. It was porridge morning with him, and his porridge had been burned. Miss Mapp already suspected something of the sort, for there had been loud angry sounds from within as she passed his dining-room window.

'That fellow whom I saw with Mrs Lucas this morning with a cape over his arm?' he said scornfully. 'Not much of a hand against the Spaniards, I should think. Ridiculous! Tea-parties with a lot of old cats more in his line. Pshaw!' And away he went to the tram, shovelling passengers off the pavement.

'Porridge burned, I expect,' said Miss Mapp, thoughtfully, 'though I couldn't say for certain. Morning, dear Irene. Another artist is coming to Tilling for August and September.'

'Hoot awa', woman,' said Irene, in recognition of the Padre's presence. 'I ken that fine, for Mistress Wyse told me half an hour agone.'

'But he'll be away for a week, though of course you know that, too,' said Miss Mapp, slightly nettled. 'Acting Francis Drake in a fête at Riseholme.'

Diva trundled up.

'I don't suppose you've heard, Elizabeth,' she said in a great hurry, 'that Mr Pillson has taken Mallards Cottage.'

Miss Mapp smiled pityingly.

'Quite correct, dear Diva,' she said. 'Mr Pillson told me himself hours ago. He's sketching the Land-gate now – a sweet picky – and insisted that I should sit down and chat to him while he worked.'

'Lor! How you draw them all in, Mapp,' said quaint Irene. 'He looks a promising young man for his age, but it's time he had his hair dyed again. Grey at the roots.'

The Padre tore himself away; he had to hurry home and tell wee wifie.

'Aweel, I mustn't stand daffing here,' he said, 'I've got my sermon to think on.'

Miss Mapp did a little more shopping, hung about on the chance of seeing Lucia again, and then went back to Mallards, to attend to her sweet flowers. Some of the beds wanted weeding, and now as she busied herself with that useful work and eradicated groundsel, each plant as she tore it up and flung it into her basket might have been Mr and Mrs Wyse. It was very annoying that they had struck their hooks (so the process represented itself to her vigorous imagery) into Lucia, for Miss Mapp had intended to have no one's hook there but her own. She wanted to run her, to sponsor her, to arrange little parties for her, and cause Lucia to arrange other little parties at her dictation, and, while keeping her in her place, show her off to

Tilling. Providence, or whatever less beneficent power ruled the world, had not been considerate of her clear right to do this, for it was she who had been put to the expense of advertising Mallards in *The Times*, and it was entirely owing to that that Lucia had come down here, and wound up that pleasant machine of sub-letting houses, so that everybody scored financially as well as got a change. But there was nothing to be done about that for the present: she must wait till Lucia arrived here, and then be both benignant and queenly. A very sweet woman, up till now, was her verdict, though possibly lacking in fine discernment, as witnessed by her having made friends with the Wyses. Then there was Georgie: she was equally well-disposed towards him for the present, but he, like Lucia, must be good, and recognize that she was the arbiter of all things social in Tilling. If he behaved properly in that regard she would propose him as an honorary member of the Tilling Art Society, and, as member of the hanging committee, see that his work had a conspicuous place on the walls of the Exhibition, but it was worth remembering (in case he was not good) that quaint Irene had said that his hair was dyed, and that Major Benjy thought that he would have been very little use against the Spaniards.

But thinking was hungry work, and weeding was dirty work, and she went indoors to wash her hands for lunch after this exciting morning.

There was a dreadful block in Porpoise Street when Lucia's car came to pick up her and Georgie after their breakfast at Starling Cottage, for Mrs Wyse's Royce was already drawn up there. The two purred and backed and advanced foot by foot, they sidled and stood on pavements meant for pedestrians, and it was not till Lucia's car had gone backwards again round the corner below Miss Mapp's garden-room, and Mrs Wyse's forward towards the High Street, that Lucia's could come to the door, and the way down Porpoise Street lie open for their departure to Riseholme. As long as they were in sight, Susan stood waving her hand, and Algernon bowing.

Often during the drive Lucia tried, but always in vain, to start the subject which had kept them both awake last night, and tell Georgie that never would she marry again, but the moment she got near the topic of friendship, or even wondered how long Mrs Plaistow had been a widow or whether Major Benjy would ever marry, Georgie saw a cow or a rainbow or something out of the window and violently directed attention to it. She could not quite make out what was going on in his mind. He shied away from such topics as friendship and widowhood, and she wondered if that was because he was not feeling quite ready yet, but was screwing himself up. If he only would let her develop those topics she could spare him the pain of a direct refusal, and thus soften the blow. But she had to give it up, determining, however, that when he came to dine with her that evening, she would not be silenced by his irrelevances: she would make it quite clear to him, before he embarked on his passionate declaration that, with all her affection for him, she could never marry him. . . . Poor Georgie!

She dropped him at his house, and as soon as he had told Foljambe about his having taken the house at Tilling (for that must be done at once), he would come across to the Hurst.

'I hope she will like the idea,' said Georgie very gravely, as he got out, 'and there is an excellent room for her, isn't there?'

Foljambe opened the door to him.

'A pleasant outing, I hope, sir,' said she.

'Very indeed, thank you, Foljambe,' said Georgie. 'And I've got great news. Mrs Lucas has taken a house at Tilling for August and September, and so have I. Quite close to hers. You could throw a stone.'

'That'll be an agreeable change,' said Foljambe.

'I think you'll like it. A beautiful bedroom for you.'

'I'm sure I shall,' said Foljambe.

Georgie was immensely relieved, and, as he went gaily across to the Hurst, he quite forgot for the time about this menace of matrimony.

'She likes the idea,' he said before he had opened the gate into Perdita's garden, where Lucia was sitting.

'Georgie, the most wonderful thing,' cried she. 'Oh, Foljambe's pleased, is she? So glad. An excellent bedroom. I knew she would. But I've found a letter from Adele Brixton; you know, Lady Brixton who always goes to America when her husband comes to England, and the other way about, so that they only pass each other on the Atlantic; she wants to take the Hurst for three months. She came down here for a Sunday, don't you remember, and adored it. I instantly telephoned to say I would let it.'

'Well, that is luck for you,' said Georgie. 'But three months – what will you do for the third?'

'Georgie, I don't know, and I'm not going to think,' she said. 'Something will happen: it's sure to. My dear, it's perfect rapture to feel the great tide of life flowing again. How I'm going to set to work on all the old interests and the new ones as well. Tilling, the age of Anne, and I shall get a translation of Pope's *Iliad* and of Plato's *Symposium* till I can rub up my Greek again. I have been getting lazy, and I have been getting – let us go in to dinner – narrow. I think you have been doing the same. We must open out, and receive new impressions, and adjust ourselves to new conditions!'

This last sentence startled Georgie very much, though it might only apply to Tilling, but Lucia did not seem to notice his faltering step as he followed her into the panelled dining-room with the refectory table, below which it was so hard to adjust the feet with any comfort, owing to the foot-rail.

'Those people at Tilling,' she said, 'how interesting it will all be. They seemed to me very much alive, especially the women, who appear to have got their majors and their padres completely under their thumbs. Delicious, isn't it, to think of the new interchange of experience which awaits us. Here, nothing happens. Our dear Daisy gets a little rounder and Mrs Arbuthnot a little deafer. We're in a rut: Riseholme is in a rut. We want, both of us, to get out of it, and now we're going to. Fresh fields and pastures new, Georgie. . . . Nothing on your mind, my dear? You were so *distrait* as we drove home.'

Some frightful revivification, thought poor Georgie, had happened to Lucia. It had been delightful, only a couple of days ago, to see her returning to her normal interests, but this repudiation of Riseholme and the craving for the *Iliad* and Tilling and the *Symposium* indicated an almost dangerous appetite for novelty. Or was it only that having bottled herself up for a year, it was natural that, the cork being now out, she should overflow in these ebullitions? She seemed to be lashing her tail, goading herself to some further revelation of her mental or spiritual needs. He shuddered at the thought of what further novelty might be popping out next. The question perhaps.

'I'm sorry I was *distrait*,' said he. 'Of course I was anxious about how Foljambe might take the idea of Tilling.'

Lucia struck the pomander, and it was a relief to Georgie to know that Grosvenor would at once glide in. ... She laughed and laid her hand affectionately on his.

'Georgie, dear, you are' – she took refuge in Italian as Grosvenor appeared – 'you are una vecchia signorina.' (That means 'old maid', thought Georgie.) 'Wider horizons, Georgie: that is what you want. Put the rest of the food on the table, Grosvenor, and we'll help ourselves. Coffee in the music-room when I ring.'

This was ghastly: Lucia, with all this talk of his being an old maid and needing to adapt himself to new conditions, was truly alarming. He almost wondered if she had been taking monkey-gland during her seclusion. Was she going to propose to him in the middle of dinner? Never, in all the years of his friendship with her, had he felt himself so strangely alien. But he was still the master of his fate (at least he hoped so), and it should not be that.

'Shall I give you some strawberry fool?' he asked miserably.

Lucia did not seem to hear him.

'Georgie, we must have 'ickle talk, before I ring for coffee,' she said. 'How long have you and I been dear friends? Longer than either of us care to think.'

'But all so pleasant,' said Georgie, rubbing his cold moist hands on his napkin. ... He wondered if drowning was anything like this.

'My dear, what do the years matter, if they have only deepened and broadened our friendship? Happy years, Georgie, bringing their sheaves with them. That lovely scene in Esmondi; Winchester Cathedral! And now we're both getting on. You're rather alone in the world, and so am I, but people like us with this dear strong bond of friendship between us can look forward to old age – can't we? – without any qualms. Tranquillity comes with years, and that horrid thing which Freud calls sex is expunged. We must read some Freud, I think; I have read none at present. That was one of the things I wanted to say all the time that you would show me cows out of the window. Our friendship is just perfect as it is.'

Georgie's relief when he found that Foljambe liked the idea of Tilling was nothing, positively nothing, to the relief he felt now.

'My dear, how sweet of you to say that,' he said. 'I, too, find the quality of our friendship perfect in every way. Quite impossible, in fact, to think of – I mean, I quite agree with you. As you say, we're getting on in years, I mean I am. You're right a thousand times.'

Lucia saw the sunlit dawn of relief in Georgie's face, and though she had been quite sincere in hoping that he would not be terribly hurt when she hinted to him that he must give up all hopes of being more to her than he was, she had not quite expected this effulgence. It was as if instead of pronouncing his sentence, she had taken from him some secret burden of terrible anxiety. For the moment her own satisfaction at having brought this off without paining him was swallowed up in surprise that he was so far from being pained. Was it possible that all his concern to interest her in cows and rainbows was due to apprehension that she might be leading up, *via* the topics of friendship and marriage, to something exceedingly different from the disclosure which had evidently gratified him rather than the reverse?

She struck the pomander quite a sharp blow.

'Let us go and have our coffee then,' she said. 'It is lovely that we are of one mind. Lovely! And there's another subject we haven't spoken about at all. Miss Mapp. What do you make of Miss Mapp? There was a look in her eye when she heard we were going to lunch with Mrs Wyse that amazed me. She would have liked to bite her or scratch her. What did it mean? It was as if Mrs Wyse – she asked me to call her Susan by the way, but I'm not sure that I can manage it just yet without practising – as if Mrs Wyse had pocketed something of hers. Most extraordinary. I don't belong to Miss Mapp. Of course it's easy to see that she thinks herself very much superior to all the rest of Tilling. She says that all her friends are angels and lambs, and then just crabs them a little. Marcate mie parole, Georgino! I believe she wants to run me. I believe Tilling is seething with intrigue. But we shall see. How I hate all that sort of thing! We have had a touch of it now and then in Riseholme. As if it mattered who took the lead! We should aim at being equal citizens of a noble republic, where art and literature and all the manifold interests of the world are our concern. Now let us have a little music.'

Whatever might be the state of affairs at Tilling, Riseholme during this month of July boiled and seethed with excitements. It was just like old times, and all circled, as of old, round Lucia. She had taken the plunge; she had come back (though just now for so brief a space before her entering upon Mallards) into her native centrality. Gradually, and in increasing areas, grey and white and violet invaded the unrelieved black in which she had spent the year of her widowhood; one day she wore a white belt, another there were grey panels in her skirt, another her garden-hat had a violet riband on it. Even Georgie, who had a great eye for female attire, could not accurately follow these cumulative changes: he could not be sure whether she had worn a grey cloak before, or whether she had had white gloves in church last Sunday. Then, instead of letting her hair droop in slack and mournful braids over her ears, it resumed its old polished and corrugated appearance, and on her pale cheeks (ashen with grief) there bloomed a little brown rouge, which made her look as if she had been playing golf again, and her lips certainly were ruddier. It was all intensely exciting, a series of subtle changes at the end of which, by the middle of July, her epiphany in church without anything black about her, and with the bloom of her vitality quite restored, passed almost unremarked.

These outward and visible signs were duly representative of what had taken place within. Time, the great healer, had visited her sick-room, laid his hand on her languid brow, and the results were truly astonishing. Lucia became as good as new, or as good as old. Mrs Arbuthnot and her tall daughters, Piggy and Goosie, Georgie and Daisy and her husband, greedy Robert, Colonel Boucher and his wife, and the rest were all bidden to dinner at the Hurst once more, and sometimes Lucia played to them the slow movement of the Moonlight Sonata, and sometimes she instructed them in such elements of Contract Bridge as she had mastered during the day. She sketched, she played the organ in church in the absence of the organist who had measles, she sang a solo, 'O for the wings of a Dove' when he recovered and the leading chorister got chicken-pox, she had lessons in book-binding at 'Ye Signe of ye Daffodille', she sat in Perdita's garden, not reading Shakespeare, but Pope's *Iliad*, and murmured half-forgotten fragments of Greek irregular verbs as she went to sleep. She had a plan for visiting Athens in the spring (' "the violet-crowned", is not that a lovely epithet, Georgie?') and in compliment to Queen Anne regaled her guests with rich thick chocolate. The hounds of spring were on the winter traces of her widowhood, and snapped up every fragment of it, and indeed spring seemed truly to have returned to her, so various and so multi-coloured were the blossoms that were unfolding. Never at all had Riseholme seen Lucia in finer artistic and intellectual fettle, and it was a long time since she had looked so gay. The world, or at any rate Riseholme, which at Riseholme came to much the same thing, had become her parish again.

Georgie, worked to the bone with playing duets, with consulting Foljambe as to questions of linen and plate (for it appeared that Isabel Poppit, in pursuance of the simple life, slept between blankets in the backyard, and ate uncooked vegetables out of a wooden bowl like a dog), with learning Vanderbilt conventions, with taking part in Royal processions across the Green, with packing his bibelots and sending them to the bank, with sketching, so that he might be in good form when he began to paint at Tilling with a view to exhibiting in the Art Society, wondered what was the true source of these stupendous activities of Lucia's, whether she was getting fit, getting in training, so to speak, for a campaign at Tilling. Somehow it seemed likely, for she would hardly think it worth while to run the affairs of Riseholme with such energy, when she was about to disappear from it for three months. Or was she intending to let Riseholme see how dreadfully flat everything would become when she left them? Very likely both these purposes were at work; it was like her to kill two birds with one stone. Indeed, she was perhaps killing three birds with one stone, for multifarious as were the interests in which she was engaged there was one, now looming large in Riseholme, namely the Elizabethan fête, of which she seemed strangely unconscious. Her drive, her powers of instilling her friends with her own fervour, never touched that: she did not seem to know that a fête was being contemplated at all, though now a day seldom passed without a procession of some sort crossing the Green or a Morris-dance getting entangled with the choristers practising madrigals, or a crowd of soldiers and courtiers being assembled near the front entrance of the 'Ambermere Arms', while Daisy harangued them from a chair put on the top of a table, pausing occasionally because she forgot her words, or in order to allow them to throw up their hats and cry 'God Save the Queen's Grace', 'To hell with Spain', and other suitable ejaculations. Daisy, occasionally now in full dress, ruff and pearls and all, came across to the gate of the Hurst, to wait for the procession to join her, and Lucia sitting in Perdita's garden would talk to her about Tilling or the importance of being prudent if you were vulnerable at contract, apparently unaware that Daisy was dressed up at all. Once Lucia came out of the Ambermere Arms when Daisy was actually mounting the palfrey that drew the milk-cart for a full-dress rehearsal, and she seemed to be positively palfrey-blind. She merely said 'Don't forget that you and Robert are dining with me tonight. Half past seven, so that we shall get a good evening's bridge,' and went on her way. . . . Or she would be passing the pond on which the framework of the *Golden Hind* was already constructed, and on which Georgie was even then kneeling down to receive the accolade amid the faint cheers of Piggy and Goosie, and she just waved her hand to Georgie and said: 'Musica after lunch, Georgie?' She made no sarcastic comments to anybody, and did not know that they were doing anything out of the ordinary.

Under this pointed unconsciousness of hers, a species of blight spread over the scheme to which Riseholme ought to have been devoting its most enthusiastic energies. The courtiers were late for rehearsals, they did not even remove their cigarettes when they bent to kiss the Queen's hand, Piggy and Goosie made steps of Morris-dances when they ought to have been holding up Elizabeth's train, and Georgie snatched up a cushion, when the accolade was imminent, to protect his shoulder. The choir-boys droned their way through madrigals, sucking peppermints, there was no life, no keenness about it all, because Lucia, who was used to inspire all Riseholme's activities, was unaware that anything was going on.

One morning when only a fortnight of July was still to run, Drake was engaged on his croquet-lawn tapping the balls about and trying to tame his white satin shoes which hurt terribly. From the garden next door came the familiar accents of the Queen's speech to her troops.

'And though I am only a weak woman,' declaimed Daisy who was determined to go through the speech without referring to her book. 'Though I am only a weak woman, a weak woman – ' she repeated.

'Yet I have the heart of a Prince,' shouted Drake with the friendly intention of prompting her.

'Thank you, Georgie. Or ought it to be Princess, do you think?'

'No: Prince,' said Georgie.

'Prince,' cried Daisy. 'Though I am only a weak woman, yet I have the heart of a Prince. . . . Let me see. . . . Prince.'

There was silence.

'Georgie,' said Daisy in her ordinary voice. 'Do stop your croquet a minute and come to the paling. I want to talk.'

'I'm trying to get used to these shoes,' said Georgie. 'They hurt frightfully. I shall have to take them to Tilling and wear them there. Oh, I haven't told you, Lady Brixton came down yesterday evening – '

'I know that,' said Daisy.

' – and she thinks that her brother will take my house for a couple of months, as long as I don't leave any servants. He'll be here for the fête, if he does, so I wonder if you could put me up. How's Robert's cold?'

'Worse,' she said. 'I'm worse too. I can't remember half of what I knew by heart a week ago. Isn't there some memory-system?'

'Lots, I believe,' said Georgie. 'But it's rather late. They don't improve your memory all in a minute. I really think you had better read your speech to the troops, as if it was the opening of Parliament.'

'I won't,' said Daisy taking off her ruff. 'I'll learn it if it costs me the last breath of blood in my body – I mean drop.'

'Well, it will be very awkward if you forget it all,' said Georgie. 'We can't cheer nothing at all. Such a pity, because your voice carries perfectly now. I could hear you while I was breakfasting.'

'And it's not only that,' said Daisy. 'There's no life in the thing. It doesn't look as if it was happening.'

'No, that's true,' said Georgie. 'These tarsome shoes of mine are real enough, though!'

'I begin to think we ought to have had a producer,' said Daisy. 'But it was so much finer to do it all ourselves, like – like Oberammergau. Does Lucia ever say anything about it? I think it's too mean for words of her to take no interest in it.'

'Well, you must remember that you asked her only to be my wife,' said Georgie. 'Naturally she wouldn't like that.'

'She ought to help us instead of going about as if we were all invisible,' exclaimed Daisy.

'My dear, she did offer to help you. At least, I told you ages ago, that I felt sure she would if you asked her to.'

'I feel inclined to chuck the whole thing,' said Daisy.

'But you can't. Masses of tickets have been sold. And who's to pay for the *Golden Hind* and the roast sheep and all the costumes?' asked Georgie. 'Not to mention all our trouble. Why not ask her to help, if you want her to?'

'Georgie, will you ask her?' said Daisy.

'Certainly not,' said Georgie very firmly. 'You've been managing it from the first. It's your show. If I were you, I would ask her at once. She'll be over here in a few minutes, as we're going to have a music. Pop in.'

A melodious cry of 'Georgino mio!' resounded from the open window of Georgie's drawing-room, and he hobbled away down the garden walk. Ever since that beautiful understanding they had arrived at, that both of them shrank, as from a cup of hemlock, from the idea of marriage, they had talked Italian or baby language to a surprising extent from mere lightness of heart.

'Me tummin',' he called. 'Oo very good girl, Lucia. O molto punctuale.'

(He was not sure about that last word, nor was Lucia, but she understood it.)

'Georgino! Che curiose scalpe!' said Lucia, leaning out of the window.

'Don't be so cattiva. They are cattivo enough,' said Georgie. 'But Drake did have shoes exactly like these.'

The mere mention of Drake naturally caused Lucia to talk about something else. She did not understand any allusion to Drake.

'Now for a good practice,' she said, as Georgie limped into the drawing-room. 'Foljambe beamed at me. How happy it all is! I hope you said you were at home to nobody. Let us begin at once. Can you manage the *sostenuto* pedal in those odd shoes?'

Foljambe entered.

'Mrs Quantock, sir,' she said.

'Daisy darling,' said Lucia effusively. 'Come to hear our little practice? We must play our best, Georgino.'

Daisy was still in queenly costume, except for the ruff. Lucia seemed as usual to be quite unconscious of it.

'Lucia, before you begin – ' said Daisy.

'So much better than interrupting,' said Lucia. 'Thank you, dear. Yes?'

'About this fête. Oh, for gracious' sake don't go on seeming to know nothing about it. I tell you there is to be one. And it's all nohow. Can't you help us?'

Lucia sprang from the music-stool. She had been waiting for

this moment, not impatiently, but ready for it if it came, as she knew it must, without any scheming on her part. She had been watching from Perdita's garden the straggling procession smoking cigarettes, the listless halberdiers not walking in step, the courtiers yawning in Her Majesty's face, the languor and the looseness arising from the lack of an inspiring mind. The scene on the *Golden Hind*, and that of Elizabeth's speech to her troops were equally familiar to her, for though she could not observe them from under her garden-hat close at hand, her husband had been fond of astronomy and there were telescopes great and small, which brought these scenes quite close. Moreover, she had that speech which poor Daisy found so elusive by heart. So easy to learn, just the sort of cheap bombast that Elizabeth would indulge in: she had found it in a small history of England, and had committed it to memory, just in case . . .

'But I'll willingly help you, dear Daisy,' she said. 'I seem to remember you told me something about it. You as Queen Elizabeth, was it not, a roast sheep on the *Golden Hind*, a speech to the troops, Morris-dances, bear-baiting, no, not bear-baiting. Isn't it all going beautifully?'

'No! It isn't,' said Daisy in a lamentable voice. 'I want you to help us, will you? It's all like dough.'

Great was Lucia. There was no rubbing in: there was no hesitation, there was nothing but helpful sunny cordiality in response to this S.O.S.

'How you all work me!' she said, 'but I'll try to help you if I can. Georgie, we must put off our practice, and get to grips with all this, if the fête is to be a credit to Riseholme. Addio, caro Mozartino for the present. Now begin, Daisy, and tell me all the trouble.'

For the next week Mozartino and the *Symposium* and contract bridge were non-existent and rehearsals went on all day. Lucia demonstrated to Daisy how to make her first appearance, and, when the trumpeters blew a fanfare, she came out of the door of the Hurst, and without the slightest hurry majestically marched down the crazy pavement. She did not fumble at the gate as Daisy always did, but with a swift imperious nod to Robert Quantock, which made him pause in the middle of a sneeze, she caused him to fly forward, open it, and kneel as she passed through. She made a wonderful curtsey to her lieges and motioned them to close up in front of her. And all this was done in the clothes of today, without a ruff or a pearl to help her.

'Something like that, do you think, dear Daisy, for the start of the procession?' she said to her. 'Will you try it like that and see how it goes? And a little more briskness, gentlemen, from the halberdiers. Would you form in front of me now, while Mrs Quantock goes into the house. ... Ah, that has more snap, hasn't it? Excellent. Quite like guardsmen. Piggy and Goosie, my dears, you must remember that you are Elizabethan Countesses. Very stately, please, and Countesses never giggle. Sweep two low curtsies, and while still down pick up the Queen's train. You opened the gate very properly, Robert. Very nice indeed. Now may we have that all over again. Queen, please,' she called to Daisy.

Daisy came out of the house in all the panoply of Majesty, and with the idea of not hurrying came so slowly that her progress resembled that of a queen following a hearse. ('A little quicker, dear,' called Lucia encouragingly. 'We're all ready.') Then she tripped over a piece of loose crazy pavement. Then she sneezed, for she had certainly caught Robert's cold. Then she forgot to bow to her lieges, until they had closed up in procession in front of her, and then bobbed to their backs.

'Hey ho, nonny, nonny,' sang Lucia to start the chorus. 'Off we go! Right, left – I beg your pardon, how stupid of me – Left, right. Crescendo, choir. Sing out, please. We're being Merrie England. Capital!'

Lucia walked by the side of the procession across the Green, beating time with her parasol, full of encouragement and enthusiasm. Sometimes she ran on in front and observed their progress, sometimes she stood still to watch them go by.

'Open out a little, halberdiers,' she cried, 'so that we can get a glimpse of the Queen from in front. Hey nonny! Hold that top G, choir-boys! Queen, dear, don't attempt to keep step with the halberdiers. Much more royal to walk as you choose. The train a little higher, Piggy and Goosie. Hey nonny, nonny HEY'

She looked round as they got near the *Golden Hind*, to see if the cooks were basting the bolster that did duty for the sheep, and that Drake's sailors were dancing their hornpipes.

'Dance, please, sailors,' she shrieked. 'Go on basting, cooks, until the procession stops, and then begins the chorus of sailors on the last "nonny Hey". Cooks must join in, too, or we shan't get enough body of sound. Open out, halberdiers, leave plenty of room for the Queen to come between you. Slowly, Elizabeth! "When the storm winds blow and the surges sweep." Louder! Are you ready, Georgie? No; don't come off the *Golden Hind*. You receive the Queen on the deck. A little faster, Elizabeth, the chorus will be over before you get here.'

Lucia clapped her hands.

'A moment, please,' she said. 'A wonderful scene. But just one suggestion. May I be Queen for a minute and show you the effect I want to get, dear Daisy? Let us go back, procession, please, twenty yards. Halberdiers still walking in front of Queen. Sailors' chorus all over again. Off we go! Now, halberdiers, open out. Half right and left turn respectively. Two more steps and halt, making an avenue.'

It was perfectly timed. Lucia moved forward up the avenue of halberdiers, and just as the last 'Yo ho' was yelled by cooks, courtiers and sailors, she stepped with indescribable majesty on to the deck of the *Golden Hind*. She stood there a moment quite still, and whispered to Georgie, 'Kneel and kiss my hand, Georgie. Now, everybody together! "God save the Queen." "Hurrah." Hats in the air. Louder, louder! Now die away! There!'

Lucia had been waving her own hat, and shrilly cheering herself, and now she again clapped her hands for attention, as she scrutinized the deck of the *Golden Hind*.

'But I don't see Drake's wife,' she said. 'Drake's wife, please.'

Drake's wife was certainly missing. She was also the grocer's wife, and as she had only to come forward for one moment, curtsey and disappear, she was rather slack at her attendance of rehearsals.

'It doesn't matter,' said Lucia. 'I'll take Drake's wife, just for this rehearsal. Now we must have that over again. It's one of the most important moments, this Queen's entry on to the *Golden*

Hind. We must make it rich in romance, in majesty, in spaciousness. Will the procession, please, go back, and do it over again?'

This time poor Daisy was much too early. She got to the *Golden Hind* long before the cooks and the chorus were ready for her. But there was a murmur of applause when Mrs Drake (so soon to be Lady Drake) ran forward and threw herself at the Queen's feet in an ecstasy of loyalty, and having kissed her hand walked backwards from the Presence with head bent low, as if in adoration.

'Now step to the Queen's left, Georgie,' said Lucia, 'and take her left hand, holding it high and lead her to the banquet. Daisy dear, you *must* mind your train. Piggy and Goosie will lay it down as you reach the deck, and then you must look after it yourself. If you're not careful you'll tread on it and fall into the Thames. You've got to move so that it follows you when you turn round.'

'May I kick it?' asked Daisy.

'No, it can be done without. You must practise that.'

The whole company now, sailors, soldiers, courtiers and all were eager as dogs are to be taken out for a walk by their mistress, and Lucia reluctantly consented to come and look at the scene of the review at Tilbury. Possibly some little idea, she diffidently said, might occur to her; fresh eyes sometimes saw something, and if they all really wanted her she was at their disposal. So off they went to the rendezvous in front of the Ambermere Arms, and the fresh eyes perceived that according to the present grouping of soldiers and populace no spectator would see anything of the Queen at all. So that was rectified, and the mob was drilled to run into its proper places with due eagerness, and Lucia sat where the front row of spectators would be to hear the great speech. When it was over she warmly congratulated the Queen.

'Oh, I'm so glad you liked it,' said the Queen. 'Is there anything that strikes you?'

Lucia sat for a while in pensive silence.

'Just one or two little tiny things, dear,' she said, thoughtfully. 'I couldn't hear very well. I wondered sometimes what the mob was cheering about. And would it perhaps be safer to read the speech? There was a good deal of prompting that was quite audible. Of course there are disadvantages in reading it. It won't seem so spontaneous and inspiring if you consult a paper all the time. Still, I daresay you'll get it quite by heart before the time comes. Indeed, the only real criticism I have to make is about your gestures, your movements. Not quite, quite majestic enough, not inspiring enough. Too much as if you were whisking flies away. More breadth!'

Lucia sighed, she appeared to be lost in meditation.

'What kind of breadth?' asked Daisy.

'So difficult to explain,' said Lucia. 'You must get more variety, more force, both in your gestures and your voice. You must be fierce sometimes, the great foe of Spain, you must be tender, the mother of your people. You must be a Tudor. The daughter of that glorious cad, King Hal. Coarse and kingly. Shall I show you for a moment the sort of thing I mean? So much easier to show than to explain.'

Daisy's heart sank: she was full of vague apprehensions. But having asked for help, she could hardly refuse this generous granting of it, for indeed Lucia was giving up her whole morning.

'Very good of you,' she said.

'Lend me your copy of the speech, then,' said Lucia, 'and might I borrow your ruff, just to encourage myself. Now let me read through the speech to myself. Yes ... yes ... crescendo, and flare up then ... pause again; a touch of tenderness .... Well, as you insist on it I'll try to show you what I mean. Terribly nervous, though.'

Lucia advanced and spoke in the most ingratiating tones to her army and the mob.

'Please have patience with me, ladies and gentlemen,' she said, 'while I go through the speech once more. Wonderful words, aren't they? I know I shan't do them justice. Let me see: the palfrey with the Queen will come out from the garden of the Ambermere Arms, will it not? Then will the whole mob, please, hurry into the garden and then come out romping and cheering and that sort of thing in front of me. When I get to where the table is, that is to say, where the palfrey will stand as I make my speech, some of the mob must fall back, and the rest sit on the grass, so that the spectators may see. Now, please.'

Lucia stalked in from the garden, joining the mob now and then to show them how to gambol, and nimbly vaulted (thanks to calisthenics) on to the table on which was the chair where she sat on horseback.

Then with a great sweep of her arm she began to speak. The copy of the speech which she carried flew out of hand, but that made no difference, for she had it all by heart, and without pause, except for the bursts of cheering from the mob, when she pointed at them, she declaimed it all, her voice now rising, now falling, now full of fire, now tender and motherly. Then she got down from the table, and passed along the line of her troops, beckoned to the mob – which in the previous scene had been cooks and sailors and all sorts of things – to close up behind her with shouts and cheers and gambollings, and went off down the garden path again.

'That sort of thing, dear Daisy, don't you think?' she said to the Queen, returning her ruff. 'So crude and awkwardly done I know, but perhaps that may be the way to put a little life into it. Ah, there's your copy of the speech. Quite familiar to me, I found. I dare say I learned it when I was at school. Now, I really must be off. I wish I could think that I had been any use.'

Next morning Lucia was too busy to superintend the rehearsal: she was sure that Daisy would manage it beautifully, and she was indeed very busy watching through a field-glass in the music-room the muddled and anaemic performance. The halberdiers strolled along with their hands in their pockets. Piggy and Goosie sat down on the grass, and Daisy knew less of her speech than ever. The collective consciousness of Riseholme began to be aware that nothing could be done without Lucia, and conspiratorial groups conferred stealthily, dispersing or dropping their voices as Queen Elizabeth approached and forming again when she had gone by. The choir which had sung so convincingly when Lucia was there with her loud 'Hey nonny nonny', never bothered about the high G at all, but simply left it out; the young Elizabethans who had gambolled like intoxicated lambkins under her stimulating eye sat down and chewed daisies; the cooks never attempted to baste the bolster; and the Queen's speech to her troops was received with the most respectful tranquillity.

Georgie, in Drake's shoes which were becoming less agonizing with use, lunched with Colonel and Mrs Boucher. Mrs Boucher was practically the only Riseholmite who was taking no part in the fête, because her locomotion was confined to the wheels of a bath-chair. But she attended every rehearsal and had views which were as strong as her voice.

'You may like it or not,' she said very emphatically, 'but the only person who can pull you through is Lucia.'

'Nobody can pull poor Daisy through,' said Georgie. 'Hopeless!'

'That's what I mean,' said she. 'If Lucia isn't the Queen, I say give it all up. Poor Daisy's bitten off, if you won't misunderstand me, as we're all such friends of hers, more than she can chew. My kitchen-cat, and I don't care who knows it, would make a better Queen.'

'But Lucia's going off to Tilling next week,' said Georgie. 'She won't be here even.'

'Well, beg and implore her not to desert Riseholme,' said Mrs Boucher. 'Why, everybody was muttering about it this morning, army and navy and all. It was like a revolution. There was Mrs Arbuthnot; she said to me, "Oh dear, oh dear, it will never do at all," and there was poor Daisy standing close beside her; and we all turned red. Most awkward. And it's up to you, Georgie, to go down on your knees to Lucia and say "Save Riseholme!" There!'

'But she refused to have anything to do with it, after Daisy asked her to be my wife,' said Georgie Drake.

'Naturally she would be most indignant. An insult. But you and Daisy must implore her. Perhaps she could go to Tilling and settle herself in and then come back for the fête, for she doesn't need any rehearsals. She could act every part herself if she could be a crowd.'

'Marvellous woman!' said Colonel Boucher. 'Every word of the Queen's speech by heart, singing with the choir, basting with the cooks, dancing with the sailors. That's what I call instinct, eh? You'd have thought she had been studying it all the time. I agree with my wife, Georgie. The difficulty is Daisy. *Would* she give it up?'

Georgie brightened.

'She did say that she felt inclined to chuck the whole thing, a few days ago,' he said.

'There you are, then,' said Mrs Boucher. 'Remind her of what she said. You and she go to Lucia before you waste time over another rehearsal without her, and implore her. Implore! I shouldn't a bit wonder if she said yes. Indeed, if you ask me, I believe that she's been keeping out of it all until you saw you couldn't do without her. Then she came to help at a rehearsal, and you all saw what you could do when she was there. Why, I burst out cheering myself when she said she had the heart of a Prince. Then she retires again as she did this morning, and more than ever you see you can't do without her. I say she's waiting to be asked. It would be like her, you know.'

That was an illuminating thought; it certainly seemed tremendously like Lucia at her very best.

'I believe you're right. She's cleverer than all of us put together,' said Georgie. 'I shall go over to Daisy at once and sound her. Thank God, my shoes are better.'

It was a gloomy queen that Georgie found, a Queen of Sheba with no spirit left in her, but only a calmness of despair.

'It went worse than ever this morning,' she remarked. 'And I daresay we've not touched bottom yet. Georgie, what is to be done?'

It was more delicate to give Daisy the chance of abdicating herself.

'I'm sure I don't know,' said he. 'But something's got to be done. I wish I could think what.'

Daisy was rent with pangs of jealousy and of consciousness of her supreme impotence. She took half a glass of port, which her regime told her was deadly poison.

'Georgie! Do you think there's the slightest chance of getting Lucia to be the Queen and managing the whole affair?' she asked quaveringly.

'We might try,' said Georgie. 'The Bouchers are for it, and everybody else as well, I think.'

'Well, come quick then, or I may repent,' said Daisy.

Lucia had seen them coming, and sat down at her piano. She had not time to open her music, and so began the first movement of the Moonlight Sonata.

'Ah, how nice!' she said. 'Georgie, I'm going to practise all afternoon. Poor fingers so rusty! And did you have a lovely rehearsal this morning? Speech going well, Daisy? I'm sure it is.'

'Couldn't remember a word,' said Daisy. 'Lucia, we all want to turn the whole thing over to you, Queen and all. Will you – ?'

'Please, Lucia,' said Georgie.

Lucia looked from one to the other in amazement.

'But, dear things, how can I?' she said. 'I shan't be here to begin with. I shall be at Tilling. And then all the trouble you've been taking, Daisy. I couldn't. Impossible. Cruel.'

'We can't do it at all without you,' said Daisy firmly. 'So that's impossible too. Please, Lucia.'

Lucia seemed quite bewildered by these earnest entreaties.

'Can't you come back for the fête?' said Georgie. 'Rehearse all day, every day, till the end of the month. Then go to Tilling, and you and I will return just for the week of the fête.'

Lucia seemed to be experiencing a dreadful struggle with herself.

'Dear Georgie, dear Daisy, you're asking a great sacrifice of me,' she said. 'I had planned my days here so carefully. My music, my Dante: all my lessons! I shall have to give them all up, you know, if I'm to get this fête into any sort of shape. No time for anything else.'

A miserable two-part fugue of 'Please, Lucia. It's the only chance. We can't do it unless you're Queen,' suddenly burst into the happy strains of 'It *is* good of you. Oh, thank you, Lucia,' and the day was won.

Instantly she became extremely business-like.

'No time to waste then,' she said. 'Let us have a full rehearsal at three, and after that I'll take the Morris-dancers and the halberdiers. You and Georgie must be my lieutenants, dear Daisy. We shall all have to pull together. By the way, what will you be now?'

'Whatever you like,' said Daisy recklessly.

Lucia looked at her fixedly with that gimlet-eye, as if appraising, at their highest, her possibilities.

'Then let us see, dear Daisy,' she said, 'what you can make of Drake's wife. Quite a short part, I know, but so important. You have to get into that one moment all the loyalty, all the devotion of the women of England to the Queen.'

She rose.

'Let us begin working at once,' she said. 'This is the *Golden Hind*: I have just stepped on to it. Now go behind the piano, and then come tripping out, full of awe, full of reverence. . . . Oh, dear me, that will never do. Shall I act it for you once more . . . ?'

4

Lucia had come back to Tilling last night from the fêteful week at Riseholme, and she was sitting next morning after breakfast at the window of the garden-room in Miss Mapp's house. It was a magic casement to anyone who was interested in life, as Lucia certainly was, and there was a tide every morning in the affairs of Tilling which must be taken at the flood. Mrs Wyse's Royce had lurched down the street, Diva had come out with her market-basket from quaint Irene's house, of which she was now the tenant, Miss Mapp's (she was already by special request 'Elizabeth') gardner had wheeled off to the greengrocer his daily barrowful of garden-produce. Elizabeth had popped in to welcome her on her return from Risehome and congratulate her on the fête of which the daily illustrated papers had been so full, and, strolling about the garden with her had absently picked a few roses (Diva's had green fly); the Padre passing by the magic casement had wished her good morrow, Mistress Lucas, and finally Major Benjy had come out of his house on the way to catch the tram to the golf-links. Lucia called 'Quai-hai' to him in silvery tones, for they had made great friends in the days she had already spent at Tilling, and reminded him that he was dining with her that night. With great gallantry he had taken off his cap, and bawled out that this wasn't the sort of engagement he was in any danger of forgetting, au reservoir.

The tide had ebbed now, and Lucia left the window. There was so much to think about that she hardly knew where to begin. First her eyes fell on the piano which was no longer the remarkable Blumenfelt belonging to Elizabeth on which she had been granted the privilege to play, but one which she had hired from Brighton. No doubt it was quite true that, as Elizabeth had said, her Blumenfelt had been considered a very fine instrument, but nobody for the last twenty years or so could have considered it anything but a remarkable curiosity. Some notes sounded like the chirping of canaries (Diva's canary was quite well again after its pip), others did not sound at all, and the *sostenuto* pedal was a thing of naught. So Lucia had hired a new piano, and had put the canary-piano in the little telephone-room off the hall. It filled it up, but it was still possible to telephone if you went in sideways. Elizabeth had shown traces of acidity about this when she discovered the substitution, and had rather pensively remarked that her piano had belonged to her dearest mamma, and she hoped the telephone-room wasn't damp. It seemed highly probable that it had been her mother's if not her grandmother's, but after all Lucia had not promised to play on it.

So much for the piano. There lay on it now a china bowl full of press-cuttings, and Lucia glanced at a few, recalling the triumphs of the past week. The fête, favoured by brilliant weather and special trains from Worcester and Gloucester and Birmingham, had been a colossal success. The procession had been cinematographed, so too had the scene on the *Golden Hind*, and the click of cameras throughout the whole performance had been like the noise of cicalas in the south. The Hurst had been the target for innumerable lenses (Lucia was most indulgent), and she was photographed at her piano and in Perdita's garden, and musing in an arbour, as Queen Elizabeth and as herself, and she had got one of those artists to take (rather reluctantly) a special photograph of Drake's poor wife. That had not been a success, for Daisy had moved, but Lucia's intention was of the kindest. And throughout, to photographers and interviewers alike, Lucia (knowing that nobody would believe it) had insisted that all the credit was due to Drake's wife, who had planned everything (or nearly) and had done all the spade-work.

There had nearly been one dreadful disaster. In fact there had been the disaster, but the amazing Lucia, quite impromptu, had wrung a fresh personal triumph out of it. It was on the last day of the fête, when the Green would hardly contain the influx of visitors, and another tier of benches had been put up round the pond where the *Golden Hind* lay, that this excruciating moment had occurred. Queen Elizabeth had just left the deck where she had feasted on a plateful of kippered cinders, and the procession was escorting her away, when the whole of the stern of the *Golden Hind*, on which was the fire and the previously roasted sheep and a mast streaming with ancients and the crowd of cheering cooks, broke off, and with a fearful splash and hiss fell into the water. Before anyone could laugh, Lucia (remembering that the water was only three feet deep at the most and so there was no danger of anyone drowning) broke into a ringing cry. 'Zounds and Zooks,' she shouted. 'Thus will I serve the damned galleons of Spain,' and with a magnificent gesture of disdain at the cooks standing waist high in the water, she swept on with her procession. The reporters singled out for special notice this wonderful piece of symbolism. A few of the most highbrow deemed it not quite legitimate business, but none questioned the superb dramatic effect of the device, for it led on with such perfect fitness to the next topic, namely the coming of the Armada. The cooks waded ashore, rushed home to change their clothes, and were in time to take their places in the mob that escorted her white palfrey. Who would mind a ducking in the service of such a resourceful Queen? Of all Lucia's triumphs during the week that inspired moment was the crown, and she could not help wondering what poor Daisy would have done, if she had been on the throne that day.

Probably she would have said: 'Oh dear, oh dear, they've all fallen into the water. We must stop.'

No wonder Riseholme was proud of Lucia, and Tilling which had been greedily devouring the picture papers was proud too. There was one possible exception, she thought, and that was Elizabeth, who in her visit of welcome just now had said, 'How dreadful all this publicity must be for you, dear! How you must shrink from it!'

But Lucia, as usual, had been quite up to the mark.

'Sweet of you to be so sympathetic, Elizabeth,' she had said. 'But it was my duty to help dear Riseholme, and I mustn't regard the consequences to myself.'

That put the lid on Elizabeth: she said no more about the fête.

Lucia, as these random thoughts suggested by that stack of press-cuttings flitted through her brain, felt that she would have soon to bring it to bear on Elizabeth, for she was becoming something of a problem. But first, for this was an immediate concern, she must concentrate on Georgie. Georgie at the present moment, unconscious of his doom, and in a state of the highest approbation with life generally, was still at Riseholme, for Adele Brixton's brother, Colonel Cresswell, had taken his house for two months and there were many bits of things, embroidery and sketches and little bottles with labels, 'For outward application only', which he must put away. He had been staying with Daisy for the fête, for Foljambe and the rest of his staff had come to Tilling at the beginning of August and it was not worth while taking them all back, though it would be difficult to get on without Foljambe for a week. Then he had stopped on for this extra day with Daisy after the fête was over, to see that everything was tidy and discreet and Lucia expected him back this morning.

She had very upsetting news for him: ghastly in fact. The vague rumours which had been rife at Riseholme were all too true, and Cadman, her chauffeur, had come to Lucia last night with the bomb-shell that he and Foljambe were thinking of getting married. She had seen Foljambe as well, and Foljambe had begged her to break the news to Georgie.

'I should take it very kind of you, ma'am, if you would,' Foljambe had said, 'for I know I could never bring myself to do it, and he wouldn't like to feel that I had made up my mind without telling him. We're in no hurry, me and Cadman, we shouldn't think of being married till after we got back to Riseholme in the autumn, and that'll give Mr Georgie several months to get suited. I'm sure you'll make him see it the right way, if anybody can.'

This handsome tribute to her tact had had its due weight, and Lucia had promised to be the messenger of these dismal tidings. Georgie would arrive in time for lunch today, and she was determined to tell him at once. But it was dreadful to think of poor Georgie on his way now, full of the pleasantest anticipations for the future (since Foljambe had expressed herself more than pleased with her bedroom) and rosy with the remarkable success of his Drake and the very substantial rent for which he had let his house for two months, with this frightful blow so soon to be dealt him by her hand. Lucia had no idea how he would take it, except that he was certain to be terribly upset. So, leaving the garden-room and establishing herself in the pleasant shade on the lawn outside, she thought out quite a quantity of bracing and valuable reflections.

She turned her thoughts towards Elizabeth Mapp. During those ten days before Lucia had gone to Riseholme for the fête, she had popped in every single day: it was quite obvious that Elizabeth was keeping her eye on her. She always had some glib excuse: she wanted a hot-water bottle, or a thimble or a screwdriver that she had forgotten to take away, and declining all assistance would go to look for them herself, feeling sure that she could put her hand on them instantly without troubling anybody. She would go into the kitchen wreathed in smiles and pleasant observations for Lucia's cook, she would pop into the servants' hall and say something agreeable to Cadman, and pry into cupboards to find what she was in search of. (It was during one of these expeditions that she had discovered her dearest mamma's piano in the telephone-room.) Often she came in without knocking or ringing the bell, and then if Lucia or Grosvenor heard her clandestine entry, and came to see who it was, she scolded herself for her stupidity in not remembering that for the present, this was not her house. So forgetful of her.

On one of these occasions she had popped out into the garden, and found Lucia eating a fig from the tree that grew against the garden-room, and was covered with fruit.

'Oh, you dear thief!' she said. 'What about garden-produce?'

Then seeing Lucia's look of blank amazement, she had given a pretty peal of laughter.

'Lulu, dear! Only my joke,' she cried. 'Poking a little fun at Queen Elizabeth. You may eat every fig in my garden, and I wish there were more of them.'

On another occasion Elizabeth had found Major Benjy having tea with Lucia, and she had said, 'Oh, how disappointed I am! I had so hoped to introduce you to each other, and now someone else has taken that treat from me. Who was the naughty person?' But perhaps that was a joke too. Lucia was not quite sure that she liked Elizabeth's jokes, any more than she liked her informal visits.

This morning, Lucia cast an eye over her garden. The lawn badly wanted cutting, the flower-beds wanted weeding, the box-edgings to them wanted clipping, and it struck her that the gardener, whose wages she paid, could not have done an hour's work here since she left. He was never in this part of the garden at all, she seemed to remember, but was always picking fruit and vegetables in the kitchen-garden, or digging over the asparagus-bed, or potting chrysanthemums, or doing other jobs that did not concern her own interests but Elizabeth's. There he was now, a nice genial man, preparing a second basketful of garden-produce to take to the greengrocer's, from whom eventually Lucia bought it. An inquiry must instantly be held.

'Good morning, Coplen,' she said. 'I want you to cut the lawn today. It's got dreadfully long.'

'Very sorry, ma'am,' said he. 'I don't think I can find time today myself. I could get a man in perhaps to do it.'

'I should prefer that you should,' said Lucia. 'You can get a man in to pick those vegetables.'

'It's not only them,' he said. 'Miss Mapp she told me to manure the strawberry-beds today.'

'But what has Miss Mapp got to do with it?' said she. 'You're in my employment.'

'Well, that does only seem fair,' said the impartial Coplen. 'But you see, ma'am, my orders are to go to Miss Mapp every morning and she tells me what she wants done.'

'Then for the future please come to me every morning and see what I want done,' she said. 'Finish what you're at now, and then start on the lawn at once. Tell Miss Mapp by all means that I've given you these instructions. And no strawberry-bed shall be manured today, nor indeed until my garden looks less like a tramp who hasn't shaved for a week.'

Supported by an impregnable sense of justice but still dangerously fuming, Lucia went back to her garden-room, to tranquillize herself with an hour's practice on the new piano. Very nice tone; she and Georgie would be able to start their musical hours again now. This afternoon, perhaps, if he felt up to it after the tragic news, a duet might prove a tonic. Not a note had she played during that triumphant week at Riseholme. Scales first then, and presently she was working away at a new Mozart, which she and Georgie would subsequently read over together.

There came a tap at the door of the garden-room. It opened a chink, and Elizabeth in her sweetest voice said:

'May I pop in once more, dear?'

Elizabeth was out of breath. She had hurried up from the High Street.

'So sorry to interrupt your sweet music, Lucia mia,' she said. 'What a pretty tune! What fingers you have! But my good Coplen has come to me in great perplexity. So much better to clear it up at once, I thought, so I came instantly though rather rushed today. A little misunderstanding, no doubt. Coplen is not clever.'

Elizabeth seemed to be labouring under some excitement which might account for this loss of wind. So Lucia waited till she was more controlled.

' – And your new piano, dear?' asked Elizabeth. 'You like it? It sounded so sweet, though not quite the tone of dearest mamma's. About Coplen then?'

'Yes, about Coplen,' said Lucia.

'He misunderstood, I am sure, what you said to him just now. So distressed he was. Afraid I should be vexed with him. I said I would come to see you and make it all right.'

'Nothing easier dear,' said Lucia. 'We can put it all right in a minute. He told me he' had not time to cut the lawn today because he had to manure your strawberry-beds, and I said "The lawn please, at once," or words to that effect. He didn't quite grasp, I think, that he's in my employment, so naturally I reminded him of it. He understands now, I hope.'

Elizabeth looked rather rattled at these energetic remarks, and Lucia saw at once that this was the stuff to give her.

'But my garden-produce, you know, dear Lulu,' said Elizabeth. 'It is not much use to me if all those beautiful pears are left to rot on the trees till the wasps eat them.'

'No doubt that is so,' said Lucia; 'but Coplen, whose wages I pay, is no use to me if he spends his entire time in looking after your garden-produce. I pay for his time, dear Elizabeth, and I intend to have it. He also told me he took his orders every morning from you. That won't do at all. I shan't permit that for a moment. If I had engaged your cook as well as your gardener, I should not allow her to spend her day in roasting mutton for you. So that's all settled.'

It was borne in upon Elizabeth that she hadn't got a leg to stand upon and she sat down.

'Lulu,' she said, 'anything would be better than that I should have a misunderstanding with such a dear as you are. I won't argue, I won't put my point of view at all. I yield. There! If you can spare Coplen for an hour in the morning to take my little fruits and vegetables to the greengrocer's I should be glad.'

'Quite impossible, I'm afraid, dear Elizabeth,' said Lucia with the greatest cordiality. 'Coplen has been neglecting the flower-garden dreadfully, and for the present it will take him all his time to get it tidy again. You must get someone else to do that.'

Elizabeth looked quite awful for a moment: then her face was wreathed in smiles again.

'Precious one!' she said. 'It shall be exactly as you wish. Now I must run away. Au reservoir. You're not free I suppose, this evening to have a little dinner with me? I would ask Major Benjy to join us, and our beloved Diva, who has a passion, positively a passion for you. Major Benjy indeed too. He raves about you. Wicked woman, stealing all the hearts of Tilling.'

Lucia felt positively sorry for the poor thing. Before she left for Riseholme last week, she had engaged Diva and Major Benjy to dine with her tonight, and it was quite incredible that Elizabeth, by this time, should not have known that.

'Sweet of you,' she said, 'but I have a tiny little party myself tonight, just one or two, dropping in.'

Elizabeth lingered a moment yet, and Lucia said to herself that the thumb-screw and the rack would not induce her to ask Elizabeth, however long she lingered.

Lucia and she exchanged kissings of the hand as Elizabeth emerged from the front door, and tripped down the street. 'I see, I must be a little firm with her,' thought Lucia, 'and when I've taught her her place, then it will be time to be kind. But I won't ask her to dinner just yet. She must learn not to ask me when she knows I'm engaged. And she shall not pop in without ringing. I must tell Grosvenor to put the door on the chain.'

Lucia returned to her practice, but shovelled the new Mozart out of sight, when, in one of her glances out of the open window she observed Georgie coming up the street, on his way from the station. He had a light and airy step, evidently he was in the best of spirits and he waved to her as he caught sight of her.

'Just going to look in at the cottage one second,' he called out, 'to see that everything's all right, and then I'll come and have a chat before lunch. Heaps to tell you.'

'So have I,' said Lucia, ruefully thinking what one of those things was. 'Hurry up, Georgie.'

He tripped along up to the cottage, and Lucia's heart was wrung for him, for all that gaiety would soon suffer a total eclipse, and she was to be the darkener of his day. Had she better tell him instantly, she wondered, or hear his news first, and outline the recent Manoeuvres of Mapp. These exciting topics might prove tonic, something to fall back on afterwards. Whereas, if she stabbed him straight away, they would be of no service as restoratives. Also there was stewed lobster for lunch, and Georgie who adored it would probably not care a bit about it if the blow fell first.

Georgie began to speak almost before he opened the door.

'All quite happy at the cottage,' he said, 'and Foljambe ever so pleased with Tilling. Everything in spick-and-span order and my paint-box cleaned up and the hole in the carpet mended quite beautifully. She must have been busy while I was away.'

('Dear, oh dear, she has,' thought Lucia.)

'And everything settled at Riseholme,' continued poor Georgie. 'Colonel Cresswell wants my house for three months, so I said yes, and now we're both homeless for October, unless we keep on our houses here. I had to put on my Drake clothes again yesterday, for the *Birmingham Gazette* wanted to photograph me. My dear, what a huge success it all was, but I'm glad to get away, for everything will be as flat as ditchwater now, all except Daisy. She began to buck up at once the moment you left, and I positively heard her say how quickly you picked up the part of the Queen after watching her once or twice.'

'No! Poor thing!' said Lucia with deep compassion.

'Now tell me all about Tilling,' said Georgie, feeling he must play fair.

'Things are beginning to move, Georgie,' said she, forgetting for the time the impending tragedy. 'Night-marches, Georgie, manoeuvres. Elizabeth, of course. I'm sure I was right, she wants to run me, and if she can't (if!) she'll try to fight me. I can see glimpses of hatred and malice in her.'

'And you'll fight her?' asked Georgie eagerly.

'Nothing of the kind my dear,' said Lucia. 'What do you take me for? Every now and then, when necessary, I shall just give her two or three hard slaps. I gave her one this morning: I did indeed. Not a very hard one, but it stung.'

'No! Do tell me,' said Georgie.

Lucia gave a short but perfectly accurate description of the gardener-crisis.

'So I stopped that,' she said, 'and there are several other things

I shall stop. I won't have her, for instance, walking into my house without ringing. So I've told Grosvenor to put up the chain. And she calls me Lulu which makes me sick. Nobody's ever called me Lulu and they shan't begin now. I must see if calling her Liblib will do the trick. And then she asked me to dinner tonight, when she must have known perfectly well that Major Benjy and Diva are dining with me. You're dining too, by the way.'

'I'm not sure if I'd better,' said Georgie. 'I think Foljambe might expect me to dine at home the first night I get back. I know she wants to go through the linen and plate with me.'

'No, Georgie, quite unnecessary,' said she. 'I want you to help me to give the others a jolly comfortable evening. We'll play bridge and let Major Benjy lay down the law. We'll have a genial evening, make them enjoy it. And tomorrow I shall ask the Wyses and talk about Countesses. And the day after I shall ask the Padre and his wife and talk Scotch. I want you to come every night. It's new in Tilling, I find, to give little dinners. Tea is the usual entertainment. And I shan't ask Liblib at all till next week.'

'But my dear, isn't that war?' asked Georgie. (It did look rather like it.)

'Not the least. It's benevolent neutrality. We shall see if she learns sense. If she does, I shall be very nice to her again and ask her to several pleasant little parties. I am giving her every chance. Also Georgie. . . .' Lucia's eyes assumed that gimlet-like expression which betokened an earnest purpose, 'I want to understand her and be fair to her. At present I can't understand her. The idea of her giving orders to a gardener to whom I give wages! But that's all done with. I can hear the click of the mowing-machine on the lawn now. Just two or three things I won't stand. I won't be patronized by Liblib, and I won't be called Lulu, and I won't have her popping in and out of my house like a cuckoo clock.'

Lunch drew to an end. There was Georgie looking so prosperous and plump with his chestnut-coloured hair no longer in the least need of a touch of dye, and his beautiful clothes. Already Major Benjy, who had quickly seen that if he wanted to be friends with Lucia he must be friends with Georgie too, had pronounced him to be the best-dressed man in Tilling, and Lucia, who invariably passed on dewdrops of this kind, had caused Georgie the deepest gratification by repeating this. And now she was about to plunge a dagger in his heart. She put her elbows on the table, so as to be ready to lay a hand of sympathy on his.

'Georgie, I've got something to tell you,' she said.

'I'm sure I shall like it,' said he. 'Go on.'

'No, you won't like it at all,' she said.

It flashed through his mind that Lucia had changed her mind about marrying him, but it could not be that, for she would never have said he wouldn't like it at all. Then he had a flash of intuition.

'Something about Foljambe,' he said in a quavering voice.

'Yes. She and Cadman are going to marry.'

Georgie turned on her a face from which all other expression except hopeless despair had vanished, and her hand of sympathy descended on his, firmly pressing it.

'When?' he said, after moistening his dry lips.

'Not for the present. Not till we get back to Riseholme.'

Georgie pushed away his untasted coffee.

'It's the most dreadful thing that's ever happened to me,' he said. 'It's quite spoiled all my pleasure. I didn't think Foljambe was so selfish. She's been with me fifteen years, and now she goes and breaks up my home like this.'

'My dear, that's rather an excessive statement,' said Lucia. 'You can get another parlour-maid. There are others.'

'If you come to that, Cadman could get another wife,' said Georgie, 'and there isn't another parlour-maid like Foljambe. I have suspected something now and then, but I never thought it would come to this. What a fool I was to leave her here when I went back to Riseholme for the fête! Or if only we had driven back there with Cadman instead of going by train. It was madness. Here they were with nothing to do but make plans behind our backs. No one will ever look after my clothes as she does. And the silver. You'll miss Cadman, too.'

'Oh, but I don't think he means to leave me,' said Lucia in

some alarm. 'What makes you think that? He said nothing about it.'

'Then perhaps Foljambe doesn't mean to leave me,' said Georgie, seeing a possible dawn on the wreck of his home.

'That's rather different,' said Lucia. 'She'll have to look after his house, you see, by day, and then at night he'd – he'd like her to be there.'

'Horrible to think of,' said Georgie bitterly. 'I wonder what she can see in him. I've got a good mind to go and live in an hotel. And I had left her five hundred pounds in my will.'

'Georgie, that was very generous of you. Very,' put in Lucia, though Georgie would not feel the loss of that large sum after he was dead.

'But now I shall certainly add a codicil to say "if still in my service",' said Georgie rather less generously. 'I didn't think it of her.'

Lucia was silent a moment. Georgie was taking it very much to heart indeed, and she racked her ingenious brain.

'I've got an idea,' she said at length. 'I don't know if it can be worked, but we might see. Would you feel less miserable about it if Foljambe would consent to come over to your house say at nine in the morning and be there till after dinner? If you were dining out as you so often are, she could go home earlier. You see Cadman's at the Hurst all day, for he does odd jobs as well, and his cottage at Riseholme is quite close to your house. You would have to give them a charwoman to do the housework.'

'Oh, that is a good idea,' said Georgie, cheering up a little. 'Of course I'll give her a charwoman or anything else she wants if she'll only look after me as before. She can sleep wherever she likes. Of course there may be periods when she'll have to be away, but I shan't mind that as long as I know she's coming back. Besides, she's rather old for that, isn't she?'

It was no use counting the babies before they were born, and Lucia glided along past this slightly indelicate subject with Victorian eyes.

'It's worth while seeing if she'll stay with you on these terms,' she said.

'Rather, I shall suggest it at once,' said Georgie. 'I think I shall

99

congratulate her very warmly, and say how pleased I am, and then ask her. Or would it be better to be very cold and preoccupied and not talk to her at all? She'd hate that, and then when I ask her after some days whether she'll stop on with me, she might promise anything to see me less unhappy again.'

Lucia did not quite approve of this Machiavellian policy.

'On the other hand, it might make her marry Cadman instantly, in order to have done with you,' she suggested. 'You'd better be careful.'

'I'll think it over,' said Georgie. 'Perhaps it would be safer to be very nice to her about it and appeal to her better nature, if she's got one. But I know I shall never manage to call her Cadman. She must keep her maiden name, like an actress.'

Lucia duly put in force her disciplinary measures for the reduction of Elizabeth. Major Benjy, Diva and Georgie dined with her that night, and there was a plate of nougat chocolates for Diva, whose inordinate passion for them was known all over Tilling, and a fiery curry for the Major to remind him of India, and a dish of purple figs bought at the greengrocer's but plucked from the tree outside the garden-room. She could not resist giving Elizabeth ever so gentle a little slap over this, and said that it was rather a roundabout process to go down to the High Street to buy the figs which Coplen plucked from the tree in the garden, and took down with other garden-produce to the shop: she must ask dear Elizabeth to allow her to buy them, so to speak, at the pit-mouth. But she was genuinely astonished at the effect this little joke had on Diva. Hastily she swallowed a nougat chocolate entire and turned bright red.

'But doesn't Elizabeth give you garden-produce?' she asked in an incredulous voice.

'Oh no,' said Lucia, 'just flowers for the house. Nothing else.'

'Well, I never!' said Diva. 'I fully understood, at least I thought I did – '

Lucia got up. She must be magnanimous and encourage no public exposure, whatever it might be, of Elizabeth's conduct, but for the pickling of the rod of discipline she would like to hear about it quietly.

'Let's go into the garden-room and have a chat,' she said. 'Look after Major Benjy, Georgie, and don't sit too long in bachelordom, for I must have a little game of bridge with him. I'm terribly frightened of him, but he and Mrs Quantock must be kind to beginners like you and me.'

The indignant Diva poured out her tale of Elizabeth's iniquities in a turgid flood.

'So like Elizabeth,' she said. 'I asked her if she gave you garden-produce, and she said she wasn't going to dig up her potatoes and carry them away. Well, of course I thought that meant she did give it you. So like her. Bismarck, wasn't it, who told the truth in order to deceive? And so of course I gave her my garden-produce and she's selling one and eating the other. I wish I'd known I ought to have distrusted her.'

Lucia smiled that indulgent Sunday-evening smile which meant she was thinking hard on week-day subjects.

'I like Elizabeth so much,' she said, 'and what do a few figs matter?'

'No, but she always scores,' said Diva, 'and sometimes it's hard to bear. She got my house with garden-produce thrown in for eight guineas a week and she lets her own without garden-produce for twelve.'

'No dear, I pay fifteen,' said Lucia.

Diva stared at her open-mouthed.

'But it was down in Woolgar's books at twelve,' she said. 'I saw it myself. She is a one: isn't she?'

Lucia maintained her attitude of high nobility, but this information added a little more pickling.

'Dear Elizabeth!' she said. 'So glad that she was sharp enough to get a few more guineas. I expect she's very clever, isn't she? And here come the gentlemen. Now for a jolly little game of bridge.'

Georgie was astonished at Lucia. She was accustomed to lay down the law with considerable firmness, and instruct partners and opponents alike, but tonight a most unusual humility possessed her. She was full of diffidence about her own skill and of praise for her partner's: she sought advice, even once asking Georgie what she ought to have played, though that was clearly a mistake, for next moment she rated him. But for the other two she had nothing but admiring envy at their declarations and their management of the hand, and when Diva revoked she took all the blame on herself for not having asked her whether her hand was bare of the suit. Rubber after rubber they played in an amity hitherto unknown in the higher gambling circles of Tilling; and when, long after the incredible hour of twelve had struck, it was found on the adjustment of accounts that Lucia was the universal loser, she said she had never bought experience so cheaply and pleasantly.

Major Benjy wiped the foam of his third (surreptitious and hastily consumed) whisky and soda from his walrus-moustache.

'Most agreeable evening of bridge I've ever spent in Tilling,' he said. 'Bless me, when I think of the scoldings I've had in this room for some little slip, and the friction there's been ... Mrs Plaistow knows what I mean.'

'I should think I did,' said Diva, beginning to simmer again at the thought of garden-produce. 'Poor Elizabeth! Lessons in self-control are what she wants and after that a few lessons on the elements of the game wouldn't be amiss. Then it would be time to think about telling other people how to play.'

This very pleasant party broke up, and Georgie, hurrying home to Mallards Cottage, thought he could discern in these comments the key to Lucia's unwonted humility at the card-table. For herself she had only kind words on the subject of Elizabeth as befitted a large-hearted woman, but Diva and Major Benjy could hardly help contrasting, brilliantly to her advantage, the charming evening they had spent with the vituperative scenes which usually took place when they played bridge in the garden-room. 'I think Lucia has begun,' thought Georgie to himself as he went noiselessly upstairs so as not to disturb the slumbers of Foljambe.

It was known, of course, all over Tilling the next morning that there had been a series of most harmonious rubbers of bridge last night at Mallards till goodness knew what hour, for

Diva spent half the morning in telling everybody about it, and the other half in advising them not to get their fruit and vegetables at the shop which dealt in the garden-produce of the Bismarckian Elizabeth. Equally well known was it that the Wyses were dining at Mallards tonight, for Mrs Wyse took care of that, and at eight o'clock that evening the Royce started from Porpoise Street, and arrived at Mallards at precisely one minute past. Georgie came on foot from the Cottage thirty yards away in the other direction, in the highest spirits, for Foljambe after consultation with her Cadman had settled to continue on day duty after the return to Riseholme. So Georgie did not intend at present to execute that vindictive codicil to his will. He told the Wyses whom he met on the doorstep of Mallards about the happy termination of this domestic crisis, while Mrs Wyse took off her sables and disclosed the fact that she was wearing the order of the M.B.E. on her ample bosom; and he observed that Mr Wyse had a soft crinkly shirt with a low collar, and velveteen dress clothes: this pretty costume caused him to look rather like a conjurer. There followed very polite conversations at dinner, full of bows from Mr Wyse; first he talked to his hostess, and when Lucia tried to produce general talk and spoke to Georgie, he instantly turned his head to the right, and talked most politely to his wife about the weather and the news in the evening paper till Lucia was ready for him again.

'I hear from our friend Miss Mapp,' he said to her, 'that you speak the most beautiful and fluent Italian.'

Lucia was quite ready to oblige.

'Ah, che bella lingua!' said she. 'Ma ho dimenticato tutto, non parla nessuno in Riseholme.'

'But I hope you will have the opportunity of speaking it before long in Tilling,' said Mr Wyse. 'My sister Amelia, Contessa Faraglione, may possibly be with us before long, and I shall look forward to hearing you and she talk together. A lovely language to listen to, though Amelia laughs at my poor efforts when I attempt it.'

Lucia smelled danger here. There had been a terrible occasion once at Riseholme when her bilingual reputation had been shattered by her being exposed to the full tempest of Italian volleyed at her by a native, and she had been unable to understand anything that he said. But Amelia's arrival was doubtful and at present remote, and it would be humiliating to confess that her knowledge was confined to a chosen though singularly limited vocabulary.

'Georgie, we must rub up our Italian again,' she said. 'Mr Wyse's sister may be coming here before long. What an opportunity for us to practise!'

'I do not imagine that you have much need of practice,' said Mr Wyse, bowing to Lucia. 'And I hear your Elizabethan fête' (he bowed to Queen Elizabeth) 'was an immense success. We so much want somebody at Tilling who can organize and carry through schemes like that. My wife does all she can, but she sadly needs someone to help, or indeed direct her. The hospital for instance, terribly in need of funds. She and I were talking as to whether we could not get up a garden fête with some tableaux or something of the sort to raise money. She has designs on you, I know, when she can get you alone, for indeed there is no one in Tilling with ability and initiative.'

Suddenly it struck Lucia that though this was very gratifying to herself, it had another purpose, namely to depreciate somebody else, and surely that could only be one person. But that name must not escape her lips.

'My services, such as they are, are completely at Mrs Wyse's disposal,' she said, 'as long as I am in Tilling. This garden for instance. Would that be a suitable place for something of the sort?'

Mr Wyse bowed to the garden.

'The ideal spot,' said he. 'All Tilling would flock here at your bidding. Never yet in my memory has the use of it been granted for such a purpose; we have often lamented it.'

There could no longer be much doubt as to the sub-current in such remarks, but the beautiful smooth surface must not be broken.

'I quite feel with you,' said Lucia. 'If one is fortunate enough, even for a short time, to possess a pretty little garden like this, it should be used for the benefit of charitable entertainment. The hospital: what more deserving object could we have? Some tableaux, you suggested. I'm sure Mr Pillson and I would be only too glad to repeat a scene or two from our fête at Rise-holme.'

Mr Wyse bowed so low that his large loose tie nearly dipped itself in an ice pudding.

'I was trying to summon my courage to suggest exactly that,' he said. 'Susan, Mrs Lucas encourages us to hope that she will give you a favourable audience about the project we talked over.'

The favourable audience began as soon as the ladies rose, and was continued when Georgie and Mr Wyse followed them. Already it had been agreed that the Padre might contribute an item to the entertainment, and that was very convenient, for he was to dine with Lucia the next night.

'His Scotch stories,' said Susan. 'I can never hear them too often, for though I've not got a drop of Scotch blood myself, I can appreciate them. Not a feature of course, Mrs Lucas, but just to fill up pauses. And then there's Mrs Plaistow. How I laugh when she does the sea-sick passenger with an orange, though I doubt if you can get oranges now. And Miss Coles. A wonderful mimic. And then there's Major Benjy. Perhaps he would read us portions of his diary.'

A pause followed. Lucia had one of those infallible pre-sentiments that a certain name hitherto omitted would follow. It did.

'And if Miss Mapp would supply the refreshment department with fruit from her garden here, that would be a great help,' said Mrs Wyse.

Lucia caught in rapid succession the respective eyes of all her guests, each of whom in turn looked away. 'So Tilling knows all about the garden-produce already,' she thought to herself.

Bridge followed, and here she could not be as humble as she had been last night, for both the Wyses abased themselves be-fore she had time to begin.

'We know already,' said Algernon, 'of the class of player that you are, Mrs Lucas,' he said. 'Any hints you will give Susan and me will be so much appreciated. We shall give you no game at all I'm afraid, but we shall have a lesson. There is no one in

Tilling who has any pretensions of being a player. Major Benjy and Mrs Plaistow and we sometimes have a well-fought rubber on our own level, and the Padre does not always play a bad game. But otherwise the less said about our bridge the better. Susan, my dear, we must do our best.'

Here indeed was a reward for Lucia's humility last night. The winners had evidently proclaimed her consummate skill, and was that, too, a reflection on somebody else, only once hitherto named, and that in connexion with garden-produce? Tonight Lucia's hands dripped with aces and kings: she denuded her adversaries of all their trumps, and then led one more for safety's sake, after which she poured forth a galaxy of winners. Whoever was her partner was in luck, and tonight it was Georgie who had to beg for change for a ten-shilling note and leave the others to adjust their portions. He recked nothing of this financial disaster, for Foljambe was not lost to him. When the party broke up Mrs Wyse begged him to allow her to give him a lift in the Royce, but as this would entail a turning of that majestic car, which would take at least five minutes followed by a long drive for them round the church square and down into the High Street and up again to Porpoise Street, he adventured forth on foot for his walk of thirty yards and arrived without undue fatigue.

Georgie and Lucia started their sketching next morning. Like charity, they began at home, and their first subjects were each other's houses. They put their camp-stools side by side, but facing in opposite directions, in the middle of the street half-way between Mallards and Mallards Cottage; and thus, by their having different objects to portray, they avoided any sort of rivalry, and secured each other's companionship.

'So good for our drawing,' said Georgie. 'We were getting to do nothing but trees and clouds which needn't be straight.'

'I've got the crooked chimney,' said Lucia proudly. 'That one beyond your house. I think I shall put it straight. People might think I had done it crooked by accident. What do you advise?'

'I think I wouldn't,' said he. 'There's character in its crookedness. Or you might make it rather more crooked than it is:

then there won't be any doubt. .... Here comes the Wyses' car. We shall have to move on to the pavement. Tarsome.'

A loud hoot warned them that that was the safer course, and the car lurched towards them. As it passed, Mr Wyse saw whom he had disturbed, stopped the Royce (which had so much better a right to the road than the artists) and sprang out, hat in hand.

'A thousand apologies,' he cried. 'I had no idea who it was, and for what artistic purpose, occupying the roadway. I am indeed distressed, I would instantly have retreated and gone round the other way had I perceived in time. May I glance? Exquisite! The crooked chimney! Mallards Cottage! The West front of the church!' He bowed to them all.

There followed that evening the third dinner-party when the Padre and wee wifie made the quartet. The Royce had called for him that day to take him to lunch in Porpoise Street (Lucia had seen it go by), and it was he who now introduced the subject of the proposed entertainment on behalf of the hospital, for he knew all about it and was ready to help in any way that Mistress Lucas might command. There were some Scottish stories which he would be happy to narrate, in order to fill up intervals between the tableaux, and he had ascertained that Miss Coles (dressed as usual as a boy) would give her most amusing parody of 'The Boy stood on the burning deck', and that Mistress Diva said she thought that an orange or two might be procured. If not, a ripe tomato would serve the purpose. He would personally pledge himself for the services of the church choir to sing catches and glees and madrigals, whenever required. He suggested also that such members of the workhouse as were not bedridden might be entertained to tea, in which case the choir would sing grace before and after buns.

'As to the expense of that, if you approve,' he said, 'put another baubee on the price of admission, and there'll be none in Tilling to grudge the extra expense wi' such entertainment as you and the other leddies will offer them.'

'Dear me, how quickly it is all taking shape,' said Lucia, finding that almost without effort on her part she had been drawn into the place of prime mover in all this, and that still a sort of conspiracy of silence prevailed with regard to Miss Mapp's name, which hitherto had only been mentioned as a suitable provider of fruit for the refreshment department. 'You must form a little committee, Padre, for putting all the arrangements in hand at once. There's Mr Wyse who really thought of the idea, and you –'

'And with yourself,' broke in the Padre, 'that will make three. That's sufficient for any committee that is going to do its work without any argle-bargle.'

There flashed across Lucia's mind a fleeting vision of what Elizabeth's face would be like when she picked up, as she would no doubt do next morning, the news of all that was becoming so solid.

'I think I had better not be on the committee,' she said, quite convinced that they would insist on it. 'It should consist of real Tillingites who take the lead among you in such things. I am only a visitor here. They will all say I want to push myself in.'

'Ah, but we can't get on wi'out ye, Mistress Lucas,' said the Padre. 'You must consent to join us. An' three, as I say, makes the perfect committee.'

Mrs Bartlett had been listening to all this with a look of ecstatic attention on her sharp but timid little face. Here she gave vent to a series of shrill minute squeaks which expressed a mouselike merriment, quite unexplained by anything that had been actually said, but easily accounted for by what had not been said. She hastily drank a sip of water and assured Lucia that a crumb of something (she was eating a peach) had stuck in her throat and made her cough. Lucia rose when the peach was finished.

'Tomorrow we must start working in earnest,' she said. 'And to think that I planned to have a little holiday in Tilling! You and Mr Wyse are regular slave-drivers, Padre.'

Georgie waited behind that night after the others had gone, and bustled back to the garden-room after seeing them off.

'My dear, it's getting too exciting,' he said. 'But I wonder if you're wise to join the committee.'

'I know what you mean,' said Lucia, 'but there really is no

reason why I should refuse, because they won't have Elizabeth. It's not me, Georgie, who is helping her out. But perhaps you're right, and I think tomorrow I'll send a line to the Padre and say that I am really too busy to be on the committee, and beg him to ask Elizabeth instead. It would be kinder. I can manage the whole thing just as well without being on the committee. She'll hear all about the entertainment tomorrow morning, and know that she's not going to be asked to do anything, except supply some fruit.'

'She knows a good deal about it now,' said Georgie. 'She came to tea with me today.'

'No! I didn't know you had asked her.'

'I didn't,' said Georgie. 'She came.'

'And what did she say about it?'

'Not very much, but she's thinking hard what to do. I could see that. I gave her the little sketch I made of the Land-gate when we first came down here, and she wants me to send in another picture for the Tilling Art Exhibition. She wants you to send something too.'

'Certainly she shall have my sketch of Mallards Cottage and the crooked chimney,' said Lucia. 'That will show good will. What else did she say?'

'She's getting up a jumble-sale in aid of the hospital,' said Georgie. 'She's busy, too.'

'Georgie, that's copied from us.'

'Of course it is; she wants to have a show of her own, and I'm sure I don't wonder. And she knows all about your three dinner-parties.'

Lucia nodded. 'That's all right then,' she said. 'I'll ask her to the next. We'll have some duets that night, Georgie. Not bridge I think, for they all say she's a perfect terror at cards. But it's time to be kind to her.'

Lucia rose.

'Georgie, it's becoming a frightful rush already,' she said. 'This entertainment which they insist on my managing will make me very busy, but when one is appealed to like that, one can't refuse. Then there's my music, and sketching, and I haven't begun to rub up my Greek.... And don't forget to send for your Drake-clothes. Good night, my dear. I'll call to you over the garden-paling tomorrow if anything happens.'

'I feel as if it's sure to,' said Georgie with enthusiasm.

5

Lucia was writing letters in the window of the garden-room next morning. One, already finished, was to Adele Brixton asking her to send to Mallards the Queen Elizabeth costume for the tableaux: a second, also finished, was to the Padre, saying that she found she would not have time to attend committees for the hospital fête, and begging him to co-opt Miss Mapp. She would, however, do all in her power to help the scheme, and make any little suggestions that occurred to her. She added that the chance of getting fruit gratis for the refreshment department would be far brighter if the owner of it was on the board.

The third letter, firmly beginning 'Dearest Liblib' (and to be signed very large, LUCIA), asking her to dine in two days' time, was not quite done when she saw dearest Liblib, with a fixed and awful smile, coming swiftly up the street. Lucia, sitting sideways to the window, could easily appear absorbed in her letter and unconscious of Elizabeth's approach, but from beneath half-lowered eyelids she watched her with the intensest interest. She was slanting across the street now, making a bee-line for the door of Mallards ('and if she tries to get in without ringing the bell, she'll find the chain on the door,' thought Lucia).

The abandoned woman, disdaining the bell, turned the handle and pushed. It did not yield to her intrusion, and she pushed more strongly. There was the sound of jingling metal, audible even in the garden-room, as the hasp that held the end of the chain gave way; the door flew open wide, and with a few swift and nimble steps she just saved herself from falling flat on the floor of the hall.

Lucia, pale with fury, laid down her pen and waited for the

situation to develop. She hoped she would behave like a lady, but was quite sure it would be a firm sort of lady. Presently up the steps to the garden-room came that fairy tread, the door was opened an inch, and that odious voice said:

'May I come in, dear?'

'Certainly,' said Lucia brightly.

'Lulu dear,' said Elizabeth, tripping across the room with little brisk steps. 'First I must apologize: so humbly. Such a stupid accident. I tried to open your front door, and gave it a teeny little push and your servants had forgotten to take the chain down. I am afraid I broke something. The hasp must have been rusty.'

Lucia looked puzzled.

'But didn't Grosvenor come to open the door when you rang?' she asked.

'That was just what I forgot to do, dear,' said Elizabeth. 'I thought I would pop in to see you without troubling Grosvenor. You and I such friends, and so difficult to remember that my dear little Mallards – Several things to talk about!'

Lucia got up.

'Let us first see what damage you have done,' she said with an icy calmness, and marched straight out of the room, followed by Elizabeth. The sound of the explosion had brought Grosvenor out of the dining-room, and Lucia picked up the dangling hasp and examined it.

'No, no sign of rust,' she said. 'Grosvenor, you must go down to the ironmonger and get them to come up and repair this at once. The chain must be made safer and you must remember always to put it on, day and night. If I am out, I will ring.'

'So awfully sorry, dear Lulu,' said Elizabeth, slightly cowed by this firm treatment. 'I had no idea the chain could be up. We all keep our doors on the latch in Tilling. Quite a habit.'

'I always used to in Riseholme,' said Lucia. 'Let us go back to the garden-room, and you will tell me what you came to talk about.'

'Several things,' said Elizabeth when they had settled themselves. 'First, I am starting a little jumble-sale for the hospital, and I wanted to look out some old curtains and rugs, laid away in cupboards, to give to it. May I just go upstairs and downstairs and poke about to find them?'

'By all means,' said Lucia. 'Grosvenor shall go round with you as soon as she has come back from the ironmonger's.'

'Thank you, dear,' said Elizabeth, 'though there's no need to trouble Grosvenor. Then another thing. I persuaded Mr Georgie to send me a sketch for our picky exhibition. Promise me that you'll send me one too. Wouldn't be complete without something by you. How you get all you do into the day is beyond me; your sweet music, your sketching, and your dinner-parties every evening.'

Lucia readily promised, and Elizabeth then appeared to lose herself in reverie.

'There *is* one more thing,' she said at last. 'I have heard a little gossip in the town both today and yesterday about a fête which it is proposed to give in my garden. I feel sure it is mere tittle-tattle, but I thought it would be better to come up here to know from you that there is no foundation for it.'

'But I hope there is a great deal,' said Lucia. 'Some tableaux, some singing, in order to raise funds for the hospital. It would be so kind of you if you would supply the fruit for the refreshment booth from your garden. Apropos I should be so pleased to buy some of it every day myself. It would be fresher than if, as at present, it is taken down to the greengrocer and brought up again.'

'Anything to oblige you, dear Lulu,' said Elizabeth. 'But that would be difficult to arrange. I have contracted to send all my garden-produce to Twistevant's – such a quaint name, is it not? – for these months, and for the same reason I should be unable to supply this fête which I have heard spoken of. The fruit is no longer mine.'

Lucia had already made up her mind that, after this affair of the chain, nothing would induce her to propose that Elizabeth should take her place on the committee. She would cling to it through storm and tempest.

'I see,' she said. 'Perhaps then you could let us have some fruit from Diva's garden, unless you have sold that also.'

Elizabeth came to the point, disregarding so futile a suggestion.

'The fête itself, dear one,' she said, 'is what I must speak about. I cannot possibly permit it to take place in my garden. The rag-tag and bob-tail of Tilling passing through my hall and my sweet little sitting-room and spending the afternoon in my garden! All my carpets soiled and my flower-beds trampled on! And how do I know that they will not steal upstairs and filch what they can find?'

Lucia's blood had begun to boil: nobody could say that she was preserving a benevolent neutrality. In consequence she presented an icy demeanour, and if her voice trembled at all, it was from excessive cold.

'There will be no admission to the rooms in the house,' she said. 'I will lock all the doors, and I am sure that nobody in Tilling will be so ill bred as to attempt to force them open.'

That was a nasty one, Elizabeth recoiled for a moment from the shock, but rallied. She opened her mouth very wide to begin again, but Lucia got in first.

'They will pass straight from the front door into the garden,' she said, 'where we undertake to entertain them, presenting their tickets of admission or paying at the door. As for the carpet in your sweet little sitting-room, there isn't one. And I have too high an opinion of the manners of Tilling in general to suppose that they will trample on your flower-beds.'

'Perhaps you would like to hire a menagerie,' said Elizabeth, completely losing her self-control, 'and have an exhibition of tigers and sharks in the garden-room.'

'No: I should particularly dislike it,' said Lucia earnestly. 'Half of the garden-room would have to be turned into a sea-water tank for the sharks and my piano would be flooded. And the rest would have to be full of horse-flesh for the tigers. A most ridiculous proposal, and I cannot entertain it.'

Elizabeth gave a dreadful gasp as if she was one of the sharks and the water had been forgotten. She adroitly changed the subject.

'Then again, there's the rumour – of course it's only rumour –

that there is some idea of entertaining such inmates of the workhouse as are not bedridden. Impossible.'

'I fancy the Padre is arranging that,' said Lucia. 'For my part, I'm delighted to give them a little treat.'

'And for my part,' said Miss Mapp, rising (she had become Miss Mapp again in Lucia's mind), 'I will not have my little home-sanctuary invaded by the rag-tag –'

'The tickets will be half a crown,' interposed Lucia.

' – and bob-tail of Tilling,' continued Miss Mapp.

'As long as I am tenant here,' said Lucia, 'I shall ask here whom I please, and when I please, and – and how I please. Or do you wish me to send you a list of the friends I ask to dinner for your sanction?'

Miss Mapp, trembling very much, forced her lips to form the syllables:

'But, dear Lulu –'

'Dear Elizabeth, I must beg you not to call me Lulu,' she said. 'Such a detestable abbreviation –'

Grosvenor had appeared at the door of the garden-room.

'Yes, Grosvenor, what is it?' asked Lucia in precisely the same voice.

'The ironmonger is here, ma'am,' she said, 'and he says that he'll have to put in some rather large screws, as they're pulled out –'

'Whatever is necessary to make the door safe,' said Lucia. 'And Miss Mapp wants to look into cupboards and take some things of her own away. Go with her, please, and give her every facility.'

Lucia, quite in the grand style, turned to look out of the window in the direction of Mallards Cottage, in order to give Miss Mapp the opportunity of a discreet exit. She threw the window open.

'Georgino! Georgino!' she called, and Georgie's face appeared above the paling.

'Come round and have 'ickle talk, Georgie,' she said. 'Sumfin I want to tell you. Presto!'

She kissed her hand to Georgie and turned back into the room. Miss Mapp was still there, but now invisible to Lucia's eye. She hummed a gay bar of Mozartino, and went back to her table in the bow-window where she tore up the letter of resignation and recommendation she had written to the Padre, and the half-finished note to Miss Mapp, which so cordially asked her to dinner, saying that it was so long since they had met, for they had met again now. When she looked up she was alone, and there was Georgie tripping up the steps by the front door. Though it was standing open (for the iron-monger was already engaged on the firm restoration of the chain) he very properly rang the bell and was admitted.

'There you are,' said Lucia brightly as he came in. 'Another lovely day.'

'Perfect. What has happened to your front door?'

Lucia laughed.

'Elizabeth came to see me,' she said gaily. 'The chain was on the door, as I have ordered it always shall be. But she gave the door such a biff that the hasp pulled out. It's being repaired.'

'No!' said Georgie, 'and did you give her what for?'

'She had several things she wanted to see me about,' said Lucia, keeping an intermittent eye on the front door. 'She wanted to get out of her cupboards some stuff for the jumble-sale she is getting up in aid of the hospital, and she is at it now under Grosvenor's superintendence. Then she wanted me to send a sketch for the picture exhibition, I said I would be delighted. Then she said she could not manage to send any fruit for our fête here. She did not approve of the fête at all, Georgie. In fact, she forbade me to give it. We had a little chat about that.'

'But what's to be done then?' asked Georgie.

'Nothing that I know of, except to give the fête,' said Lucia. 'But it would be no use asking her to be on the committee for an object of which she disapproved, so I tore up the letter I had written to the Padre about it.'

Lucia suddenly focused her eyes and her attention on the front door, and a tone of warm human interest melted the deadly chill of her voice.

'Georgie, there she goes,' she said. 'What a quantity of things! There's an old kettle and a boot-jack, and a rug with a hole in it, and one stair-rod. And there's a shaving from the front door where they are putting in bigger screws, stuck to her skirt. . . . And she's dropped the stair-rod. . . . Major Benjy's picking it up for her.'

Georgie hurried to the window to see these exciting happenings, but Miss Mapp, having recovered the stair-rod, was already disappearing.

'I wish I hadn't given her my picture of the Land-gate,' said he. 'It was one of my best. But aren't you going to tell me all about your interview? Properly, I mean: everything.'

'Not worth speaking of,' said Lucia. 'She asked me if I would like to have a menagerie and keep tigers and sharks in the garden-room. That sort of thing. Mere raving. Come out, Georgie. I want to do a little shopping. Coplen told me there were some excellent greengages from the garden which he was taking down to Twistevant's.'

It was the hour when the collective social life of Tilling was at its briskest. The events of the evening before, tea-parties, and games of bridge had become known and were under discussion, as the ladies of the place with their baskets on their arms collided with each other as they popped in and out of shops and obstructed the pavements. Many parcels were being left at Wasters which Miss Mapp now occupied, for jumble-sales on behalf of deserving objects were justly popular, since everybody had a lot of junk in their houses, which they could not bear to throw away, but for which they had no earthly use. Diva had already been back from Taormina to her own house (as Elizabeth to hers) and had disinterred from a cupboard of rubbish a pair of tongs, the claws of which twisted round if you tried to pick up a lump of coal and dropped it on the carpet, but which were otherwise perfect. Then there was a scuttle which had a hole in the bottom, through which coal dust softly dribbled, and a candlestick which had lost one of its feet, and a glass inkstand once handsome, but now cracked. These treasures, handsome donations to a jumble-sale, but otherwise of no particular value, she carried to her own hall, where donors were requested to leave their offerings, and she learned from Withers, Miss Mapp's palour-maid, the disagreeable news that the jumble-sale was to be held here. The thought revolted her; all the rag-tag and bob-tail of Tilling would come wandering about her house, soiling her carpets and smudging her walls. At this moment Miss Mapp herself came in carrying the tea-kettle and the boot-jack and the other things. She had already thought of half a dozen withering retorts she might have made to Lucia.

'Elizabeth, this will never do,' said Diva. 'I can't have the jumble-sale held here. They'll make a dreadful mess of the place.'

'Oh no, dear,' said Miss Mapp, with searing memories of a recent interview in her mind. 'The people will only come into your hall where you see there's no carpet, and make their purchases. What a beautiful pair of tongs! For my sale? Fancy! Thank you, dear Diva.'

'But I forbid the jumble-sale to be held here,' said Diva. 'You'll be wanting to have a menagerie here next.'

This was amazing luck.

'No, dear, I couldn't dream of it,' said Miss Mapp. 'I should hate to have tigers and sharks all over the place. Ridiculous!'

'I shall put up a merry-go-round in quaint Irene's studio at Taormina,' said Diva.

'I doubt if there's room, dear,' said Miss Mapp, scoring heavily again, 'but you might measure. Perfectly legitimate, of course, for if my house may be given over to parties for paupers, you can surely have a merry-go-round in quaint Irene's and I a jumble-sale in yours.'

'It's not the same thing,' said Diva. 'Providing beautiful tableaux in your garden is quite different from using my panelled hall to sell kettles and coal-scuttles with holes in them.'

'I dare say I could find a good many holes in the tableaux,' said Miss Mapp.

Diva could think of no adequate verbal retort to such coruscations, so for answer she merely picked up the tongs, the coal-scuttle, the candlestick and the inkstand, and put them back in the cupboard from which she had just taken them, and left her tenant to sparkle by herself.

Most of the damaged objects for the jumble-sale must have

arrived by now, and after arranging them in tasteful groups Miss Mapp sat down in a rickety basket-chair presented by the Padre for fell meditation. Certainly it was not pretty of Diva (no one could say that Diva was pretty) to have withdrawn her treasures, but that was not worth thinking about. What did demand her highest mental activities was Lucia's conduct. How grievously different she had turned out to be from that sweet woman for whom she had originally felt so warm an affection, whom she had planned to take so cosily under her wing, and administer in small doses as treats to Tilling society! Lucia had turned upon her and positively bitten the caressing hand. By means of showy little dinners and odious flatteries, she had quite certainly made Major Benjy and the Padre and the Wyses and poor Diva think that she was a very remarkable and delightful person and in these manoeuvres Miss Mapp saw a shocking and sinister attempt to set herself up as the Queen of Tilling society. Lucia had given dinner-parties on three consecutive nights since her return, she had put herself on the committee for this fête, which (however much Miss Mapp might say she could not possibly permit it) she had not the slightest idea how to stop, and though Lucia was only a temporary resident here, these weeks would be quite intolerable if she continued to inflate herself in this presumptuous manner. It was certainly time for Miss Mapp to reassert herself before this rebel made more progress, and though dinner-giving was unusual in Tilling, she determined to give one or two most amusing ones herself, to none of which, of course, she would invite Lucia. But that was not nearly enough: she must administer some frightful snub (or snubs) to the woman. Georgie was in the same boat and must suffer too, for Lucia would not like that. So she sat in this web of crippled fire-irons and napless rugs like a spider, meditating reprisals. Perhaps it was a pity, when she needed allies, to have quarrelled with Diva, but a dinner would set that right. Before long she got up with a pleased expression. 'That will do to begin with: he won't like that at all,' she said to herself and went out to do her belated marketing.

She passed Lucia and Georgie, but decided not to see them, and, energetically waving her hand to Mrs Bartlett, she popped into Twistevant's, from the door of which they had just come out. At that moment quaint Irene, after a few words with the Padre, caught sight of Lucia, and hurried across the street to her. She was hatless, as usual, and wore a collarless shirt and knickerbockers unlike any other lady of Tilling, but as she approached Lucia her face assumed an acid and awful smile, just like somebody else's, and then she spoke in a cooing velvety voice that was quite unmistakable.

'The boy stood on the burning deck, Lulu,' she said. 'Whence all but he had fled, dear. The flames that lit the battle-wreck, sweet one, shone round him –'

Quaint Irene broke off suddenly, for within a yard of her at the door of Twistevant's appeared Miss Mapp. She looked clean over all their heads, and darted across the street to Wasters, carrying a small straw basket of her own delicious greengages.

'Oh, lor!' said Irene. 'The Mapp's in the fire, so that's done. Yes. I'll recite for you at your fête. Georgie, what a saucy hat! I was just going to Taormina to rout out some old sketches of mine for the Art Show, and then this happens. I wouldn't have had it not happen for a hundred pounds.'

'Come and dine tonight,' said Lucia warmly, breaking all records in the way of hospitality.

'Yes, if I needn't dress, and you'll send me home afterwards. I'm half a mile out of the town and I may be tipsy, for Major Benjy says you've got jolly good booze, quai hai, the King, God bless him! Good-bye.'

'Most original!' said Lucia. 'To go on with what I was telling you, Georgie, Liblib said she would not have her little home-sanctuary – Good morning, Padre. Miss Mapp shoved her way into Mallards this morning without ringing, and broke the chain which was on the door, such a hurry was she in to tell me that she will not have her little home-sanctuary, as I was just saying to Georgie, invaded by the rag-tag and bob-tail of Tilling.'

'Hoots awa!' said the Padre. 'What in the world has Mistress Mapp got to do with it? An' who's holding a jumble-sale in Mistress Plaistow's? I keeked in just now wi' my bit o' rubbish and never did I see such a mess. Na, na! Fair play's a jool, an' we'll go richt ahead. Excuse me, there's wee wifie wanting me.'

'It's war,' said Georgie as the Padre darted across to the Mouse, who was on the other side of the street, to tell her what had happened.

'No, I'm just defending myself,' said Lucia. 'It's right that people should know she burst my door-chain.'

'Well, I feel like the fourth of August, 1914,' said Georgie. 'What do you suppose she'll do next?'

'You may depend upon it, Georgie, that I shall be ready for her whatever it is,' said Lucia. 'I shan't raise a finger against her, if she behaves. But she *shall* ring the bell and I *won't* be dictated to and I *won't* be called Lulu. However, there's no immediate danger of that. Come, Georgie, let us go home and finish our sketches. Then we'll have them framed and send them Liblib for the picture exhibition. Perhaps that will convince her of my general good will, which I assure you is quite sincere.'

The jumble-sale opened next day, and Georgie, having taken his picture of Lucia's house and her picture of his to be framed in a very handsome manner, went on to Wasters with the idea of buying anything that could be of the smallest use for any purpose, and thus showing more good will towards the patroness. Miss Mapp was darting to and fro with lures for purchasers, holding the kettle away from the light so that the hole in its bottom should not be noticed, and she gave him a smile that looked rather like a snarl, but after all very like the smile she had for others. Georgie selected a hearth-brush, some curtain rings and a kettle-holder.

Then in a dark corner he came across a large cardboard tray, holding miscellaneous objects with the label 'All 6d. Each.' There were thimbles, there were photographs with slightly damaged frames, there were chipped china ornaments and cork-screws, and there was the picture of the Land-gate which he had painted himself and given Miss Mapp. Withers, Miss Mapp's parlour-maid, was at a desk for the exchange of custom by the door, and he exhibited his purchases for her inspection.

'Ninepence for the hearth-brush and threepence for the curtain rings,' said Georgie in a trembling voice, 'and sixpence for the kettle-holder. Then there's this little picture out of the sixpenny tray, which makes just two shillings.'

Laden with these miscellaneous purchases he went swiftly up the street to Mallards. Lucia was at the window of the garden-room, and her gimlet-eye saw that something had happened. She threw the sash up.

'I'm afraid the chain is on the door, Georgie,' she called out. 'You'll have to ring. What is it?'

'I'll show you,' said Georgie.

He deposited the hearth-brush, the curtain rings and the kettle-holder in the hall, and hurried out to the garden-room with the picture.

'The sketch I gave her,' he said. 'In the sixpenny tray. Why, the frame cost a shilling.'

Lucia's face became a flint.

'I never heard of such a thing, Georgie,' said she. 'The monstrous woman!'

'It may have got there by mistake,' said Georgie, frightened at this Medusa countenance.

'Rubbish, Georgie,' said Lucia.

Pictures for the annual exhibition of the Art Society of which Miss Mapp was President had been arriving in considerable numbers at Wasters, and stood stacked round the walls of the hall where the jumble-sale had been held a few days before, awaiting the judgement of the hanging committee which consisted of the President, the Treasurer and the Secretary: the two latter were Mr and Mrs Wyse. Miss Mapp had sent in half a dozen water-colours, the Treasurer a study in still life of a teacup, an orange and a wallflower, the Secretary a pastel portrait of the King of Italy, whom she had seen at a distance in Rome last spring. She had reinforced the vivid impression he had made on her by photographs. All these, following the precedent of the pictures of Royal Academicians at Burlington House, would be hung on the line without dispute, and there could not be any friction concerning them. But quaint Irene had sent some at which Miss Mapp felt lines must be drawn. They were, as usual, very strange and modern: there was one, harmless but insane, that purported to be Tilling Church by moonlight: a bright green pinnacle all crooked (she supposed it was a pinnacle) rose up against a strip of purple sky and the whole of the rest of the canvas was black. There was the back of somebody with no clothes on lying on an emerald-green sofa; and, worst of all, there was a picture called 'Women Wrestlers', from which Miss Mapp hurriedly averted her eyes. A proper regard for decency alone, even if Irene had not mimicked her reciting 'The Boy stood on the burning deck', would have made her resolve to oppose, tooth and nail, the exhibition of these shameless athletes. Unfortunately Mr Wyse had the most unbounded admiration for quaint Irene's work, and if she had sent in a picture of mixed wrestlers he would probably have said, 'Dear me, very powerful!' He was a hard man to resist, for if he and Miss Mapp had a very strong difference of opinion concerning any particular canvas he broke off and fell into fresh transports of admiration at her own pictures and this rather disarmed opposition.

The meeting of the hanging committee was to take place this morning at noon. Half an hour before that time, an errand boy arrived at Wasters from the frame-maker's bringing, according to the order he had received, two parcels which contained Georgie's picture of Mallards and Lucia's picture of Mallards Cottage: they had the cards of their perpetrators attached. 'Rubbishy little daubs,' thought Miss Mapp to herself, 'but I suppose those two Wyses will insist.' Then an imprudent demon of revenge suddenly took complete possession of her, and she called back the boy, and said she had a further errand for him.

At a quarter before twelve the boy arrived at Mallards and rang the bell. Grosvenor took down the chain and received from him a thin square parcel labelled 'With care'. One minute afterwards he delivered a similar parcel to Foljambe at Mallards Cottage, and had discharged Miss Mapp's further errand. The two maids conveyed these to their employers, and Georgie and Lucia, tearing off the wrappers, found themselves simultaneously confronted with their own pictures. A type-written slip accompanied each, conveying to them the cordial thanks of the hanging committee and its regrets that the limited wall space at its disposal would not permit of these works of art being exhibited.

Georgie ran out into his little yard and looked over the paling of Lucia's garden. At the same moment Lucia threw open the window of the garden-room which faced towards the paling.

'Georgie, have you received – ' she called.

'Yes,' said Georgie.

'So have I.'

'What are you going to do?' he asked.

Lucia's face assumed an expression eager and pensive, the far-away look with which she listened to Beethoven. She thought intently for a moment.

'I shall take a season ticket for the exhibition,' she said, 'and constantly – '

'I can't quite hear you,' said Georgie.

Lucia raised her voice.

'I shall buy a season ticket for the exhibition,' she shouted, 'and go there every day. Believe me, that's the only way to take it. They don't want our pictures, but we mustn't be small about it. Dignity, Georgie.'

There was nothing to add to so sublime a declaration, and Lucia went across to the bow-window, looking down the street. At that moment the Wyses' Royce lurched out of Porpoise Street, and turned down towards the High Street. Lucia knew they were both on the hanging committee which had just rejected one of her own most successful sketches (for the crooked chimney had turned out beautifully), but she felt not the smallest resentment towards them. No doubt they had acted quite conscientiously and she waved her hand in answer to a flutter of sables from the interior of the car. Presently she went down herself to the High Street to hear the news of the morning, and there was the Wyses' car drawn up in front of Wasters. She remembered then that the hanging committee met this morning, and a suspicion, too awful to be credible, flashed through her mind. But she thrust it out, as being unworthy of entertainment by a clean mind. She did her shopping and on her return took down a pale straw-coloured sketch by Miss Mapp that hung in the garden-room, and put in its place her picture of Mallards Cottage and the crooked chimney. Then she called to mind that powerful platitude, and said to herself that time would show . . .

Miss Mapp had not intended to be present at the desecration of her garden by paupers from the workhouse and such low haunts. She had consulted her solicitor, about her power to stop the entertainment, but he assured her that there was no known statute in English law, which enabled her to prevent her tenant giving a party. So she determined, in the manner of Lucia and the Elizabethan fête at Riseholme, to be unaware of it, not to know that any fête was contemplated, and never afterwards to ask a single question about it. But as the day approached she suspected that the hot tide of curiosity, rapidly rising in her, would probably end by swamping and submerging her principles. She had seen the Padre dressed in a long black cloak, and carrying an axe of enormous size, entering Mallards; she had seen Diva come out in a white satin gown and scuttle down the street to Taormina, and those two prodigies taken together suggested that the execution of Mary Queen of Scots was in hand. (Diva as the Queen!) She had seen boards and posts carried in by the garden-door and quantities of red cloth, so there was perhaps to be a stage for these tableaux. More intriguing yet was the apparition of Major Benjy carrying a cardboard crown glittering with gold paper. What on earth did that portend? Then there was her fruit to give an eye to: those choir-boys, scampering all over the garden in the intervals between their glees would probably pick every pear from the tree. She starved to know what was going on, but since she avoided all mention of the fête herself, others were most amazingly respectful to her reticence. She knew nothing, she could only make these delirious guesses, and there was *that* Lucia, being the centre of executioners and queens and choir-boys, instead of in her proper place, made much of by kind Miss Mapp, and enjoying such glimpses of Tilling society as she chose to give her. 'A fortnight ago,' thought kind Miss Mapp, 'I was popping in and out of the house, and she was Lulu. Anyhow, that was a nasty one she got over her picture, and I must bear her no grudge. I shall go to the fête because I can't help it, and I shall be very cordial to her and admire her tableaux. We're all Christians together, and I despise smallness.'

It was distressing to be asked to pay half a crown for admittance to her own Mallards, but there seemed positively no other way to get past Grosvenor. Very distressing, too, it was to see Lucia in full fig as Queen Elizabeth, graciously receiving newcomers on the edge of the lawn, precisely as if this was her party and these people who had paid half a crown to come in, her invited guests. It was a bitter thought that it ought to be herself who (though not dressed in all that flummery, so unconvincing by daylight) welcomed the crowd; for to whom, pray, did Mallards belong, and who had allowed it (since she could not stop it) to be thrown open? At the bottom of the steps into the garden-room was a large placard 'Private' but of course that would not apply to her. Through the half-opened door, as she passed, she caught a glimpse of a familiar figure, though sadly travestied, sitting in a robe and a golden crown and pouring something into a glass: no doubt then the garden-room was the green-room of performers in the tableaux, who, less greedy of publicity than Lulu, hid themselves here till the time of their exposure brought them out. She would go in there presently, but her immediate duty, bitter but necessary, was to greet her hostess. With a very happy inspiration she tripped up to Lucia and dropped a low curtsey.

'Your Majesty's most obedient humble servant,' she said, and then trusting that Lucia had seen that this obeisance was made in a mocking spirit, abounded in geniality.

'My dear, what a love of a costume!' she said. 'And what a lovely day for your fête! And what a crowd! How the half-crowns have been pouring in! All Tilling seems to be here, and I'm sure I don't wonder.'

Lucia rivalled these cordialities with equal fervour and about as much sincerity.

'Elizabeth! How nice of you to look in!' she said. 'Ecco, le due

Elizabethe! And you like my frock? Sweet of you! Yes. Tilling has indeed come to the aid of the hospital! And your jumble-sale too was a wonderful success, was it not? Nothing left, I am told.'

Miss Mapp had a moment's hesitation as to whether she should not continue to stand by Lucia and shake hands with new arrivals and give them a word of welcome, but she decided she could do more effective work if she made herself independent and played hostess by herself. Also this mention of the jumble-sale made her slightly uneasy. Withers had told her that Georgie had bought his own picture of the Land-gate from the sixpenny tray, and Lucia (for all her cordiality) might be about to spring some horrid trap on her about it.

'Yes, indeed,' she said. 'My little sale-room was soon as bare as Mother Hubbard's cupboard. But I mustn't monopolize you, dear, or I shall be lynched. There's a whole *queue* of people waiting to get a word with you. How I shall enjoy the tableaux! Looking forward to them so!'

She sidled off into the crowd. There were those dreadful old wretches from the workhouse, snuffy old things, some of them smoking pipes on her lawn and scattering matches, and being served with tea by Irene and the Padre's curate.

'So pleased to see you all here,' she said, 'sitting in my garden and enjoying your tea. I must pick a nice nosegay for you to take back home. How de do, Mr Sturgis. Delighted you could come and help to entertain the old folks for us. Good afternoon, Mr Wyse; yes, my little garden is looking nice, isn't it? Susan, dear! Have you noticed my bed of delphiniums? I must give you some seed. Oh, there is the town-crier ringing his bell! I suppose that means we must take our places for the tableaux. What a good stage! I hope the posts will not have made very big holes in my lawn. Oh, one of those naughty choir-boys is hovering about my fig-tree. I cannot allow that.'

She hurried off to stop any possibility of such depredation, and had made some telling allusions to the eighth commandment when on a second peal of the town-crier's bell, the procession of mummers came down the steps of the garden-room and advancing across the lawn disappeared behind the stage. Poor Major Benjy (so weak of him to allow himself to be dragged into this sort of thing) looked a perfect guy in his crown (who could he be meant for?) and as for Diva – Then there was Georgie (Drake indeed), and last of all Queen Elizabeth with her train held up by two choir-boys. Poor Lucia! Not content with a week of mumming at Riseholme she had to go on with her processions and dressings-up here. Some people lived on limelight.

Miss Mapp could not bring herself to take a seat close to the stage, and be seen applauding – there seemed to be some hitch with the curtain: no, it righted itself, what a pity! – and she hung about on the outskirts of the audience. Glees were interposed between the tableaux; how thin were the voices of those little boys out of doors! Then Irene, dressed like a sailor, recited that ludicrous parody. Roars of laughter. Then Major Benjy was King Cophetua: that was why he had a crown. Oh dear, oh dear! It was sad to reflect that an elderly, sensible man (for when at his best, he was that) could be got hold of by a pushing woman. The final tableau, of course (anyone might have guessed that), was the knighting of Drake by Queen Elizabeth. Then amid sycophantic applause the procession of guys returned and went back into the garden-room. Mr and Mrs Wyse followed them, and it seemed pretty clear that they were going to have a private tea there. Doubtless she would be soon sought for among the crowd with a message from Lucia to hope that she would join them in her own garden-room, but as nothing of the sort came, she presently thought that it would be only kind to Lucia to do so, and add her voice to the general chorus of congratulation that was no doubt going on. So with a brisk little tap on the door, and the inquiry 'May I come in?' she entered.

There they all were, as pleased as children with dressing-up. King Cophetua still wore his crown, tilted slightly to one side like a forage cap, and he and Queen Elizabeth and Queen Mary were seated round the tea-table and calling each other your Majesty. King Cophetua had a large whisky and soda in front of him and Miss Mapp felt quite certain it was not his first. But though sick in soul at these puerilities she pulled herself together and made a beautiful curtsey to the silly creatures.

And the worst of it was that there was no one left of her own intimate circle to whom she could in private express her disdain, for they were all in it, either actively or, like the Wyses, truckling to Lucia.

Lucia for the moment seemed rather surprised to see her, but she welcomed her and poured her out a cup of rather tepid tea, nasty to the taste. She must truckle, too, to the whole lot of them, though that tasted nastier than the tea.

'How I congratulate you all,' she cried. 'Padre, you looked too cruel as executioner, your mouth so fixed and stern. It was quite a relief when the curtain came down. Irene, quaint one, how you made them laugh! Diva, Mr Georgie, and above all our wonderful Queen Lucia. What a treat it has all been! The choir! Those beautiful glees. A thousand pities, Mr Wyse, that the Contessa was not here.'

There was still Susan to whom she ought to say something pleasant, but positively she could not go on, until she had eaten something solid. But Lucia chimed in.

'And your garden, Elizabeth,' she said. 'How they are enjoying it. I believe if the truth was known they are all glad that our little tableaux are over, so that they can wander about and admire the flowers. I must give a little party some night soon with Chinese lanterns and fairy-lights in the beds.'

'Upon my word, your Majesty is spoiling us all,' said Major Benjy. 'Tilling's never had a month with so much pleasure provided for it. Glorious.'

Miss Mapp had resolved to stop here if it was anyhow possible, till these sycophants had dispersed, and then have one private word with Lucia to indicate how ready she was to overlook all the little frictions that had undoubtedly arisen. She fully meant, without eating a morsel of humble pie herself, to allow Lucia to eat proud pie, for she saw that just for the present she herself was nowhere and Lucia everywhere. So Lucia should glut herself into a sense of complete superiority, and then it would be time to begin fresh manoeuvres. Major Benjy and Diva soon took themselves off: she saw them from the garden-window going very slowly down the street, ever so pleased to have people staring at them, and Irene, at the Padre's request, went out to dance a hornpipe on the lawn in her sailor clothes. But the two Wyses (always famous for sticking) remained and Georgie.

Mr Wyse got up from the tea-table and passed round behind Miss Mapp's chair. Out of the corner of her eye she could see he was looking at the wall where a straw-coloured picture of her own hung. He always used to admire it, and it was pleasant to feel that he was giving it so careful and so respectful a scrutiny. Then he spoke to Lucia.

'How well I remember seeing you paint that,' he said, 'and how long I took to forgive myself for having disturbed you in my blundering car. A perfect little masterpiece, Mallards Cottage and the crooked chimney. To the life.'

Susan heaved herself up from the sofa and joined in the admiration.

'Perfectly delightful,' she said. 'The lights, the shadows. Beautiful! What a touch!'

Miss Mapp turned her head slowly as if she had a stiff neck, and verified her awful conjecture that it was no longer a picture of her own that hung there, but the very picture of Lucia's which had been rejected for the Art Exhibition. She felt as if no picture but a bomb hung there, which might explode at some chance word, and blow her into a thousand fragments. It was best to hurry from this perilous neighbourhood.

'Dear Lucia,' she said, 'I must be off. Just one little stroll, if I may, round my garden, before I go home. My roses will never forgive me, if I go away without noticing them.'

She was too late.

'How I wish I had known it was finished!' said Mr Wyse. 'I should have begged you to allow us to have it for our Art Exhibition. It would have been the gem of it. Cruel of you, Mrs Lucas!'

'But I sent it in to the hanging committee,' said Lucia. 'Georgie sent his, too, of Mallards. They were both sent back to us.'

Mr Wyse turned from the picture to Lucia with an expression of incredulous horror, and Miss Mapp quietly turned to stone.

'But impossible,' he said. 'I am on the hanging committee

myself, and I hope you cannot think I should have been such an imbecile. Susan is on the committee too: so is Miss Mapp. In fact, we are the hanging committee. Susan, that gem, that little masterpiece never came before us.'

'Never,' said Susan. 'Never. Never, never.'

Mr Wyse's eye transferred itself to Miss Mapp. She was still stone and her face was as white as the wall of Mallards Cottage in the masterpiece. Then for the first time in the collective memory of Tilling Mr Wyse allowed himself to use slang.

'There has been some hanky-panky,' he said. 'That picture never came before the hanging committee.'

The stone image could just move its eyes and they looked, in a glassy manner, at Lucia. Lucia's met them with one short gimlet thrust, and she whisked round to Georgie. Her face was turned away from the others, and she gave him a prodigious wink, as he sat there palpitating with excitement.

'Georgino mio,' she said. 'Let us recall exactly what happened. The morning, I mean, when the hanging committee met. Let me see: let me see. Don't interrupt me: I will get it all clear.'

Lucia pressed her hands to her forehead.

'I have it,' she said. 'It is perfectly vivid to me now. You had taken our little pictures down to the framer's, Georgie, and told him to send them in to Elizabeth's house direct. That was it. The errand boy from the framer's came up here that very morning, and delivered mine to Grosvenor, and yours to Foljambe. Let me think exactly when that was. What time was it, Mr Wyse, that the hanging committee met?'

'At twelve, precisely,' said Mr Wyse.

'That fits in perfectly,' said Lucia. 'I called to Georgie out of the window here, and we told each other that our pictures had been rejected. A moment later, I saw your car go down to the High Street and when I went down there soon afterwards, it was standing in front of Miss – I mean Elizabeth's house. Clearly what happened was that the framer misunderstood Georgie's instructions, and returned the pictures to us before the hanging committee sat at all. So you never saw them, and we imagined all the time – did we not, Georgie? – that you had simply sent them back.'

'But what must you have thought of us?' said Mr Wyse, with a gesture of despair.

'Why, that you did not conscientiously think very much of our art,' said Lucia. 'We were perfectly satisfied with your decision. I felt sure that my little picture had a hundred faults and feeblenesses.'

Miss Mapp had become unpetrified. Could it be that by some miraculous oversight she had not put into those parcels the formal, typewritten rejection of the committee? It did not seem likely, for she had a very vivid remembrance of the gratification it gave her to do so, but the only alternative theory was to suppose a magnanimity on Lucia's part which seemed even more miraculous. She burst into speech.

'How we all congratulate ourselves,' she cried, 'that it has all been cleared up! Such a stupid errand-boy! What are we to do next, Mr Wyse? Our exhibition must secure Lucia's sweet picture, and of course Mr Pillson's too. But how are we to find room for them? Everything is hung.'

'Nothing easier,' said Mr Wyse. 'I shall instantly withdraw my paltry little piece of still life, and I am sure that Susan – '

'No, that would never do,' said Miss Mapp, currying favour all round. 'That beautiful wallflower, I could almost smell it: that King of Italy. Mine shall go: two or three of mine. I insist on it.'

Mr Wyse bowed to Lucia and then to Georgie.

'I have a plan better yet,' he said. 'Let us put – if we may have the privilege of securing what was so nearly lost to our exhibition – let us put these two pictures on easels as showing how deeply we appreciate our good fortune in getting them.'

He bowed to his wife, he bowed – was it quite a bow? – to Miss Mapp, and had there been a mirror, he would no doubt have bowed to himself.

'Besides,' he said, 'our little sketches will not thus suffer so much from their proximity to – ' and he bowed to Lucia. 'And if Mr Pillson will similarly allow us – ' he bowed to Georgie.

Georgie, following Lucia's lead, graciously offered to go

round to the Cottage and bring back his picture of Mallards, but Mr Wyse would not hear of such a thing. He and Susan would go off in the Royce now, with Lucia's masterpiece, and fetch Georgie's from Mallards Cottage, and the sun should not set before they both stood on their distinguished easels in the enriched exhibition. So off they went in a great hurry to procure the easels before the sun went down and Miss Mapp, unable alone to face the reinstated victims of her fraud, scurried after them in a tumult of mixed emotions. Outside in the garden Irene, dancing hornpipes, was surrounded by both sexes of the enraptured youth of Tilling, for the boys knew she was a girl, and the girls thought she looked so like a boy. She shouted out 'Come and dance, Mapp,' and Elizabeth fled from her own sweet garden as if it had been a plague-stricken area, and never spoke to her roses at all.

The Queen and Drake were left alone in the garden-room.

'Well, I never!' said Georgie. 'Did you? She sent them back all by herself.'

'I'm not the least surprised,' said Lucia. 'It's like her.'

'But why did you let her off?' he asked. 'You ought to have exposed her and have done with her.'

Lucia showed a momentary exultation, and executed a few steps from a Morris-dance.

'No, Georgie, that would have been a mistake,' she said. 'She knows that we know, and I can't wish her worse than that. And I rather think, though he makes me giddy with so much bowing, that Mr Wyse has guessed. He certainly suspects something of the sort.'

'Yes, he said there had been some hanky-panky,' said Georgie. 'That was a strong thing for him to say. All the same – '

Lucia shook her head.

'No, I'm right,' she said. 'Don't you see I've taken the moral stuffing out of that woman far more completely than if I had exposed her?'

'But she's a cheat,' cried Georgie. 'She's a liar, for she sent back our pictures with a formal notice that the committee had rejected them. She hasn't got any moral stuffing to take out.'

Lucia pondered this.

'That's true, there doesn't seem to be much,' she said. 'But even then, think of the moral stuffing that I've put into myself. A far greater score, Georgie, than to have exposed her, and it must be quite agonizing for her to have that hanging over her head. Besides, she can't help being deeply grateful to me if there are any depths in that poor shallow nature. There may be: we must try to discover them. Take a broader view of it all, Georgie.... Oh, and I've thought of something fresh! Send round to Mr Wyse for the exhibition your picture of the Land-gate, which poor Elizabeth sold. He will certainly hang it and she will see it there. That will round everything off nicely.'

Lucia moved across to the piano and sat down on the treble music-stool.

'Let us forget all about these *piccoli disturbi*, Georgie,' she said, 'and have some music to put us in tune with beauty again. No you needn't shut the door: it is so hot, and I am sure that no one else will dream of passing that notice of "Private", or come in here unasked. Ickle bit of divine Mozartino?'

Lucia found the duet at which she had worked quietly at odd moments.

'Let us try this,' she said: 'though it looks rather diffy. Oh, one thing more, Georgie. I think you and I had better keep those formal notices of rejection from the hanging committee just in case. We might need them some day, though I'm sure I hope we shan't. But one must be careful in dealing with that sort of woman. That's all I think. Now let us breathe harmony and loveliness again. Uno, due . . . pom.'

6

It was a mellow morning of October, the season, as Lucia reflected, of mists and mellow fruitfulness, wonderful John Keats. There was no doubt about the mists, for there had been several sea-fogs in the English Channel, and the mellow fruitfulness of the garden at Mallards was equally indisputable. But now the fruitfulness of that sunny plot concerned Lucia far more than it had done during August and September, for she had taken Mallards for another month (Adele Brixton having taken the Hurst, Riseholme, for three), not on those original Shylock terms of fifteen guineas a week, and no garden-produce – but of twelve guineas a week, and all the garden-produce. It was a wonderful year for tomatoes: there were far more than a single widow could possibly eat, and Lucia, instead of selling them, constantly sent little presents of them to Georgie and Major Benjy. She had sent one basket of them to Miss Mapp, but these had been returned and Miss Mapp had written an effusive note saying that they would be wasted on her. Lucia had applauded that; it showed a very proper spirit.

The chain of consequences, therefore, of Lucia's remaining at Mallards was far-reaching. Miss Mapp took Wasters for another month at a slightly lower rent, Diva extended her lease of Taormina, and Irene still occupied the four-roomed labourer's cottage outside Tilling, which suited her so well, and the labourer and his family remained in the hop-picker's shanty. It was getting chilly of nights in the shanty, and he looked forward to the time when, Adele having left the Hurst, his cottage could be restored to him. Nor did the chain of consequences end here, for Georgie could not go back to Riseholme without Foljambe, and Foljambe would not go back there and leave her Cadman, while Lucia remained at Mallards. So Isabel Poppit continued to inhabit her bungalow by the sea, and Georgie remained in Mallards Cottage. With her skin turned black with all those sun-baths, and her hair spiky and wiry with so many sea-baths, Isabel resembled a cross between a kipper and a sea-urchin.

September had been full of events. The Art Exhibition had been a great success, and quantities of the pictures had been sold. Lucia had bought Georgie's picture of Mallards, Georgie had bought Lucia's picture of Mallards Cottage, Mr Wyse had bought his wife's pastel of the King of Italy, and sent it as a birthday present to Amelia, and Susan Wyse had bought her husband's tea-cup and wallflower and kept them herself. But the greatest gesture of all had been Lucia's purchase of one of Miss Mapp's six exhibits, and this had practically forced Miss Mapp, so powerful was the suggestion hidden in it, to buy Georgie's picture of the Land-gate, which he had given her, and which she had sold (not even for her own benefit but for that of the hospital) for sixpence at her jumble-sale. She had had to pay a guinea to regain what had once been hers, so that in the end the revengeful impulse which had prompted her to put it in the sixpenny tray had been cruelly expensive. But she had still felt herself to be under Lucia's thumb in the whole matter of the exhibition (as indeed she was) and this purchase was of the nature of a propitiatory act. They had met one morning at the show, and Lucia had looked long at this sketch of Georgie's and then, looking long at Elizabeth, she had said it was one of the most charming and exquisite of his water-colours. Inwardly raging, yet somehow impotent to resist, Elizabeth had forked up. But she was now busily persuading herself that this purchase had something to do with the hospital, and that she need not make any further contributions to its funds this year: she felt there was a very good chance of persuading herself about this. No one had bought quaint Irene's pictures, and she had turned the women wrestlers into men.

Since then Miss Mapp had been very busy with the conversion of the marvellous crop of apples, plums and red currants in Diva's garden into jam and jelly. Her cook could not tackle so big a job alone, and she herself spent hours a day in the kitchen, and the most delicious odours of boiling preserves were wafted out of the windows into the High Street. It could not be supposed that they would escape Diva's sharp nose, and there had been words about it. But garden-produce (Miss Mapp believed) meant what it said, or would dear Diva prefer that she let the crop rot on the trees, and be a portion for wasps. Diva acknowledged that she would. And when the fruit was finished Miss Mapp proposed to turn her attention to the vegetable marrows, which, with a little ginger, made a very useful preserve for the household. She would leave a dozen of these pots for Diva.

But the jam-making was over now and Miss Mapp was glad of that, for she had scalded her thumb: quite a blister. She was even gladder that the Art Exhibition was over. All the important works of the Tilling school (except the pastel of the King of

Italy) remained in Tilling, she had made her propitiatory sacrifice about Georgie's sketch of the Land-gate, and she had no reason to suppose that Lucia had ever repented of that moment of superb magnanimity in the garden-room, which had averted an exposure of which she still occasionally trembled to think. Lucia could not go back on that now, it was all over and done with like the jam-making (though, like the jam-making, it had left a certain seared and sensitive place behind) and having held her tongue then, Lucia could not blab afterwards. Like the banns in church, she must for ever hold her peace. Miss Mapp had been deeply grateful for that clemency at the time, but no one could go on being grateful indefinitely. You were grateful until you had paid your debt of gratitude, and then you were free. She would certainly be grateful again, when this month was over and Lucia and Georgie left Tilling, never, she hoped, to return, but for the last week or two she had felt that she had discharged in full every groat of gratitude she owed Lucia, and her mind had been busier than usual over plots and plans and libels and inductions with regard to her tenant who, with those cheeseparing ways so justly abhorred by Miss Mapp, had knocked down the rent to twelve guineas a week and grabbed the tomatoes.

But Miss Mapp did not yet despair of dealing Lucia some nasty blow, for the fact of the matter was (she felt sure of it) that Tilling generally was growing a little restive under Lucia's autocratic ways. She had been taking them in hand, she had been patronizing them, which Tilling never could stand, she had been giving them treats, just like that! She had sent out cards for an evening party (not dinner at all) with 'un po' di musica' written in the left-hand corner. Even Mr Wyse, that notorious sycophant, had raised his eyebrows over this, and had allowed that this was rather an unusual inscription: 'musica' (he thought) would have been more ordinary, and he would ask Amelia when she came. That had confirmed a secret suspicion which Miss Mapp had long entertained that Lucia's Italian (and, of course, Georgie's too) was really confined to such words as 'ecco' and 'bon giorno', and 'bello', and she was earnestly hoping that Amelia would come before October was over, and they would all see what these great talks in Italian to which Mr Wyse was so looking forward, would amount to.

And what an evening that 'po-di-mu' (as it was already referred to with faint little smiles) had been! It was a wet night and in obedience to her command (for at that time Lucia was at the height of the ascendancy she had acquired at the hospital fête), they had all put mackintoshes over their evening clothes, and goloshes over their evening shoes, and slopped up to Mallards through the pouring rain. A couple of journeys of Lucia's car could have brought them all in comfort and dryness, but she had not offered so obvious a convenience. Mrs Wyse's Royce was being overhauled, so they had to walk too, and a bedraggled and discontented company had assembled. They had gone into the garden-room dripped on by the wistaria, and an interminable po-di-mu ensued. Lucia turned off all the lights in the room except one on the piano, so that they saw her profile against a black background, like the head on a postage stamp, and first she played the slow movement out of the Moonlight Sonata. She stopped once, just after she had begun, because Diva coughed, and when she had finished there was a long silence. Lucia sighed and Georgie sighed, and everyone said 'Thank you' simultaneously. Major Benjy said he was devoted to Chopin and Lucia playfully told him that she would take his musical education in hand.

Then she had allowed the lights to be turned up again, and there was a few minutes' pause to enable them to conquer the poignancy of emotion aroused by that exquisite rendering of the Moonlight Sonata, to disinfect it so to speak with cigarettes, or drown it, as Major Benjy did, in rapid whiskies and sodas, and when they felt braver the po-di-mu began again, with a duet, between her and Georgie, of innumerable movements by Mozart, who must indeed have been a most prolific composer if he wrote all that. Diva fell quietly asleep, and presently there were indications that she would soon be noisily asleep. Miss Mapp hoped that she would begin to snore properly, for that would be a good set down for Lucia, but Major Benjy poked her stealthily on the knee to rouse her. Mr Wyse began to stifle yawns, though he sat as upright as ever, with his eyes fixed rather glassily on the ceiling, and ejaculated 'Charming' at the end of every movement. When it was all over there were some faintly murmured requests that Lucia would play to them again, and without any further pressing, she sat down. Her obtuseness was really astounding.

'How you all work me!' she said. 'A fugue by Bach then, if you insist on it, and if Georgie will promise not to scold me if I break down.'

Luckily amid suppressed sighs of relief, she did break down, and though she was still perfectly willing to try again, there was a general chorus of unwillingness to take advantage of her great good nature, and after a wretched supper, consisting largely of tomato-salad, they trooped out into the rain, cheered by the promise of another musical evening next week when she would have that beautiful fugue by heart.

It was not the next week but the same week that they had all been bidden to a further evening of harmony, and symptoms of revolt, skilfully fomented by Miss Mapp, were observable. She had just received her note of invitation one morning, when Diva trundled in to Wasters.

'Another po-di-mu already,' said she sarcastically. 'What are you – '

'Isn't it unfortunate?' interrupted Elizabeth, 'for I hope, dear Diva, you have not forgotten that you promised to come in that very night – Thursday, isn't it – and play piquet with me.'

Diva returned Elizabeth's elaborate wink. 'So I did,' she said. 'Anyhow, I do.'

'Consequently we shall have to refuse dear Lucia's invitation,' said Elizabeth regretfully. 'Lovely, wasn't it, the other night? And so many movements of Mozart. I began to think he must have discovered the secret of perpetual motion, and that we should be stuck there till Doomsday.'

Diva was fidgeting about the room in her restless manner ('Rather like a spinning top,' thought Miss Mapp, 'bumping into everything. I wish it would die').

'I don't think she plays bridge very well,' said Diva. 'She began, you know, by saying she was so anxious to learn, and that we all played marvellously, but now she lays down the law like anything, telling us what we ought to have declared, and how we ought to have played. It's quite like – '

She was going to say 'It's quite like playing with you,' but luckily stopped in time.

'I haven't had the privilege of playing with her. Evidently I'm not up to her form,' said Elizabeth, 'but I hear, only report, mind, that she doesn't know the elements of the game.'

'Well, not much more,' said Diva. 'And she says she will start a bridge class if we like.'

'She spoils us! And who will the pupils be?' asked Elizabeth.

'I know one who won't,' said Diva darkly.

'And one and one makes two,' observed Elizabeth. 'A pity that she sets herself up like that. Saying the other night that she would take Major Benjy's musical education in hand! I always thought education began at home, and I'm sure I never heard so many wrong notes in my life.'

Diva ruminated a moment, and began spinning again. 'She offered to take the choir practices in church, only the Padre wouldn't hear of it,' she said. 'And there's talk of a class to read Homer in Pope's translation.'

'She has every accomplishment,' said Elizabeth, 'including push.'

Diva bumped into another topic.

'I met Mr Wyse just now,' she said. 'Countess Amelia Faraglione is coming tomorrow.'

Miss Mapp sprang up.

'Not really?' she cried. 'Why, she'll be here for Lucia's po-di-mu on Thursday. And the Wyses will be going, that's certain, and they are sure to ask if they may bring the Faradidleone with them. Diva, dear, we must have our piquet another night. I wouldn't miss that for anything.'

'Why?' asked Diva.

'Just think what will happen! She'll be forced to talk Italian, for Mr Wyse has often said what a treat it will be to hear them talk it together, and I'm sure Lucia doesn't know any. I must be there.'

'But if she does know it, it will be rather a sell,' said Diva. 'We shall have gone there for nothing except to hear all that Mozart over again and to eat tomatoes. I had heart-burn half the night afterwards.'

'Trust me, Diva,' said Elizabeth. 'I swear she doesn't know any Italian. And how on earth will she be able to wriggle out of talking it? With all her ingeniousness, it can't be done. She can't help being exposed.'

'Well, that would be rather amusing,' said Diva. 'Being put down a peg or two certainly wouldn't hurt her. All right. I'll say I'll come.'

Miss Mapp's policy was now of course the exact reverse of what she had first planned. Instead of scheming to get all Tilling to refuse Lucia's invitation to listen to another po-di-mu, her object was to encourage everyone to go, in order that they might listen not so much to Mozart as to her rich silences or faltering replies when challenged to converse in the Italian language. She found that the Padre and Mrs Bartlett had hurriedly arranged a choir practice and a meeting of the girl-guides respectively to take place at the unusual hour of half past nine in the evening in order to be able to decline the po-di-mu, but Elizabeth, throwing economy to the winds, asked them both to dine with her on the fatal night, and come on to Lucia's delicious music afterwards. This added inducement prevailed, and off they scurried to tell choir-boys and girl-guides that the meetings were cancelled and would be held at the usual hour of the day after. The curate needed no persuasion, for he thought that Lucia had a wonderful touch on the piano, and was already looking forward to more; Irene similarly had developed a violent *schwärm* for Lucia and had accepted, so that Tilling, thanks to Elizabeth's friendly offices, would now muster in force to hear Lucia play duets and fugues and not speak Italian. And when, in casual conversation with Mr Wyse, Elizabeth learned that he had (as she had anticipated) ventured to ask Lucia if she would excuse the presumption of one of her greatest admirers, and bring his sister Amelia to her *soirée* and that Lucia had sent him her most cordial permission to do so, it seemed that nothing could stand in the way of the fulfilment of Elizabeth's romantic revenge on that upstart visitor for presuming to set herself up as Queen of the social life of Tilling.

It was, as need hardly be explained, this aspect of the affair which so strongly appealed to the sporting instincts of the place. Miss Mapp had long been considered by others as well as herself the first social citizen of Tilling, and though she had often been obliged to fight desperately for her position, and had suffered from time to time manifold reverses, she had managed to maintain it, because there was no one else of so commanding and unscrupulous a character. Then, this alien from Riseholme had appeared and had not so much challenged her as just taken her sceptre and her crown and worn them now for a couple of months. At present all attempts to recapture them had failed, but Lucia had grown a little arrogant, she had offered to take choir practice, she had issued her invitations (so thought Tilling) rather as if they had been commands, and Tilling would not have been sorry to see her suffer some set-back. Nobody wanted to turn out in the evening to hear her play Mozart (except the curate), no one intended to listen to her read Pope's translation of Homer's *Iliad*, or to be instructed how to play bridge, and though Miss Mapp was no favourite, they would have liked to see her score. But there was little partisanship; it was the sporting instinct which looked forward to witnessing an engagement between two well-equipped Queens, and seeing whether one really could speak Italian or not, even if they had to listen to all the fugues of Bach first. Everyone, finally, except Miss Mapp, wherever their private sympathies might lie, regretted that now in less than a month, Lucia would have gone back to her own kingdom of Riseholme, where it appeared she had no rival of any sort, for these encounters were highly stimulating to students of human nature and haters of Miss Mapp. Never before had Tilling known so exciting a season.

On this mellow morning, then, of October, Lucia, after practising her fugue for the coming po-di-mu, and observing Coplen bring into the house a wonderful supply of tomatoes, had received that appalling note from Mr Wyse, conveyed by the Royce, asking if he might bring Contessa Amelia di Faraglione to the musical party to which he so much looked forward. The gravity of the issue was instantly clear to Lucia, for Mr Wyse had made no secret about the pleasure it would give him to hear his sister and herself mellifluously converse in the Italian tongue, but without hesitation she sent back a note by the chauffeur and the Royce, that she would be charmed to see the Contessa. There was no getting out of that, and she must accept the inevitable before proceeding irresistibly to deal with it. From the window she observed the Royce backing and advancing and backing till it managed to turn and went round the corner to Porpoise Street.

Lucia closed the piano, for she had more cosmic concerns to think about than the fingerings of a fugue. Her party of course (that required no consideration) would have to be cancelled, but that was only one point in the problem that confronted her. For that baleful bilinguist the Contessa di Faraglione was not coming to Tilling (all the way from Italy) for one night but she was to stay here, so Mr Wyse's note had mentioned, for 'about a week', after which she would pay visits to her relations the Wyses of Whitchurch and others. So for a whole week (or about) Lucia would be in perpetual danger of being called upon to talk Italian. Indeed, the danger was more than mere danger, for if anything in this world was certain, it was that Mr Wyse would ask her to dinner during this week, and exposure would follow. Complete disappearance from Tilling during the Contessa's sojourn here was the only possible plan, yet how was that to be accomplished? Her house at Riseholme was let, but even if it had not been, she could not leave Tilling tomorrow, when she had invited everybody to a party in the evening.

The clock struck noon: she had meditated for a full half-hour, and now she rose.

'I can only think of influenza,' she said to herself. 'But I shall consult Georgie. A man might see it from another angle.'

He came at once to her S.O.S.

'Georgino mio,' began Lucia, but then suddenly corrected herself. 'Georgie,' she said. 'Something very disagreeable. The Contessa Thingummy is coming to the Wyses tomorrow, and he's asked me if he may bring her to our musica. I had to say yes; no way out of it.'

Georgie was often very perceptive. He saw what this meant at once.

'Good Lord,' he said. 'Can't you put it off? Sprain your thumb.'

The man's angle was not being of much use so far.

'Not a bit of good,' she said. 'She'll be here about a week, and naturally I have to avoid meeting her altogether. The only thing I can think of is influenza.'

Georgie never smoked in the morning, but the situation seemed to call for a cigarette.

'That would do it,' he said. 'Rather a bore for you, but you could live in the secret garden a good deal. It's not over-looked.'

He stopped: the unusual tobacco had stimulated his perceptive powers.

'But what about me?' he said.

'I'm sure I don't know,' said Lucia.

'You're not looking far enough,' said Georgie. 'You're not taking the long view which you so often talk to me about. I can't have influenza too, it would be too suspicious. So I'm bound to meet the Faraglione and she'll see in a minute I can't talk Italian.'

'Well?' said Lucia in a very selfish manner, as if he didn't matter at all.

'Oh, I'm not thinking about myself only,' said Georgie in self-defence. 'Not so at all. It'll react on you. You and I are supposed to talk Italian together, and when it's obvious I can't say more than three things in it, the fat's in the fire, however much influenza you have. How are you going to be supposed to jabber away in Italian to me when it's seen that I can't understand a word of it?'

Here indeed was the male angle, and an extremely awkward angle it was. For a moment Lucia covered her face with her hands.

'Georgie, what are we to do?' she asked in a stricken voice.

Georgie was a little ruffled at having been considered of such absolute unimportance until he pointed out to Lucia that her fate was involved with his, and it pleased him to echo her words.

'I'm sure I don't know,' he said stiffly.

Lucia hastened to smooth his smart.

'My dear, I'm so glad I thought of consulting you,' she said. 'I knew it would take a man's mind to see all round the question, and how right you are! I never thought of that.'

'Quite,' said Georgie. 'It's evident you haven't grasped the situation at all.'

She paced up and down the garden-room in silence, recoiling once from the window, as she saw Elizabeth go by and kiss her hand with that awful hyaena grin of hers.

'Georgie, oo not cross with poor Lucia?' she said, resorting to the less dangerous lingo which they used in happier days. This softened Georgie.

'I was rather,' said Georgie, 'but never mind that now. What am I to do? Che faro, in fact.'

Lucia shuddered.

'Oh, for goodness' sake, don't talk Italian,' she said. 'It's that we've got to avoid. It's odd that we have to break ourselves of the habit of doing something we can't do.... And you can't have influenza too. It would be too suspicious if you began simultaneously with me tomorrow. I've often wondered, now I come to think of it, if that woman, that Mapp, hasn't suspected that our Italian was a fake, and if we both had influenza exactly as the Faraglione arrived, she might easily put two and two together. Her mind is horrid enough for anything.'

'I know she suspects,' said Georgie. 'She said some word in Italian to me the other day, which meant paperknife, and she looked surprised when I didn't understand, and said it in English. Of course she had looked it out in a dictionary: it was a trap.'

A flood of horrid light burst in on Lucia.

'Georgie,' she cried. 'She tried me with the same word. I've forgotten it again, but it did mean paperknife. I didn't know it either, though I pretended it was her pronunciation that puzzled me. There's no end to her craftiness. But I'll get the better of her yet. I think you'll have to go away, while the Faraglione is here and I have influenza.'

'But I don't want to go away,' began Georgie. 'Surely we can think of – '

Lucia paid no heed to this attempt at protest: it is doubtful if she even heard it, for the spark was lit now, and it went roaring through her fertile brain like a prairie fire in a high gale.

'You must go away tomorrow,' she said. 'Far better than influenza, and you must stop away till I send you a telegram, that the Faraglione has left. It will be very dull for me because I shall be entirely confined to the house and garden all the time you are gone. I think the garden will be safe. I cannot remember that it is overlooked from any other house and I shall do a lot of reading, though even the piano won't be possible. . . . Georgie, I see it all. You have not been looking very well lately (my dear, you're the picture of health really, I have never seen you looking younger or better) and so you will have gone off to have a week at Folkestone or Littlestone, whichever you prefer. Sea air: you needn't bathe. And you can take my car, for I shan't be able to use it, and why not take Foljambe as well to valet you, as you often do when you go for a jaunt? She'll have her Cadman: we may as well make other people happy, Georgie, as it all seems to fit in so beautifully. And one thing more: this little jaunt of yours is entirely undertaken for my sake, and I must insist on paying it all. Go to a nice hotel and make yourself thoroughly comfortable; half a bottle of champagne whenever you want it in the evening, and what extras you like, and I will telephone to you to say when you can come back. You must start tomorrow morning before the Faraglione gets here.'

Georgie knew it was useless to protest when Lucia got that loud, inspired, gabbling ring in her voice; she would cut through any opposition, as a steam saw buzzes through the most solid oak board till, amid a fountain of flying sawdust, it has sliced its way. He did not want to go away, but when Lucia exhibited that calibre of determination that he should, it was better to yield at once than to collapse later in a state of wretched exhaustion. Besides, there were bright points in her scheme. Foljambe would be delighted at the plan, for it would give her and Cadman leisure to enjoy each other's society; and it would not be disagreeable to stay for a week at some hotel in

Folkestone and observe the cargoes of travellers from abroad arriving at the port after a billowy passage. Then he might find some bibelots in the shops, and he would listen to a municipal band, and have a bathroom next his bedroom, and do some sketches, and sit in a lounge in a series of those suits which had so justly earned him the title of the best-dressed man in Tilling. He would have a fine Rolls-Royce in the hotel garage, and a smart chauffeur coming to ask for orders every morning, and he would be seen, an interesting and opulent figure, drinking his half-bottle of champagne every evening and he would possibly pick up an agreeable acquaintance or two. He had no hesitation whatever in accepting Lucia's proposal to stand the charges of this expedition, for, as she had most truly said, it was undertaken in her interests, and naturally she paid (besides, she was quite rich) for its equipment.

The main lines of this defensive campaign being thus laid down, Lucia, with her Napoleonic eye for detail, plunged into minor matters. She did not, of course, credit 'that Mapp' with having procured the visit of the Faraglione, but a child could see that if she herself met the Faraglione during her stay here the grimmest exposure of her ignorance of the language she talked in such admired snippets must inevitably follow. 'That Mapp' would pounce on this, and it was idle to deny that she would score heavily and horribly. But Georgie's absence (cheap at the cost) and her own invisibility by reason of influenza made a seemingly unassailable position and it was with a keen sense of exhilaration in the coming contest that she surveyed the arena.

Lucia sent for the trusty Grosvenor and confided in her sufficiently to make her a conspirator. She told her that she had a great mass of arrears to do in reading and writing, and that for the next week she intended to devote herself to them, and lead the life of a hermit. She wanted no callers, and did not mean to see anyone, and the easiest excuse was to say that she had influenza. No doubt there would be many inquiries, and so day by day she would issue to Grosvenor her own official bulletin. Then she told Cadman that Mr Georgie was far from well, and she had bundled him off with the car to Folkestone for about a week: he and Foljambe would accompany him. Then she made a careful survey of the house and garden to ascertain what freedom of movement she could have during her illness. Playing the piano, except very carefully with the soft pedal down, would be risky, but by a judicious adjustment of the curtains in the garden-room window, she could refresh herself with very satisfactory glances at the world outside. The garden, she was pleased to notice, was quite safe, thanks to its encompassing walls, from any prying eyes in the houses round: the top of the church tower alone overlooked it, and that might be disregarded, for only tourists ascended it.

Then forth she went for the usual shoppings and chats in the High Street and put in some further fine work. The morning tide was already on the ebb, but by swift flittings this way and that she managed to have a word with most of those who were coming to her po-di-mu tomorrow, and interlarded all she said to them with brilliant scraps of Italian. She just caught the Wyses as they were getting back into the Royce and said how molto amabile it was of them to give her the gran' piacere of seeing the Contessa next evening: indeed she would be a welcome guest, and it would be another gran' piacere to talk la bella lingua again. Georgie, alas, would not be there for he was un po' ammalato, and was going to spend a settimana by the mare per stabilirsi. Never had she been so fluent and idiomatic, and she accepted with mille grazie Susan's invitation to dine the evening after her music and renew the conversations to which she so much looked forward. She got almost tipsy with Italian. ... Then she flew across the street to tell the curate that she was going to shut herself up all afternoon in order to get the Bach fugue more worthy of his critical ear, she told Diva to come early to her party in order that they might have a little chat first, and she just managed by a flute-like 'Cooee' to arrest Elizabeth as she was on the very doorstep of Wasters. With glee she learned that Elizabeth was entertaining the Padre and his wife and Major Benjy to dinner before she brought them on to her party, and then, remembering the trap which that woman had laid for her and Georgie over the Italian paperknife, she could not refrain from asking her to dine and play bridge on the third night of her coming illness. Of course she would be obliged to put her off, and that would be about square. . . . This half-hour's active work produced the impression that, however little pleasure Tilling anticipated from tomorrow's po-di-mu, the musician herself looked forward to it enormously, and was thirsting to talk Italian.

From the window of her bedroom next morning Lucia saw Georgie and Cadman and Foljambe set off for Folkestone, and it was with a Lucretian sense of pleasure in her own coming tranquillity that she contemplated the commotion and general upset of plans which was shortly to descend on Tilling. She went to the garden-room, adjusted the curtains and brewed the tempest which she now sent forth in the shape of a series of notes charged with the bitterest regrets. They were written in pencil (the consummate artist) as if from bed, and were traced in a feeble hand not like her usual firm script. 'What a disappointment!' she wrote to Mrs Wyse. 'How cruel to have got the influenza – where could she have caught it? – on the very morning of her party, and what a blow not to be able to welcome the Contessa today or to dine with dear Susan tomorrow!' There was another note to Major Benjy, and others to Diva and quaint Irene and the curate and the Padre and Elizabeth. She still hoped that possibly she might be well enough for bridge and dinner the day after tomorrow, but Elizabeth must remember how infectious influenza was, and again she herself might not be well enough. That seemed pretty safe, for Elizabeth had a frantic phobia of infection, and Wasters had reeked of carbolic all the time the jumble-sale was being held, for fear of some bit of rubbish having come in contact with tainted hands. Lucia gave these notes to Grosvenor for immediate delivery and told her that the bulletin for the day in answer to callers was that there was no anxiety, for the attack though sharp was not serious, and only demanded warmth and complete quiet. She then proceeded to get both by sitting in this warm October sun in her garden, reading Pope's translation of the *Iliad* and seeing what the Greek for it was.

Three impregnable days passed thus. From behind the adjusted curtains of the garden-room she observed the coming of many callers and Grosvenor's admirable demeanour to them.

The Royce lurched up the street, and there was Susan in her sables, and, sitting next her, a vivacious gesticulating woman with a monocle, who looked the sort of person who could talk at the most appalling rate. This without doubt was the fatal Contessa, and Lucia felt that to see her thus was like observing a lion at large from behind the bars of a comfortable cage. Miss Mapp on the second day came twice, and each time she glanced piercingly at the curtains, as if she knew that trick, and listened as if hoping to hear the sound of the piano. The Padre sent a note almost entirely in Highland dialect, the curate turned away from the door with evident relief in his face at the news he had received, and whistled the Bach fugue rather out of tune.

On the fifth day of her illness new interests sprang up for Lucia that led her to neglect Pope's *Iliad* altogether. By the first post there came a letter from Georgie, containing an enclosure which Lucia saw (with a slight misgiving) was written in Italian. She turned first to Georgie's letter.

'The most wonderful thing has happened,' wrote Georgie,

and you will be pleased. ... There's a family here with whom I've made friends, an English father, an Italian mother and a girl with a pig-tail. Listen! The mother teaches the girl Italian, and sets her little themes to write on some subject or other, and then corrects them and writes a fair copy. Well, I was sitting in the lounge this morning while the girl was having her lesson, and Mrs Brocklebank (that's her name) asked me to suggest a subject for the theme, and I had the most marvellous idea. I said 'Let her write a letter to an Italian Countess whom she has never seen before, and say how she regretted having been obliged to put off her musical party to which she had asked the Countess and her brother because she had caught influenza. She was so sorry not to meet her, and she was afraid that as the Countess was only staying a week in the place, she would not have the pleasure of seeing her at all.' Mrs B. thought that would do beautifully for a theme, and I repeated it over again to make sure. Then the girl wrote it, and Mrs B. corrected it and made a fair copy. I begged her to give it me, because I adored Italian (though I couldn't speak it) and it was so beautifully expressed. I haven't told this very well, because I'm in a hurry to catch the post, but I enclose Mrs B's Italian letter, and you just see whether it doesn't do the trick too marvellously. I'm having quite a gay time, music and drives and seeing the Channel boat come in, and aren't I clever?

Your devoted,
GEORGIE.

Foljambe and Cadman have had a row, but I'm afraid they've made it up.

Lucia, with her misgivings turned to joyful expectation, seized and read the enclosure. Indeed it was a miraculous piece of manna to one whom the very sight of it made hungry. It might have been the result of telepathy between Mrs Brocklebank and her own subconscious self, so aptly did that lady grasp her particular unspoken need. It expressed in the most elegant idiom precisely what met the situation, and she would copy out and send it today, without altering a single word. And how clever of Georgie to have thought of it. He deserved all the champagne he could drink.

Lucia used her highest art in making a copy (on Mallards paper) of this document, as if writing hastily in a familiar medium. Occasionally she wrote a word (it did not matter what), erased it so as to render it illegible to the closest scrutiny, and then went on with Mrs Brocklebank's manuscript; occasionally she omitted a word of it and then inserted it with suitable curves of direction above. No one receiving her transcript could imagine that it was other than her own extempore scribble. Mrs Brocklebank had said that in two or three days she hoped to be able to see her friends again, and that fitted beautifully, because in two or three days now the Contessa's visit would have come to an end, and Lucia could get quite well at once.

The second post arrived before Lucia had finished this thoughtful copy. There was a letter in Lady Brixton's handwriting, and hastily scribbling the final florid salutations to the Contessa, she opened this, and thereupon forgot Georgie and Mrs Brocklebank and everything else in the presence of the tremendous question which was brought for her decision. Adele had simply fallen in love with Riseholme; she affirmed that life was no longer worth living without a house there, and, of all houses, she would like best to purchase, unfurnished, the Hurst.

Failing that there was another that would do, belonging to round red little Mrs Quantock, who, she had ascertained, might consider selling it. Could darling Lucia therefore let her know with the shortest possible delay whether she would be prepared to sell the Hurst? If she had no thought of doing so Adele would begin tempting Mrs Quantock at once. But if she had, let genteel indications about price be outlined at once.

There are certain processes of mental solidification which take place with extraordinary rapidity, because the system is already soaked and super-saturated with the issues involved. It was so now with Lucia. Instantly, on the perusal of Adele's inquiries her own mind solidified. She had long been obliquely contemplating some such step as Adele's letter thrust in front of her, and she was surprised to find that her decision was already made. Riseholme, once so vivid and significant, had during these weeks at Tilling been fading like an ancient photograph exposed to the sun, and all its features, foregrounds and backgrounds had grown blurred and dim. If she went back to Riseholme at the end of the month, she would find there nothing to occupy her energies, or call out her unique powers of self-assertion. She had so swept the board with her management of the Elizabethan fête that no further progress was possible. Poor dear Daisy might occasionally make some minute mutinies, but after being Drake's wife (what a lesson for her!) there would be no real fighting spirit left in her. It was far better, while her own energies still bubbled within her, to conquer this fresh world of Tilling than to smoulder at Riseholme. Her work there was done, whereas here, as this week of influenza testified, there was a very great deal to do. Elizabeth Mapp was still in action and capable of delivering broadsides; innumerable crises might still arise, volcanoes smoked, thunder-clouds threatened, there were hostile and malignant forces to be thwarted. She had never been better occupied and diverted, the place suited her, and it bristled with opportunities. She wrote to Adele at once saying that dear as Riseholme (and especially the Hurst) was to her, she was prepared to be tempted, and indicated a sum before which she was likely to fall.

Miss Mapp by this fifth day of Lucia's illness was completely baffled. She did not yet allow herself to despair of becoming unbaffled, for she was certain that there was a mystery here, and every mystery had an explanation if you only worked at it enough. The coincidence of Lucia's illness with the arrival of the Contessa and Georgie's departure, supported by the trap she had laid about the paperknife, was far too glaring to be overlooked by any constructive mind, and there must be something behind it. Only a foolish ingenuous child (and Elizabeth was anything but that) could have considered these as isolated phenomena. With a faith that would have removed mountains, she believed that Lucia was perfectly well, but all she had been able to do at present was to recite her creed to Major Benjy and Diva and others, and eagerly wait for any shred of evidence to support it. Attempts to pump Grosvenor and lynx-like glances at the window of the garden-room had yielded nothing, and her anxious inquiry addressed to Dr Dobbie, the leading physician of Tilling, had yielded a snub. She did not know who Lucia's doctor was, so with a view to ascertaining that, and possibly getting other information, she had approached him with her most winning smile, and asked how the dear patient at Mallards was.

'I am not attending any dear patient at Mallards,' had been his unpromising reply, 'and if I was I need hardly remind you that, as a professional man, I should not dream of answering any inquiry about my patients without their express permission to do so. Good morning.'

'A very rude man,' thought Miss Mapp, 'but perhaps I had better not try to get at it that way.'

She looked up at the church, wondering if she would find inspiration in that beautiful grey tower, which she had so often sketched, outlined against the pellucid blue of the October sky. She found it instantly, for she remembered that the leads at the top of it which commanded so broad a view of the surrounding country commanded also a perfectly wonderful view of her own little secret garden. It was a small chance, but no chance however small must be neglected in this famine of evidence, and it came to her in a flash that there could be no more pleasant way of spending the morning than making a sketch of the green, green marsh and the line of the blue, blue sea beyond. She hurried back to Wasters, pausing only at Mallards to glance at the garden-room where the curtains were adjusted in the most exasperatingly skilful manner, and to receive Grosvenor's assurance that the patient's temperature was quite normal today.

'Oh, that is good news,' said Miss Mapp. 'Then tomorrow perhaps she will be about again.'

'I couldn't say, miss,' said Grosvenor, holding on to the door.

'Give her my fondest love,' said Miss Mapp, 'and tell her how rejoiced I am, please, Grosvenor.'

'Yes, miss,' said Grosvenor, and before Miss Mapp could step from the threshold, she heard the rattle of the chain behind the closed door.

She was going to lunch that day with the Wyses, a meal which Mr Wyse, in his absurd affected fashion always alluded to as breakfast, especially when the Contessa was staying with them. Breakfast was at one, but there was time for an hour at the top of the church-tower first. In order to see the features of the landscape better, she took up an opera-glass with her sketching things. She first put a blue watery wash on her block for the sky and sea, and a green one for the marsh, and while these were drying she examined every nook of her garden with the opera-glass. No luck, and she picked up her sketch again on which the sky was rapidly inundating the land.

Lucia had learned this morning *via* Grosvenor and her cook and Figgis, Mr Wyse's butler, that the week of the Contessa's stay here was to be curtailed by one day and that the Royce would convey her to Whitchurch next morning on her visit to the younger but ennobled branch of the family. Further intelligence from the same source made known that the breakfast today to which Miss Mapp was bidden was a Belshazzar breakfast, eight if not ten. This was good news: the period of Lucia's danger of detection would be over in less than twenty-four hours, and about the time that Miss Mapp at the top of the tower of Tilling Church was hastily separating the firmament from the dry land, Lucia wrote out a telegram to Georgie that he might return the following day and find all clear. Together with that she sent a request to Messrs Woolgar and Pipstow that they should furnish her with an order to view a certain house she had seen just outside Tilling, near quaint Irene's cottage, which she had observed was for sale.

She hesitated about giving Grosvenor the envelope addressed to Contessa di Faraglione, which contained the transcript, duly signed, of Mrs Brocklebank's letter to a Countess, and decided, on the score of dramatic fitness, to have it delivered shortly after one o'clock when Mrs Wyse's breakfast would be in progress, with orders that it should be presented to the Contessa at once.

Lucia was feeling the want of vigorous exercise, and bethought herself of the Ideal System of Callisthenics for those no longer Young. For five days she had been confined to house and garden, and the craving to skip took possession of her. Skipping was an exercise highly recommended by the ideal system, and she told Grosvenor to bring back for her, with the order to view from Messrs Woolgar and Pipstow, a simple skipping-rope from the toyshop in the High Street. While Grosvenor was gone this desire for free active moment in the open air awoke a kindred passion for the healthful action of the sun on the skin, and she hurried up to her sick-room, changed into a dazzling bathing-suit of black and yellow, and, putting on a very smart dressing-gown gay with ribands, was waiting in the garden-room when Grosvenor returned, recalling to her mind the jerks and swayings which had kept her in such excellent health when grief forbade her to play golf.

The hour was a quarter to one when Lucia tripped into the secret garden, shed her dressing-gown and began skipping on the little lawn with the utmost vigour. The sound of the church-clock immediately below Miss Mapp's eyrie on the tower warned her that it was time to put her sketching things away. deposit them at Wasters and go out to breakfast. During the last half-hour she had cast periodical but fruitless glances at her garden, and had really given it up as a bad job. Now she looked down once more, and there close beside the bust of good Queen

Anne was a gay striped figure of waspish colours skipping away like mad. She dropped her sketch, she reached out a trembling hand for her opera-glasses, the focus of which was already adjusted to a nicety, and by their aid she saw that this athletic wasp who was skipping with such exuberant activity was none other than the invalid.

Miss Mapp gave a shrill crow of triumph. All came to him who waited, and if she had known Greek she would undoubtedly have exclaimed 'Eureka': as it was she only crowed. It was all too good to be true, but it was all too distinct not to be. 'Now I've got her,' she thought. 'The whole thing is as clear as daylight. I was right all the time. She has not had influenza any more than I, and I'll tell everybody at breakfast what I have seen.' But the sight still fascinated her. What shameless vigour, when she should have been languid with fever! What abysses of falsehood, all because she could not talk Italian! What expense to herself in that unnecessary dinner to the Padre and Major Benjy! There was no end to it . . .

Lucia stalked about the lawn with a high prancing motion when she had finished her skipping. Then she skipped again, and then she made some odd jerks, as if she was being electrocuted. She took long deep breaths, she lifted her arms high above her head as if to dive, she lay down on the grass and kicked, she walked on tiptoe like a ballerina, she swung her body round from the hips. All this had for Miss Mapp the fascination that flavours strong disgust and contempt. Eventually, just as the clock struck one, she wrapped herself in her dressing-gown, the best was clearly over. Miss Mapp was already late, and she must hurry straight from the tower to her breakfast, for there was no time to go back to Wasters first. She would be profuse in pretty apologies for her lateness; the view from the church-tower had been so entrancing (this was perfectly true) that she had lost all count of time. She could not show her sketch to the general company, because the firmament had got dreadfully muddled up with the waters which were below it, but instead she would tell them something which would muddle up Lucia.

The breakfast-party was all assembled in Mrs Wyse's

drawing-room with its dark oak beams and its silver-framed photographs and its morocco-case containing the order of the M.B.E., still negligently open. Everybody had been waiting, everybody was rather grumpy at the delay, and on her entry the Contessa had clearly said 'Ecco! Now at last!'

They would soon forgive her when they learned what had really made her late, but it was better to wait for a little before imparting her news, until breakfast had put them all in a more appreciative mood. She hastened on this desired moment by little compliments all round: what a wonderful sermon the Padre had preached last Sunday: how well dear Susan looked: what a delicious dish these eggs *à la Capri* were, she must really be greedy and take a teeny bit more. But these dewdrops were only interjected, for the Contessa talked in a loud continuous voice as usual, addressing the entire table, and speaking with equal fluency whether her mouth was full or empty.

At last the opportunity arrived. Figgis brought in a note on an immense silver (probably plated) salver, and presented it to the Contessa: it was to be delivered at once. Amelia said 'Scusi' which everybody understood – even Lucia might have understood that – and was silent for a space as she tore it open and began reading it.

Miss Mapp decided to tantalize and excite them all before actually making her revelation.

'I will give anybody three guesses as to what I have seen this morning,' she said. 'Mr Wyse, Major Benjy, Padre, you must all guess. It is about someone whom we all know, who is still an invalid. I was sketching this morning at the top of the tower, and happened to glance down into my pet little secret garden. And there was Lucia in the middle of the lawn. How was she dressed, and what was she doing? Three guesses each, shall it be?'

Alas! The introductory tantalization had been too long, for before anybody could guess anything the Contessa broke in again.

'But never have I read such a letter!' she cried. 'It is from Mrs Lucas. All in Italian, and such Italian! Perfect. I should not have thought that any foreigner could have had such command of idiom and elegance. I have lived in Italy for ten years, but my Italian is a bungle compared to this. I have always said that no foreigner ever can learn Italian perfectly, and Cecco too, but we were wrong. This Mrs Lucas proves it. It is composed by the ear, the spoken word on paper. Dio mio! What an escape I have had, Algernon! You had a plan to bring me and your Mrs Lucas together to hear us talk. But she would smile to herself, and I should know what she was thinking, for she would be thinking how very poorly I talk Italian compared with herself. I will read her letter to you all, and though you do not know what it means you will recognize a fluency, a music . . .'

The Contessa proceeded to do so, with renewed exclamations of amazement, and all that bright edifice of suspicion, so carefully reared by the unfortunate Elizabeth, that Lucia knew no Italian collapsed like a house built of cards when the table is shaken. Elizabeth had induced everybody to accept invitations to the second po-di-mu in order that all Tilling might hear Lucia's ignorance exposed by the Contessa, and when she had wriggled out of that, Elizabeth's industrious efforts had caused the gravest suspicions to be entertained that Lucia's illness was feigned in order to avoid any encounter with one who did know Italian, and now not only was not one pane of that Crystal Palace left unshattered, but the Contessa was congratulating herself on her own escape.

Elizabeth stirred feebly below the ruins: she was not quite crushed.

'I'm sure it sounds lovely,' she said when the recitation was over. 'But did not you yourself, dear Mr Wyse, think it odd that anyone who knew Italian should put un po' di musica on her invitation-card?'

'Then he was wrong,' said the Contessa. 'No doubt that phrase is a little humorous quotation from something I do not know. Rather like you ladies of Tilling who so constantly say "au reservoir". It is not a mistake: it is a joke.'

Elizabeth made a final effort.

'I wonder if dear Lucia wrote that note herself,' she said pensively.

'Pish! Her parlour-maid, doubtless,' said the Contessa. 'For me,

I must spend an hour this afternoon to see if I can answer that letter in a way that will not disgrace me.'

There seemed little more to be said on that subject and Elizabeth hastily resumed her tantalization.

'Nobody has tried to guess yet what I saw from the church-tower,' she said. 'Major Benjy, you try! It was Lucia, but how was she dressed and what was she doing?'

There was a coldness about Major Benjy. He had allowed himself to suspect, owing to Elizabeth's delicate hints, that there was perhaps some Italian mystery behind Lucia's influenza, and now he must make amends.

'Couldn't say, I'm sure,' he said. 'She was sure to have been very nicely dressed from what I know of her.'

'I'll give you a hint then,' said she. 'I've never seen her dressed like that before.'

Major Benjy's attention completely wandered. He made no attempt to guess but sipped his coffee.

'You then, Mr Wyse, if Major Benjy gives up,' said Elizabeth, getting anxious. Though the suspected cause of Lucia's illness was disproved, it still looked as if she had never had influenza at all, and that was something.

'My ingenuity, I am sure, will not be equal to the occasion,' said Mr Wyse, very politely. 'You will be obliged to tell me. I give up.'

Elizabeth emitted a shrill little titter.

'A dressing-gown,' she said. 'A bathing costume. And she was skipping! Fancy! With influenza!'

There was a dreadful pause. No babble of excited inquiry and comment took place at all. The Contessa put up her monocle, focused Elizabeth for a moment, and this pause somehow was like the hush that succeeds some slight *gaffe*, some small indelicacy that had better have been left unsaid. Her host came to her rescue.

'That is indeed good news,' said Mr Wyse. 'We may encourage ourselves to hope that our friend is well on the road to convalescence. Thank you for telling us that, Miss Mapp.'

Mrs Bartlett gave one of her little mouselike squeals, and Irene said:

'Hurrah! I shall try to see her this afternoon. I am glad.'

That again was an awful thought. Irene no doubt, if admitted, would give an account of the luncheon-party which would lose nothing in the telling, and she was such a ruthless mimic. Elizabeth felt a sinking feeling.

'Would that be wise, dear?' she said. 'Lucia is probably not yet free from infection, and we mustn't have you down with it. I wonder where she caught it, by the way?'

'But your point is that she's never had influenza at all,' said Irene with that dismal directness of hers.

Choking with this monstrous dose of fiasco, Elizabeth made for the present no further attempt to cause her friends to recoil from the idea of Lucia's skippings, for they only rejoiced that she was sufficiently recovered to do so. The party presently dispersed, and she walked away with her sketching things and Diva, and glanced up the street towards her house. Irene was already standing by the door, and Elizabeth turned away with a shudder, for Irene waved her hand to them and was admitted.

'It's all very strange, dear Diva, isn't it?' she said. 'It's impossible to believe that Lucia's been ill, and it's useless to try to do so. Then there's Mr Georgie's disappearance. I never thought of that before.'

Diva interrupted.

'If I were you, Elizabeth,' she said, 'I should hold my tongue about it all. Much wiser.'

'Indeed?' said Elizabeth, beginning to tremble.

'Yes, I tell you so as a friend,' continued Diva firmly. 'You got hold of a false scent. You made us think that Lucia was avoiding the Faraglione. All wrong from beginning to end. One of your worst shots. Give it up.'

'But there is something queer,' said Elizabeth wildly. 'Skipping – '

'If there is,' said Diva, 'you're not clever enough to find it out. That's my advice. Take it or leave it. I don't care. Au reservoir.'

7

Had Miss Mapp been able to hear what went on in the garden-room that afternoon, as well as she had been able to see what had gone on that morning in the garden, she would never have found Irene more cruelly quaint. Her account of this luncheon-party was more than graphic, for so well did she reproduce the Contessa's fervid monologue and poor Elizabeth's teasings over what she wanted them all to guess, that it positively seemed to be illustrated. Almost more exasperating to Miss Mapp would have been Lucia's pitiful contempt for the impotence of her malicious efforts.

'Poor thing!' she said. 'Sometimes I think she is a little mad. Una pazza: un po' pazza. ... But I regret not seeing the Contessa. Nice of her to have approved of my scribbled note, and I daresay I should have found that she talked Italian very well indeed. Tomorrow – for after my delicious exercise on the lawn this morning, I do not feel up to more today – tomorrow I should certainly have hoped to call – in the afternoon – and have had a chat with her. But she is leaving in the morning, I understand.'

Lucia, looking the picture of vigour and vitality, swept across to the curtained window and threw back those screenings with a movement that made the curtain-rings chime together.

'Poor Elizabeth!' she repeated. 'My heart aches for her, for I am sure all that carping bitterness makes her wretched. I daresay it is only physical: liver perhaps, or acidity. The ideal system of callisthenics might do wonders for her. I cannot, as you will readily understand, dear Irene, make the first approaches to her after her conduct to me, and the dreadful innuendoes she has made, but I should like her to know that I bear her no malice at all. Do convey that to her some time. Tactfully, of course. Women like her who do all they can on every possible occasion to hurt and injure others are usually very sensitive themselves, and I would not add to the poor creature's other chagrins. You must all be kind to her.'

'My dear, you're too wonderful!' said Irene, in a sort of ecstasy. 'What a joy you are! But, alas, you're leaving us so soon. It's too unkind of you to desert us.'

Lucia had dropped on to the music-stool by the piano which had so long been dumb, except for a few timorous chords muffled by the *unsostenuto* pedal, and dreamily recalled the first bars of the famous slow movement.

Irene sat down on the cold hot-water pipes and yearned at her.

'You can do everything,' she said. 'You play like an angel, and you can knock out Mapp with your little finger, and you can skip and play bridge, and you've got such a lovely nature that you don't bear Mapp the slightest grudge for her foul plots. You are adorable! Won't you ask me to come and stay with you at Riseholme sometime?'

Lucia, still keeping perfect time with her triplets while this recital of her perfections was going on, considered whether she should not tell Irene at once that she had practically determined not to desert them. She had intended to tell Georgie first, but she would do that when he came back tomorrow, and she wanted to see about getting a house here without delay. She played a nimble arpeggio on the chord of C sharp minor and closed the piano.

'Too sweet of you to like me, dear,' she said, 'but as for your staying with me at Riseholme, I don't think I shall ever go back there myself. I have fallen in love with this dear Tilling, and I fully expect I shall settle here for good.'

'Angel!' said Irene.

'I've been looking about for a house that might suit me,' she continued when Irene had finished kissing her, 'and the house-agents have just sent me the order to view one which particularly attracts me. It's that white house on the road that skirts the marsh, half a mile away. A nice garden sheltered from the north wind. Right down on the level, it is true, but such a divine view. Broad, tranquil! A dyke and a bank just across the road, keeping back the high tides in the river.'

'But of course I know it; you mean Grebe,' cried Irene. 'The cottage I am in now adjoins the garden. Oh, do take it! While you're settling in, I'll let Diva have Taormina, and Diva will let Mapp have Wasters, and Mapp will let you have Mallards till Grebe's ready for you. And I shall be at your disposal all day to help you with your furniture.'

Lucia decided that there was no real danger of meeting the Contessa if she drove out there: besides the Contessa now wanted to avoid her for fear of showing how inferior was her Italian.

'It's such a lovely afternoon,' she said, 'that I think a little drive would not hurt me. Unfortunately Georgie, who comes back tomorrow, has got my car. I lent it him for his week by the sea.'

'Oh, how like you!' cried Irene. 'Always unselfish!'

'Dear Georgie! So pleased to give him a little treat,' said Lucia. 'I'll ring up the garage and get them to send me something closed. Come with me, dear, if you have nothing particular to do, and we'll look over the house.'

Lucia found much to attract her in Grebe. Though it was close to the road it was not overlooked, for a thick hedge of hornbeam made a fine screen: besides, the road did not lead anywhere particular. The rooms were of good dimensions, there was a hall and dining-room on the ground floor, with a broad staircase leading up to the first floor where there were two or three bedrooms and a long admirable sitting-room with four windows looking across the road to the meadows and the high bank bounding the river. Beyond that lay the great empty levels of the marsh, with the hill of Tilling rising out of it half a mile away to the west. Close behind the house was the cliff which had once been the coast-line before the marshes were drained and reclaimed, and this would be a rare protection against northerly and easterly winds. All these pleasant rooms looked south, and all had this open view away seawards; they had character and dignity, and at once Lucia began to see herself living here. The kitchen and offices were in a wing by themselves, and here again there was character, for the kitchen had evidently been a coach-house, and still retained the big double doors appropriate to such. There had once been a road from it to the end of the kitchen garden, but with its disuse as a coach-house, the road had been replaced by a broad cinder-path now bordered with beds of useful vegetables.

'Ma molto conveniente,' said Lucia more than once, for it was now perfectly safe to talk Italian again, since the Contessa, no less than she, was determined to avoid a duet in that language. 'Mi piace molto. È un bel giardino.'

'How I love hearing you talk Italian,' ejaculated Irene, 'especially since I know it's the very best. Will you teach it me? Oh, I am so pleased you like the house.'

'But I am charmed with it,' said Lucia. 'And there's a garage with a very nice cottage attached which will do beautifully for Cadman and Foljambe.'

She broke off suddenly, for in the fervour of her enthusiasm for the house, she had not thought about the awful catastrophe which must descend on Georgie, if she decided to live at Tilling. She had given no direct thought to him, and now for the first time she realized the cruel blow that would await him, when he came back tomorrow, all bronzed from his week at Folkestone. He had been a real *Deus ex machina* to her: his stroke of genius had turned a very hazardous moment into a blaze of triumph, and now she was going to plunge a dagger into his domestic heart by the news that she and therefore Cadman and therefore Foljambe were not coming back to Riseholme at all . . .

'Oh, are they going to marry?' asked Irene. 'Or do you mean they just live together? How interesting!'

'Dear Irene, do not be so modern,' said Lucia, quite sharply. 'Marriage of course, and banns first. But never mind that for the present. I like those great double doors to the kitchen. I shall certainly keep them.'

'How ripping that you're thinking about kitchen-doors already,' said Irene. 'That really sounds as if you did mean to buy the house. Won't Mapp have a fit when she hears it! I must be there when she's told. She'll say "Darling Lulu, what a joy," and then fall down and foam at the mouth.'

Lucia gazed out over the marsh where the level rays of sunset turned a few low-lying skeins of mist to rose and gold. The tide was high and the broad channel of the river running out to sea was brimming from edge to edge. Here and there, where the banks were low, the water had overflowed on to adjacent margins of land; here and there, spread into broad lakes, it lapped the confining dykes. There were sheep cropping the meadows, there were sea-gulls floating on the water, and half a mile away to the west the red roofs of Tilling glowed as if molten not only with the soft brilliance of the evening light, but (to the discerning eye) with the intensity of the interests that burned beneath them. . . . Lucia hardly knew what gave her the most satisfaction, the magic of the marsh, her resolve to live here, or the recollection of the complete discomfiture of Elizabeth.

Then again the less happy thought of Georgie recurred, and she wondered what arguments she could use to induce him to leave Riseholme and settle here. Tilling with all its manifold interests would be incomplete without him, and how dismally incomplete Riseholme would be to him without herself and Foljambe. Georgie had of late taken his painting much more seriously than ever before, and he had often during the summer put off dinner to an unheard-of lateness in order to catch a sunset, and had risen at most inconvenient hours to catch a sunrise. Lucia had strongly encouraged this zeal, she had told him that if he was to make a real career as an artist he had no time to waste. Appreciation and spurring-on was what he needed: perhaps Irene could help.

She pointed to the glowing landscape.

'Irene, what would life be without sunsets?' she asked. 'And to think that this miracle happens every day, except when it's very cloudy!'

Irene looked critically at the view.

'Generally speaking, I don't like sunsets,' she said. 'The composition of the sky is usually childish. But good colouring about this one.'

'There are practically no sunsets at Riseholme,' said Lucia. 'I suppose the sun goes down, but there's a row of hills in the way. I often think that Georgie's development as an artist is starved there. If he goes back there he will find no one to make him work. What do you think of his painting, dear?'

'I don't think of it at all,' said Irene.

'No? I am astonished. Of course your own is so different in

character. Those wrestlers! Such movement! But personally I find very great perception in Georgie's work. A spaciousness, a calmness! I wish you would take an interest in it and encourage him. You can find beauty anywhere if you look for it.'

'Of course I'll do my best if you want me to,' said Irene. 'But it will be hard work to find beauty in Georgie's little valentines.'

'Do try. Give him some hints. Make him see what you see. All that boldness and freedom. That's what he wants. . . . Ah, the sunset is fading. Buona notte, bel sole! We must be getting home too. Addio, mia bella casa. But Georgie must be the first to know, Irene, do not speak of it until I have told him. Poor Georgie: I hope it will not be a terrible blow to him.'

Georgie came straight to Mallards on his arrival next morning from Folkestone with Cadman and Foljambe. His recall, he knew, meant that the highly dangerous Contessa had gone, and his admission by Grosvenor, after the door had been taken off the chain, that Lucia's influenza was officially over. He looked quite bronzed, and she gave him the warmest welcome.

'It all worked without a hitch,' she said as she told him of the plots and counter-plots which had woven so brilliant a tapestry of events. 'And it was that letter of Mrs Brocklebank's which you sent me that clapped the lid on Elizabeth. I saw at once what I could make of it. Really, Georgie, I turned it into a stroke of genius.'

'But it was a stroke of genius already,' said Georgie. 'You only had to copy it out and send it to the Contessa.'

Lucia was slightly ashamed of having taken the supreme credit for herself: the habit was hard to get rid of.

'My dear, all the credit shall be yours then,' she said handsomely. 'It was your stroke of genius. I copied it out very carelessly as if I had scribbled it off without thought. That was a nice touch, don't you think? The effect? Colossal, so Irene tells me, for I could not be there myself. That was only yesterday. A few desperate wriggles from Elizabeth, but of course no good. I do not suppose there was a more thoroughly thwarted woman in all Sussex than she.'

Georgie gave a discreet little giggle.

'And what's so terribly amusing is that she was right all the time about your influenza and your Italian and everything,' he said. 'Perfectly maddening for her.'

Lucia sighed pensively.

'Georgie, she was malicious,' she observed, 'and that never pays.'

'Besides, it serves her right for spying on you,' Georgie continued.

'Yes, poor thing. But I shall begin now at once to be kind to her again. She shall come to lunch tomorrow, and you of course. By the way, Georgie, Irene takes so much interest in your painting. It was news to me, for her style is so different from your beautiful, careful work.'

'No! That's news to me too,' said Georgie. 'She never seemed to see my sketches before: they might have been blank sheets of paper. Does she mean it? She's not pulling my leg?'

'Nothing of the sort. And I couldn't help thinking it was a great opportunity for you to learn something about more modern methods. There is something you know in those fierce canvasses of hers.'

'I wish she had told me sooner,' said Georgie. 'We've only got a fortnight more here. I shall be very sorry when it's over, for I felt terribly pleased to be getting back to Tilling this morning. It'll be dull going back to Riseholme. Don't you feel that too? I'm sure you must. No plots: no competition.'

Lucia had just received a telegram from Adele concerning the purchase of the Hurst, and it was no use putting off the staggering moment. She felt as if she was Zeus about to discharge a thunderbolt on some unhappy mortal.

'Georgie, I'm not going back to Riseholme at all,' she said. 'I have sold the Hurst: Adele Brixton has bought it. And, practically, I've bought that white house with the beautiful garden, which we admired so much, and that view over the marsh (how I thought of you at sunset yesterday), and really charming rooms with character.'

Georgie sat open-mouthed, and all expression vanished from his face. It became as blank as a piece of sunburnt paper. Then slowly, as if he was coming round from an anaesthetic while the surgeon was still carving dexterously at living tissue, a look of intolerable anguish came into his face.

'But Foljambe, Cadman!' he cried. 'Foljambe can't come back here every night from Riseholme. What am I to do? Is it all irrevocable?'

Lucia bridled. She was quite aware that this parting (if there was to be one) between him and Foljambe would be a dagger; but it was surprising, to say the least, that the thought of the parting between herself and him should not have administered him the first shock. However, there it was. Foljambe first by all means.

'I knew parting from Foljambe would be a great blow to you,' she said, with an acidity that Georgie could hardly fail to notice. 'What a pity that row you told me about came to nothing! But I am afraid that I can't promise to live in Riseholme for ever in order that you may not lose your parlour-maid.'

'But it's not only that,' said Georgie, aware of this acidity and hastening to sweeten it. 'There's you as well. It will be ditch-water at Riseholme without you.'

'Thank you, Georgie,' said Lucia. 'I wondered if and when, as the lawyers say, you would think of that. No reason why you should, of course.'

Georgie felt that this was an unjust reproach.

'Well, after all, you settled to live in Tilling,' he retorted, 'and said nothing about how dull it would be without me. And I've got to do without Foljambe as well.'

Lucia had recourse to the lowest artifice.

'Georgie-orgie, oo not cwoss with me?' she asked in an innocent, childish voice.

Georgie was not knocked out by this sentimental stroke below the belt. It was like Lucia to settle everything in exactly the way that suited her best, and then expect her poor pawns to be stricken at the thought of losing their queen. Besides, the loss of Foljambe *had* occurred to him first. Comfort, like charity, began at home.

'No, I'm not cross,' he said, utterly refusing to adopt baby-talk which implied surrender. 'But I've got every right to be hurt with you for settling to live in Tilling and not saying a word about how you would miss me.'

'My dear, I knew you would take that for granted,' began Lucia.

'Then why shouldn't you take it for granted about me?' he observed.

'I ought to have,' she said. 'I confess it, so that's all right. But why don't you leave Riseholme too and settle here, Georgie? Foljambe, me, your career, now that Irene is so keen about your pictures, and this marvellous sense of not knowing what's going to happen next. Such stimulus, such stuff to keep the soul awake. And you don't want to go back to Riseholme: you said so yourself. You'd moulder and vegetate there.'

'It's different for you,' said Georgie. 'You've sold your house and I haven't sold mine. But there it is: I shall go back, I suppose, without Foljambe or you – I mean you or Foljambe. I wish I had never come here at all. It was that week when we went back for the fête, leaving Cadman and her here, which did all the mischief.'

There was no use in saying anything more at present, and Georgie, feeling himself the victim of an imperious friend and of a faithless parlour-maid, went sadly back to Mallards Cottage. Lucia had settled to leave Riseholme without the least thought of what injury she inflicted on him by depriving him at one fell blow of Foljambe and her own companionship. He was almost sorry he had sent her that wonderful Brocklebank letter, for she had been in a very tight place, especially when Miss Mapp had actually seen her stripped and skipping in the garden as a cure for influenza; and had he not, by his stroke of genius, come to her rescue, her reputation here might have suffered an irretrievable eclipse, and they might all have gone back to Riseholme together. As it was, he had established her on the most exalted pinnacle and her thanks for that boon were expressed by dealing this beastly blow at him.

He threw himself down, in deep dejection, on the sofa in the little parlour of Mallards Cottage, in which he had been so comfortable. Life at Tilling had been full of congenial pleasures, and what a spice all these excitements had added to it! He had done a lot of painting, endless subjects still awaited his brush, and it had given him a thrill of delight to know that quaint Irene, with all her modern notions about art, thought highly of his work. Then there was the diversion of observing and nobly assisting in Lucia's campaign for the sovereignty, and her wars, as he knew, were far from won yet, for Tilling certainly had grown restive under her patronizings and acts of autocracy, and there was probably life in the old dog (meaning Elizabeth Mapp) yet. It was dreadful to think that he would not witness the campaign that was now being planned in those Napoleonic brains. These few weeks that remained to him here would be blackened by the thought of the wretched future that awaited him, and there would be no savour in them, for in so short a time now he would go back to Riseholme in a state of the most pitiable widowerhood, deprived of the ministering care of Foljambe, who all these years had made him so free from household anxieties, and of the companion who had spurred him on to ambitions and activities. Though he had lain awake shuddering at the thought that perhaps Lucia expected him to marry her, he felt he would almost sooner have done that than lose her altogether. 'It may be better to have loved and lost,' thought Georgie, 'than never to have loved at all, but it's very poor work not having loved and also to have lost.' . . .

There was Foljambe singing in a high buzzing voice as she unpacked his luggage in his room upstairs, and though it was a rancid noise, how often had it filled him with the liveliest satisfaction, for Foljambe seldom sang, and when she did, it meant that she was delighted with her lot in life and was planning fresh efforts for his comfort. Now, no doubt, she was planning all sorts of pleasures for Cadman, and not thinking of him at all. Then there was Lucia: through his open window he could already hear the piano in the garden-room, and that showed a horrid callousness to his miserable plight. She didn't care; she was rolling on like the moon or the car of Juggernaut. It was heartless of her to occupy herself with those gay tinkling tunes, but the fact was that she was odiously selfish, and cared about nothing but her own successes. . . . He abstracted himself from those painful reflections for a moment and listened more attentively. It was clearly Mozart that she was practising, but the melody was new to him. 'I bet,' thought Georgie, 'that this evening or tomorrow she'll ask me to read over a new Mozart, and it'll be that very piece that she's practising now.'

His bitterness welled up within him again, as that pleasing reflection faded from his mind, and almost involuntarily he began to revolve how he could pay her back for her indifference to him. A dark but brilliant thought (like a black pearl) occurred to him. What if he dismissed his own chauffeur, Dickie, at present in the employment of his tenant at Riseholme, and, by a prospect of a rise in wages, seduced Cadman from Lucia's service, and took him and Foljambe back to Riseholme? He would put into practice the plan that Lucia herself had suggested, of establishing them in a cottage of their own, with a charwoman, so that Foljambe's days should be his, and her nights Cadman's. That would be a nasty one for Lucia, and the idea was feasible, for Cadman didn't think much of Tilling, and might easily fall in with it. But hardly had this devilish device occurred to him than his better nature rose in revolt against it. It would serve Lucia right, it is true, but it was unworthy of him. 'I should be descending to her level,' thought Georgie very nobly, 'if I did such a thing. Besides, how awful it would be if Cadman said no, and then told her that I had tempted him. She would despise me for doing it, as much as I despise her, and she would gloat over me for having failed. It won't do. I must be more manly about it all somehow. I must be like Major Benjy and say "Damn the woman! Faugh!" and have a drink. But I feel sick at the idea of going back to Riseholme alone. . . . I wish I had eyebrows like a pastebrush, and could say damn properly.'

With a view to being more manly he poured himself out a very small whisky and soda, and his eye fell on a few letters lying for him on the table, which must have come that morning. There was one with the Riseholme postmark, and the envelope was of that very bright blue which he always used. His own stationery evidently, of which he had left a supply, without charge, for the use of his tenant. He opened it, and behold there was dawn breaking on his dark life, for Colonel Cresswell wanted to know if he had any thoughts of selling his house. He was much taken by Riseholme, his sister had bought the Hurst, and he would like to be near her. Would Georgie therefore let him have a line about this as soon as possible, for there was another house, Mrs Quantock's, about which he would enter into negotiations, if there was no chance of getting Georgie's . . .

The revulsion of feeling was almost painful. Georgie had another whisky and soda at once, not because he was depressed, but because he was so happy. 'But I mustn't make a habit of it,' he thought, as he seized his pen.

Georgie's first impulse when he had written his letter to Colonel Cresswell was to fly round to Mallards with this wonderful news, but now he hesitated. Some hitch might arise, the price Colonel Cresswell proposed might not come up to his expectations, though – God knew – he would not dream of haggling over any reasonable offer. Lucia would rejoice at the chance of his staying in Tilling, but she did not deserve to have such a treat of pleasurable expectation for the present. Besides, though he had been manly enough to reject with scorn the wiles of the devil who had suggested the seduction of Cadman, he thought he would tease her a little even if his dream came true. He had often told her that if he was rich enough he would have a flat in London, and now, if this sale of his house came off, he would pretend that he was not meaning to live in Tilling at all, but would live in Town, and he would see how she would take that. It would be her turn to be hurt, and serve her right. So instead of interrupting the roulades of Mozart that were pouring from the window of the garden-room, he walked briskly down to the High Street to see how Tilling was taking the news that it would have Lucia always with it, if her purchase of Grebe had become public property. If not, he would have the pleasure of disseminating it.

There was a hint of seafaring about Georgie's costume as befitted one who had lately spent so much time on the pier at Folkestone. He had a very nautical-looking cap, with a black shining brim, a dark-blue double-breasted coat, white trousers and smart canvas shoes: really he might have been supposed to have come up to Tilling in his yacht, and have landed to see the town. . . . A piercing whistle from the other side of the street showed him that his appearance had at once attracted attention, and there was Irene planted with her easel in the middle of the pavement, and painting a row of flayed carcases that hung in the butcher's shop. Rembrandt had better look out ...

'Avast there, Georgie,' she cried. 'Home is the sailor, home from sea. Come and talk.'

This was rather more attention than Georgie had anticipated, but as Irene was quite capable of shouting nautical remarks after him if he pretended not to hear, he tripped across the street to her.

'Have you seen Lucia, Commodore?' she said. 'And has she told you?'

'About her buying Grebe?' asked Georgie. 'Oh, yes.'

'That's all right then. She told me not to mention it till she'd seen you. Mapp's popping in and out of the shops, and I simply must be the first to tell her. Don't cut in in front of me, will you? Oh, by the way, have you done any sketching at Folke-stone?'

'One or two,' said Georgie. 'Nothing very much.'

'Nonsense. Do let me come and see them. I love your handling. Just cast your eye over this and tell me what's wrong with – There she is. Hi! Mapp!'

Elizabeth, like Georgie, apparently thought it more prudent to answer that summons and avoid further public proclamation of her name, and came hurrying across the street.

'Good morning, Irene mine,' she said. 'What a beautiful picture! All the poor skinned piggies in a row, or are they sheep? Back again, Mr Georgie? How we've missed you. And how do you think dear Lulu is looking after her illness?'

'Mapp, there's news for you,' said Irene, remembering the luncheon-party yesterday. 'You must guess: I shall tease you. It's about your Lulu. Three guesses.'

'Not a relapse, I hope?' said Elizabeth brightly.

'Quite wrong. Something much nicer. You'll enjoy it tremendously.'

'Another of those beautiful musical parties?' asked Elizabeth. 'Or has she skipped a hundred times before breakfast?'

'No, much nicer,' said Irene. 'Heavenly for us all.'

A look of apprehension had come over Elizabeth's face, as an awful idea occurred to her.

'Dear one, give over teasing,' she said. 'Tell me.'

'She's not going away at the end of the month,' said Irene. 'She's bought Grebe.'

Blank dismay spread over Elizabeth's face.

'Oh, what a joy!' she said. 'Lovely news.'

She hurried off to Wasters, too much upset even to make Diva, who was coming out of Twistevant's, a partner in her joy. Only this morning she had been consulting her calendar and observing that there were only fifteen days more before Tilling was quit of Lulu, and now at a moderate estimate there might be at least fifteen years of her. Then she found she could not bear the weight of her joy alone and sped back after Diva.

'Diva dear, come in for a minute,' she said. 'I've heard something.'

Diva looked with concern at that lined and agitated face.

'What's the matter?' she said. 'Nothing serious?'

'Oh no, lovely news,' she said with bitter sarcasm. 'Tilling will rejoice. *She's* not going away. *She's* going to stop here for ever.'

There was no need to ask who 'she' was. For weeks Lucia had been 'she'. If you meant Susan Wyse, or Diva or Irene, you said so. But 'she' was Lucia.

'I suspected as much,' said Diva. 'I know she had an order to view Grebe.'

Elizabeth, in a spasm of exasperation, banged the door of Wasters so violently after she and Diva had entered, that the house shook and a note leaped from the wire letter-box on to the floor.

'Steady on with my front door,' said Diva, 'or there'll be some dilapidations to settle.'

Elizabeth took no notice of this petty remark, and picked up the note. The handwriting was unmistakable, for Lucia's study of Homer had caused her (subconsciously or not) to adopt a modified form of Greek script, and she made her 'a' like alpha and her 'e' like epsilon. At the sight of it Elizabeth suffered a complete loss of self-control, she held the note on high as if exposing a relic to the gaze of pious worshippers, and made a low curtsey to it.

'And this is from Her,' she said. 'Oh, how kind of Her Majesty to write to me in her own hand with all those ridiculous twiddles. Not content with speaking Italian quite perfectly, she must also write in Greek. I daresay she talks it beautifully too.'

'Come, pull yourself together, Elizabeth,' said Diva.

'I am not aware that I am coming to bits, dear,' said Elizabeth, opening the note with the very tips of her fingers, as if it had been written by someone infected with plague or at least influenza. 'But let me see what Her Majesty says. . . . "Dearest Liblib" . . . the impertinence of it! Or is it Riseholme humour?'

'Well, you call her Lulu,' said Diva. 'Do get on.'

Elizabeth frowned with the difficulty of deciphering this crabbed handwriting.

' "Now that I am quite free of infection," she read – (Infection indeed. She never had flu at all) – "of infection, I can receive my friends again, and hope so much you will lunch with me tomorrow. I hasten also to tell you of my change of plans, for I have so fallen in love with your delicious Tilling that I have bought a house here – (Stale news!) – and shall settle into it next month. An awful wrench, as you may imagine, to leave my dear Riseholme – (Then why wrench yourself?) – and poor Georgie is in despair, but Tilling and all you dear people have wrapt yourselves round my heart. (Have we? The same to you!) – and it is no use my struggling to get free. I wonder therefore if you would consider letting me take your beautiful Mallards at the same rent for another month, while Grebe is being done up, and my furniture being installed? I should be so grateful if this is possible, otherwise I shall try to get Mallards Cottage when my Georgie – (My!) – goes back to Riseholme. Could you, do you think, let me know about this tomorrow, if, as I hope, you will send me 'un' amabile "si" ' – (What in the world is an amabile si?) – and come to lunch? – Tanti saluti, Lucia." '

'I understand,' said Diva. 'It means "an amiable yes", about going to lunch.'

'Thank you, Diva. You are quite an Italian scholar too,' said

Elizabeth. 'I call that a thoroughly heartless letter. And all of us, mark you, must serve her convenience. I can't get back into Mallards, because She wants it, and even if I refused, She would be next door at Mallards Cottage. I've never been so long out of my own house before.'

Both ladies felt that it would be impossible to keep up any semblance of indignation that Lucia was wanting to take Mallards for another month, for it suited them both so marvellously well.

'You are in luck,' said Diva, 'getting another month's let at that price. So am I too, if you want to stop here, for Irene is certain to let me stay on at her house, because her cottage is next to Grebe, and she'll be in and out all day – '

'Poor Irene seems to be under a sort of spell,' said Elizabeth in parenthesis. 'She can think about nothing except that woman. Her painting has fallen off terribly. Coarsened. ... Yes, dear, I think I will give the Queen of the Italian language an amabile si about Mallards. I don't know if you would consider taking rather a smaller rent for November. Winter prices are always lower.'

'Certainly not,' said Diva. 'You're going to get the same as before for Mallards.'

'That's my affair, dear,' said Elizabeth.

'And this is mine,' said Diva firmly. 'And will you go to lunch with her tomorrow?'

Elizabeth, now comparatively calm, sank down in the window seat, which commanded so good a view of the High Street.

'I suppose I shall have to,' she said. 'One must be civil, whatever has happened. Oh, there's Major Benjy. I wonder if he's heard.'

She tapped at the window and threw it open. He came hurrying across the street and began to speak in a loud voice before she could get in a word.

'That amusing guessing game of yours, Miss Elizabeth,' he said, just like Irene. 'About Mrs Lucas. I'll give you three – '

'One's enough: we all know,' said Elizabeth. 'Joyful news, isn't it?'

'Indeed, it is delightful to know that we are not going to lose one who – who has endeared herself to us all so much,' said he very handsomely.

He stopped. His tone lacked sincerity; there seemed to be something in his mind which he left unsaid. Elizabeth gave him a piercing and confidential look.

'Yes, Major Benjy?' she suggested.

He glanced round like a conspirator to see there was no one eavesdropping.

'Those parties, you know,' he said. 'Those entertainments which we've all enjoyed so much. Beautiful music. But Grebe's a long way off on a wet winter night. Not just round the corner. Now if she was settling in Mallards – '

He saw at once what an appalling interpretation might be put on this, and went on in a great hurry.

'You'll have to come to our rescue, Miss Elizabeth,' he said, dropping his voice so that even Diva could not hear. 'When you're back in your own house again, you'll have to look after us all as you always used to. Charming woman, Mrs Lucas, and most hospitable, I'm sure, but in the winter, as I was saying, that long way out of Tilling, just to hear a bit of music, and have a tomato, if you see what I mean.'

'Why, of course I see what you mean,' murmured Elizabeth. 'The dear thing, as you say, is so hospitable. Lovely music and tomatoes, but we must make a stand.'

'Well, you can have too much of a good thing,' said Major Benjy, 'and for my part a little Mozart lasts me a long time, especially if it's a long way on a wet night. Then I'm told there's an idea of callisthenic classes, though no doubt they would be for ladies only – '

'I wouldn't be too sure about that,' said Elizabeth. 'Our dear friend has got enough – shall we call it self-confidence? – to think herself capable of teaching anybody anything. If you aren't careful, Major Benjy, you'll find yourself in a skipping match on the lawn at Grebe, before you know what you're doing. You've been King Cophetua already, which I, for one, never thought to see.'

'That was just once in a way,' said he. 'But when it comes to callisthenic classes – '

Diva, in an agony at not being able to hear what was going on, had crept up behind Elizabeth, and now crouched close to her as she stood leaning out of the window. At this moment, Lucia, having finished her piano-practice, came round the corner from Mallards into the High Street. Elizabeth hastily withdrew from the window and bumped into Diva.

'So sorry: didn't know you were there, dear,' she said. 'We must put our heads together another time, Major Benjy. Au reservoir.'

She closed the window.

'Oh, do tell me what you're going to put your heads together about,' said Diva. 'I only heard just the end.'

It was important to get allies: otherwise Elizabeth would have made a few well-chosen remarks about eavesdroppers.

'It is sad to find that just when Lucia has settled never to leave us any more,' she said, 'that there should be so much feeling in Tilling about being told to do this and being made to listen to that. Major Benjy – I don't know if you heard that part, dear – spoke very firmly, and I thought sensibly about it. The question really is if England is a free country or not, and whether we're going to be trampled upon. We've been very happy in Tilling all these years, going our own way, and living in sweet harmony together, and I for one, and Major Benjy for another, don't intend to put our necks under the yoke. I don't know how you feel about it. Perhaps you like it, for after all you were Mary Queen of Scots just as much as Major Benjy was King Cophetua.'

'I won't go to any po-di-mus, after dinner at Grebe,' said Diva. 'I shouldn't have gone to the last, but you persuaded us all to go. Where was your neck then, Elizabeth? Be fair.'

'Be fair yourself, Diva,' said Elizabeth with some heat. 'You know perfectly well that I wanted you to go in order that you might all get your necks from under her yoke, and hear that she couldn't speak a word of Italian.'

'And a nice mess you made of that,' said Diva. 'But never mind. She's established now as a perfect Italian linguist, and there it is. Don't meddle with that again, or you'll only prove that she can talk Greek too.'

Elizabeth rose and pointed at her like one of Raphael's Sibyls.

'Diva, to this day I don't believe she can talk Italian. It was a conjuring trick, and I'm no conjurer but a plain woman, and I can't tell you how it was done. But I will swear it was a trick. Besides, answer me this! Why doesn't she offer to give us Italian lessons if she knows it? She has offered to teach us bridge and Homer and callisthenics and take choir-practices and arrange tableaux. Why not Italian?'

'That's curious,' said Diva thoughtfully.

'Not the least curious. The reason is obvious. Everyone snubbed me and scolded me, you among others, at that dreadful luncheon-party, but I know I'm right, and some day the truth will come out. I can wait. Meantime what she means to do is to take us all in hand, and I won't be taken in hand. What is needed from us all is a little firmness.'

Diva went home thrilled to the marrow of her bones at the thought of the rich entertainment that these next months promised to provide. Naturally she saw through Elizabeth's rodomontade about yokes and free countries: what she meant was that she intended to assert herself again, and topple Lucia over. Two could not reign in Tilling, as everybody could see by this time. 'All most interesting,' said Diva to herself. 'Elizabeth's got hold of Major Benjy for the present, and Lucia's going to lose Georgie, but then men don't count for much in Tilling: it's brains that do it. There'll be more bridge-parties and teas this winter than ever before. Really, I don't know which of them I would back. Hullo, there's a note from her. Lunch tomorrow, I expect. . . . I thought so.'

Lucia's luncheon-party next day was to be of the nature of a banquet to celebrate the double event of her recovery and of the fact that Tilling, instead of mourning her approaching departure, was privileged to retain her, as Elizabeth had said, for ever and ever. The whole circle of her joyful friends would be there, and she meant to give them to eat of the famous dish of lobster à la Riseholme, which she had provided for Georgie, a few weeks ago, to act as a buffer to break the shock of Foljambe's engagement. It had already produced a great deal of wild surmise in the minds of the housewives at Tilling, for no one could conjecture how it was made, and Lucia had been deaf to all requests for the recipe: Elizabeth had asked her twice to give it her, but Lucia had merely changed the subject without attempt at transition: she had merely talked about something quite different. This secretiveness was considered unamiable, for the use of Tilling was to impart its culinary mysteries to friends, so that they might enjoy their favourite dishes at each other's houses, and lobster *à la Riseholme* had long been an agonizing problem to Elizabeth. She had made an attempt at it herself, but the result was not encouraging. She had told Diva and the Padre that she felt sure she had 'guessed it', and, when bidden to come to lunch and partake of it, they had both anticipated a great treat. But Elizabeth had clearly guessed wrong, for lobster *à la Riseholme à la Mapp* had been found to consist of something resembling lumps of india-rubber (so tough that the teeth positively bounced away from them on contact) swimming in a dubious pink gruel, and both of them left a great deal on their plates, concealed as far as possible under their knives and forks, though their hostess continued manfully to chew, till her jaw-muscles gave out. Then Elizabeth had had recourse to underhand methods. Lucia had observed her more than once in the High Street, making herself suspiciously pleasant to her cook, and from the window of the garden-room just before her influenza, she had seen her at the back door of Mallards again in conversation with the lady of the kitchen. On this occasion, with an unerring conviction in her mind, she had sent for her cook and asked her what Miss Mapp wanted. It was even so: Elizabeth's ostensible inquiry was for an egg-whisk, which she had left by mistake at Mallards three months ago, but then she had unmasked her batteries, and, actually fingering a bright half-crown, had asked point-blank for the recipe of this lobster *à la Riseholme*. The cook had given her a polite but firm refusal, and Lucia was now more determined than ever that Elizabeth should never know the exquisite secret. She naturally felt that it was beneath her to take the slightest notice of this low and paltry attempt to obtain by naked bribery a piece of private knowledge, and she never let Elizabeth know that she was cognizant of it.

During the morning before Lucia's luncheon-party a telegram had come for Georgie from Colonel Cresswell making a firm and very satisfactory offer for his house at Riseholme, unfurnished. That had made him really busy: first he had to see Foljambe and tell her (under seal of secrecy, for he had his little plot of teasing Lucia in mind) that he was proposing to settle in Tilling. Foljambe was very pleased to hear it, and in a burst of most unusual feeling, had said that it would have gone to her heart to leave his service, after so many harmonious years, when he went back to Riseholme, and that she was very glad to adopt the plan, which she had agreed to, when it was supposed that they would all go back to Riseholme together. She would do her work all day in Georgie's house, and retire in the evening to the connubialities of the garage at Grebe. When this affecting interview was over, she went back to her jobs, and again Georgie heard her singing as she cleaned the silver. 'So that's beautiful,' he said to himself, 'and the cloud has passed for ever. Now I must instantly see about getting a house here.'

He hurried out. There was still an hour before he was due at the lobster lunch. Though he had left the seaside twenty-four hours ago, he put on his yachtsman's cap and, walking on air, set off for the house-agent's. Of all the houses in the place which he had seen, he was sure that none would suit him as well as this dear little Mallards Cottage which he now occupied; he liked it, Foljambe liked it, they all liked it, but he had no idea whether he could get a lease from kippered Isabel. As he crossed the High Street, a wild hoot from a motor-horn just behind him gave him a dreadful fright, but he jumped nimbly for the pavement, reached it unhurt, and though his cap fell off and landed in a puddle, he was only thankful to have escaped being run down by Isabel Poppit on her motor-cycle. Her hair was like a twisted mop, her skin incredibly tanned, and mounted on her cycle she looked like a sort of modernized Valkyrie in rather bad repair. . . . Meeting her just at this moment, when he was on his way to inquire about Mallards Cottage, seemed a good omen to Georgie, and he picked up his cap and ran back across the street, for in her natural anxiety to avoid killing him she had swerved into a baker's cart, and had got messed up in the wheels.

'I do apologize, Miss Poppit,' he said. 'Entirely my fault for not looking both ways before I crossed.'

'No harm done,' said she. 'Oh, your beautiful cap. I am sorry. But after all the wonderful emptiness and silence among the sand-dunes, a place like a town seems to me a positive nightmare.'

'Well, the emptiness and silence does seem to suit you,' said Georgie, gazing in astonishment at her mahogany face. 'I never saw anybody looking so well.'

Isabel, with a tug of her powerful arms, disentangled her cycle.

'It's the simple life,' said she, shaking her hair out of her eyes. 'Never again will I live in a town. I have taken the bungalow I am in now for six months more, and I only came into Tilling to tell the house-agent to get another tenant for Mallards Cottage, as I understand that you're going back to Riseholme at the end of this month.'

Georgie had never felt more firmly convinced that a wise and beneficent Providence looked after him with the most amiable care.

'And I was also on my way to the house-agent's,' he said, 'to see if I could get a lease of it.'

'Gracious! What a good thing I didn't run over you just now,' said Isabel, with all the simplicity derived from the emptiness and silence of sand-dunes. 'Come on to the agent's.'

Within half an hour the whole business was as good as settled. Isabel held a lease from her mother of Mallards Cottage, which had five years yet to run, and she agreed to transfer this to Georgie, and store her furniture. He had just time to change into his new mustard-coloured suit with its orange tie and its topaz tie-pin, and arrived at the luncheon-party in the very highest spirits. Besides, there was his talk with Lucia, when other guests had gone, to look forward to. How he would tease her about settling in London!

Though Tilling regarded the joyful prospect of Lucia's never going away again with certain reservations, and, in the case of Elizabeth, with nothing but reservations, her guests vied with each other in the fervency of their self-congratulations, and

Elizabeth outdid them all, as she took into her mouth small fragments of lobster, in the manner of a wine-taster, appraising subtle flavours. There was cheese, there were shrimps, there was cream: there were so many things that she felt like Adam giving names to the innumerable procession of different animals. She had helped herself so largely that when the dish came to Georgie there was nothing left but a little pink juice, but he hardly minded at all, so happy had the events of the morning made him. Then when Elizabeth felt that she would choke if she said anything more in praise of Lucia, Mr Wyse took it up, and Georgie broke in and said it was cruel of them all to talk about the delicious busy winter they would have, when they all knew that he would not be here any longer but back at Riseholme. In fact, he rather overdid his lamentations, and Lucia, whose acute mind detected the grossest insincerity in Elizabeth's raptures, began to wonder whether Georgie for some unknown reason was quite as woeful as he professed to be. Never had he looked more radiant, not a shadow of disappointment had come over his face when he inspected the casserole that had once contained his favourite dish, and found nothing left for him. There was something up – what on earth could it be? Had Foljambe jilted Cadman? – and just as Elizabeth was detecting flavours in the mysterious dish, so Lucia was trying to arrive at an analysis of the gay glad tones in which Georgie expressed his misery.

'It's too tarsome of you all to go on about the lovely things you're going to do,' he said. 'Callisthenic classes and Homer and bridge, and poor me far away. I shall tell myself every morning that I hate Tilling; I shall say like Coué, "Day by day in every way, I dislike it more and more," until I've convinced myself that I shall be glad to go.'

Mr Wyse made him a beautiful bow.

'We too shall miss you very sadly, Mr Pillson,' he said, 'and for my part I shall be tempted to hate Riseholme for taking from us one who has so endeared himself to us.'

'I ask to be allowed to associate myself with those sentiments,' said Major Benjy, whose contempt for Georgie and his sketches and his needlework had been intensified by the sight of his yachting cap, which he had pronounced to be only fit for a popinjay. It had been best to keep on good terms with him while Lucia was at Mallards, for he might poison her mind about himself, and now that he was going, there was no harm in these handsome remarks. Then the Padre said something Scotch and sympathetic and regretful, and Georgie found himself, slightly to his embarrassment, making bows and saying 'thank you' right and left in acknowledgement of these universal expressions of regret that he was so soon about to leave them. It was rather awkward, for within a few hours they would all know that he had taken Mallards Cottage unfurnished for five years, which did not look like an immediate departure. But this little deception was necessary if he was to bring off his joke against Lucia, and make her think that he meant to settle in London. And after all, since everybody seemed so sorry that (as they imagined) he was soon to leave Tilling, they ought to be very much pleased to find that he was doing nothing of the kind.

The guests dispersed soon after lunch and Georgie, full of mischief and naughtiness, lingered with his hostess in the garden-room. All her gimlet glances during lunch had failed to fathom his high good humour: here was he on the eve of parting with his Foljambe and herself, and yet his face beamed with content. Lucia was in very good spirits also, for she had seen Elizabeth's brow grow more and more furrowed as she strove to find a formula for the lobster.

'What a lovely luncheon-party, although I got no lobster at all,' said Georgie, as he settled himself for his teasing. 'I did enjoy it. And Elizabeth's rapture at your stopping here! She must have an awful blister on her tongue.'

Lucia sighed.

'Sapphira must look to her laurels, poor thing,' she observed pensively. 'And how sorry they all were that you are going away.'

'Wasn't it nice of them?' said Georgie. 'But never mind that now: I've got something wonderful to tell you. I've never felt happier in my life, for the thing I've wanted for so many years can be managed at last. You will be pleased for my sake.'

Lucia laid a sympathetic hand on his. She felt that she had shown too little sympathy with one who was to lose his parlour-maid and his oldest friend so soon. But the gaiety with which he bore this double stroke was puzzling . . .

'Dear Georgie,' she said, 'anything that makes you happy makes me happy. I am rejoiced that something of the sort has occurred. Really rejoiced. Tell me what it is instantly.'

Georgie drew a long breath. He wanted to give it out all in a burst of triumph like a fanfare.

'Too lovely,' he said. 'Colonel Cresswell has bought my house at Riseholme – such a good price – and now at last I shall be able to settle in London. I was just as tired of Riseholme as you, and now I shall never see it again or Tilling either. Isn't it a dream? Riseholme, stuffy little Mallards Cottage, all things of the past! I shall have a nice little home in London, and you must promise to come up and stay with me sometimes. How I looked forward to telling you! Orchestral concerts at Queen's Hall, instead of our fumbling little arrangements of Mozartino for four hands. Pictures, a club if I can afford it, and how nice to think of you so happy down at Tilling! As for all the fuss I made yesterday about losing Foljambe, I can't think why it seemed to me so terrible.'

Lucia gave him one more gimlet glance, and found she did not believe a single word he was saying except as regards the sale of his house at Riseholme. All the rest must be lies, for the Foljambe-wound could not possibly have healed so soon. But she instantly made up her mind to pretend to believe him, and clapped her hands for pleasure.

'Dear Georgie! What splendid news!' she said. 'I am pleased. I've always felt that you, with all your keenness and multifarious interests in life, were throwing your life away in these little backwaters like Riseholme and Tilling. London is the only place for you! Now tell me: Are you going to get a flat or a house? And where is it to be? If I were you I should have a house!'

This was not quite what Georgie had expected. He had thought that Lucia would suggest that now that he was quit of Riseholme, he positively must come to Tilling, but not only did she fail to do that, but she seemed delighted that no such thought had entered into his head.

'I haven't really thought about that yet,' he said. 'There's something to be said for a flat.'

'No doubt. It's more compact, and then there's no bother about rates and taxes. And you'll have your car, I suppose. And will your cook go with you? What does she say to it all?'

'I haven't told her yet,' said Georgie, beginning to get a little pensive.

'Really? I should have thought you would have done that at once. And isn't Foljambe pleased that you are so happy again?'

'She doesn't know yet,' said Georgie. 'I thought I would tell you first.'

'Dear Georgie, how sweet of you,' said Lucia. 'I'm sure Foljambe will be as pleased as I am. You'll be going up to London, I suppose, constantly now till the end of this month, so that you can get your house or your flat, whichever it is, ready as soon as possible. How busy you and I will be, you settling into London and I into Tilling. Do you know, supposing you had thought of living permanently here, now that you've got rid of your house at Riseholme, I should have done my best to persuade you not to, though I know in my selfishness that I did suggest that yesterday. But it would never do, Georgie. It's all very well for elderly women like me, who just want a little peace and quietness, or for retired men like Major Benjy or for dilettantes like Mr Wyse, but for you, a thousand times no. I am sure of it.'

Georgie got thoughtfuller and thoughtfuller. It had been rather a mistake to try to tease Lucia, for so far from being teased she was simply pleased. The longer she went on like this, and there seemed no end to her expressions of approval, the harder it would be to tell her.

'Do you really think that?' he said.

'Indeed I do. You would soon be terribly bored with Tilling. Oh, Georgie, I am so pleased with your good fortune and your good sense. I wonder if the agents here have got any houses or flats in London on their books. Let's go down there at once and see. We might find something. I'll run and put on my hat.'

Georgie threw in his hand. As usual Lucia had come out on top.

'You're too tarsome,' he said. 'You don't believe a single word I've been telling you of my plans.'

'My dear, of course I don't,' said Lucia brightly. 'I never heard such a pack of rubbish. Ananias is not in it. But it is true about selling your Riseholme house, I hope?'

'Yes, that part is,' said Georgie.

'Then of course you're going to live here,' said she. 'I meant you to do that all along. Now how about Mallards Cottage? I saw that Yahoo in the High Street this morning, and she told me she wanted to let it for the winter. Let's go down to the agent's as I suggested, and see.'

'I've done that already,' said Georgie, 'for I met her too, and she nearly knocked me down. I've got a five years' lease of it.'

It was not in Lucia's nature to crow over anybody. She proved her quality and passed on to something else.

'Perfect!' she said. 'It has all come out just as I planned, so that's all right. Now, if you've got nothing to do, let us have some music.'

She got out the new Mozart which she had been practising.

'This looks a lovely duet,' she said, 'and we haven't tried it yet. I shall be terribly rusty, for all the time I had influenza, I hardly dared to play the piano at all.'

Georgie looked at the new Mozart.

'It does look nice,' he said. 'Tum-ti-tum. Why, that's the one I heard you practising so busily yesterday morning.'

Lucia took not the slightest notice of this.

'We begin together,' she said, 'on the third beat, Now. ... Uno, due, TRE!'

8

The painting and decorating of Grebe began at once. Irene offered to do all the painting with her own hands, and recommended as a scheme for the music-room, a black ceiling and four walls of different colours, vermilion, emerald green, ultra-marine and yellow. It would take a couple of months or so to execute, and the cost would be considerable as lapis lazuli must certainly be used for the ultramarine wall, but she assured Lucia that the result would be unique and marvellously stimu-lating to the eye, especially if she would add a magenta carpet and a nickel-plated mantelpiece.

'It sounds too lovely, dear,' said Lucia, contemplating the sample of colours which Irene submitted to her, 'but I feel sure I shan't be able to afford it. Such a pity! Those beautiful hues!'

Then Irene besought her to introduce a little variety into the shape of the windows. It would be amusing to have one win-dow egg-shaped, and another triangular, and another with five or six or seven irregular sides, so that it looked as if it was a hole in the wall made by a shell. Or how about a front-door that, instead of opening sideways, let down like a portcullis?

Irene rose to more daring conceptions yet. One night she had dined on a pot of strawberry jam and half a pint of very potent cocktails, because she wanted her eye for colour to be at its keenest round about eleven o'clock when the moon would rise over the marsh, and she hoped to put the lid for ever on Whistler's naïve old-fashioned attempts to paint moonlight. After this salubrious meal she had come round to Mallards, waiting for the moon to rise and sat for half an hour at Lucia's piano, striking random chords, and asking Lucia what colour they were. These musical rainbows suggested a wonderful idea, and she shut down the piano with a splendid purple bang.

'Darling, I've got a new scheme for Grebe,' she said. 'I want you to furnish a room sideways, if you understand what I mean.'

'I don't think I do,' said Lucia.

'Why, like this,' said Irene very thoughtfully. 'You would open the door of the room and find you were walking about on wallpaper with pictures hanging on it. (I'll do the pictures for you.) Then one side of the room where the window is would be whitewashed as if it was a ceiling and the window would be the skylight. The opposite side would be the floor; and you would have the furniture screwed on to it. The other walls, including the one which would be the ceiling in an ordinary room, would be covered with wallpaper and more pictures and a bookcase. It would all be sideways, you see: you'd enter through the wall, and the room would be at right angles to you; ceiling on the left, floor on the right, or vice versa. It would give you a perfectly new perception of the world. You would see everything from a new angle, which is what we want so much in life nowadays. Don't you think so?'

Irene's speech was distinct and clear cut, she walked up and down the garden-room with a firm unwavering step, and Lucia put from her the uneasy suspicion that her dinner had gone to her head.

'It would be most delightful,' she said, 'but slightly too experimental for me.'

'And then, you see,' continued Irene, 'how useful it would be if somebody tipsy came in. It would make him sober at once, for tipsy people see everything crooked, and so your sideways-room, being crooked, would appear to him straight, and so he would be himself again. Just like that.'

'That would be splendid,' said Lucia, 'but I can't provide a room where tipsy people could feel sober again. The house isn't big enough.'

Irene sat down by her, and passionately clasped one of her hands.

'Lucia, you're too adorable,' she said. 'Nothing defeats you. I've been talking the most abject nonsense, though I do think that there may be something in it, and you remain as calm as the moon which I hope will rise over the marsh before long, unless the almanack in which I looked it out is last year's. Don't tell anybody else about the sideways-room, will you, or they might think I was drunk. Let it be our secret, darling.'

Lucia wondered for a moment if she ought to allow Irene to spend the night on the marsh, but she was perfectly capable of coherent speech and controlled movements, and possibly the open air might do her good.

'Not a soul shall know, dear,' she said. 'And now if you're really going to paint the moon, you had better start. You feel quite sure you can manage it, don't you?'

'Of course I can manage the moon,' said Irene stoutly. 'I've managed it lots of times. I wish you would come with me. I always hate leaving you. Or shall I stop here, and paint you instead? Or do you think Georgie would come? What a lamb, isn't he? Pass the mint-sauce please, or shall I go home?'

'Perhaps that would be best,' said Lucia. 'Paint the moon another night.'

Lucia next day hurried up the firm to which she had entrusted the decoration of Grebe, in case Irene had some new schemes, and half-way through November, the house was ready to receive her furniture from Riseholme. Georgie simultaneously was settling into Mallards Cottage, and in the course of it went through a crisis of the most agitating kind. Isabel had assured him that by noon on a certain day men would arrive to take her furniture to the repository where it was to be stored, and as the vans with his effects from Riseholme had arrived in Tilling the night before, he induced the foreman to begin moving everything out of the house at nine next morning and bring his furniture in. This was done, and by noon all Isabel's tables and chairs and beds and crockery were standing out in the street ready for her van. They completely blocked it for wheeled traffic, though pedestrians could manage to squeeze by in single file. Tilling did not mind this little inconvenience in the least, for it was all so interesting, and tradesmen's carts coming down the street were cheerfully backed into the churchyard again and turned round in order to make a more circuitous route, and those coming up were equally obliging, while foot-passengers, thrilled with having the entire contents of a house exposed for their inspection, were unable to tear themselves away from so intimate an exhibition. Then Georgie's furniture was moved in, and there were dazzling and fascinating objects for inspection, pictures that he had painted, screens and bedspreads that he had worked, very pretty woollen pyjamas for the winter and embroidered covers for hot-water bottles. These millineries roused Major Benjy's manliest indignation, and he was nearly late for the tram to take him out to play golf, for he could not tear himself away from the revolting sight. In a few hours Georgie's effects had passed into the house, but still there was no sign of anyone coming to remove Isabel's from the street, and, by dint of telephoning, it was discovered that she had forgotten to give any order at all about them, and the men from the repository were out on other jobs. It then began to rain rather heavily, and though Georgie called heaven and earth to witness that all this muddle was not his fault he felt compelled, out of mere human compassion, to have Isabel's furniture moved back into his house again. In consequence the rooms and passages on the ground floor were completely blocked with stacks of cupboards and tables piled high with books and crockery and saucepans, the front door would not shut, and Foljambe, caught upstairs by the rising tide, could not come down. The climax of intensity arrived when she let down a string from an upper window, and Georgie's cook attached a small basket of nourishing food to it. Diva was terribly late for lunch at the Wyses, for she was rooted to the spot, though it was raining heavily, till she was sure that Foljambe would not be starved.

But by the time that the month of November was over, the houses of the newcomers were ready to receive them, and a general post of owners back to their homes took place after a remunerative let of four months. Elizabeth returned to Mallards from Wasters, bringing with her, in addition to what she had taken there, a cargo of preserves made from Diva's garden of such bulk that Coplen had to make two journeys with her large wheelbarrow. Diva returned to Wasters from Taormina, quaint Irene came back to Taormina from the labourer's cottage with a handcart laden with striking canvases including that of the women wrestlers who had become men, and the labourer and his family were free to trek to their own abode from the hop-picker's shanty which they had inhabited so much longer than they had intended.

There followed several extremely busy days for most of the returning emigrants. Elizabeth in particular was occupied from morning till night in scrutinizing every corner of Mallards and making out a list of dilapidations against Lucia. There was a teacup missing, the men who removed Lucia's hired piano from the garden-room had scraped a large piece of paint off the wall,

Lucia had forgotten to replace dearest mamma's piano which still stood in the telephone-room, and there was no sign of a certain egg-whisk. Simultaneously Diva was preparing a similar list for Elizabeth which would astonish her, but was pleased to find that the tenant had left an egg-whisk behind; while the wife of the labourer, not being instructed in dilapidations, was removing from the white-washed wall of her cottage the fresco which Irene had painted there in her spare moments. It wasn't fit to be seen, that it wasn't, but a scrubbing-brush and some hot water made short work of all those naked people. Irene, for her part, was frantically searching among her canvases for a picture of Adam and Eve with quantities of the sons of God shouting for joy: an important work. Perhaps she had left it at the cottage, and then remembering that she had painted it on the wall, she hurried off there in order to varnish it against the inclemencies of weather. But it was already too late, for the last of the sons of God was even then disappearing under the strokes of the scrubbing-brush.

Gradually, though not at once, these claims and counter-claims were (with the exception of the fresco) adjusted to the general dissatisfaction. Lucia acknowledged the charge for the re-establishment of dearest mamma's piano in the garden-room, but her cook very distinctly remembered that on the day when Miss Mapp tried to bribe her to impart the secret of lobster *à la Riseholme*, she took away the egg-whisk, which had formed the gambit of Miss Mapp's vain attempt to corrupt her. So Lucia reminded Elizabeth that not very long ago she had called at the back door of Mallards and had taken it away herself. Her cook believed that it was in two if not three pieces. So Miss Mapp, having made certain it had not got put by mistake among the pots of preserves she had brought from Wasters, went to see if she had left it there, and found not it alone, but a preposterous list of claims against her from Diva. But by degrees these billows, which were of annual occurrence, subsided, and apart from Elizabeth's chronic grievance against Lucia for her hoarding the secret of the lobster, they and other differences in the past faded away and Tilling was at leisure to turn its attention again to the hardly more important problems and perplexities of life and the menaces that might have to be met in the future.

Elizabeth, on this morning of mid-December, was quite settled into Mallards again, egg-whisk and all, and the window of her garden-room was being once more used by the rightful owner for the purpose of taking observations. It had always been a highly strategic position; it commanded, for instance, a perfect view of the front door of Taormina, which at the present moment quaint Irene was painting in stripes of salmon pink and azure. She had tried to reproduce the lost fresco on it, but there had been earnest remonstrances from the Padre, and also the panels of the door broke it up and made it an unsuitable surface for such a cartoon. She therefore was contenting herself with brightening it up. Then Elizabeth could see the mouth of Porpoise Street and register all the journeys of the Royce. These, after a fortnight's intermission, had become frequent again, for the Wyses had just come back from 'visiting friends in Devonshire', and though Elizabeth had strong reason to suspect that friends in Devonshire denoted nothing more than an hotel in Torquay, they had certainly taken the Royce with them, and during its absence the streets of Tilling had been far more convenient for traffic. Then there was Major Benjy's house as before, under her very eye, and now Mallards Cottage as well was a point that demanded frequent scrutiny. She had never cared what that distraught Isabel Poppit did, but with Georgie there it was different, and neither Major Benjy nor he (nor anybody else visiting them) could go in or out of either house without instant detection. The two most important men in Tilling, in fact, were powerless to evade her observation.

Nothing particular was happening at the moment, and Elizabeth was making a mental retrospect rather as if she was the King preparing his speech for the opening of Parliament. Her relations with foreign powers were excellent, and though during the last six months there had been disquieting incidents, there was nothing immediately threatening. . . . Then round the corner of the High Street came Lucia's car and the King's speech was put aside.

The car stopped at Taormina. Quaint Irene instantly put

down her painting paraphernalia on the pavement, and stood talking into the window of the car for quite a long time. Clearly therefore Lucia, though invisible, was inside it. Eventually Irene leaned her head forward into the car, exactly as if she was kissing something, and stepping back again upset one of her paint-pots. This was pleasant, but not of first-rate importance compared with what the car would do next. It turned down into Porpoise Street: naturally there was no telling for certain what happened to it there, for it was out of sight, but a tyro could conjecture that it had business at the Wyses, even if she had been so deaf as not to hear the clanging of that front-door bell. Then it came backing out again, went through the usual manoeuvres of turning, and next stopped at Major Benjy's. Lucia was still invisible, but Cadman got down and delivered a note. The tyro could therefore conjecture by this time that invitations were coming from Grebe.

She slid her chair a little farther back behind the curtain, feeling sure that the car would stop next at her own door. But it turned the corner below the window without drawing up, and Elizabeth got a fleeting glance into the interior, where Lucia was sitting with a large book open in her lap. Next it stopped at Mallards Cottage: no note was delivered there, but Cadman rang the bell, and presently Georgie came out. Like Irene, he talked for quite a long time into the window of the car, but, unlike her, did not kiss anything at the conclusion of the interview. The situation was therefore perfectly clear: Lucia had asked Irene and Major Benjy and Georgie and probably the Wyses to some entertainment, no doubt the house-warming of which there had been rumours, but had not asked her. Very well. The relations with foreign powers therefore had suddenly become far from satisfactory.

Elizabeth quitted her seat in the window, for she had observed enough to supply her with plenty of food for thought, and went back, in perfect self-control, to the inspection of her household books; adding up figures was a purely mechanical matter, which allowed the intenser emotions full play. Georgie would be coming in here presently, for he was painting a sketch of the interior of the garden-room; this was to be his Christmas present to Lucia (a surprise, about which she was to know nothing), to remind her of the happy days she had spent in it. He usually left his sketch here, for it was not worth while to take it backwards and forwards, and there it stood, propped up on the book-case. He had first tried an Irene-ish technique, but he had been obliged to abandon that, since the garden-room with this handling persisted in looking like Paddington Station in a fog, and he had gone back to the style he knew, in which book-cases, chairs and curtains were easily recognizable. It needed a few mornings' work yet, and now the idea of destroying it, and, when he arrived, of telling him that she was quite sure he had taken it back with him yesterday darted unbidden into Elizabeth's mind. But she rejected it, though it would have been pleasant to deprive Lucia of her Christmas present ... and she did not believe for a moment that she had ordered a dozen eggs on Tuesday and a dozen more on Thursday. The butcher's bill seemed to be correct, though extortionate, and she must find out as soon as possible whether the Padre and his wife and Diva were asked to Grebe too. If they were – but she banished the thought of what was to be done if they were: it was difficult enough to know what to do even if they weren't.

The books were quickly done, and Elizabeth went back to finish reading the morning paper in the window. Just as she got there Georgie, with his little cape over his shoulders and his paint-box in his hand, came stepping briskly along from Mallards Cottage. Simultaneously Lucia's great bumping car returned round the corner by the churchyard, in the direction of Mallards.

An inspiration of purest ray serene seized Elizabeth. She waited till Georgie had rung the front-door bell, at which psychological moment Lucia's car was straight below the window. Without a second's hesitation Elizabeth threw up the sash, and, without appearing to see Lucia at all, called out to Georgie in a high cheerful voice, using baby-language.

'Oo is very naughty boy, Georgie!' she cried. 'Never ring Elizabeth's belly-pelly. Oo walk straight in always, and sing out for her. There's no chain up.'

Georgie looked round in amazement. Never had Elizabeth

called him Georgie before, or talked to him in the language consecrated for his use and Lucia's. And there was Lucia's car close to him. She must have heard this affectionate welcome, and what would she think? But there was nothing to do but to go in.

Still without seeing (far less cutting) Lucia, Elizabeth closed the window again, positively dazzled by her own brilliance. An hour's concentrated thought could not have suggested to her anything that Lucia would dislike more thoroughly than hearing that gay little speech, which parodied her and revealed such playful intimacy with Georgie. Georgie came straight out to the garden-room, saying 'Elizabeth, Elizabeth' to himself below his breath, in order to get used to it, for he must return this token of friendship in kind.

'Good morning, Elizabeth,' he said firmly (and the worst was over until such time as he had to say it again in Lucia's presence).

'Good morning, Georgie,' she said by way of confirmation. 'What a lovely light for your painting this morning. Here it is ready for you, and Withers will bring you out your glass of water. How you've caught the feel of my dear little room!'

Another glance out of the window as she brought him his sketch was necessary, and she gasped. There was Cadman on the doorstep just handing Withers a note. In another minute she came into the garden-room.

'From Mrs Lucas,' she said. 'She forgot to leave it when she went by before.'

'That's about the house-warming, I'm sure,' said Georgie, getting his paint-box ready.

What was done, was done, and there was no use in thinking about that. Elizabeth tore the note open.

'A house-warming?' she said. 'Dear Lucia! What a treat that will be. Yes, you're quite right.'

'She's sending her car up for the Padre and his wife and Irene and Mrs Plaistow,' said Georgie, 'and asked me just now if I would bring you and Major Benjy. Naturally I will.'

Elizabeth's brilliant speech out of the window had assumed

the aspect of a gratuitous act of war. But she could not have guessed that Lucia had merely forgotten to leave her invitation. The most charitable would have assumed that there was no invitation to leave.

'How kind of you!' she said. 'Tomorrow night, isn't it? Rather short notice. I must see if I'm disengaged.'

As Lucia had asked the whole of the élite of Tilling, this proved to be the case. But Elizabeth still pondered as to whether she should accept or not. She had committed one unfriendly act in talking baby-language to Georgie, with a pointed allusion to the door-chain, literally over Lucia's head, and it was a question whether, having done that, it would not be wiser to commit another (while Lucia, it might be guessed, was still staggering) by refusing to go to the house-warming. She did not doubt that there would be war before long; the only question was if she was ready now.

As she was pondering Withers came in to say that Major Benjy had called. He would not come out into the garden-room, but he would like to speak to her a minute.

'Evidently he has heard that Georgie is here,' thought Elizabeth to herself as she hurried into the house. 'Dear me, how men quarrel with each other, and I only want to be on good terms with everybody. No doubt he wants to know if I'm going to the house-warming. – Good morning, Major Benjy.'

'Thought I wouldn't come out,' said this bluff fellow, 'as I heard your Miss Milliner Michael-Angelo, ha, was with you – '

'Oh Major Benjy, fie!' said Elizabeth. 'Cruel of you.'

'Well, leave it at that. Now about this party tomorrow. I think I shall make a stand straight away, for I'm not going to spend the whole of the winter evenings tramping through the mud to Grebe. To be sure it's dinner this time, which makes a difference.'

Elizabeth found that she longed to see what Lucia had made of Grebe, and what she had made of her speech from the window.

'I quite agree in principle,' she said, 'but a house-warming, you know. Perhaps it wouldn't be kind to refuse. Besides, Georgie – '

'Eh?' said the Major.

'Mr Pillson, I mean,' said Elizabeth, hastily correcting herself, 'has offered to drive us both down.'

'And back?' asked he suspiciously.

'Of course. So just for once, shall we?'

'Very good. But none of those after-dinner musicals, or lessons in bridge for me.'

'Oh, Major Benjy!' said Elizabeth. 'How can you talk so? As if poor Lucia would attempt to teach *you* bridge.'

This could be taken in two ways, one interpretation would read that he was incapable of learning, the other that Lucia was incapable of teaching. He took the more obvious one.

'Upon my soul she did, at the last game I had with her,' said he. 'Laid out the last three tricks and told me how to play them. Beyond a joke. Well, I won't keep you from your dressmaker.'

'O fie!' said Elizabeth again. 'Au reservoir.'

Lucia, meantime, had driven back to Grebe with that mocking voice still ringing in her ears, and a series of most unpleasant images, like some diabolical film, displaying themselves before her inward eye. Most probably Elizabeth had seen her when she called out to Georgie like that, and was intentionally insulting her. Such conduct called for immediate reprisals and she must presently begin to think these out. But the alternative, possible though not probable, that Elizabeth had not seen her, was infinitely more wounding, for it implied that Georgie was guilty of treacheries too black to bear looking at. Privately, when she herself was not present, he was on Christian-name terms with that woman, and permitted and enjoyed her obvious mimicry of herself. And what was Georgie doing popping in to Mallards like this, and being scolded in baby-voice for ringing the bell instead of letting himself in, with allusions of an absolutely unmistakable kind to that episode about the chain? Did they laugh over that together: did Georgie poke fun at his oldest friend behind her back? Lucia positively writhed at the thought. In any case, whether or no he was guilty of this monstrous infidelity, he must be in the habit of going into Mallards, and now she remembered that he had his paint-box in his hand. Clearly then he was going there to paint, and in all their talks when he so constantly told her what he had been doing, he had never breathed a word of that. Perhaps he was painting Elizabeth, for in this winter weather he could never be painting in the garden. Just now too, when she called at Mallards Cottage, and they had had a talk together, he had refused to go out and drive with her, because he had some little jobs to do indoors, and the moment he had got rid of her – no less than that – he had hurried off to Mallards with his paint-box. With all this evidence, things looked very dark indeed, and the worst and most wounding of these two alternatives began to assume probability.

Georgie was coming to tea with her that afternoon, and she must find out what the truth of the matter was. But she could not imagine herself saying to him: 'Does she really call you Georgie, and does she imitate me behind my back, and are you painting her?' Pride absolutely forbade that: such humiliating inquiries would choke her. Should she show him an icy aloof demeanour, until he asked her if anything was the matter? But that wouldn't do, for either she must say that nothing was the matter, which would not help, or she must tell him what the matter was, which was impossible. She must behave to him exactly as usual, and he would probably do the same. 'So how am I to find out?' said the bewildered Lucia quite aloud.

Another extremely uncomfortable person in tranquil Tilling that morning was Georgie himself. As he painted this sketch of the garden-room for Lucia, with Elizabeth busying herself with dusting her piano and bringing in chrysanthemums from her greenhouse, and making bright little sarcasms about Diva who was in ill odour just now, there painted itself in his mind, in colours growing ever more vivid, a most ominous picture of Lucia. If he knew her at all, and he was sure he did, she would say nothing whatever about that disconcerting scene on the doorstep. Awkward as it would be, he would be obliged to protest his innocence, and denounce Elizabeth. Most disagreeable, and who could foresee the consequences? For Lucia (if he knew her) would see red, and there would be war. Bloody war of the most devastating sort. 'But it will be rather exciting too,' thought he, 'and I back Lucia.'

Georgie could not wait for tea-time, but set forth on his un-comfortable errand soon after lunch. Lucia had seen him coming up the garden, and abandoned her musings and sat down hastily at the piano. Instantly on his entry she sprang up again, and plunged into mixed Italian and baby-talk.

'Ben arrivato, Georgino,' she cried. 'How early you are, and so we can have cosy ickle chat-chat before tea. Any newsy-pewsy?'

Georgie took the plunge.

'Yes,' he said.

'Tell Lucia, presto. Oo think me like it?'

'It'll interest you,' said Georgie guardedly. 'Now! When I was standing on Mallards doorstep this morning, did you hear what that old witch called to me out of the garden-room win-dow?'

Lucia could not repress a sigh of relief. The worst could not be true. Then she became herself again.

'Let me see now!' she said. 'Yes. I think I did. She called you Georgie, didn't she: she scolded you for ringing. Something of that sort.'

'Yes. And she talked baby-talk like you and me,' interrupted Georgie, 'and she said the door wasn't on the chain. I want to tell you straight off that she never called me Georgie before, and that we've never talked baby-talk together in my life. I owe it to myself to tell you that.'

Lucia turned her piercing eye on to Georgie. There seemed to be a sparkle in it that boded ill for somebody.

'And you think she saw me, Georgie?' she asked.

'Of course she did. Your car was directly below her win-dow.'

'I am afraid there is no doubt about it,' said Lucia. 'Her re-marks, therefore, seem to have been directed at me. A singularly ill-bred person. There's one thing more. You were taking your paint-box with you – '

'Oh, that's all right,' said he. 'I'm doing a sketch of the garden-room. You'll know about that in time. And what are you going to do?' he asked greedily.

Lucia laughed in her most musical manner.

'Well, first of all I shall give her a very good dinner tomorrow, as she has not had the decency to say she was engaged. She telephoned to me just now telling me what a joy it would be, and how she was looking forward to it. And mind you call her Elizabeth.'

'I've done that already,' said Georgie proudly. 'I practised saying it to myself.'

'Good. She dines here then tomorrow night, and I shall be her hostess and shall make the evening as pleasant as I can to all my guests. But apart from that, Georgie, I shall take steps to teach her manners if she's not too old to learn. She will be sorry; she will wish she had not been so rude. And I can't see any objection to our other friends in Tilling knowing what occurred this morning, if you feel inclined to speak of it. I shan't, but there's no reason why you shouldn't.'

'Hurrah, I'm dining with the Wyses tonight,' said Georgie. 'They'll soon know.'

Lucia knitted her brows in profound thought.

'And then there's that incident about our pictures, yours and mine, being rejected by the hanging committee of the Art Club,' said she. 'We have both kept the forms we received saying that they regretted having to return them, and I think, Georgie, that while you are on the subject of Elizabeth Mapp, you might show yours to Mr Wyse. He is a member, so is Susan, of the committee, and I think they have a right to know that our pictures were rejected on official forms without ever coming before the committee at all. I behaved towards our poor friend with a magnanimity that now appears to me excessive, and since she does not appreciate magnanimity we will try her with something else. That would not be amiss.' Lucia rose.

'And now let us leave this very disagreeable subject for the present,' she said, 'and take the taste of it out of our mouths with a little music. Beethoven, noble Beethoven, don't you think? The fifth symphony, Georgie, for four hands. Fate knocking at the door.'

Georgie rather thought that Lucia smacked her lips as she said, 'this very disagreeable subject', but he was not certain, and presently Fate was knocking at the door with Lucia's firm fingers, for she took the treble.

They had a nice long practice, and when it was time to go home Lucia detained him.

'I've got one thing to say to you, Georgie,' she said, 'though not about that paltry subject. I've sold the Hurst, I've bought this new property, and so I've made a new will. I've left Grebe and all it contains to you, and also, well, a little sum of money. I should like you to know that.'

Georgie was much touched.

'My dear, how wonderful of you,' he said. 'But I hope it will be ages and ages before – '

'So do I, Georgie,' she said in her most sincere manner.

Tilling had known tensions before and would doubtless know them again. Often it had been on a very agreeable rack of suspense, as when, for instance, it had believed (or striven to believe) that Major Benjy might be fighting a duel with that old crony of his, Captain Puffin, lately deceased. Now there was a suspense of a more intimate quality (for nobody would have cared at all if Captain Puffin had been killed, nor much, if Major Benjy), for it was as if the innermost social guts of Tilling were attached to some relentless windlass, which, at any moment now, might be wound, but not relaxed. The High Street next morning, therefore, was the scene of almost painful excitement. The Wyses' Royce, with Susan smothered in sables, went up and down, until she was practically certain that she had told everybody that she and Algernon had retired from the hanging committee of the Arts' Club, pending explanations which they had requested Miss (no longer Elizabeth) Mapp to furnish, but which they had no hope of receiving. Susan was perfectly explicit about the cause of this step, and Algernon who, at a very early hour, had interviewed the errand-boy at the frame-shop, was by her side, to corroborate all she said. His high-bred reticence, indeed, had been even more weighty than Susan's volubility. 'I am afraid it is all too true,' was all that could be got out of him. Two hours had now elapsed since their resignations had been sent in, and still no reply had come from Mallards.

But that situation was but an insignificant fraction of the

prevalent suspense, for the exhibition had been opened and closed months before, and if Tilling was to make a practice of listening to such posthumous revelations, life would cease to have any poignant interest, but be wholly occupied in retrospective retributions. Thrilling therefore as was the past, as revealed by the stern occupants of the Royce, what had happened only yesterday on the door-step of Mallards was far more engrossing. The story of that, by 11.30 a.m., already contained several remarkable variants. The Padre affirmed that Georgie had essayed to enter Mallards without knocking, and that Miss Mapp (the tendency to call her Miss Mapp was spreading) had seen Lucia in her motor just below the window of the garden-room, and had called out 'Tum in, Georgino mio, no tarsame chains now that Elizabeth has got back to her own housie-pousie.' Diva had reason to believe that Elizabeth (she still stuck to that) had not seen Lucia in her motor, and had called out of the window to Georgie 'Ring the belly-pelly, dear, for I'm afraid the chain is on the door.' Mrs Bartlett (she was no use at all) said, 'All so distressing and exciting and Christmas Day next week, and very little goodwill, oh dear me!' Irene had said, 'That old witch will get what for.'

Again, it was known that Major Benjy had called at Mallards soon after the scene, whatever it was, had taken place, and had refused to go into the garden-room, when he heard that Georgie was painting Elizabeth's portrait. Withers was witness (she had brought several pots of jam to Diva's house that morning, not vegetable marrow at all, but raspberry, which looked like a bribe) that the Major had said 'Faugh!' when she told him that Georgie was there. Major Benjy himself could not be cross-examined because he had gone out by the eleven o'clock tram to play golf. Lucia had not been seen in the High Street at all, nor had Miss Mapp, and Georgie had only passed through it in his car, quite early, going in the direction of Grebe. This absence of the principals, in these earlier stages of development, was felt to be in accordance with the highest rules of dramatic technique, and everybody, as far as was known, was to meet that very night at Lucia's house-warming. Opinion as to what would happen then was as divergent as the rumours of what had happened already. Some said that Miss Mapp had declined the invitation on the plea that she was engaged to dine with Major Benjy. This was unlikely, because he never had anybody to dinner. Some said that she had accepted, and that Lucia no doubt intended to send out a message that she was not expected, but that George's car would take her home again. So sorry. All this, however, was a matter of pure conjecture, and it was work enough to sift out what had happened, without wasting time (for time was precious) in guessing what would happen.

The church clock had hardly struck half past eleven (winter time) before the first of the principals appeared on the stage of the High Street. This was Miss Mapp, wreathed in smiles, and occupied in her usual shopping errands. She trotted about from grocer to butcher, and butcher to general stores, where she bought a mouse-trap, and was exceedingly affable to tradespeople. She nodded to her friends, she patted Mr Woolgar's dog on the head, she gave a penny to a ragged individual with a lugubrious baritone voice who was singing 'The Last Rose of Summer', and said 'Thank you for your sweet music.' Then after pausing for a moment on the pavement in front of Wasters, she rang the bell. Diva, who had seen her from the window, flew to open it.

'Good morning, Diva dear,' she said. 'I just looked in. Any news?'

'Good gracious, it's I who ought to ask you that,' said Diva. 'What *did* happen really?'

Elizabeth looked very much surprised.

'How? When? Where?' she asked.

'As if you didn't know,' said Diva, fizzing with impatience. 'Mr Georgie, Lucia, paint-boxes, no chain on the door, you at the garden-room window, belly-pelly. Etcetera. Yesterday morning.'

Elizabeth put her finger to her forehead, as if trying to recall some dim impression. She appeared to succeed.

'Dear gossipy one,' she said, 'I believe I know what you mean. Georgie came to paint in the garden-room, as he so often does – '

'Do you call him Georgie?' asked Diva in an eager parenthesis.

'Yes, I fancy that's his name, and he calls me Elizabeth.'

'No!' said Diva.

'Yes,' said Elizabeth. 'Do not interrupt me, dear. ... I happened to be at the window as he rang the bell, and I just popped my head out, and told him he was a naughty boy not to walk straight in.'

'In baby-talk?' asked Diva. 'Like Lucia?'

'Like any baby you chance to mention,' said Elizabeth. 'Why not?'

'But with her sitting in her car just below?'

'Yes, dear, it so happened that she was just coming to leave an invitation on me for her house-warming tonight. Are you going?'

'Yes, of course, everybody is. But how could you do it?'

Elizabeth sat wrapped in thought.

'I'm beginning to see what you mean,' she said at length. 'But what an absurd notion. You mean, don't you, that dear Lulu thinks – goodness, how ridiculous – that I was mimicking her.'

'Nobody knows what she thinks,' said Diva. 'She's not been seen this morning.'

'But gracious goodness me, what have I done? asked Elizabeth. 'Why this excitement? Is there a law that only Mrs Lucas of Grebe may call Georgie, Georgie? So ignorant of me if there is. Ought I to call him Frederick? And pray, why shouldn't I talk baby-talk? Another law perhaps. I must get a book of the laws of England.'

'But you knew she was in the car just below you and must have heard.'

Elizabeth was now in possession of what she wanted to know. Diva was quite a decent barometer of Tilling weather, and the weather was stormy.

'Rubbish, darling,' she said. 'You are making mountains out of mole-hills. If Lulu heard – and I don't know that she did, mind – what cause of complaint has she? Mayn't I say Georgie? Mayn't I say "vewy naughty boy"? Let us hear no more about it. You will see this evening how wrong you all are. Lulu will be just as sweet and cordial as ever. And you will hear with your own ears how Georgie calls me Elizabeth.'

These were brave words, and they very fitly represented the stout heart that inspired them. Tilling had taken her conduct to be equivalent to an act of war, exactly as she had meant it to be, and if anyone thought that E. M. was afraid they were wrong. . . . Then there was that matter of Mr Wyse's letter, resigning from the hanging committee. She must tap the barometer again.

'I think everybody is a shade mad this morning,' she observed, 'and I should call Mr Wyse, if anybody asked me to be candid, a raving lunatic. There was a little misunderstanding months and months ago – I am vague about it – concerning two pictures that Lulu and Georgie sent in to the Art Exhibition in the summer. I thought it was all settled and done with. But I did act a little irregularly. Technically I was wrong, and when I have been wrong about a thing, as you very well know, dear Diva, I am not ashamed to confess it.'

'Of course you were wrong,' said Diva cordially, 'if Mr Wyse's account of it is correct. You sent the pictures back, such beauties, too, with a formal rejection from the hanging committee when they had never seen them at all. So rash, too: I wonder at you.'

These unfavourable comments did not make the transaction appear any the less irregular.

'I said I was wrong, Diva,' remarked Elizabeth with some asperity, 'and I should have thought that was enough. And now Mr Wyse, raking bygones up again in the way he has, has written to me to say that he and Susan resign their places on the hanging committee.'

'I know: they told everybody,' said Diva. 'Awkward. What are you going to do?'

The barometer had jerked alarmingly downwards on this renewed tapping.

'I shall cry peccavi,' said Elizabeth, with the air of doing something exceedingly noble. 'I shall myself resign. That will show that whatever anybody else does, I am doing the best in my power to put right a technical error. I hope Mr Wyse will appreciate that, and be ashamed of the letter he wrote me. More than that, I shall regard his letter as having been written in a fit of temporary insanity, which I trust will not recur.'

'Yes; I suppose that's the best thing you can do,' said Diva. 'It will show him that you regret what you did, now that it's all found out.'

'That is not generous of you, Diva,' cried Elizabeth, 'I am sorry you said that.'

'More than I am,' said Diva. 'It's a very fair statement. Isn't it now? What's wrong with it?'

Elizabeth suddenly perceived that at this crisis it was unwise to indulge in her usual tiffs with Diva. She wanted allies.

'Diva, dear, we mustn't quarrel,' she said. 'That would never do. I felt I had to pop in to consult you as to the right course to take with Mr Wyse, and I'm so glad you agree with me. How I trust your judgement! I must be going. What a delightful evening we have in store for us. Major Benjy was thinking of declining, but I persuaded him it would not be kind. A housewarming, you know. Such a special occasion.'

The evening to which everybody had looked forward so much was, in the main, a disappointment to bellicose spirits. Nothing could exceed Lucia's cordiality to Elizabeth unless it was Elizabeth's to Lucia: they left the dining-room at the end of dinner with arms and waists intertwined, a very bitter sight. They then played bridge at the same table, and so loaded each other with compliments while deploring their own errors, that Diva began to entertain the most serious fears that they had been mean enough to make it up on the sly, or that Lucia in a spirit of Christian forbearance, positively unnatural, had decided to overlook all the attacks and insults with which Elizabeth had tried to provoke her. Or did Lucia think that this degrading display of magnanimity was a weapon by which she would secure victory, by enlisting for her the sympathy and applause of Tilling? If so, that was a great mistake; Tilling did not want to witness a demonstration of forgiveness or white feathers but a combat without quarter. Again, if she thought that such nobility would soften the malevolent heart of Mapp, she showed a distressing ignorance of Mapp's nature, for she would quite properly construe this as not being nobility at all but the most ignoble cowardice. There was Georgie, under Lucia's very nose, interlarding his conversation with far more 'Elizabeths' than was in the least necessary to show that he was talking to her, and she volleyed 'Georgies' at him in return. Every now and then, when these discharges of Christian names had been particularly resonant, Elizabeth caught Diva's eye with a glance of triumph as if to remind her that she had prophesied that Lulu would be all sweetness and cordiality, and Diva turned away sick at heart.

On the other hand, there were still grounds for hope, and, as the evening went on, these became more promising: they were like small caps of foam and catspaws of wind upon a tranquil sea. To begin with, it was only this morning that the baseness of Elizabeth in that matter concerning the Art Committee had come to light. Georgie, not Lucia, had been directly responsible for that damning disclosure, but it must be supposed that he had acted with her connivance, if not with her express wish, and this certainly did not look so much like forgiveness as a nasty one for Elizabeth. That was hopeful, and Diva's eagle eye espied other signs of bad weather. Elizabeth, encouraged by Lucia's compliments and humilities throughout a long rubber, began to come out more in her true colours, and to explain to her partner that she had lost a few tricks (no matter) by not taking a finesse, or a whole game by not supporting her declaration, and Diva thought she detected a certain dangerous glitter in Lucia's eye as she bent to these chastisements. Surely, too, she bit her lip when Elizabeth suddenly began to call her Lulu again. Then there was Irene's conduct to consider: Irene was fizzing and fidgeting in her chair, she cast glances of black hatred at Elizabeth, and once Diva distinctly saw Lucia frown and shake her head at her. Again, at the voluptuous supper which succeeded many rubbers of bridge, there was the famous lobster *à la Riseholme*. It had become, as all Tilling knew, a positive obsession with Elizabeth to get the secret of that delicious dish, and now, flushed with continuous victories at bridge and with Lucia's persevering pleasantness, she made another direct request for it.

'Lulu dear,' she said, 'It would be sweet of you to give me the recipe of your lobster. So good . . .'

Diva felt this to be a crucial moment: Lucia had often refused it before, but now if she was wholly Christian and cowardly she would consent. But once more she gave no reply, and asked the Padre on what day of the week Christmas fell. So Diva heaved a sigh of relief, for there was still hope.

In spite of this rebuff, it was hardly to be wondered at that Elizabeth felt in a high state of elation when the evening was over. The returning revellers changed the order of their going, and Georgie took back her and Diva. He went outside with Dicky, for, during the last half-hour, Mapp (as he now mentally termed her in order to be done with Elizabeth) had grown like a mushroom in complaisance and self-confidence, and he could not trust himself, if she went on, as she would no doubt do, in the same strain, not to rap out something very sharp. 'Let her just wait,' he thought, 'she'll soon be singing a different tune.'

Georgie's precautions in going outside, well wrapped up in his cap and his fur tippet and his fur rug were well founded, for hardly had Mapp kissed her hand for the last time to Lulu (who would come to the door to see them off), and counted over the money she had won, than she burst into staves of intolerable triumph and condescension.

'So that's that!' she said, pulling up the window. 'And if I was to ask you, dear Diva, which of us was right about how this evening would go off, I don't think there would be very much doubt about the answer. Did you ever see Lulu so terribly anxious to please me? And did you happen to hear me say Georgie and him say Elizabeth? Lulu didn't like it, I am sure, but she had to swallow her medicine, and she did so with a very good grace, I am bound to say. She just wanted a little lesson, and I think I may say I've given it her. I had no idea, I will confess, that she would take it lying down like that. I just had to lean out of the window, pretend not to see her, and talk to Georgie in that silly voice and language and the thing was done.'

Diva had been talking simultaneously for sometime, but Elizabeth only paused to take breath, and went on in a slightly louder tone. So Diva talked louder too; until Georgie turned round to see what was happening. They both broke off, and smiled at him, and then both began again.

'If you would allow me to get a word in edgeways,' said Diva, who had some solid arguments to produce, and had she not been a lady, could have slapped Mapp's face in impotent rage –

'I don't think,' said Elizabeth, 'that we shall have much more trouble with her and her queenly airs. Quite a pleasant house-warming, and there was no doubt that the house wanted it, for it was bitterly cold in the dining-room, and I strongly suspect that chicken-cream of being rabbit. She only had to be shown that whatever Riseholme may have stood from her in the way of condescensions and graces, she had better not try them on at Tilling. She was looking forward to teaching us, and ruling us and guiding us. Pop! Elizabeth (that's me, dear!) has a little lamb, which lives at Grebe and gives a house-warming, so you may guess who *that* is. The way she flattered and sued tonight over our cards when but a few weeks ago she was thinking of holding bridge-classes – '

'You were just as bad,' shouted Diva. 'You told her she played beauti—'

'She was "all over me", to use that dreadful slang expression of Major Benjy's,' continued Mapp. 'She was like a dog that has had a scolding and begs – so prettily – to be forgiven. Mind, dear, I do not say that she is a bad sort of woman by any means, but she required to be put in her place, and Tilling ought to thank me for having done so. Dear me, here we are already at your house. How short the drive has seemed!'

'Anyhow, you didn't get the recipe for the lobster *à la Riseholme*,' said Diva, for this was one of the things she most wanted to say.

'A little final wriggle,' said Mapp. 'I have not the least doubt that she will think it over and send it me tomorrow. Good night, darling. I shall be sending out invitations for a cosy evening at bridge some time at the end of this week.'

The baffled Diva let herself into Wasters in low spirits, so convinced and lucid had been Mapp's comments on the evening. It was such a dismal conclusion to so much excitement; and all that thrilling tension, instead of snapping, had relaxed into the most depressing slackness. But she did not quite give up hope, for there had been catspaws and caps of foam on the tranquil sea. She fell asleep visualizing these.

9

Though Georgie had thought that the garden-room would have to give him at least two more sittings before his sketch arrived at the high state of finish which he, like the pre-Raphaelites, regarded as necessary to any work of art, he decided that he would leave it in a more impressionist state, and sent it next morning to be framed. In consequence the glass of water which Elizabeth had brought out for him in anticipation of his now usual visit at eleven o'clock remained unsullied by washings from his brush, and at twelve, Elizabeth, being rather thirsty in consequence of so late a supper the night before, drank it herself. On the second morning, a very wet one, Major Benjy did not go out for his usual round of golf, and again Georgie did not come to paint. But at a few minutes to one she observed that his car was at the door of Mallards Cottage; it passed her window, it stopped at Major Benjy's, and he got in. It was impossible not to remember that Lucia always lunched at one in the winter because a later hour for *colazione* made the afternoon so short. But it was a surprise to see Major Benjy driving away with Miss Milliner Michael-Angelo, and difficult to conjecture where else it was at all likely that they could have gone.

There was half an hour yet to her own luncheon, and she wrote seven post cards inviting seven friends to tea on Saturday, with bridge to follow. The Wyses, the Padres, Diva, Major Benjy and Georgie were the *destinataires* of these missives: these, with herself, made eight, and there would thus be two tables of agreeable gamblers. Lucia was not to be favoured: it would be salutary for her to be left out every now and then, just to impress upon her the lesson of which she had stood so sadly in need. She must learn to go to heel, to come when called, and to produce recipes when desired, which at present she had not done.

There had been several days of heavy rain, but early in the afternoon it cleared up, and Elizabeth set out for a brisk healthy walk. The field-paths would certainly make very miry going, for she saw from the end of the High Street that there was much water lying in the marsh, and she therefore kept to that excellent road, which, having passed Grebe, went nowhere particular. She was prepared to go in and thank Lucia for her lovely house-warming, in order to make sure whether Georgie and Major Benjy had gone to lunch with her, but no such humiliating need occurred, for there in front of the house was drawn up Georgie's motor-car, so (whether she liked it or not, and she didn't) *that* problem was solved. The house stood quite close to the road: a flagged pathway of half a dozen yards, flanked at the entrance-gate by thick hornbeam hedges on which the leaf still lingered, separated it from the road, and just as Elizabeth passed Georgie's car drawn up there, the front-door opened, and she saw Lucia and her two guests on the threshold. Major Benjy was laughing in that fat voice of his, and Georgie was giving forth his shrill little neighs like a colt with a half-cracked voice.

The temptation to know what they were laughing at was irresistible. Elizabeth moved a few steps on and, screened by the hornbeam hedge, held her breath.

Major Benjy gave another great haw-haw and spoke.

'Pon my word, did she really?' he said. 'Do it again, Mrs Lucas. Never laughed so much in my life. Infernal impertinence!'

There was no mistaking the voice and the words that followed.

'Oo is vewy naughty boy, Georgie,' said Lucia. 'Never ring Elizabeth's belly-pelly – '

Elizabeth hurried on, as she heard steps coming down that short flagged pathway. But hurry as she might, she heard a little more.

'Oo walk straight in always and sing out for her,' continued the voice, repeating word for word the speech of which she had been so proud. 'There's no chain up' – and then came loathsome parody – 'now that Liblib has ritornata to Mallardino.'

It was in a scared mood, as if she had heard or seen a ghost, that Elizabeth hastened along up the road that led nowhere in particular, before Lucia's guests could emerge from the gate. Luckily at the end of the kitchen-garden the hornbeam hedge turned at right angles, and behind this bastion she hid herself till she heard the motor move away in the direction of Tilling, the prey of the most agitated misgivings. Was it possible that her own speech, which she had thought had scarified Lucia's pride, was being turned into a mockery and a derision against herself? It seemed not only possible but probable. And how dare Mrs Lucas invent and repeat as if spoken by herself that rubbish about ritornata and Mallardino? Never in her life had she said such a thing.

When the coast was clear, she took the road again, and walked quickly on away from Tilling. The tide was very high, for the river was swollen with rain, and the waters over-brimmed its channel and extended in a great lake up to the foot of the bank and dyke which bounded the road. Perturbed as she was, Miss Mapp could not help admiring that broad expanse of water, now lit by a gleam of sun, in front of which to the westward, the hill of Tilling rose dark against a sky already growing red with the winter sunset. She had just turned a corner in the road, and now she perceived that close ahead of her somebody else was admiring it too in a more practical manner, for there by the roadside within twenty yards of her sat quaint Irene, with her mouth full of paintbrushes and an easel set up in front of her. She had not seen Irene since the night of the house-warming, when the quaint one had not been very cordial, and so, thinking she had walked far enough, she turned back. But Irene had quite evidently seen her, for she shaded her eyes for a moment against the glare, took some of the paintbrushes out of her mouth and called to her with words that seemed to have what might be termed a dangerous undertow.

'Hullo, Mapp,' she said. 'Been lunching with Lulu – '

'What a lovely sketch, dear,' said Mapp. 'No, just a brisk little walk. Not been lunching at Grebe today.'

Irene laughed hoarsely.

'I didn't think it was very likely, but thought I would ask,' she said. 'Yes; I'm rather pleased with my sketch. A bloody look about the sunlight, isn't there, as if the Day of Judgement was coming. I'm going to send it to the winter exhibition of the Art Club.'

'Dear girlie, what do you mean?' asked Mapp. 'We don't have winter exhibitions.'

'No, but we're going to,' said girlie. 'A new hanging committee, you see, full of pep and pop and vim. Haven't they asked you to send them something. . . . Of course the space at their disposal is very limited.'

Mapp laughed, but not with any great exuberance. This undertow was tweaking at her disagreeably.

'That's news to me,' she said. 'Most enterprising of Mr Wyse and dear Susan.'

'Sweet Lulu's idea,' said Irene. 'As soon as you sent in your resignation, of course they asked her to be President.'

'That is nice for her,' said Mapp enthusiastically. 'She will like that. I must get to work on some little picky to send them.'

'There's that one you did from the church-tower when Lucia had influenza,' said this awful Irene. 'That would be nice. . . . Oh, I forgot. Stupid of me. It's by invitation: the committee are asking a few people to send pickies. No doubt they'll beg you for one. Such a good plan. There won't be any mistakes in the future about rejecting what is sent in.'

Mapp gave a gulp but rallied.

'I see. They'll be all Academicians together, and be hung on the line,' said she unflinchingly.

'Yes. On the line or be put on easels,' said Irene. 'Curse the light! It's fading. I must pack up. Hold these brushes, will you – '

'And then we'll walk back home together, shall we? A cup of tea with me, dear?' asked Mapp, anxious to conciliate and to know more.

'I'm going into Lucia's, I'm afraid. Wyses tummin' to play bridgey and hold a committee meeting,' said Irene.

'You are a cruel thing to imitate poor Lulu,' said Mapp. 'How well you've caught that silly baby-talk of hers. Just her voice. Bye-bye.'

'Same to you,' said Irene.

There was undoubtedly, thought Mapp, as she scudded swiftly homewards alone, a sort of mocking note about quaint Irene's conversation, which she did not relish. It was full of hints and awkward allusions; it bristled with hidden menace, and even her imitation of Lucia's baby-talk was not wholly satisfactory, for quaint Irene might be mimicking her imitation of Lucia, even as Lucia herself had done, and there was very little humour in that. Presently she passed the Wyses' Royce going to Grebe. She kissed her hand to a mound of sables inside, but it was too dark to see if the salute was returned. Her brisk afternoon's walk had not freshened her up; she was aware of a feeling of fatigue, of a vague depression and anxiety. And mixed with that was a hunger not only for tea but for more information. There seemed to be things going on of which she was sadly ignorant, and even when her ignorance was enlightened, they remained rather sad. But Diva (such a gossip) might know more about this winter exhibition, and she popped in to Wasters. Diva was in, and begged her to wait for tea: she would be down in a few minutes.

It was a cosy little room, looking out on to the garden which had yielded her so many pots of excellent preserves during the summer, but dreadfully untidy, as Diva's house always was. There was a litter of papers on the table, notes half-thrust back into their envelopes, crossword puzzles cut out from the *Evening Standard* and partially solved: there was her own post card to Diva sent off that morning and already delivered, and there was a sheet of paper with the stamp of Grebe upon it and Lucia's monogram, which seemed to force itself on Elizabeth's eye. The most cursory glance revealed that this was a request from the Art Committee that Mrs Plaistow would do them the honour to send them a couple of her sketches for the forthcoming winter exhibition. All the time there came from Diva's bedroom, directly overhead, the sound of rhythmical steps or thumps most difficult to explain. In a few minutes these ceased, and Diva's tread on the stairs gave Elizabeth sufficient warning to enable her to snatch up the first book that came to hand, and sink into a chair by the fire. She saw, with some feeling of apprehension similar to those which had haunted her all afternoon, that this was a copy of *An Ideal System of Callisthenics for those no longer Young*, of which she seemed to have heard. On the title-page was an inscription 'Diva from Lucia', and in brackets, like a prescription, 'Ten minutes at the exercises in Chapter I, twice a day for the present.'

Diva entered very briskly. She was redder in the face than usual, and, so Elizabeth instantly noticed, lifted her feet very high as she walked, and held her head well back and her breast out like a fat little pigeon. This time there was to be no question about getting a word in edgeways, for she began to talk before the door was fully open.

'Glad to see you, Elizabeth,' she said, 'and I shall be very pleased to play bridge on Saturday. I've never felt so well in my life, do you know, and I've only been doing them two days. Oh, I see you've got the book.'

'I heard you stamping and thumping, dear,' said Elizabeth. 'Was that them?'

'Yes, twice a day, ten minutes each time. It clears the head, too. If you sit down to a cross-word puzzle afterwards you find you're much brighter than usual.'

'Callisthenics *a la Lucia*?' asked Elizabeth.

'Yes. Irene and Mrs Barlett and I all do them, and Mrs Wyse is going to begin, but rather more gently. Hasn't Lucia told you about them?'

Here was another revelation of things happening. Elizabeth met it bravely.

'No. Dear Lulu knows my feelings about that sort of fad. A brisk walk such as I've had this afternoon is all I require. Such lovely lights of sunset and a very high tide. Quaint Irene was sketching on the road just beyond Grebe.'

'Yes. She's going to send it in and three more for the winter exhibition. Oh, perhaps you haven't heard. There's to be an exhibition directly after Christmas.'

'Such a good idea: I've been discussing it,' said Elizabeth.

Diva's eye travelled swiftly and suspiciously to the table where this flattering request to her lay on the top of the litter. Elizabeth did not fail to catch the significance of this.

'Irene told me,' she said hastily, 'I must see if I can find time to do them something.'

'Oh, then they have asked you,' said Diva with a shade of disappointment in her voice. 'They've asked me too – '

'No! Really?' said Elizabeth.

' – so of course I said Yes, but I'm afraid I'm rather out of practice. Lucia is going to give an address on modern Art at the opening, and then we shall all go round and look at each other's pictures.'

'What fun!' said Elizabeth cordially.

Tea had been brought in. There was a pot of greenish jam and Elizabeth loaded her buttered toast with it, and put it into her mouth. She gave a choking cry and washed it down with a gulp of tea.

'Anything wrong?' asked Diva.

'Yes, dear. I'm afraid it's fermenting,' said Elizabeth, laying down the rest of her toast. 'And I can't conceive what it's made of.'

Diva looked at the pot.

'You ought to know,' she said. 'It's one of the pots you gave me. Labelled vegetable marrow. So sorry it's not eatable. By the way, talking of food, did Lucia sent you the recipe for the lobster?'

Elizabeth smiled her sweetest.

'Dear Lucia,' she said. 'She's been so busy with art and callisthenics. She must have forgotten. I shall jog her memory.'

The afternoon had been full of rather unpleasant surprises, thought Elizabeth to herself, as she went up to Mallards that evening. They were concerned with local activities, art and gymnastics, of which she had hitherto heard nothing, and they all seemed to show a common origin: there was a hidden hand directing them. This was disconcerting, especially since, only a few nights ago, she had felt so sure that that hand had been upraised to her, beseeching pardon. Now it rather looked as if that hand had spirited itself away and was very busy and energetic on its own account.

She paused on her doorstep. There was a light shining out

through chinks behind the curtains in Mallards Cottage, and she thought it would be a good thing to pop in on Georgie and see if she could gather some further gleanings. She would make herself extremely pleasant: she would admire his needlework if he was at it, she would praise the beautiful specklessness of his room, for Georgie always appreciated any compliment to Foljambe, she would sing the praises of Lucia, though they blistered her tongue.

Foljambe admitted her. The door of the sitting-room was ajar, and as she put down her umbrella, she heard Georgie's voice talking to the telephone.

'Saturday, half past four,' he said. 'I've just found a post card. Hasn't she asked you?'

Georgie, as Elizabeth had often observed, was deafer than he knew (which accounted for his not hearing all the wrong notes he played in his duets with Lucia) and he had not heard her entry, though Foljambe spoke her name quite loud. He was listening with rapt attention to what was coming through and saying 'My dear!' or 'No!' at intervals. Now, however, he turned and saw her, and with a scared expression hung up the receiver.

'Dear me, I never heard you come in!' he said. 'How nice! I was just going to tell Foljambe to bring up tea. Two cups, Foljambe.'

'I'm interrupting you,' said Elizabeth. 'I can see you were just settling down to your sewing and a cosy bachelor evening.'

'Not a bit,' said Georgie. 'Do have a chair near the fire.'

It was not necessary to explain that she had already had tea with Diva, even if one mouthful of fermenting vegetable could properly be called tea, and she took the chair he pulled up for her.

'Such beautiful work,' she said, looking at Georgie's tambour of *petit point*, which lay near by. 'What eyes you must have to be able to do it.'

'Yes, they're pretty good yet,' said Georgie, slipping his spectacle-case into his pocket. 'And I shall be delighted to come to tea and bridge on Saturday. Thanks so much. Just got your invitation.'

Miss Mapp knew that already.

'That's charming,' she said. 'And how I envy you your Foljambe. Not a speck of dust anywhere. You could eat your tea off the floor, as they say.'

Georgie noticed that she did not use his Christian name. This confirmed his belief that the employment of it was reserved for Lucia's presence as an annoyance to her. Then the telephone-bell rang again.

'May I?' said Georgie.

He went across to it, rather nervous. It was as he thought: Lucia was at it again, explaining that somebody had cut her off. Listen as she might, Miss Mapp, from where she sat, could only hear a confused quacking noise. So to show how indifferent she was to the conversation, she put her fingers close to her ears ready to stop them when Georgie turned round again, and listened hard to what he said.

'Yes ... yes,' said Georgie. 'Thanks so much – lovely. I'll pick him up then, shall I? Quarter to eight, is it? Yes, her too. Yes, I've done them once today: not a bit giddy. ... I can't stop now, Lucia. Miss Ma— Elizabeth's just come in for a cup of tea. ... I'll tell her.'

Elizabeth felt she understood all this; she was an adept at telephonic reconstruction. There was evidently another party at Grebe. 'Him' and 'Her' no doubt were Major Benjy and herself, whom Georgie would pick up as before. 'Them' were exercises, and Georgie's promise to tell her clearly meant that he should convey an invitation. This was satisfactory: evidently Lucia was hoping to propitiate. Then Georgie turned round and saw Elizabeth smiling gaily at the fire with her hands over her ears. He moved into her field of vision and she uncorked herself.

'Finished?' she said. 'Hope you did not cut it short because of me.'

'Not at all,' said Georgie, for she couldn't (unless she was pretending) have heard him say that he had done precisely that. 'It was Lucia ringing up. She sends you her love.'

'Sweet of her, such a pet,' said Elizabeth, and waited for more about picking up and that invitation. But Lucia's love appeared to be all, and Georgie asked her if she took sugar. She did, and tried if he in turn would take another sort of sugar, both for himself and Lucia.

'Such a lovely house-warming,' she said, 'and how we all enjoyed ourselves. Lucia seems to have time for everything, bridge, those lovely duets with you, Italian, Greek (though we haven't heard much about that lately), a winter art exhibition, and an address (how I shall look forward to it!) on modern art, callisthenics – '

'Oh, you ought to try those,' said Georgie. 'You stretch and stamp and feel ever so young afterwards. We're all doing them.'

'And does she take classes as she threat— promised to do?' asked Elizabeth.

'She will when we've mastered the elements,' said Georgie. 'We shall march round the kitchen-garden at Grebe – cinder paths you know, so good in wet weather – keeping time, and then skip and flex and jerk. And if it's raining we shall do them in the kitchen. You can throw open those double doors, and have plenty of fresh air which is so important. There's that enormous kitchen table too, to hold on to, when we're doing that swimming movement. It's like a great raft.'

Elizabeth had not the nerve to ask if Major Benjy was to be of that company. It would be too bitter to know that he, who had so sternly set his face against Lucia's domination, was in process of being sucked down in that infernal whirlpool of her energetic grabbings. Almost she wished that she had asked her to be one of her bridge-party tomorrow: but it was too late now. Her seven invitations – seven against Lucia – had gone forth, and not till she got home would she know whether her two bridge tables were full.

'And this winter exhibition,' she asked. 'What a good idea! We're all so idle in the winter at dear old Tilling, and now there's another thing to work for. Are you sending that delicious picture of the garden-room? How I enjoyed our lovely chatty mornings when you were painting it!'

By the ordinary rules of polite conversation, Georgie ought to have asked her what she was sending. He did nothing of the kind, but looked a little uncomfortable. Probably then, as Irene had told her, the exhibition was to consist of pictures sent by request of the committee, and at present they had not requested her. She felt that she must make sure about that, and determined to send in a picture without being asked. That would show for certain what was going on.

'Weren't those mornings pleasant?' said the evasive Georgie. 'I was quite sorry when my picture was finished.'

Georgie appeared unusually reticent: he did not volunteer any more information about the winter exhibition, nor about Lucia's telephoning, nor had he mentioned that he and Major Benjy had lunched with her today. She would lead him in the direction of that topic . . .

'How happy dear Lucia is in her pretty Grebe,' she said. 'I took my walk along the road there today. Her garden, so pleasant! A high tide this afternoon. The beautiful river flowing down to the sea, and the tide coming up to meet it. Did you notice it?'

Georgie easily saw through that: he would talk about tides with pleasure, but not lunch.

'It looked lovely,' he said, 'but they tell me that in ten days' time the spring tides are on, and they will be much higher. The water has been over the road in front of Lucia's house sometimes.'

Elizabeth went back to Mallards more uneasy than ever. Lucia was indeed busy arranging callisthenic classes and winter exhibitions and, clearly, some party at Grebe, but not a word had she said to her about any of these things, nor had she sent the recipe of lobster *à la Riseholme*. But there was nothing more to be done tonight except to take steps concerning the picture exhibition to which she had not been asked to contribute. The house was full of her sketches, and she selected quite the best of them and directed Withers to pack it up and send it, with her card, to the Committee of the Art Club, Grebe.

The winter bridge-parties in Tilling were in their main features of a fixed and invariable pattern. An exceedingly substantial tea, including potted-meat sandwiches, was served at half past four, and, after that was disposed of, at least three hours of bridge followed. After such a tea, nobody, as was perfectly well known, dreamed of having dinner: and though round about eight o'clock, the party broke up, with cries of astonishment at the lateness of the hour, and said it must fly back home to dress, this was a mere fashion of speech. 'A tray' was the utmost refreshment that anyone could require, and nobody dressed for a solitary tray. Elizabeth was a great upholder of the dress-and-dinner fiction, and she had been known to leave a bridge-party at nine, saying that Withers would scold her for being so late, and that her cook would be furious.

So this Saturday afternoon the party of eight (for all seven had accepted) assembled at Mallards. They were exceedingly cordial: it was as if they desired to propitiate their hostess for something presently to emerge. Also it struck that powerful observer that there was not nearly so much eaten as usual. She had provided the caviare sandwiches of which Mrs Wyse had been known absentmindedly to eat nine, she had provided the nougat-chocolates of which Diva had been known to have eaten all, but though the chocolates were in front of Diva, and the caviare in front of Susan, neither of them exhibited anything resembling their usual greed. There was Scotch shortbread for the Padre, who, though he came from Birmingham, was insatiable with regard to that national form of biscuit, and there was whisky and soda for Major Benjy, who had no use for tea, and both of them, too, were mysteriously abstemious. Perhaps this wet muggy weather, thought Elizabeth, had made them all a trifle liverish, or very likely those callisthenics had taken away their appetites. It was noticeable, moreover, that throughout tea nobody mentioned the name of Lucia.

They adjourned to the garden-room where two tables were set out for bridge, and till half past six nothing momentous occurred. At that hour Elizabeth was partner to Major Benjy, and she observed with dark misgivings that when she had secured the play of the hand (at a staggering sacrifice, as it was soon to prove) he did not as usual watch her play, but got up and standing by the fire-place indulged in some very antic movements. He bent down, apparently trying to touch his toes with his fingers and a perfect fusillade of small crackling noises from his joints (knee or hip it was impossible to tell) accompanied these athletic flexings. Then he whisked himself round to right and left as if trying to look down his back, like a parrot. This was odd and ominous conduct, this strongly suggested that he had been sucked into the callisthenic whirlpool, and what was more ominous yet was that when he sat down again he whispered to Georgie, who was at the same table, 'That makes my ten minutes, old boy.' Elizabeth did not like that at all. She knew now what the ten minutes must refer to, and that endearing form of address to Miss Milliner Michael-Angelo was a little worrying. The only consolation was that Georgie's attention was diverted from the game, and that he trumped his partner's best card. At the conclusion of the hand, Elizabeth was three tricks short of her contract, and another very puzzling surprise awaited her, for instead of Major Benjy taking her failure in very ill part, he was more than pleasant about it. What could be the matter with him?

'Very well played, Miss Elizabeth,' he said. 'I was afraid that after my inexcusable declaration we should lose more than that.'

Elizabeth began to feel more keenly puzzled as to why none of them had any appetites, and why they were all so pleasant to her. Were they rallying round her again, or was their silence about Lucia a tactful approval of her absence? Or was there some hidden connexion between their abstemiousness, their reticence and their unwontedly propitiatory attitude? – If there was, it quite eluded her. Then as Diva dealt in her sloppy manner Lucia's name came up for the first time.

'Mr Georgie, you ought not to have led trumps,' she said. 'Lucia always says – Oh, dear me, I believe I've misdealt. Oh no, I haven't. That's all right.'

Elizabeth pondered this as she sorted her cards. Nobody inquired what Lucia said, and Diva's swift changing of the subject as if that name had slipped out by accident, looked as if possibly they none of them desired any allusion to be made to her. Had they done with her, she wondered? But if so what about the callisthenics?

She was dummy now and was absorbed in watching Major Benjy's tragical mismanagement of the hand, for he was getting into a sadder bungle than anyone, except perhaps Lucia, could have involved himself in. Withers entered while this was going on, and gave Elizabeth a parcel. With her eye and her mind still glued to the cards, she absently unwrapped it, and took its contents from its coverings just as the last trick was being played. It was the picture she had sent to the Art Committee the day before and with it was a typewritten form to convey its regrets that the limited wall space at its disposal would not permit of Miss Mapp's picture being exhibited. This slip floated out on to the floor, and Georgie bent down and returned it to her. She handed it and the picture and the wrappings to Withers, and told her to put them in the cupboard. Then she leaned over the table to her partner, livid with mixed and uncontrollable emotions.

'Dear Major Benjy, what a hash!' she said. 'If you had pulled out your cards at random from your hand, you could not, bar revokes, have done worse. I think you must have been having lessons from dear Lulu. Never mind: live and unlearn.'

There was an awful pause. Even the players at the other table were stricken into immobility and looked at each other with imbecile eyes. Then the most surprising thing of all happened.

' 'Pon my word, partner,' said Major Benjy, 'I deserve all the scoldings you can give me. I played it like a baby. I deserve to pay all our losings. A thousand apologies.'

Elizabeth, though she did not feel like it, had to show that she was generous too. But why didn't he answer her back in the usual manner?

'Naughty Major Benjy!' she said. 'But what does it matter? It's only a game, and we all have our ups and downs. I have them myself. That's the rubber, isn't it? Not very expensive after all. Now let us have another and forget all about this one.'

Diva drew a long breath, as if making up her mind to something, and glanced at the watch set with false pearls (Elizabeth was sure) on her wrist.

'Rather late to begin again,' she said. 'I make it ten minutes to seven. I think I ought to be going to dress.'

'Nonsense, dear,' said Elizabeth. 'Much too early to leave off. Cut, Major Benjy.'

He also appeared to take his courage in his hands, not very successfully.

'Well, upon my word, do you know, really Miss Elizabeth,' he babbled, 'a rubber goes on sometimes for a very long while, and if it's close on seven now, if, you know what I mean. . . . What do you say, Pillson?'

It was Georgie's turn.

'Too tarsome,' he said, 'but I'm afraid personally that I must stop. Such a delightful evening. Such good rubbers . . .'

They all got up together, as if some common mechanism controlled their movements. Diva scuttled away to the other table, without even waiting to be paid the sum of one and threepence which she had won from Elizabeth.

'I'll see how they're getting on here,' she said. 'Why they're just adding up, too.'

Elizabeth sat where she was and counted out fifteen pennies. That would serve Diva right for going at ten minutes to seven. Then she saw that the others had got up in a hurry, for Susan Wyse said to Mrs Bartlett, 'I'll pay you later on,' and her husband held up her sable coat for her.

'Diva, your winnings,' said Elizabeth, piling up the coppers.

Diva whisked round, and instead of resenting this ponderous discharge of the debt, received it with enthusiasm.

'Thank you, Elizabeth,' she said. 'All coppers: how nice! So useful for change. Good night, dear. Thanks ever so much.'

She paused a moment by the door, already open, by which Georgie was standing.

'Then you'll call for me at twenty minutes to eight,' she said to him in the most audible whisper, and Georgie with a nervous glance in Elizabeth's direction gave a silent assent. Diva vanished into the night where Major Benjy had gone. Elizabeth rose from her deserted table.

'But you're not all going too?' she said to the others. 'So early yet.'

Mr Wyse made a profound bow.

'I regret that my wife and I must get home to dress,' he said. 'But one of the most charming evenings of bridge I have ever spent, Miss Mapp. So many thanks. Come along, Susan.'

'Delicous bridge,' said Susan. 'And those caviare sandwiches. Good night, dear. You must come round and play with us some night soon.'

'A grand game of bridge, Mistress Mapp,' said the Padre. 'Ah, wee wifie's callin' for me. Au reservoir.'

Next moment Elizabeth was alone. Georgie had followed on the heels of the others, closing the door very carefully, as if she had fallen asleep. Instead of that she hurried to the window and peeped out between the curtains. There were three or four of them standing on the steps while the Wyses got into the Royce, and they dispersed in different directions like detected conspirators, as no doubt they were.

The odd disconnected little incidents of the evening, the lack of appetites, the propitiatory conduct to herself, culminating in this unexampled departure a full hour before bridge-parties had ever been known to break up, now grouped themselves together in Elizabeth's constructive mind. They fitted on to other facts that had hitherto seemed unrelated, but now were charged with significance. Georgie, for instance, had telephoned the day and the hour of this bridge-party to Lucia, he had accepted an invitation to something at a quarter to eight: he had promised to call for 'him' and 'her'. There could be no reasonable doubt that Lucia had purposely broken up Elizabeth's party at this early hour by bidding to dinner the seven guests who had just slunk away to dress. . . . And her picture had been returned by the Art Committee, two of whom (though she did them the justice to admit that they were but the catspaws of a baleful intelligence) had hardly eaten any caviare sandwiches at all, for fear that they should not have good appetites for dinner. Hence also Diva's abstention from nougat-chocolate, Major Benjy's from whisky, and the Padre's from shortbread. Nothing could be clearer.

Elizabeth was far from feeling unhappy or deserted, and very very far from feeling beaten. Defiance and hatred warmed her blood most pleasantly, and she spent half an hour sitting by the window, thoroughly enjoying herself. She meant to wait here till twenty minutes to eight, and if by that time she had not seen the Royce turning the corner of Porpoise Street, and Georgie's car calling at the perfidious Major Benjy's house, she would be ready to go barefoot to Grebe, and beg Lucia's pardon for having attributed to her so devilish a device. But no such humiliating pilgrimage awaited her, for all happened exactly as she knew it would. The great glaring head-lights of the Royce blazed on the house opposite the turning to Porpoise Street, its raucous foghorn sounded, and the porpoise car lurched into view scaring everybody by its lights and its odious voice, and by its size making foot passengers flatten themselves against the walls. Hardly had it cleared the corner into the High Street when Georgie's gay bugle piped out and his car came under the window of the garden-room, and stopped at Major Benjy's. Elizabeth's intellect unaided by any direct outside information, except that which she had overheard on the telephone, had penetrated this hole-and-corner business, and ringing the bell for her tray, she ate the large remainder of caviare sandwiches and nougat-chocolate and fed her soul with schemes of reprisals. She could not off-hand think of any definite plan of sufficiently withering a nature, and presently, tired with mental activity, she fell into a fireside doze and had a happy dream that Dr Dobbie had popped in to tell her that Lucia had developed undoubted symptoms of leprosy.

During the positively voluptuous week that followed Elizabeth's brief bridge-party, no fresh development occurred of the drama on which Tilling was concentrated, except that Lucia asked Elizabeth to tea and that Elizabeth refused. The rivals therefore did not meet, and neither of them seemed aware of the existence of the other. But both Grebe and Mallards had been inordinately gay; at Grebe there had been many lunches with bridge afterwards, and the guests on several occasions had hurried back for tea and more bridge at Mallards. Indeed, Tilling had never had so much lunch or tea in its life or enjoyed so brilliant a winter season, for Diva and the Wyses and Mrs Padre followed suit in lavish hospitality, and Georgie on one notable morning remembered that he had not had lunch or tea at home for five days; this was a record that beat Riseholme all to fits.

In addition to these gaieties there were celebrated the nuptials of Foljambe and Cadman, conducted from the bride's home, and the disposition of Foljambe's time between days with Georgie and nights with Cadman was working to admiration: everybody was pleased. At Grebe there had been other entertainments as well; the callisthenic class met on alternate days and Lucia in a tunic rather like Artemis, but with a supplementary skirt and scarlet stockings, headed a remarkable procession, consisting of Diva and the Wyses and Georgie and Major Benjy and the Padres and quaint Irene, out on to the cinder path of the kitchen-garden, and there they copied her jerks and flexings and whirlings of the arms and touchings of the toes to the great amazement of errand-boys who came legitimately to the kitchen door, and others who peered through the hornbeam hedge. On wet days the athletes assembled in the kitchen with doors flung wide to the open air, and astonished the cook with their swimming movements, an arm and leg together, while they held on with the other hand to the great kitchen table. 'Uno, due, tre,' counted Lucia, and they all kicked out like frogs. And quaint Irene in her knickerbocks sometimes stood on her head, but nobody else attempted that. Lucia played them soothing music as they rested afterwards in her drawing-room; she encouraged Major Benjy to learn his notes on the piano, for she would willingly teach him: she persuaded Susan to take up her singing again, and played 'La ci darem' for her, while Susan sang it in a thin shrill voice, and Mr Wyse said 'Brava! How I wish Amelia was here.' Sometimes Lucia read them Pope's translation of the *Iliad* as they drank their lemonade and Major Benjy his whisky and soda, and not content with these diversions (the wonderful creature) she was composing the address on modern art which she was to deliver at the opening of the exhibition on the day following Boxing Day. She made notes for it and then dictated to her secretary (Elizabeth Mapp's face was something awful to behold when Diva told her that Lucia had a secretary) who took down what she said on a typewriter. Indeed, Elizabeth's face had never been more awful when she heard that, except when Diva informed her that she was quite certain that Lucia would be delighted to let her join the callisthenic class.

But though, during these days, no act of direct aggression like that of Lucia's dinner-party causing Elizabeth's bridge-party to break up had been committed on either side, it was generally believed that Elizabeth was not done for yet, and Tilling was on tiptoe, expectant of some 'View halloo' call to show that the chase was astir. She had refused Lucia's invitation to tea, and if she had been done for or gone to earth she would surely have accepted. Probably she took the view that the invitation was merely a test question to see how she was getting on, and her refusal showed that she was getting on very nicely. It would be absolutely unlike Elizabeth (to adopt a further metaphor) to throw up the sponge like that, for she had not yet been seriously hurt, and the bridge-party-round had certainly been won by Lucia; there would be fierce boxing in the next. It seemed likely that, in this absence of aggressive acts, both antagonists were waiting till the season of peace and good will was comfortably over and then they would begin again. Elizabeth would have a God-sent opportunity at the opening of the exhibition, when Lucia delivered her address. She could sit in the front row and pretend to go to sleep or suppress an obvious inclination to laugh. Tilling felt that she must have thought of that and of many other acts of reprisal unless she was no longer the Elizabeth they all knew and (within limits) respected, and (on numerous occasions) detested.

The pleasant custom of sending Christmas cards prevailed in Tilling, and most of the world met in the stationer's shop on Christmas Eve, selecting suitable salutations from the threepenny, the sixpenny and the shilling trays. Elizabeth came in rather early and had almost completed her purchases when some of her friends arrived, and she hung about looking at the backs of volumes in the lending-library, but keeping an eye on what they purchased. Diva, she observed, selected nothing from the shilling tray any more than she had herself; in fact, she thought that Diva's purchases this year were made entirely from the threepenny tray. Susan, on the other hand, ignored the threepenny tray and hovered between the sixpennies and the shillings and expressed an odiously opulent regret that there were not some 'choicer' cards to be obtained. The Padre and Mrs Bartlett were certainly exclusively threepenny, but that was always the case. However they, like everybody else, studied the other trays, so that when, next morning, they all received seasonable coloured greetings from their friends, a person must have a shocking memory if he did not know what had been the precise cost of all that were sent him. But Georgie and Lucia as was universally noticed, though without comment, had not been in at all, in spite of the fact that they had been seen about in the High Street together and going into other shops. Elizabeth therefore decided that they did not intend to send any Christmas cards and before paying for what she had chosen, she replaced in the threepenny tray a pretty picture of a robin sitting on a sprig of mistletoe which she had meant to send Georgie. There was no need to put back what she had chosen for Lucia, since the case did not arise.

Christmas Day dawned, a stormy morning with a strong gale from the south-west, and on Elizabeth's breakfast table was a pile of letters, which she tore open. Most of them were threepenny Christmas cards, a sixpenny from Susan, smelling of musk, and none from Lucia or Georgie. She had anticipated that, and it was pleasant to think that she had put back into the threepenny tray the one she had selected for him, before purchasing it.

The rest of her post was bills, some of which must be stoutly disputed when Christmas was over, and she found it difficult to realize the jollity appropriate to the day. Last evening various choirs of amateur riffraffs and shrill bobtails had rendered night hideous by repetitions of Good King Wenceslas and the First Noël, church-bells borne on squalls of wind and rain had awakened her while it was still dark and now sprigs of holly kept falling down from the picture-frames where Withers had perched them. Bacon made her feel rather better, and she went to church, with a mackintosh against these driving gusts of rain, and a slightly blue nose against this boisterous wind. Diva was coming to a dinner-lunch: this was an annual institution held at Wasters and Mallards alternately.

Elizabeth hurried out of church at the conclusion of the service by a side door, not feeling equal to joining in the gay group of her friends who with Lucia as their centre were gathered at the main entrance. The wind was stronger than ever, but the rain had ceased, and she battled her way round the square surrounding the church before she went home. Close to Mallards Cottage she met Georgie holding his hat on against the gale. He wished her a merry Christmas, but then his hat had been whisked off his head, and something very strange happened to his hair, which seemed to have been blown off his skull, leaving a quite bare place there, and he vanished in frenzied pursuit of his hat with long tresses growing from the side of his head streaming in the wind, A violent draught eddying round the corner by the garden-room propelled her into Mallards holding on to the knocker, and it was with difficulty that she closed the door. On the table in the hall stood a substantial package, which had certainly not been there when she left. Within its wrappings was a *terrine* of *pâté de foie gras* with a most distinguished label on it, and a card fluttered on to the floor, proclaiming that wishes for a merry Christmas from Lucia and Georgie accompanied it. Elizabeth instantly conquered the feeble temptation of sending this gift back again in the manner in which she had returned that basket of tomatoes from her own garden. Tomatoes were not *pâté*. But what a treat for Diva!

Diva arrived, and they went straight in to the banquet. The *terrine* was wrapped in a napkin, and Withers handed it to Diva. She helped herself handsomely to the truffles and the liver.

'How delicious!' she said. 'And such a monster!'

'I hope it's good,' said Elizabeth, not mentioning the donors. 'It ought to be. Paris.'

Diva suddenly caught sight of a small label pasted below the distinguished one. It was that of the Tilling grocer, and a flood of light poured in upon her.

'Lucia and Mr Georgie have sent such lovely Christmas presents to everybody,' she said. 'I felt quite ashamed of myself for only having given them threepenny cards.'

'How sweet of them,' said Elizabeth. 'What were they – '

'A beautiful box of hard chocolates for me,' said Diva. 'And a great pot of caviare for Susan, and an umbrella for the Padre – his blew inside out in the wind yesterday – and – '

'And this beautiful *pâté* for me,' interrupted Elizabeth, grasping the nettle, for it was obvious that Diva had guessed. 'I was just going to tell you.'

Diva knew that was a lie, but it was no use telling Elizabeth so, because she knew it too, and she tactfully changed the subject.

'I shall have to do my exercises three times today after such a lovely lunch,' she said, as Elizabeth began slicing the turkey. But that was not a well-chosen topic, for subjects connected with Lucia might easily give rise to discord and she tried again and again and again, bumping, in her spinning-top manner, from one impediment to another.

'Major Benjy can play the scale of C with his right hand' – (No, that wouldn't do.) 'What an odd voice Susan's got: she sang an Italian song the other day at' – (Worse and worse.) 'I sent two pictures to the winter exhibition' – (Worse if possible: there seemed to be no safe topic under the sun.) 'A terrific gale, isn't it? There'll be three days of tremendous high tides for the wind is heaping them up. I should not wonder if the road by Grebe – ' (she gave it up: it was no use) – 'isn't flooded tomorrow.'

Elizabeth behaved like a perfect lady. She saw that Diva was doing her best to keep off disagreeable subjects on Christmas Day, but there were really no others. All topics led to Lucia.

'I hope not,' she said, 'for with all the field-paths soaked from the rain it is my regular walk just now. But not very likely, dear, for after the last time that the road was flooded, they built the bank opposite – opposite that house much higher.'

They talked for quite a long while about gales and tides and dykes in complete tranquillity. Then the proletarian diversions of Boxing Day seemed safe.

'There's a new film tomorrow at the Picture Palace about tadpoles,' said Elizabeth. 'So strange to think they become toads: or is it frogs? I think I must go.'

'Lucia's giving a Christmas-tree for the choir-boys in the evening, in that great kitchen of hers,' said Diva.

'How kind!' said Elizabeth hastily, to show she took no offence.

'And in the afternoon there's a whist drive at the Institute,' said Diva. 'I'm letting both my servants go, and Lucia's sending all hers too. I'm not sure I should like to be quite alone in a house along that lonely road. We in the town could scream from a top window if burglars got into our houses and raise the alarm.'

'It would be a very horrid burglar who was so wicked on Boxing Day,' observed Elizabeth sententiously. 'Ah, here's the plum pudding! Blazing beautifully, Withers! So pretty!'

Diva became justifiably somnolent when lunch was over, and after half an hour's careful conversation she went off home to have a nice long nap, which she expressed by the word exercises. Elizabeth wrote two notes of gratitude to the donors of the *pâté* and sat herself down to think seriously of what she could do. She had refused Lucia's invitation to tea a few days before, thus declaring her attitude, and now it seemed to her that that was a mistake, for she had cut herself off from the opportunities of reprisals which intercourse with her might have provided. She had been unable, severed like this, to devise anything at all effective; all she could do was to lie awake at night hating Lucia, and this seemed to be quite barren of results. It might be better (though bitter) to join that callisthenic class in order to get a foot in the enemy's territory. Her note of thanks for the *pâté* would have paved the way towards such a step, and though it would certainly be eating humble pie to ask to join an affair that she had openly derided, it would be pie with a purpose. As it was, for a whole week she had had no opportunities, she had surrounded herself with a smoke-cloud, she heard nothing about Lucia any more, except when clumsy Diva let out things by accident. All she knew was that Lucia, busier than any bee known to science, was undoubtedly supreme in all the social activities which she herself had been accustomed to direct, and to remain, like Achilles in his tent, did not lead to anything. Also she had an idea that Tilling expected of her some exhibition of spirit and defiance, and no one was more anxious than she to fulfil those expectations to the utmost. So she settled she would go to Grebe tomorrow, and, after thanking her in person for the *pâté*, ask to join the callisthenic class. Tilling, and Lucia too, no doubt would take that as a sign of surrender, but let them wait a while, and they should see.

'I can't fight her unless I get in touch with her,' reflected Elizabeth; 'at least I don't see how, and I'm sure I've thought enough.'

10

In pursuance of this policy Elizabeth set out early in the afternoon next day to walk out to Grebe, and there eat pie with a purpose. The streets were full of holiday folk, and by the railings at the end of the High Street, where the steep steps went down to the levels below, there was a crowd of people looking at the immense expanse of water that lay spread over the marsh. The south-westerly gale had piled up the spring tides, the continuous rains had caused the river to come down in flood, and the meeting of the two, the tide now being at its height, formed a huge lake, a mile and more wide, which stretched seawards. The gale had now quite ceased, the sun shone brilliantly from the pale blue of the winter sky, and this enormous estuary sparkled in the gleam. Far away to the south a great bank of very thick vapour lay over the horizon, showing that out in the Channel there was thick fog, but over Tilling and the flooded marsh the heavens overhead were of a dazzling radiance.

Many of Elizabeth's friends were there, the Padre and his wife (who kept exclaiming in little squeaks, 'Oh dear me, what a quantity of water!'), the Wyses who had dismounted from the Royce, which stood waiting, to look at the great sight, before they proceeded on their afternoon drive. Major Benjy was saying that it was nothing to the Jumna in flood, but then he always held up India as being far ahead of England in every way (he had even once said on an extremely frosty morning, that this was nothing to the bitterness of Bombay): Georgie was there and Diva. With them all Elizabeth exchanged the friendliest greetings, and afterwards, when the great catastrophe had happened, everyone agreed that they had never known her more cordial and pleasant, poor thing. She did not of course tell them what her errand was, for it would be rash to do that till she saw how Lucia received her, but merely said that she was going for her usual brisk walk on this lovely afternoon, and should probably pop into the Picture Palace to learn about tadpoles. With many flutterings of her hand and enough au reservoirs to provide water for the world, she tripped down the hill, through the Land-gate, and out on to the road that led to Grebe and nowhere else particular.

She passed, as she neared Grebe, Lucia's four indoor servants and Cadman coming into the town, and, remembering that they were going to a whist drive at the Institute, wished them a merry Christmas and hoped that they would all win. (Little kindly remarks like that always pleased servants, thought Elizabeth; they showed a human sympathy with their pleasures and cost nothing; so much better than Christmas boxes.) Her brisk pace made short work of the distance, and within quite a few minutes of her leaving her friends, she had come to the thick hornbeam hedge which shielded Grebe from the road. She stopped opposite it for a moment: there was that prodigious sheet of dazzling water now close to the top of the restraining bank to admire: there was herself to screw up to the humility required for asking Lucia if she might join her silly callisthenic class. Finally, coming from nowhere, there flashed into her mind the thought of lobster à la Riseholme, the recipe for which Lucia had so meanly withheld from her. Instantly that thought fructified into apples of Desire.

She gave one glance at the hornbeam hedge to make sure that she was not visible from the windows of Grebe. (Lucia used often to be seen spying from the windows of the garden-room during her tenancy of Mallards, and she might be doing the same thing here.) But the hedge was quite impenetrable to human eye, as Elizabeth had often regretfully observed already, and now instead of going in at the high wooden gate which led to the front door, she passed quickly along till she came to the far corner of the hedge bordering the kitchen-garden. So swift was thought to a constructive mind like hers already stung with desire, that, brisk though was her physical movement, her mind easily outstripped it, and her plan was laid before she got to the corner. Viz.:

The servants were all out – of that she had received ocular evidence but a few moments before – and the kitchen would certainly be empty. She would therefore go round to the gate at the end of the kitchen-garden and approach the house that way. The cinder path, used for the prancing of the callisthenic class in fine weather, led straight to the big coach-house doors of the kitchen, and she would ascertain by the simple device of trying the handle if these were unlocked. If they were locked, there was an end to her scheme, but if they were unlocked, she would quietly pop in, and see whether the cook's book of recipes was not somewhere about. If it was she would surely find in it the recipe for lobster à la Riseholme. A few minutes would suffice to copy it, and then tiptoeing out of the kitchen again, with the key to the mystery in her pocket, she would go round to the front door as cool as a cucumber, and ring the bell. Should Lucia (alone in the house and possibly practising for more po-di-mus) not hear the bell, she would simply postpone the eating of her humble pie till the next day. If, by ill chance, Lucia was in the garden and saw her approaching by this unusual route, nothing was easier than to explain that, returning from her walk, she thought she would look in to thank her for the pâté and ask if she might join her callisthenic class. Knowing that the servants were all out (she would glibly explain) she felt sure that the main gate on to the road would be locked, and therefore she tried the back way. ... The whole formation of the scheme was instantaneous; it was as if she had switched on the lights at the door of a long gallery, and found it lit from end to end.

Without hurrying at all she walked down the cinder path and tested the kitchen-door. It was unlocked, and she slipped in, closing it quietly behind her. In the centre of the kitchen, decked and ready for illumination, stood the Christmas-tree designed for the delectation of the choir-boys that evening, and the great kitchen-table, with its broad skirting of board halfway down the legs, had been moved away and stood on its side against the dresser in order to give more room for the tree. Elizabeth hardly paused a second to admire the tapers, the reflecting glass balls, the bright tinselly decorations, for she saw a small shelf of books on the wall opposite, and swooped like a merlin on it. There were a few trashy novels, there was a hymn-book and a prayer-book, and there was a thick volume, with no title on the back, bound in American cloth. She opened it and saw at once that her claws had at last gripped the prey, for on one page was pasted a cutting from the daily press concerning *oeufs à l'aurore*, on the next was a recipe in manuscript for cheese straws. Rapidly she turned the leaves, and there manifest at last was the pearl of great price, lobster *à la Riseholme*. It began with the luscious words, 'Take two hen lobsters.'

Out came her pencil; that and a piece of paper in which had been wrapped a present for a choir-boy was all she needed. In a couple of minutes she had copied out the mystic spell, replaced the sacred volume on its shelf and put in her pocket the information for which she had pined so long. 'How odd,' she cynically reflected, 'that only yesterday I should have said to Diva that it must be a very horrid burglar who was so wicked as to steal things on Boxing Day. Now I'll go round to the front door.'

At the moment when this Mephistophelian thought came into her mind, she heard with a sudden stoppage of her heart-beat, a step on the crisp path outside, and the handle of the kitchen-door was turned. Elizabeth took one sideways stride behind the gaudy tree and, peering through its branches, saw Lucia standing at the entrance. Lucia came straight towards her, not yet perceiving that there was a Boxing Day burglar in her own kitchen, and stood admiring her tree. Then with a startled exclamation she called out, 'Who's that?' and Elizabeth knew that she was discovered. Further dodging behind the decorated fir would be both undignified and ineffectual, however skilful her footwork.

'It's me, dear Lucia,' she said. 'I came to thank you in person for that delicious *pâté* and to ask if – '

From somewhere close outside there came a terrific roar and rush as of great water-floods released. Reunited for the moment by a startled curiosity, they ran together to the open door, and saw, already leaping across the road and over the hornbeam hedge, a solid wall of water.

'The bank has given way,' cried Lucia. 'Quick, into the house through the door in the kitchen, and up the stairs.'

They fled back past the Christmas-tree, and tried the door into the house. It was locked: the servants had evidently taken this precaution before going out on their pleasuring.

'We shall be drowned,' wailed Elizabeth, as the flood came foaming into the kitchen.

'Rubbish,' cried Lucia. 'The kitchen-table! We must turn it upside down and get on to it.'

It was but the work of a moment to do this, for the table was already on its side, and the two stepped over the high boarding that ran round it. Would their weight be too great to allow it to float on the rushing water that now deepened rapidly in the kitchen? That anxiety was short-lived, for it rose free from the floor and bumped gently into the Christmas-tree.

'We must get out of this,' cried Lucia. 'One doesn't know how much the water will rise. We may be drowned yet if the table legs come against the ceiling. Catch hold of the dresser and pull.'

But there was no need for such exertion, for the flood, eddying fiercely round the submerged kitchen, took them out of the doors that it had flung wide, and in a few minutes they were floating away over the garden and the hornbeam hedge. The tide had evidently begun to ebb before the bank gave way, and now the kitchen-table, occasionally turning round in an eddy, moved off in the direction of Tilling and of the sea. Luckily it had not got into the main stream of the river but floated smoothly and swiftly along, with the tide and the torrent of the flood to carry it. Its two occupants, of course, had no control whatever over its direction, but soon, with an upspring of hope, they saw that the current was carrying it straight towards the steep slope above the Land-gate, where not more than a quarter of an hour ago Elizabeth had interchanged greetings and au reservoirs with her friends who had been looking at the widespread waters. Little had she thought that so soon she would be involved in literal reservoirs of the most gigantic sort – but this was no time for light conceits.

The company of Tillingites was still there when the bank opposite Grebe gave way. All but Georgie had heard the rush and roar of the released waters, but his eyes were sharper than others, and he had been the first to see where the disaster had occurred.

'Look, the bank opposite Grebe has burst!' he cried. 'The road's under water, her garden's under water: the rooms downstairs must be flooded. I hope Lucia's upstairs, or she'll get dreadfully wet.'

'And that road is Elizabeth's favourite walk,' cried Diva. 'She'll be on it now.'

'But she walks so fast,' said the Padre, forgetting to speak Scotch. 'She'll be past Grebe by now, and above where the bank has burst.'

'Oh dear, oh dear, and on Boxing Day!' wailed Mrs Bartlett.

The huge flood was fast advancing on the town, but with this outlet over the fields, it was evident that it would get no deeper at Grebe, and that, given Lucia was upstairs and that Elizabeth had walked as fast as usual, there was no real anxiety for them. All eyes now watched the progress of the water. It rose like a wave over a rock when it came to the railway line that crossed the marsh and in a couple of minutes more it was foaming over the fields immediately below the town.

Again Georgie uttered woe like Cassandra.

'There's something coming,' he cried. 'It looks like a raft with its legs in the air. And there are two people on it. Now it's spinning round and round; now it's coming straight here ever so fast. There are two women, one without a hat. It's Them! It's Lucia and Miss Mapp! What *has* happened?'

The raft, with legs sometimes madly waltzing, sometimes floating smoothly along, was borne swiftly towards the bottom of the cliff, below which the flood was pouring by. The Padre, with his new umbrella, ran down the steps that led to the road below in order to hook it in, if it approached within umbrella-distance. On and on it came, now clearly recognizable as Lucia's great kitchen-table upside down, until it was within a yard or two of the bank. To attempt to wade out to it, for any effective purpose, was useless: the strongest would be swept away in such a headlong torrent, and even if he reached the raft there would be three helpless people on it instead of two and it would probably sink. To hook it with the umbrella was the only chance, for there was no time to get a boat-hook or a rope to throw out to the passengers. The Padre made a desperate lunge at it, slipped and fell flat into the water, and was only saved from being carried away by clutching at the iron railing along-side the lowest of the submerged steps. Then some fresh current tweaked the table and, still moving in the general direction of the flood water, it sheered off across the fields. As it receded Lucia showed the real stuff of which she was made. She waved her hand and her clear voice rang out gaily across the waste of water.

'Au reservoir, all of you,' she cried. 'We'll come back: just wait till we come back,' and she was seen to put her arm round the huddled form of Mapp, and comfort her.

The kitchen-table was observed by the watchers to get into the main channel of the river, where the water was swifter yet. It twirled round once or twice as if waving a farewell, and then shot off towards the sea and that great bank of thick mist which hung over the horizon.

There was not yet any reason to despair. A telephone-message was instantly sent to the fishermen at the port, another to the coast-guards, another to the lifeboat, that a kitchen-table with a cargo of ladies on it was coming rapidly down the river, and no effort must be spared to arrest its passage out to sea. But, one after the other, as the short winter afternoon waned, came dis-couraging messages from the coast. The flood had swept from their moorings all the fishing boats anchored at the port or drawn up on the shore above high-water mark, and a coast-guardsman had seen an unintelligible object go swiftly past the mouth of the river before the telephone-message was received.

He could not distinguish what it was, for the fog out in the Channel had spread to the coastline, and it had seemed to him more like the heads and necks of four sea-serpents playing together than anything else. But when interrogated as to whether it might be the legs of a kitchen-table upside down he acknowledged that the short glimpse which he obtained of it before it got lost in the fog would suit a kitchen-table as well as sea-serpents. He had said sea-serpents because it was in the sea, but it was just as like the legs of a kitchen-table, which had never occurred to him as possible. His missus had just such a kitchen-table – but as he seemed to be diverging into domestic reminiscences, the Mayor of Tilling, who himself conducted in-quiries instead of opening the whist drive at the Institute with a short speech on the sin of gambling, cut him off. It was only too clear that this imaginative naturalist had seen – too late – the kitchen-table going out to sea.

The lifeboat had instantly responded to the S.O.S. call on its services, and the great torrent of the flood having now gone by, the crew had been able to launch the boat and had set off to search the English Channel, in the blinding fog, for the table. The tide was setting west down the coast, the flood pouring out from the river mouth was discharged east, but they had gone off to row about in every direction, where the kitchen-table might have been carried. Rockets had been sent up from the station in case the ladies didn't know where they were. That, so the Mayor reflected, might conceivably show the ladies where they were, but it didn't really enable them to get anywhere else.

Dusk drew on and the friends of the missing went back to their respective houses, for there was no good in standing about in this dreadful cold fog which had now crept up from the marsh. Pneumonia wouldn't help matters. Four of them, Georgie and Major Benjy and Diva and quaint Irene, lived soli-tary and celibate, and the prospect of a lonely evening with only suspense and faint hopes to feed upon was perfectly ghastly. In consequence, when each of them in turn was rung up by Mr Wyse, who hoped, in a broken voice, that he might find them disengaged and willing to come round to his house for supper (not dinner), they all gladly accepted. Mr Wyse requested them not to dress for dinner, and this was felt to show a great delicacy: not dressing would be a sort of symbol of their common anxiety. Supper would be at half past eight, and Mr Wyse trusted that there would be encouraging news before that hour.

The Padre and Mrs Bartlett had been bidden as well, so that there was a supper-party of eight. Supper began with the most delicious caviare, and on the black oak mantelpiece were two threepenny Christmas cards. Susan helped herself plentifully to the caviare. There was no use in not eating.

'Dear Lucia's Christmas present to me,' she said. 'Hers and yours I should say, Mr Georgie.'

'Lucia sent me a wonderful box of nougat-chocolates,' said Diva. 'She and you, I mean, Mr Georgie.'

Major Benjy audibly gulped.

'Mrs Lucia,' he said, 'if I may call her so, sent me half a dozen bottles of pre-war whisky.'

The Padre had pulled himself together by this time, and spoke Scotch.

'I had a wee mischance wi' my umbrella two days agone,' he said, 'and Mistress Lucia, such a menseful woman, sent me a new one. An' now that's gone bobbin' out to sea.'

'You're too pessimistic, Kenneth,' said Mrs Bartlett. 'An umbrella soon gets waterlogged and sinks, I tell you. The chances are it will be picked up in the marsh tomorrow, and it'll find its way back to you, for there's that beautiful silver band on the handle with your name engraved on it.'

'Eh, 'twould be a bonnie thing to recover it,' said her husband.

Mr Wyse thought that the conversation was getting a little too much concerned with minor matters; the recovery of an umbrella, though new, was a loss that might be lamented later. Besides, the other missing lady had not been mentioned yet. He pointed to the two threepenny Christmas cards on the mantelpiece.

'Our friend Elizabeth Mapp sent those to my wife and me yesterday,' he said. 'We shall keep them always among our most cherished possessions in case – I mean in any case. Pretty designs. Roofs covered with snow. Holly. Robins. She had a very fine artistic taste. Her pictures had always something striking and original about them.'

Everybody cudgelled their brains for something appropriate to say about Elizabeth's connexion with Art. The effort was quite hopeless, for her ignoble trick in rejecting Lucia's and Georgie's pictures for the last exhibition, and the rejection by the new committee of her own for the forthcoming exhibition were all that could occur to the most nimble brain, and while the artist was in direst peril on the sea, or possibly now at rest beneath it, it would be in the worst taste to recall those discordant incidents. A very long pause of silence followed, broken only by the crashing of toast in the mouths of those who had not yet finished their caviare.

Irene had eaten no caviare, nor hitherto had she contributed anything to the conversation. Now she suddenly burst into shrieks of hysterical laughter and sobs.

'What rubbish you're all talking,' she cried, wiping her eyes. 'How can you be so silly? I'm sure I beg your pardons, but there it is. I'll go home, please.'

She fled from the room and banged the front door so loudly that the house shook, and one of Miss Mapp's cards fell into the fireplace.

'Poor thing. Very excitable and uncontrolled,' said Susan. 'But I think she's better alone.'

There was a general feeling of relief that Irene had gone, and as Mrs Wyse's excellent supper progressed, with its cold turkey and its fried slices of plum pudding, its toasted cheese and its figs stuffed with almonds sent by Amelia from Capri, the general numbness caused by the catastrophe began to pass off. Consumed with anxiety as all were for the two (especially one of them) who had vanished into the Channel fogs on so unusual a vehicle, they could not fail to recognize what problems of unparalleled perplexity and interest were involved in what all still hoped might not turn out to be a tragedy. But whether it proved so or not, the whole manner of these happenings, the cause, the conditions, the circumstances which led to the two unhappy ladies whisking by on the flood must be discussed, and presently Major Benjy broke into this unnatural reticence.

'I've seen many floods on the Jumna,' he said, refilling his glass of port, 'but I never saw one so sudden and so – so fraught with enigmas. They must have been in the kitchen. Now we all know there was a Christmas-tree there – '

A conversational flood equal to the largest ever seen on the Jumna was unloosed; a torrent of conjectures, and reconstruction after reconstruction of what could have occurred to produce what they had all seen, was examined and rejected as containing some inherent impossibility. And then what did the gallant Lucia's final words mean, when she said, 'Just wait till we come back'? By now discussion had become absolutely untrammelled, the rivalry between the two, Miss Mapp's tricks and pointless meannesses, Lucia's scornful victories, and, no less, her domineering ways were openly alluded to.

'But "Just wait till we come back" is what we're talking about,' cried Diva. 'We must keep to the point, Major Benjy. I believe she simply meant "Don't give up hope. We *shall* come back." And I'm sure they will.'

'No, there's more in it than that,' said Georgie, interrupting. 'I know Lucia better than any of you. She meant that she had something frightfully interesting to tell us when she did come back, as of course she will, and I'd bet it was something about Elizabeth. Some new thing she'd found her out in.'

'But at such a solemn moment,' said the Padre, again forgetting his pseudo-Highland origin, 'when they were being whirled out to sea with death staring them in the face, I hardly think that such trivialities as those which had undoubtedly before caused between those dear ladies the frictions which we all deplored – '

'Nonsense, Kenneth,' said his wife, rather to his relief, for he did not know how he was to get out of this sentence, 'you enjoyed those rows as much as anybody.'

'I don't agree with you, Padre,' said Georgie. 'To begin with, I'm sure Lucia didn't think she was facing death and even if she did, she'd still have been terribly interested in life till she went phut.'

'Thank God I live on a hill,' exclaimed Major Benjy, thinking, as usual, of himself.

Mr Wyse held up his hand. As he was the host, it was only kind to give him a chance, for he had had none as yet. 'Your pardon,' he said, 'if I may venture to suggest what may combine the ideas of our reverend friend and of Mr Pillson' – he made them two bows – 'I think Mrs Lucas felt she was facing death – who wouldn't? – but she was of that vital quality which never gives up interest in life, until, in fact (which we trust with her is not the case) all is over. But like a true Christian, she was, as we all saw, employed in comforting the weak. She could not have been using her last moments, which we hope are nothing of the sort, better. And if there had been frictions, they arose only from the contact of two highly vitalized – '

'She kissed Elizabeth too,' cried Mrs Bartlett. 'I saw her. She hasn't done that for ages. Fancy!'

'I want to get back to the kitchen,' said Diva. 'What could have taken Elizabeth to the kitchen – I've got a brilliant idea, though I don't know what you'll think of it. She knew Lucia was giving a Christmas-tree to the choir-boys, because I told her so yesterday – '

'I wonder what's happened to that,' said the Padre. 'If it wasn't carried away by the flood, and I think we should have seen it go by, it might be dried.'

Diva, as usual when interrupted, had held her mouth open, and went straight on.

' – and she knew the servants were out, because I'd told her that too, and she very likely wanted to see the Christmas-tree. So I suggest that she went round the back way into the kitchen – that would be extremely like her, you know – in order to have a look at it, without asking a favour of – '

'Well, I do call that clever,' interrupted Georgie admiringly. 'Go on. What happened next?'

Diva had not got further than that yet, but now a blinding brilliance illuminated her and she clapped her hands.

'I see, I see,' she cried. 'In she went into the kitchen and while she was looking at it, Lucia came in too, and then the flood came in too. All three of them. That would explain what was be- hind her words, "Just wait till we come back." She meant that she wanted to tell us that she'd found Elizabeth in her kitchen.'

It was universally felt that Diva had hit it, and after such a stroke of reconstructive genius, any further discussion must be bathos. Instantly a sad reaction set in, and they all looked at each other much shocked to find how wildly interested they had become in these trivial affairs, while their two friends were, to put the more hopeful view of the case, on a kitchen-table somewhere in the English Channel. But still Lucia had said that she and her companion were coming back, and though no news had arrived of the castaways, every one of her friends, at the bottom of their hearts, felt that these were not idle words, and that they must keep alive their confidence in Lucia. Miss Mapp alone would certainly have been drowned long ago, but Lucia, whose power of resource all knew to be unlimited, was with her. No one could suggest what she could possibly do in such difficult circumstances, but never yet had she been floored, nor failed to emerge triumphant from the most menacing situations.

Mrs Wyse's cuckoo clock struck the portentous hour of 1 a.m. They all sighed, they all got up, they all said good night with melancholy faces, and groped their ways home in the cold fog. Above Georgie's head as he turned the corner by Mallards there loomed the gable of the garden-room, where so often a chink of welcoming light had shone between the curtains, as the sound of Mozartino came from within. Dark and full of suspense as was the present, he could still, without the sense of something for ever passed from his life, imagine himself sitting at the piano again with Lucia, waiting for her Uno, due, TRE as they tried over for the first time the secretly familiar duets.

The whole of the next day this thick fog continued both on land and water, but no news came from seawards save the bleating and hooting of fog-horns, and as the hours passed, anxiety grew more acute. Mrs Wyse opened the picture exhibition on behalf of Lucia, for it was felt that in any case she would have wished that, but owing to the extreme inclemency of the weather only Mr Wyse and Georgie attended this inaugural ceremony. Mrs Wyse in the lamented absence of the authoress read Lucia's lecture on modern Art from the typewritten copy which she had sent Georgie to look through and criticize. It lasted an hour and twenty minutes, and after Georgie's applause had died away at the end, Mr Wyse read the speech he had composed to propose a vote of thanks to Lucia for her most enthralling address. This also was rather long, but written in the most classical and urbane style. Georgie seconded this in a shorter speech, and Mrs Wyse (*vice* Lucia) read another longer speech of Lucia's which was appended in manuscript to her lecture, in which she thanked them for thanking her, and told them how diffident she had felt in thus appearing before them. There was more applause, and then the three of them wandered round the room and peered at each other's pictures through the dense fog. Evening drew in again, without news, and Tilling began to fear the worst.

Next morning there came a mute and terrible message from the sea. The fog had cleared, the day was of crystalline brightness, and since air and exercise would be desirable after sitting at home all the day before, and drinking that wonderful pre-war whisky, Major Benjy set off by the eleven o'clock tram to play a round of golf with the Padre. Though hope was fast expiring, neither of them said anything definitely indicating that they no longer really expected to see their friends again, but there had been talk indirectly bearing on the catastrophe; the Major had asked casually whether Mallards was a freehold, and the Padre replied that both it and Grebe were the property of their occupiers and not held on lease; he also made a distant allusion to memorial services, saying he had been to one lately, very affecting. Then Major Benjy lost his temper with the caddie, and their game assumed a more normal aspect.

They had now come to the eighth hole, the tee of which was perched high like a pulpit on the sand-dunes and overlooked the sea. The match was most exciting: hole after hole had been halved in brilliant sixes and sevens, the players were both on the top of their form, and in their keenness had quite banished from their minds the overshadowing anxiety. Here Major Benjy topped his ball into a clump of bents immediately in front of the tee, and when he had finished swearing at his caddie for moving on the stroke, the Padre put his iron shot on to the green.

'A glorious day,' he exclaimed, and, turning to pick up his clubs, gazed out seawards. The tide was low, and an immense stretch of 'shining sands' as in Charles Kingsley's poem was spread in front of him. Then he gave a gasp.

'What's that?' he said to Major Benjy, pointing with a shaking finger.

'Good God,' said Major Benjy. 'Pick up my ball, caddie.'

They scrambled down the steep dunes and walked across the sands to where lay this object which had attracted the Padre's attention. It was an immense kitchen-table upside down with its legs in the air, wet with brine but still in perfect condition. Without doubt it was the one which they had seen two days before whirling out to sea. But now it was by itself, no ladies were sitting upon it. The Padre bared his head.

'Shall we abandon our game, Major?' he said. 'We had better telephone from the Club-house to the Mayor. And I must arrange to get some men to bring the table back. It's far too heavy for us to think of moving it.'

The news that the table had come ashore spread swiftly through Tilling, and Georgie, hearing that the Padre had directed that when it had passed the Custom House it should be brought to the Vicarage, went round there at once. It seemed almost unfeeling in this first shock of bereavement to think about tables, but it would save a great deal of bother afterwards to see to this now. The table surely belonged to Grebe.

'I quite understand your point of view,' he said to the Padre, 'and of course what is found on the seashore in a general way belongs to the finder, if it's a few oranges in a basket, because nobody knows who the real owner is. But we all know, at least we're afraid we do, where this came from.'

The Padre was quite reasonable.

'You mean it ought to go back to Grebe,' he said. 'Yes, I agree. Ah, I see it has arrived.'

They went out into the street, where a trolly, bearing the table, had just drawn up. Then a difficulty arose. It was late, and the bearers demurred to taking it all the way out to Grebe tonight and carrying it through the garden.

'Move it in here then for the night,' said the Padre. 'You can get it through the backyard and into the outhouse.'

Georgie felt himself bound to object to this: the table belonged to Grebe, and it looked as if Grebe, alas, belonged to him.

'I think it had better come to Mallards Cottage,' said he firmly. 'It's only just round the corner, and it can stand in my yard.'

The Padre was quite willing that it should go back to Grebe, but why should Georgie claim this object with all the painful interest attached to it? After all, he had found it.

'And so I don't quite see why you should have it,' he said a little stiffly.

Georgie took him aside.

'It's dreadful to talk about it so soon,' he said, 'but that is what I should like done with it. You see Lucia left me Grebe and all its contents. I still cling – I can't help it – to the hope that neither it nor they may ever be mine, but in the interval which may elapse – '

'No! Really!' said the Padre with a sudden thrill of Tillingite interest which it was no use trying to suppress. 'I congrat— Well, well. Of course the kitchen-table is yours. Very proper.'

The trolly started again and by dint of wheedlings and cunning coaxing the sad substantial relic was induced to enter the backyard of Mallards Cottage. Here for the present it would have to remain, but pickled as it was with long immersion in sea water, the open air could not possibly hurt it, and if it rained, so much the better, for it would wash the salt out.

Georgie, very tired and haggard with these harrowing arrangements, had a little rest on his sofa, when he had seen the table safely bestowed. His cook gave him a succulent and most nutritious dinner by way of showing her sympathy, and Foljambe waited on him with peculiar attention, constantly holding a pocket handkerchief to the end of her nose, by way of expressing her own grief. Afterwards he moved to his sitting-room and took up his needlework, that 'sad narcotic exercise', and looked his loss in the face.

Indeed, it was difficult to imagine what life would be like

without Lucia, but there was no need to imagine it, for he was experiencing it already. There was nothing to look forward to, and he realized how completely Lucia and her manoeuvres and her indomitable vitality and her deceptions and her greatnesses had supplied the salt to life. He had never been in the least in love with her, but somehow she had been as absorbing as any wayward and entrancing mistress. 'It will be too dull for anything,' thought he, 'and there won't be a single day in which I shan't miss her most dreadfully. It's always been like that: when she was away from Riseholme, I never seemed to care to paint or to play, except because I should show her what I had done when she came back, and now she'll never come back.'

He abandoned himself for quite a long time to despair with regard to what life would hold for him. Nobody else, not even Foljambe, seemed to matter at all. But then through the black, deep waters of his tribulation there began to appear little bubbles on the surface. It was like comparing a firefly with the huge night itself to weigh them against this all-encompassing darkness, but where for a moment each pricked the surface there was, it was idle to deny, just a spark that stood out momentarily against the blackness. The table, for instance: he would have a tablet fixed on it, with a suitable inscription to record the tragic rôle it had played, a text, so to speak, as on a cenotaph. How would Lucia's last words do? 'Just wait till we come back.' But if this was a memorial table, it must record that Lucia was not coming back.

He fetched a writing-pad and began again. 'This is the table – ' but that wouldn't do. It suggested 'This is the house that Jack built.' Then, 'It was upon this table on Boxing Day afternoon, 1930, that Mrs Emmeline Lucas, of Grebe, and Miss Elizabeth Mapp, of Mallards – ' that was too prolix. Then: 'In memory of Emmeline Lucas and Elizabeth Mapp. They went to sea' – but that sounded like a nursery rhyme by Edward Lear, or it might suggest to future generations that they were sailors. Then he wondered if poetry would supply anything, and the lines, 'And may there be no sadness of farewell, when I embark,' occurred to him. But that wouldn't do: people would wonder why she had embarked on a kitchen-table, and even now, when the event was so lamentably recent, nobody actually knew.

'I hadn't any idea,' thought Georgie, 'how difficult it is to write a few well-chosen and heart-felt words. I shall go and look at the tombstones in the churchyard tomorrow. Lucia would have thought of something perfect at once.'

Tiny as were these bubbles and others (larger ones) which Georgie refused to look at directly, they made a momentary, an evanescent brightness. Some of them made quite loud pops as they burst, and some presented problems. This catastrophe had conveyed a solemn warning against living in a house so low-lying, and Major Benjy had already expressed that sentiment when he gave vent to that self-centred *cri de coeur*, 'Thank God I live on a hill,' but for Georgie that question would soon become a practical one, though he would not attempt to make up his mind yet. It would be absurd to have two houses in Tilling, to be the tenant of Mallards Cottage, and the owner of Grebe. Or should he live in Grebe during the summer, when there was no fear of floods, and Mallards Cottage in the winter?

He got into bed: the sympathetic Foljambe, before going home had made a beautiful fire, and his hot-water bottle was of such a temperature that he could not put his feet on it at all. . . . If he lived at Grebe she would only have to go back across the garden to her Cadman, if Cadman remained in his service. Then there was Lucia's big car. He supposed that would be included in the contents of Grebe. Then he must remember to put a black bow on Lucia's picture in the Art Exhibition. Then he got sleepy . . .

I I

Though Georgie had thought that there would be nothing interesting left in life now that Lucia was gone, and though Tilling generally was conscious that the termination of the late rivalries would take all thrill out of existence as well as eclipsing its gaieties most dreadfully, it proved one morning when the sad days had begun to add themselves into weeks, that there was a great deal for him to do, as well as a great deal for Tilling to talk about. Lucia had employed a local lawyer over the making of her will, and today Mr Causton (*re* the affairs of Mrs Emmeline Lucas) came to see Georgie about it. He explained to him with a manner subtly compounded of sympathy and congratulation that the little sum of money to which Lucia had alluded was no less than £80,000. Georgie was, in fact, apart from certain legacies, her heir. He was much moved.

'Too kind of her,' he said. 'I had no idea – '

Mr Causton went on with great delicacy.

'It will be some months,' he said, 'before in the absence of fresh evidence, the death of my client can be legally assumed – '

'Oh, the longer, the better,' said Georgie rather vaguely, wiping his eyes, 'but what do you mean about fresh evidence?'

'The recovery, by washing ashore or other identification, of the lamented corpses,' said Mr Causton. 'In the interval the – the possibly late Mrs Lucas has left no provision for the contingency we have to face. If and when her death is proved, the staff of servants will receive their wages up to date, and a month's notice. Until then the estate, I take it, will be liable for the outgoings and the upkeep of Grebe. I would see to all that, but I felt that I must get your authority first.'

'Of course, naturally,' said Georgie.

'But here a difficulty arises,' said Mr Causton. 'I have no authority for drawing on the late – or, we hope, the present Mrs Lucas's balance at the bank. There is, you see, no fund out of which the current expenses of the upkeep of the house can be paid. There is more than a month's food and wages for her servants already owing.'

Georgie's face changed a little. A very little.

'I had better pay them myself,' he said. 'Would not that be the proper course?'

'I think, under the circumstances, that it would,' said Mr Causton. 'In fact, I don't see what else is to be done, unless all the servants were discharged at once, and the house shut up.'

'No, that would never do,' said Georgie. 'I must go down there and arrange about it all. If Mrs Lucas returns, how horrid for her to find all her servants who had been with her so long, gone.

Everything must carry on as if she had only gone for a visit somewhere and forgotten to send a cheque for expenses.'

Here then, at any rate, was something to do already, and Georgie, thinking that he would like a little walk on this brisk morning, and also feeling sure that he would like a little conversation with friends in the High Street, put on his thinner cape, for a hint of spring was in the air, and there were snowdrops abloom in the flower border of his little garden. Lucia, he remembered, always detested snowdrops: they hung their heads and were feeble; they typified for her slack though amiable inefficiency. In order to traverse the whole length of the High Street and get as many conversations as possible he went down by Mallards and Major Benjy's house. The latter, from the window of his study, where he so often enjoyed a rest or a little refreshment before and after his game of golf, saw him pass, and beckoned him in.

'Good morning, old boy,' he said. 'I've had a tremendous slice of luck: at least that is not quite the way to put it, but what I mean is – In fact, I've just had a visit from the solicitor of our lamented friend Elizabeth Mapp, God bless her, and he told me the most surprising news. I was monstrously touched by it: hadn't a notion of it, I assure you.'

'You don't mean to say – ' began Georgie.

'Yes I do. He informed me of the provisions of that dear woman's will. In memory of our long friendship, these were the very words – and I assure you I was not ashamed to turn away and wipe my eyes, when he told me – in memory of our long friendship she has left me that beautiful Mallards and the sum of ten thousand pounds, which I understand was the bulk of her fortune. What do you think of that?' he asked, allowing his exultation to get the better of him for the moment.

'No!' said Georgie, 'I congratulate – at least in case – '

'I know,' said Major Benjy. 'If it turns out to be too true that our friends have gone for ever, you're friendly enough to be glad that what I've told you is too true, too. Eh?'

'Quite, and I've had a visit from Mr Causton,' said Georgie, unable to contain himself any longer, 'and Lucia's left me Grebe and eighty thousand pounds.'

'My word! What a monstrous fortune,' cried the Major with a spasm of chagrin. 'I congrat— Anyhow, the same to you. I shall get a motor instead of going to my golf on that measly tram. Then there's Mallards for me to arrange about. I'm thinking of letting it furnished, servants and all. It'll be snapped up at ten guineas a week. Why, she got fifteen last summer from the other poor corpse.'

'I wouldn't,' said Georgie. 'Supposing she came back and found she couldn't get into her house for another month because you had let it – '

'God grant she may come back,' said the Major, without falling dead on the spot. 'But I see your point: it would be awkward. I'll think it over. Anyhow, of course, after a proper interval, when the tragedy is proved, I shall go and live there myself. Till then I shall certainly pay the servants' wages and the upkeep. Rather a drain, but it can't be helped. Board wages of twelve shillings a week is what I shall give them: they'll live like fighting cocks on that. By Jove, when I think of that terrible sight of the kitchen-table lying out there on the beach, it causes me such a sinking still. Have a drink: wonderful pre-war whisky.'

Georgie had not yet visited Grebe, and he found a thrilling though melancholy interest in seeing the starting-point of the catastrophe. The Christmas-tree, he ascertained, had stuck in the door of the kitchen, and the Padre had already been down to look at it, but had decided that the damage to it was irreparable. It was lying now in the garden from which soil and plants had been swept away by the flood, but Georgie could not bear to see it there, and directed that it should be put up, as a relic, in an empty outhouse. Perhaps a tablet on that as well as on the table. Then he had to interview Grosvenor, and make out a schedule of the servants' wages, the total of which rather astonished him. He saw the cook and told her that he had the kitchen-table in his yard, but she begged him not to send it back, as it had always been most inconvenient. Mrs Lucas, she told him, had had a feeling for it; she thought there was luck about it. Then she burst into tears and said it hadn't brought her mistress much luck after all. This was all dreadfully affecting, and Georgie told her that in this period of waiting during which they must not give up hope, all their wages would be paid as usual, and they must carry on as before, and keep the house in order. Then there were some unpaid bills of Lucia's, a rather appalling total, which must be discharged before long, and the kitchen must be renovated from the effects of the flood. It was after dark when he got back to Mallards Cottage again.

In the absence of what Mr Causton called further evidence in the way of corpses, and of alibis in the way of living human bodies, the Padre settled in the course of the next week to hold a memorial service, for unless one was held soon, they would all have got used to the bereavement, and the service would lose point and poignancy. It was obviously suitable that Major Benjy and Georgie, being the contingent heirs of the defunct ladies, should sit by themselves in a front pew as chief mourners, and Major Benjy ordered a black suit to be made for him without delay for use on this solemn occasion. The church-bell was tolled as if for a funeral service, and the two walked in side by side after the rest of the congregation had assembled, and took their places in a pew by themselves immediately in front of the reading-desk.

The service was of the usual character, and the Padre gave a most touching address on the text 'They were lovely and pleasant in their lives and in their death they were not divided.' He reminded his hearers how the two whom they mourned were as sisters, taking the lead in social activities, and dispensing to all who knew them their bountiful hospitalities. Their lives had been full of lovable energy. They had been at the forefront in all artistic and literary pursuits: indeed he might almost have taken the whole of the verse of which he had read them only the half as his text, and have added that they were swifter than eagles, they were stronger than lions. One of them had been known to them all for many years, and the name of Elizabeth Mapp was written on their hearts. The other was a newer comer, but she had wonderfully endeared herself to them in her briefer sojourn here, and it was typical of her beautiful nature that on the very day on which the disaster occurred, she had been busy with a Christmas-tree for the choristers in whom she took so profound an interest.

As regards the last sad scene, he need not say much about it, for never would any of them forget that touching, that ennobling, that teaching sight of the two, gallant in the face of death as they had ever been in that of life, being whirled out to sea. Mrs Lucas, in the ordeal which they would all have to face one day, gave that humorous greeting of hers, 'au reservoir' which they all knew so well, to her friends standing in safety on the shore, and then turned again to her womanly work of comforting and encouraging her weaker sister. 'May we all,' said the Padre, with a voice trembling with emotion, 'go to meet death in that serene and untroubled spirit, doing our duty to the last. And now – '

This sermon, at the request of a few friends, he had printed in the Parish Magazine next week, and copies were sent to everybody.

It was only natural that Tilling should feel relieved when the ceremony was over, for the weeks since the stranding of the kitchen-table had been like the period between a death and a funeral. The blinds were up again now, and life gradually resumed a more normal complexion. January ebbed away into February, February into March, and as the days lengthened with the returning sun, so the mirths and squabbles of Tilling grew longer and brighter.

But a certain stimulus which had enlivened them all since Lucia's advent from Riseholme was lacking. It was not wholly that there was no Lucia, nor, wholly, that there was no Elizabeth, it was the intense reactions which they had produced together that everyone missed so fearfully. Day after day those who were left met and talked in the High Street, but never was there news of that thrilling kind which since the summer had keyed existence up to so exciting a level. But it was interesting to see Major Benjy in his new motor, which he drove himself, and watch his hairbreadth escapes from collisions at sharp corners and to hear the appalling explosions of military language if any other vehicle came within a yard of his green bonnet.

'He seems to think,' said Diva to Mrs Bartlett, as they met on shopping errands one morning, 'that now he has got a motor nobody else may use the road at all.'

'A trumpery little car,' said Mrs Bartlett, 'I should have thought, with ten thousand pounds as good as in his pocket, he might have got himself something better.'

They were standing at the corner looking up towards Mallards, and Diva suddenly caught sight of a board on Major Benjy's house, announcing that it was for sale.

'Why, whatever's that?' she cried. 'That must have been put up only today. Good morning, Mr Georgie. What about Major Benjy's house?'

Georgie still wore a broad black band on his sleeve.

'Yes, he told me yesterday that he was going to move into Mallards next week,' he said. 'And he's going to have a sale of his furniture almost immediately.'

'That won't be much to write home about,' said Diva scornfully. 'A few moth-eaten tiger-skins which he said he shot in India.'

'I think he wants some money,' said Georgie. 'He's bought a motor, you see, and he has to keep up Mallards as well as his own house.'

'I call that very rash,' said Mrs Bartlett. 'I call that counting your chickens before they're hatched. Oh dear me, what a thing to have said! Dreadful!'

Georgie tactfully covered this up by a change of subject.

'I've made up my mind,' he said, 'and I'm going to put up a cenotaph in the churchyard to dear Lucia and Elizabeth.'

'What? Both?' asked Diva.

'Yes, I've thought it carefully over, and it's going to be both.'

'Major Benjy ought to go halves with you then,' said Diva.

'Well, I told him I was intending to do it,' said Georgie, 'and he didn't catch on. He only said "Capital idea", and took some whisky and soda. So I shan't say any more. I would really just as soon do it all myself.'

'Well, I do think that's mean of him,' said Diva. 'He ought anyhow to bear some part of the expense, considering everything. Instead of which he buys a motor-car which he can't drive. Go on about the cenotaph.'

'I saw it down at the stonemason's yard,' said Georgie, 'and that put the idea into my head. Beautiful white marble on the lines, though of course much smaller, of the one in London. It had been ordered, I found, as a tombstone, but then the man who ordered it went bankrupt, and it was on the stonemason's hands.'

'I've heard about it,' said Mrs Bartlett, in rather a superior voice. 'Kenneth told me you've told him, and we both think that it's a lovely idea.'

'The stonemason ought to let you have it cheap then,' said Diva.

'It wasn't very cheap,' said Georgie, 'but I've bought it, and they'll put it in its place today, just outside the south transept, and the Padre is going to dedicate it. Then there's the inscription. I shall have in loving memory of them, by me, and a bit of the Padre's text at the memorial service. Just "In death they were not divided".'

'Quite right. Don't put in about the eagles and the lions,' said Diva.

'No, I thought I would leave that out. Though I liked that part,' said Georgie for the sake of Mrs Bartlett.

'Talking of whisky,' said Diva, flying back, as her manner was, to a remote allusion, 'Major Benjy's finished all the pre-war whisky that Lucia gave him. At least I heard him ordering some more yesterday. Oh, and there's the notice of his sale. Old English furniture – yes, that may mean two things, and I know which of them it is. Valuable works of Art. Well, I never! A print of the "Monarch of the Glen" and a photograph of the "Soul's Awakening". Rubbish! Fine tiger-skins! The skins may be all right, but they're bald.'

'My dear, how severe you are,' said Georgie. 'Now I must go and see how they're getting on with the inscription. Au reservoir.'

Diva nodded at Evie Bartlett.

'Nice to hear that again,' she said. 'I've not heard it – well, since.'

The cenotaph with its inscription in bold leaded letters to say that Georgie had erected it in memory of the two undivided ladies, roused much admiration, and a full-page reproduction of it appeared in the Parish Magazine for April, which appeared on the last day of March. The stone-cutter had slightly mis-calculated the space at his disposal for the inscription, and the words 'Elizabeth Mapp' were considerably smaller than the words 'Emmeline Lucas' in order to get them into the line. Though Tilling said nothing about that, it was felt that the error was productive of a very suitable effect, if a symbolic meaning was interpreted into it. Georgie was considered to have done it very handsomely and to be behaving in a way that contrasted most favourably with the conduct of Major Benjy, for whereas Georgie was keeping up Grebe at great expense, and restoring, all at his own charge, the havoc the flood had wrought in the garden, Major Benjy, after unsuccessfully trying to let Mallards at ten guineas a week, had moved into the house, and, with a precipitation that was as rash as it was indelicate, was already negotiating about the disposal of his own, and was to have a sale of his furniture on April the first. He had bought a motor, he had replenished the cellars at Mallards with strong wines and more pre-war whisky, he was spending money like water and on the evening of this last day of March he gave a bridge-party in the garden-room.

Georgie and Diva and Mrs Padre were the guests at this party: there had been dinner first, a rich elaborate dinner, and bridge afterwards up till midnight. It had been an uncomfortable even-ing, and before it was over they all wished they had not come, for Major Benjy had alluded to it as a house-warming, which showed that either his memory was going, or that his was a very callous nature, for no one whose perceptions were not of the commonest could possibly have used that word so soon. He had spoken of his benefactress with fulsome warmth, but it was painfully evident from what source this posthumous affection sprang. He thought of having the garden-room redecorated, the house wanted brightening up a bit, he even offered each of them one of Miss Mapp's water-colour sketches, of which there was a profusion on the walls, as a memento of their friend, God bless her. . . . There he was straddling in the doorway with the air of a vulgar *nouveau riche* owner of an ancestral property, as they went their ways homewards into the night, and they heard him bolt and lock the door and put up the chain which Lucia in her tenancy had had repaired in order to keep out the uninvited and informal visits of Miss Mapp. 'It would serve him jolly well right,' thought Georgie, 'if she came back.'

12

It was a calm and beautiful night with a high tide that overflowed the channel of the river. There was spread a great sheet of moonlit water over the submerged meadows at the margin, and it came up to the foot of the rebuilt bank opposite Grebe. Between four and five of the morning of April the first, a trawler entered the mouth of the river, and just at the time when the stars were growing pale and the sky growing red with the coming dawn, it drew up at the little quay to the east of the town, and was moored to the shore. There stepped out of it two figures clad in overalls and tarpaulin jackets.

'I think we had better go straight to Mallards, dear,' said Elizabeth, 'as it's so close, and have a nice cup of tea to warm ourselves. Then you can telephone from there to Grebe, and tell them to send the motor up for you.'

'I shall ring up Georgie too,' said Lucia. 'I can't bear to think that his suspense should last a minute more than is necessary.'

Elizabeth pointed upwards.

'See, there's the sun catching the top of the church-tower,' she said. 'Little did I think I should ever see dear Tilling again.'

'I never had the slightest doubt about it,' said Lucia. 'Look, there are the fields we floated across on the kitchen-table. I wonder what happened to it.'

They climbed the steps at the south-east angle of the town, and up the slope to the path across the churchyard. This path led close by the south side of the church, and the white marble of the cenotaph gleamed in the early sunlight.

'What a handsome tomb,' said Elizabeth. 'It's quite new. But how does it come here? No one has been buried in the church-yard for a hundred years.'

Lucia gave a gasp as the polished lead letters caught her eye. 'But it's us!' she said.

They stood side by side in their tarpaulins, and together in a sort of chant read the inscription aloud.

THIS STONE WAS ERECTED BY
GEORGE PILLSON
IN LOVING MEMORY OF
EMMELINE LUCAS AND Elizabeth Mapp
LOST AT SEA ON BOXING DAY, 1930

———

'IN DEATH THEY WERE NOT DIVIDED.'

'I've never heard of such a thing,' cried Lucia. 'I call it most premature of Georgie, assuming that I was dead like that. The inscription must be removed instantly. All the same it was kind of him and what a lot of money it must have cost him! Gracious me, I suppose he thought – Let us hurry, Elizabeth.'

Elizabeth was still staring at the stone.

'I am puzzled to know why my name is put in such exceed-ingly small letters,' she said acidly. 'You can hardly read it. As you say, dear, it was most premature of him. I should call it impertinent, and I'm very glad dear Major Benjy had nothing to do with it. There's an indelicacy about it.'

They went quickly on past Mallards Cottage where the blinds were still down, and there was the window of the garden-room from which each had made so many thrilling observations, and the red-brick front, glowing in the sunlight, of Mallards itself. As they crossed the cobbled way to the front door, Elizabeth looked down towards the High Street and saw on Major Benjy's house next door the house-agent's board announcing that the freehold of this desirable residence was for disposal. There were bills pasted on the walls announcing the sale of furniture to take place there that very day.

Her face turned white, and she laid a quaking hand on Lucia's arm.

'Look, Major Benjy's house is for sale,' she faltered. 'Oh, Lucia, what has happened? Have we come back from the dead, as it were, to find that it's our dear old friend instead? And to think – ' She could not complete the sentence.

'My dear, you mustn't jump at any such terrible conclusions,' said Lucia. 'He may have changed his house – '

Elizabeth shook her head; she was determined to believe the worst, and indeed it seemed most unlikely that Major Benjy who had lived in the same house for a full quarter of a century could have gone to any new abode but one. Meantime, eager to put an end to this suspense, Elizabeth kept pressing the bell, and Lucia plying the knocker of Mallards.

'They all sleep on the attic floor,' said Elizabeth, 'but I think they must hear us soon if we go on. Ah, there's a step on the stairs. Someone is coming down.'

They heard the numerous bolts on the door shot back, they heard the rattle of the released chain. The door was opened and there within stood Major Benjy. He had put on his dinner jacket over his Jaeger pyjamas, and had carpet slippers on his feet. He was sleepy and bristly and very cross.

'Now what's all this about, my men,' he said, seeing two tarpaulined figures on the threshold. 'What do you mean by waking me up with that infernal – '

Elizabeth's suspense was quite over.

'You wretch,' she cried in a fury. 'What do *you* mean? Why are you in my house? Ah, I guess! He! He! You learned about my will, did you? You thought you wouldn't wait to step into a dead woman's shoes, but positively tear them off my living feet. My will shall be revoked this day: I promise you that. . . . Now out you go, you horrid supplanter! Off to your own house with you, for you shan't spend another minute in mine.'

During this impassioned address Major Benjy's face changed to an expression of the blankest dismay, as if he had seen something much worse (as indeed he had) than a ghost. He pulled pieces of himself together.

'But, my dear Miss Elizabeth,' he said. 'You'll allow me surely to get my clothes on, and above all to say one word of my deep thankfulness that you and Mrs Lucas – it is Mrs Lucas, isn't it? – '

'Get out!' said Elizabeth, stamping her foot. 'Thankfulness indeed! There's a lot of thankfulness in your face! Go away! Shoo!'

Major Benjy had faced wounded tigers (so he said) in India, but then he had a rifle in his hand. He could not face his benefactress, and, with first one slipper and then the other dropping off his feet, he hurried down the few yards of pavement to his own house. The two ladies entered: Elizabeth banged the door and put up the chain.

'So that's that,' she observed (and undoubtedly it was). 'Ah, here's Withers. Withers, we've come back, and though you ought never to have let the Major set foot in my house, I don't blame you, for I feel sure he bullied you into it.'

'Oh, miss!' said Withers. 'Is it you? – Fancy! Well, that is a surprise!'

'Now get Mrs Lucas and me a cup of tea,' said Elizabeth, 'and then she's going back to Grebe. That wretch hasn't been sleeping in my room, I trust?'

'No, in the best spare bedroom,' said Withers.

'Then get my room ready and I shall go to bed for a few hours. We've been up all night. Then, Withers, take all Major Benjy's clothes and his horrid pipes, and all that belongs to him, and put them on the steps outside. Ring him up, and tell him where he will find them. But not one foot shall he set in my house again.'

Lucia went to the telephone and rang up Cadman's cottage for her motor. She heard his exclamation of 'My Gawd', she heard (what she supposed was) Foljambe's cry of astonishment, and then she rang up Georgie. He and his household were all a-bed and asleep when the telephone began its summons, but presently the persistent tinkle penetrated into his consciousness, and made him dream that he was again watching Lucia whirling down the flood on the kitchen-table and ringing an enormous dinner bell as she swept by the steps. Then he became completely awake and knew it was only the telephone.

'The tarsome thing!' he muttered. 'Who on earth can it be ringing one up at this time? Go on ringing then till you're tired. I shall go to sleep again.'

In spite of these resolutions, he did nothing of the kind. So ceaseless was the summons that in a minute or two he got out of bed, and putting on his striped dressing-gown (blue and yellow) went down to his sitting-room.

'Yes. Who is it? What do you want?' he said crossly.

There came a little merry laugh, and then a voice, which he had thought was silent for ever, spoke in unmistakable accents.

'Georgie! Georgino mio!' it said.

His heart stood still.

'What – What?' he cried.

'Yes, it's Lucia,' said the voice. 'Me's tum home, Georgie.'

Eighty thousand pounds (less death duties) and Grebe seemed to sweep by him like an avalanche, and fall into the gulf of things that might have been. But it was not the cold blast of that ruin that filled his eyes with tears.

'Oh my dear!' he cried. 'Is it really you? Lucia, where are you? Where are you talking from?'

'Mallards. Elizabeth and I – '

'What, both of you?' called Georgie. 'Then – where's Major Benjy?'

'Just gone home,' said Lucia discreetly. 'And as soon as I've had a cup of tea I'm going to Grebe.'

'But I must come round and see you at once,' said Georgie. 'I'll just put some things on.'

'Yes, do,' said Lucia. 'Presto, presto, Georgie.'

Careless of his reputation for being the best-dressed man in Tilling, he put on his dress trousers and a pullover, and his thick brown cape, and did not bother about his *toupet*. The front door of Mallards was open, and Elizabeth's servants were laying out on the top step a curious collection of golf clubs and toothbrushes and clothes. From mere habit – everyone in Tilling had

263

the habit – he looked up at the window of the garden-room as he passed below it, and was astonished to see two mariners in sou'wester caps and tarpaulin jackets kissing their hands to him. He had only just time to wonder who these could possibly be when he guessed. He flew into Lucia's arms, then wondered if he ought to kiss Elizabeth too. But, there was a slight reserve about her which caused him to refrain. He was not brilliant enough at so early an hour to guess that she had seen the smaller lettering in which her loving memory was recorded.

There was but time for a few ejaculations and a promise from Georgie to dine at Grebe that night, before Lucia's motor arrived, and the imperturbable Cadman touched his cap and said to Lucia, 'Very pleased to see you back, ma'am,' as she picked her way between the growing deposits of socks and other more intimate articles of male attire which were now being ranged on the front steps. Georgie hurried back to Mallards Cottage to dress in a manner more worthy of his reputation, and Elizabeth up to her bedroom for a few hours' sleep. Below her oil-skins she still wore the ragged remains of the clothes in which she had left Tilling on Boxing Day, and now she drew out of the pocket of her frayed and sea-stained jacket, a halfsheet of discoloured paper. She unfolded it and having once more read the mystic words 'Take two hen lobsters', she stowed it safely away for future use.

Meantime Major Benjy next door had been the prey of the most sickening reflections; whichever way he turned, fate gave him some stinging blow that set him staggering and reeling in another direction. Leaning out of an upper window of his own house, he observed his clothes and boots and articles of toilet being laid out like a bird's breakfast on the steps of Mallards, and essaying to grind his teeth with rage he discovered that his upper dental plate must still be reposing in a glass of water in the best spare bedroom which he had lately quitted in such haste. To recover his personal property was the first necessity, and when from his point of observation he saw that the collection had grown to a substantial size, he crept up the pavement, seized a bundle of miscellaneous articles, as many as he could carry, then stole back again, dropping a nail-brush here and a sock-suspender there, and dumped them in his house. Three times he must go on these degrading errands, before he had cleared all the birds' breakfast away; indeed he was an early bird feeding on the worms of affliction.

Tilling was beginning to awake now: the milkman came clattering down the street and, looking in amazement at his dishevelled figure, asked whether he wanted his morning supply left at his own house or at Mallards: Major Benjy turned on him so appalling a face that he left no milk at either and turned swiftly into the less alarming air of Porpoise Street. Again he had to make the passage of his Via Dolorosa to glean the objects which had dropped from his overburdened arms, and as he returned he heard a bumping noise behind him, and saw his new portmanteau hauled out by Withers rolling down the steps into the street. He emerged again when Withers had shut the door, put more gleanings into it and pulled it into his house. There he made a swift and sorry toilet, for there was business to be done which would not brook delay. Already the preparations for the sale of his furniture were almost finished; the carpet and hearth-rug in his sitting-room were tied up together and labelled Lot 1: the fire-irons and a fishing-rod and a rhinoceros-hide whip were Lot 2; a kitchen tray with packs of cards, a tobacco jar, a piece of chipped cloisonné ware and a roll of toilet paper formed an unappetizing Lot 3. The sale must be stopped at once and he went down to the auctioneer's in the High Street and informed him that owing to circumstances over which he had no control he was compelled to cancel it. It was pointed out to him that considerable expense had already been incurred for the printing and display of the bills that announced it, for the advertisements in the local press, for the time and trouble already spent in arranging and marking the lots, but the Major bawled out: 'Damn it all, the things are mine and I won't sell one of them. Send me in your bill.' Then he had to go to the house agent's and tell him to withdraw his house from the market and take down his board, and coming out of the office he ran into Irene, already on her way to Grebe, who cried out: 'They've come back, old Benjy-wenjy. Joy! Joy!'

The most immediate need of having a roof over his head and

a chair to sit on was now provided for, and as he had already dismissed his own servants, taking those of Mallards, he must go to another agency to find some sort of cook or charwoman till he could get his establishment together again. They promised to send an elderly lady, highly respectable though rather deaf and weak in the legs, tomorrow if possible. Back he came to his house with such cold comfort to cheer him, and observed on the steps of Mallards half a dozen bottles of wine. 'My God, my cellar,' muttered the Major, 'there are dozens and dozens of my wine and my whisky in the house!' Again he crept up to the abhorred door and, returning with the bottles, put a kettle on to boil, and began cutting the strings that held the lots together. Just then the church-bells burst out into a joyful peal, and it was not difficult to conjecture the reason of their unseemly mirth. All this before breakfast . . .

A cup of hot strong tea without any milk restored not only his physical stability but also his mental capacity for suffering, and he sat down to think. There was the financial side of the disaster first of all, a thing ghastly to contemplate. He had bought (but not yet paid for) a motor, some dozens of wine, a suit of new clothes, as well as the mourning habiliments in which he had attended the memorial service, quantities of stationery with the Mallards stamp on it, a box of cigars and other luxuries too numerous to mention. It was little comfort to remember that he had refused to contribute to the cenotaph; a small saving like that did not seem to signify. Then what view, he wondered, would his benefactress, when she knew all, take of his occupation of Mallards? – She might find out (indeed being who she was, she would not fail to do so) that he had tried to let it at ten guineas a week and she might therefore send him in a bill on that scale for the fortnight he had spent there, together with that for her servants' wages, and for garden-produce and use of her piano. Luckily he had only eaten some beetroot out of the garden, and he had had the piano tuned. Out of all these staggering expenses, the only items which were possibly recoverable were the wages he had paid to the staff of Mallards between Boxing Day and the date of his tenancy: these Elizabeth might consent to set against the debits. Not less hideous than this financial débâcle that stared him in the face, was the loss of prestige in Tilling. Tilling, he knew, had disapproved of his precipitancy in entering into Mallards, and Tilling, full, like Irene, of joy, joy for the return of the lost, would simply hoot with laughter at him. He could visualize with awful clearness the chatting groups in the High Street which would vainly endeavour to suppress their smiles as he approached. The day of swank was past and done, he would have to be quiet and humble and grateful to anybody who treated him with the respect to which he had been accustomed.

He unrolled a tiger-skin to lay down again in his hall: a cloud of dust and deciduous hair rose from it, pungent like snuff, and the remaining glass eye fell out of the socket. He bawled 'Quai-hai' before he remembered that till tomorrow at least he would be alone in the house, and that even then his attendant would be deaf. He opened his front door and looked out into the street again, and there on the door-step of Mallards was another dozen or so of wine and a walking-stick. Again he stole out to recover his property with the hideous sense that perhaps Elizabeth was watching him from the garden-room. His dental plate – thank God – was there too on the second step, all by itself, gleaming in the sun, and seeming to grin at him in a very mocking manner. After that throughout the morning he looked out at intervals as he rested from the awful labour of laying carpets and putting beds together, and there were usually some more bottles waiting for him, with stray golf clubs, bridge-markers and packs of cards. About one o'clock just as he was collecting what must surely be the last of these bird breakfasts, the door of Mallards opened and Elizabeth stepped carefully over his umbrella and a box of cigars. She did not appear to see him. It seemed highly probable that she was going to revoke her will.

Georgie, as well as Major Benjy, had to do a little thinking, when he returned from his visit at dawn to Mallards. It concerned two points, the cenotaph and the kitchen-table. The cenotaph had not been mentioned in those few joyful ejaculations he had exchanged with Lucia, and he hoped that the ladies had not seen it. So after breakfast he went down to the stonemason's and begged him to send a trolly and a hefty lot of men up to the churchyard at once, and remove the monument to the back-yard of Mallards Cottage, which at present was chiefly occupied by the kitchen-table under a tarpaulin. But Mr Marble (such was his appropriate name) shook his head over this, the cenotaph had been dedicated, and he felt sure that a faculty must be procured before it could be removed. That would never do: Georgie could not wait for a faculty, whatever that was, and he ordered that the inscription, anyhow, should be effaced without delay: surely no faculty was needed to destroy all traces of a lie. Mr Marble must send some men up to chip, and chip and chip for all they were worth till these beautiful lead letters were detached and the surface of the stone cleared of all that erroneous information.

'And then I'll tell you what,' said Georgie, with a sudden splendid thought. 'Why not paint on to it (I can't afford any more cutting) the inscription that was to have been put on it when that man went bankrupt and I bought the monument instead? He'll get his monument for nothing, and I shall get rid of mine, which is just what I want. ... That's beautiful. Now you must send a trolly to my house and take a very big kitchen-table, *the* one in fact, back to Grebe. It must go in through the door of the kitchen-garden and be put quietly into the kitchen. And I particularly want it done today.'

All went well with these thoughtful plans. Georgie saw with his own eyes the last word of his inscription disappear in chips of marble; and he carried away all the lead letters in case they might come in useful for something, though he could not have said what: perhaps he would have 'Mallards Cottage' let into the threshold of his house for that long inscription would surely contain the necessary letters. Rather a pretty and original idea. Then he ascertained that the kitchen-table had been restored to its place while Lucia slept, and he drove down at dinner-time feeling that he had done his best. He wore his white waistcoat with onyx buttons for the happy occasion.

Lucia was looking exceedingly well and much sunburnt. By way of resting she had written a larger number of post cards to all her friends, both here and elsewhere, than Georgie had ever seen together in one place.

'Georgino,' she cried. 'There's so much to say that I hardly know where to begin. I think my adventures first, quite shortly, for I shall dictate a full account of them to my secretary, and have a party next week for all Tilling, and read them out to you. Two parties, I expect, for I don't think I shall be able to read it all in one evening. Now we go back to Boxing Day.'

'I went into the kitchen that afternoon,' she said as they sat down to dinner, 'and there was Elizabeth. I asked her, naturally, don't you think? – why she was there, and she said, "I came to thank you for that delicious *pâté*, and to ask if – " That was as far as she got – I must return to that later – when the bank burst with a frightful roar, and the flood poured in. I was quite calm. We got on to, I should really say into the table – By the way, was the table ever washed up?'

'Yes,' said Georgie, 'it's in your kitchen now. I sent it back.'

'Thank you, my dear. We got into the kitchen-table, really a perfect boat, I can't think why they don't make more like it, flew by the steps – oh, did the Padre catch a dreadful cold? Such a splash it was, and that was the only drop of water that we shipped at all.'

'No, but he lost his umbrella, the one you'd given him,' said Georgie, 'and the Padre of the Roman Catholic Church found it, a week afterwards and returned it to him. Wasn't that a co-incidence? Go on. Oh no, wait a minute. What did you mean by calling out "Just wait till we get back"?'

'Why of course I wanted to tell you that I had found Elizabeth in my kitchen,' said Lucia.

'Hurrah! I guessed you meant something of the kind,' said Georgie.

'Well, out we went – I've never been so fast in a kitchen-table before – out to sea in a blinding sea-fog. My dear; poor Elizabeth! No nerve of any kind! I told her that if we were rescued, there was nothing to cry about, and if we weren't all our troubles would soon be over.'

Grosvenor had put some fish before Lucia. She gave an awful shudder.

'Oh, take it away,' she said. 'Never let me see fish again, par-ticularly cod, as long as I live. Tell the cook. You'll see why

269

presently, Georgie. Elizabeth got hysterical and said she wasn't fit to die, so I scolded her – the best plan always with hysterical people – and told her that the longer she lived, the less fit she would be, and that did her a little good. Then it got dark, and there were fog-horns hooting all round us, and we called and yelled, but they had much more powerful voices than we, and nobody heard us. One of them grew louder and louder, until I could hardly bear it, and then we bumped quite gently into it, the fog-horn's boat I mean.'

'Gracious, you might have upset,' said Georgie.

'No, it was like a liner coming up to the quay,' said Lucia. 'No shock of any kind. Then when the fog-horn stopped, they heard us shouting, and took us aboard. It was an Italian trawler on its way to the cod fishery (that's why I never want to see cod again) on the Gallagher banks.'

'That was lucky too,' said Georgie, 'you could make them understand a little. Better than if they had been Spanish.'

'About the same, because I'm convinced, as I told Elizabeth, that they talked a very queer Neapolitan dialect. It was rather unlucky, in fact. But as the Captain understood English perfectly, it didn't matter. They were most polite, but they couldn't put us ashore, for we were miles out in the Channel by this time, and also quite lost. They hadn't an idea where the coast of England or any other coast was.'

'Wireless?' suggested Georgie.

'It had been completely smashed up by the dreadful gale the day before. We drifted about in the fog for two days, and when it cleared and they could take the sun again – a nautical expression, Georgie – we were somewhere off the coast of Devonshire. The captain promised to hail any passing vessel bound for England that he saw but he didn't see any. So he continued his course to the Gallagher bank, which is about as far from Ireland as it is from America, and there we were for two months. Cod, cod, cod, nothing but cod, and Elizabeth snoring all night in the cabin we shared together. Bitterly cold very often: how glad I was that I knew so many callisthenic exercises! I shall tell you all about that time at my lecture. Then we found that there was a Tilling trawler on the bank, and when it was ready to start home we transhipped – they call it – and got back, as you know, this morning. That's the skeleton.'

'It's the most wonderful skeleton I ever heard,' said Georgie. 'Do write your lecture quick.'

Lucia fixed Georgie with her gimlet eye. It had lost none of its penetrative power by being so long at sea.

'Now it's your turn for a little,' she said. 'I expect I know rather more than you think. First about that memorial service.'

'Oh, do you know about that?' he asked.

'Certainly. I found the copy of the Parish Magazine waiting for me, and read it in bed. I consider it to have been very premature. You attended it, I think.'

'We all did,' said Georgie. 'And after all the Padre said extremely nice things about you.'

'I felt very much flattered. But all the same it was too early. And you and Major Benjy were chief mourners.'

Georgie considered for a moment.

'I'm going to make a clean breast of it,' he said. 'You told me you had left me Grebe, and a small sum of money, and your lawyer told me what that meant. My dear, I was too touched, and naturally, it was proper that I should be chief mourner. It was the same with Major Benjy. He had seen Elizabeth's will, so there we were.'

Suddenly an irresistible curiosity seized him.

'Major Benjy hasn't been seen all day,' he said. 'Do tell me what happened this morning at Mallards. You only said on the telephone that he had just gone home.'

'Yes, bag and baggage,' said Lucia. 'At least he went first and his bag and baggage followed. Socks and things, you saw some of them on the top step. Elizabeth was mad with rage, a perfect fishwife. So suitable after coming back from the Gallagher bank. But tell me more. What was the next thing after the memorial service?'

The hope of keeping the knowledge of the cenotaph from Lucia became very dim. If Lucia had seen the February number of the Parish Magazine she had probably also seen the April number in which appeared the full page reproduction of that monument. Besides, there was the gimlet eye.

'The next thing was that I put up a beautiful cenotaph to you and Elizabeth,' said Georgie firmly. ' "In loving memory of by me". But I've had the inscription erased today.'

Lucia laid her hand on his.

'Dear Georgie, I'm glad you told me,' she said. 'As a matter of fact I knew, because Elizabeth and I studied it this morning. I was vexed at first, but now I think it's rather dear of you. It must have cost a lot of money.'

'It did,' said Georgie. 'And what did Elizabeth think about it?'

'Merely furious because her name was in smaller letters than mine,' said Lucia. 'So like the poor thing.'

'Was she terribly tarsome all these months?' asked Georgie.

'Tiresome's not quite the word,' said Lucia judicially. 'Deficient rather than tiresome, except incidentally. She had no idea of the tremendous opportunities she was getting. She never rose to her chances, nor forgot our little discomforts and that everlasting smell of fish. Whereas I learned such lots of things, Georgie: the Italian for starboard and port – those are the right and left sides of the ship – and how to tie an anchor-knot and a running noose, and a clove-hitch, and how to splice two ends of fishing-line together, and all sorts of things of the most curious and interesting kind. I shall show you some of them at my lecture. I used to go about the deck barefoot (Lucia had very pretty feet) and pull on anchors and capstans and things, and managed never to tumble out of my berth on to the floor when the ship was rolling frightfully, and not to be seasick. But poor Elizabeth was always bumping on to the floor, and sometimes being sick there. She had no spirit. Little moans and sighs and regrets that she ever came down the Tilling hill on Boxing Day.'

Lucia leaned forward and regarded Georgie steadfastly.

'I couldn't fathom her simply because she was so superficial,' she said. 'But I feel sure that there was something on her mind all the time. She used often to seem to be screwing herself up to confess something to me, and then not to be able to get it out.

No courage. And though I can make no guess as to what it actually was, I believe I know its general nature.'

'How thrilling!' cried Georgie. 'Tell me!'

Lucia's eye ceased to bore, and became of far-off focus, keen still but speculative, as if she was Einstein concentrating on some cosmic deduction.

'Georgie, why did she come into my kitchen like a burglar on Boxing Day?' she asked. 'She told me she had come to thank me for that *pâté* I sent her. But that wasn't true: anyone could see that it wasn't. Nobody goes into kitchens to thank people for *pâté*.'

'Diva guessed that she had gone there to see the Christmas-tree,' said Georgie. 'You weren't on very good terms at the time. We all thought that brilliant of her.'

'Then why shouldn't she have said so?' asked Lucia. 'I believe it was something much meaner and more underhand than that. And I am convinced – I have those perceptions sometimes, as you know very well – that all through the months of our Odyssey she wanted to tell me why she was there, and was ashamed of doing so. Naturally I never asked her, because if she didn't choose to tell me, it would be beneath me to force a confidence. There we were together on the Gallagher Bank, she all to bits all the time, and I should have scorned myself for attempting to worm it out of her. But the more I think of it, Georgie, the more convinced I am, that what she had to tell me and couldn't, concerned that. After all, I had unmasked every single plot she made against me before, and I knew the worst of her up till that moment. She had something on her mind, and that something was why she was in my kitchen.'

Lucia's far-away prophetic aspect cleared.

'I shall find out all right,' she said. 'Poor Elizabeth will betray herself some time. But Georgie, how in those weeks I missed my music! Not a piano on board any of the trawlers assembled there! Just a few concertinas and otherwise nothing except cod. Let us go, in a minute, into my music-room and have some Mozartino again. But first I want to say one thing.'

Georgie took a rapid survey of all he had done in his

conviction that Lucia had long ago been drowned. But if she knew about the memorial service and the cenotaph there could be nothing more except the kitchen-table, and that was now in its place again. She knew all that mattered. Lucia began to speak baby-talk.

'Georgie,' she said. 'Oo have had dweffel disappointy – '

That was too much. Georgie thumped the table quite hard.

'I haven't,' he cried. 'How dare you say that?'

'Ickle joke, Georgie,' piped Lucia. 'Haven't had joke for so long with that melancholy Liblib. 'Pologize. Oo not angry wif Lucia?'

'No, but don't do it again,' said Georgie. 'I won't have it.'

'You shan't then,' said Lucia, relapsing into the vernacular of adults. 'Now all this house is spick and span, and Grosvenor tells me you've been paying all their wages, week by week.'

'Naturally,' said Georgie.

'It was very dear and thoughtful of you. You saw that my house was ready to welcome my return, and you must send me in all the bills and everything tomorrow and I'll pay them at once, and I thank you enormously for your care of it. And send me in the bill for the cenotaph too. I want to pay for it, I do indeed. It was a loving impulse of yours, Georgie, though, thank goodness, a hasty one. But I can't bear to think that you're out of pocket because I'm alive. Don't answer: I shan't listen. And now let's go straight to the piano and have one of our duets, the one we played last, that heavenly Mozartino.'

They went into the next room. There was the duet ready on the piano, which much looked as if Lucia had been at it already, and she slid on to the top music-stool.

'We both come in on the third beat,' said she. 'Are you ready? Now! Uno, due, TRE!'

13

The wretched Major Benjy, who had not been out all day except for interviews with agents and miserable traverses between his house and the doorsteps of Mallards, dined alone that night (if you could call it dinner) on a pork pie and a bottle of Burgundy. A day's hard work had restored the lots of his abandoned sale to their proper places, and a little glue had restored its eye to the bald tiger. He felt worse than bald himself, he felt flayed, and God above alone knew what fresh skinnings were in store for him. All Tilling must have had its telephone-bells (as well as the church bells) ringing from morning till night with messages of congratulation and suitable acknowledgements between the returned ladies and their friends, and he had never felt so much like a pariah before. Diva had just passed his windows (clearly visible in the lamplight, for he had not put up the curtains of his snuggery yet) and he had heard her knock on the door of Mallards. She must have gone to dine with the fatal Elizabeth, and what were they talking about now? Too well he knew, for he knew Elizabeth.

If in spirit he could have been present in the dining-room, where only last night he had so sumptuously entertained Diva and Georgie and Mrs Bartlett, and had bidden them punish the port, he would not have felt much more cheerful.

'In my best spare room, Diva, would you believe it?' said Elizabeth, 'with all the drawers full of socks and shirts and false teeth, wasn't it so, Withers? and the cellar full of wine. What he has consumed of my things, goodness only knows. There was that *pâté* which Lucia gave me only the day before we were whisked out to sea – '

'But that was three months ago,' said Diva.

' – and he used my coal and my electric light as if they were his own, not to mention firing,' said Elizabeth, going on exactly where she had left off, 'and a whole row of beetroot.'

Diva was bursting to hear the story of the voyage. She knew that Georgie was dining with Lucia, and he would be telling everybody about it tomorrow, but if only Elizabeth would leave the beetroot alone and speak of the other she herself would be another focus of information instead of being obliged to listen to Georgie.

'Dear Elizabeth,' she said 'what does a bit of beetroot matter compared to what you've been through? When an old friend like you has had such marvellous experiences as I'm sure you must have, nothing else counts. Of course I'm sorry about your beetroot: most annoying, but I do want to hear about your adventures.'

'You'll hear all about them soon,' said Elizabeth, 'for tomorrow I'm going to begin a full history of it all. Then, as soon as it's finished, I shall have a big tea-party, and instead of bridge afterwards I shall read it to you. That's absolutely confidential, Diva. Don't say a word about it, or Lucia may steal my idea or do it first.'

'Not a word,' said Diva. 'But surely you can tell me some bits.'

'Yes, there is a certain amount which I shan't mention publicly,' Elizabeth said. 'Things about Lucia which I should never dream of stating openly.'

'Those are just the ones I should like to hear about most,' said Diva. 'Just a few little titbits.'

Elizabeth reflected a moment.

'I don't want to be hard on her,' she said, 'for after all we were together, and what would have happened if I had not been there, I can't think. A little off her head perhaps with panic: that is the most charitable explanation. As we swept by the town on our way out to sea she shrieked out – perhaps you heard her – "Au reservoir: just wait till we come back." Diva, I am not easily shocked, but I must say I was appalled. Death stared us in the face and all she could do was to make jokes! There was I sitting quiet and calm, preparing myself to meet the solemn moment as a Christian should, with this screaming hyaena for my companion. Then out we went to sea, in that blinding fog, tossing and pitching on the waves, till we went crash into the side of a ship which was invisible in the darkness.'

'How awful!' said Diva. 'I wonder you didn't upset,'

'Certainly it was miraculous,' said Elizabeth. 'We were battered about, the blows against the table were awful, and if I hadn't kept my head and clung on to the ship's side, we must have upset. They had heard our calls by then, and I sprang on to the rope-ladder they put down, without a moment's pause, so as to lighten the table for Lucia, and then she came up too.'

Elizabeth paused a moment.

'Diva, you will bear me witness that I always said, in spite of Amelia Faraglione, that Lucia didn't know a word of Italian, and it was proved I was right. It was an Italian boat, and our great Italian scholar was absolutely flummoxed, and the Captain had to talk to us in English. There!'

'Go on,' said Diva breathlessly.

'The ship was a fishing trawler bound for the Gallagher Banks, and we were there for two months, and then we found another trawler on its way home to Tilling, and it was from that we landed this morning. But I shan't tell you of our life and adventures, for I'm reserving that for my reading to you.'

'No, never mind then,' said Diva. 'Tell me intimate things about Lucia.'

Elizabeth sighed.

'We mustn't judge anybody,' she said, 'and I won't: but oh, the nature that revealed itself! The Italians were a set of coarse, lascivious men of the lowest type, and Lucia positively revelled in their society. Every day she used to walk about the deck, often with bare feet, and skip and do her callisthenics, and learn a few words of Italian; she sat with this one or that, with her fingers actually entwined with his, while he pretended to teach her to tie a knot or a clove-hitch or something that probably had an improper meaning as well. Such flirtation (at her age too), such promiscuousness, I have never seen. But I don't judge her, and I beg you won't.'

'But didn't you speak to her about it?' asked Diva.

'I used to try to screw myself up to it,' said Elizabeth, 'but her lightness positively repelled me. We shared a cabin about as big as a dog kennel, and oh, the sleepless nights when I used to be thrown from the shelf where I lay! Even then she wanted to instruct me, and show me how to wedge myself in. Always that dreadful superior attitude, that mania to teach everybody everything except Italian, which we have so often deplored. But that was nothing. It was her levity from the time when the flood poured into the kitchen at Grebe – '

'Do tell me about that,' cried Diva. 'That's almost the most interesting thing of all. Why had she taken you into the kitchen?'

Elizabeth laughed.

'Dear thing!' she said. 'What a lovely appetite you have for details! You might as well expect me to remember what I had for breakfast that morning. She and I had both gone into the kitchen; there we were, and we were looking at the Christmas-tree. Such a tawdry tinselly tree! Rather like her. Then the flood poured in, and I saw that our only chance was to embark on the kitchen-table. By the way, was it ever washed up?'

'Oh yes, without a scratch on it,' said Diva, thinking of the battering it was supposed to have undergone against the side of the trawler . . .

Elizabeth had evidently not reckoned on its having come ashore, and rose.

'I am surprised that it didn't go to bits,' she said. 'But let us go into the garden-room. We must really talk about that wretched sponger next door. Is it true he's bought a motor-car out of the money he hoped my death would bring him? And all that wine: bottles and bottles, so Withers told me. Oceans of champagne. How is he to pay for it all now with his miserable little income on which he used to pinch and scrape along before?'

'That's what nobody knows,' said Diva. 'An awful crash for him. So rash and hasty, as we all felt.'

They settled themselves comfortably by the fire, after Elizabeth had had one peep between the curtains.

'I'm not the least sorry for having been a little severe with him this morning,' she said. 'Any woman would have done the same.'

Withers entered with a note. Elizabeth glanced at the hand-writing, and turned pale beneath the tan acquired on the cod-banks.

'From him,' she said. 'No answer, Withers.'

'Shall I read it?' said Elizabeth, when Withers had left the room, 'or throw it, as it deserves, straight into the fire.'

'Oh, read it,' said Diva, longing to know what was in it. 'You must see what he has to say for himself.'

Elizabeth adjusted her pince-nez and read it in silence.

'Poor wretch,' she said. 'But very proper as far as it goes. Shall I read it you?'

'Do, do, do,' said Diva.

Elizabeth read:

'MY DEAR MISS ELIZABETH (if you will still permit me to call you so)' –

'Very proper,' said Diva.

'Don't interrupt, dear, or I shan't read it,' said Elizabeth.

' – call you so. I want first of all to congratulate you with all my heart on your return after adventures and privations which I know you bore with Christian courage.

'Secondly I want to tender you my most humble apologies for my atrocious conduct in your absence, which was unworthy of a soldier and Christian, and, in spite of all, a gentleman. Your forgiveness, should you be so gracious as to extend it to me, will much mitigate my present situation.

'Most sincerely yours (if you will allow me to say so),

BENJAMIN FLINT.'

'I call that very nice,' said Diva. 'He didn't find that easy to write!'

'And I don't find it very easy to forgive him,' retorted Elizabeth.

'Elizabeth, you must make an effort,' said Diva energetically. 'Tilling society will all fly to smithereens if we don't take care. You and Lucia have come back from the dead, so that's a very good opportunity for showing a forgiving spirit and beginning again. He really can't say more than he has said.'

'Nor could he possibly, if he's a soldier, a Christian and a gentleman, have said less,' observed Elizabeth.

'No, but he's done the right thing.'

Elizabeth rose and had one more peep out of the window.

'I forgive him,' she said. 'I shall ask him to tea tomorrow.'

Elizabeth carried up to bed with her quantities of food for thought and lay munching it till a very late hour. She had got rid of a good deal of spite against Lucia, which left her head the clearer and she would be very busy tomorrow writing her account of the great adventure. But it was the thought of Major Benjy that most occupied her. Time had been when he had certainly come very near making honourable proposals to her which she always was more than ready to accept. They used to play golf together in those days before that firebrand Lucia descended on Tilling; he used to drop in casually, and she used to put flowers in his buttonhole for him. Tilling had expected their union, and Major Benjy had without doubt been on the brink. Now, she reflected, was the precise moment to extend to him a forgiveness so plenary that it would start a new chapter in the golden book of pardon. Though only this morning she had ejected his golf-clubs and his socks and his false teeth with every demonstration of contempt, this appeal of his revived in her hopes that had hitherto found no fruition. There should be fatted calves for him as for a prodigal son, he should find in this house that he had violated a cordiality and a welcome for the future and an oblivion of the past that could not fail to undermine his celibate propensities. Discredited owing to his precipitate occupation of Mallards, humiliated by his degrading expulsion from it, and impoverished by the imprudent purchase of wines, motor-car and steel-shafted drivers, he would surely take advantage of the wonderful opportunity which she presented to him. He might be timid at first, unable to believe the magnitude of his good fortune, but with a little tact, a proffering of saucers of milk, so to speak, as to a stray and friendless cat with comfortable invitations to sweet Pussie to be fed and stroked, with stealthy butterings of his paws, and with, frankly, a sudden slam of the door when sweet Pussie had begun to make himself at home, it seemed that unless Pussie was a lunatic, he could not fail to wish to domesticate himself. 'I think I can manage it,' thought Elizabeth, 'and then poor Lulu will only be a widow and I a married woman with a well-controlled husband. How will she like that?'

Such sweet thoughts as these gradually lulled her to sleep.

It was soon evident that the return of the lost, an event in itself of the first magnitude, was instantly to cause a revival of those rivalries which during the autumn had rendered life at Tilling so thrilling a business. Georgie, walking down to see Lucia three days after her return, found a bill-poster placarding the High Street with notices of a lecture to be delivered at the Institute in two days' time by Mrs Lucas, admission free and no collection of any sort before, during, or after. 'A modern Odyssey' was the title of the discourse. He hurried on to Grebe, and found her busy correcting the typewritten manuscript which she had been dictating to her secretary all yesterday with scarcely a pause for meals.

'Why, I thought it was to be just an after-dinner reading,' he said, straight off, without any explanation of what he was talking about.

Lucia put a paper-knife in the page she was at, and turned back to the first.

'My little room would not accommodate all the people who, I understand, are most eager to hear about what I went through,' she said. 'You see, Georgie, I think it is a duty laid upon those who have been privileged to pass unscathed through tremendous adventures to let others share, as far as is possible, their experiences. In fact that is how I propose to open my lecture. I was reading the first sentence. What do you think of it?'

'Splendid,' said Georgie. 'So well expressed.'

'Then I make some allusion to Nansen, and Stanley and Amundsen,' said Lucia, 'who have all written long books about their travels, and say that as I do not dream of comparing my adventure to theirs, a short verbal recital of some of the strange things that happened to me will suffice. I calculate that it will not take much more than two hours, or at most two and a half. I finished it about one o'clock this morning.'

'Well, you have been quick about it,' said Georgie. 'Why, you've only been back three days.'

Lucia pushed the pile of typewritten sheets aside.

'Georgie, it has been terrific work,' she said. 'But I had to rid myself of the incubus of these memories by writing them down. Aristotle, you know; the purging of the mind. Besides, I'm sure I'm right in hurrying up. It would be like Elizabeth to be intending to do something of the sort. I've hired the Institute anyhow – '

'Now that is interesting,' said Georgie. 'Practically every time that I've passed Mallards during these last two days Elizabeth had been writing in the window of the garden-room. Frightfully busy: hardly looking up at all. I don't know for certain that she is writing her Odyssey – such a good title – but she is writing something, and surely it must be that. And two of those times Major Benjy was sitting with her on the piano stool and she was reading to him from a pile of blue foolscap. Of course I couldn't hear the words, but there were her lips going on like anything. So busy that she didn't see me, but I think he did.'

'No!' said Lucia, forgetting her lecture for the moment. 'Has she made it up with him then?'

'She must have. He dined there once, for I saw him going in, and he lunched there once, for I saw him coming out, and then there was tea, when she was reading to him, and I passed them just now in his car. All their four hands were on the wheel, and I think he was teaching her to drive, or perhaps learning himself.'

'And fancy his forgiving all the names she called him, and putting his teeth on the doorstep,' said Lucia. 'I believe there's more than meets the eye.'

'Oh, much more,' said he. 'You know she wanted to marry him and nearly got him, Diva says, just before we came here. She's having another go.'

'Clever of her,' said Lucia appreciatively. 'I didn't think she had so much ability. She's got him on the hop, you see, when he's ever so grateful for her forgiving him. But cunning, Georgie, rather low and cunning. And it's quite evident she's writing our adventures as hard as she can. It's a good thing I've wasted no time.'

'I should like to see her face when she comes back from her drive,' said Georgie. 'They were pasting the High Street with you, as I came. Friday afternoon, too: that's a good choice because it's early closing.'

'Yes, of course, that's why I chose it,' said Lucia. 'I don't think she can possibly be ready a whole day before me, and if she hires the Institute the day after me, nobody will go, because I shall have told them everything already. Then she can't have hired the Institute on the same day as I, because you can't have two lectures, especially on the same subject, going on in the same room simultaneously. Impossible.'

Grosvenor came in with the afternoon post.

'And one by hand, ma'am,' she said.

Lucia, of course, looked first at the one by hand. Nothing that came from outside Tilling could be as urgent as a local missive.

'Georgie!' she cried. 'Delicious complication! Elizabeth asks me – me – to attend her reading in the garden-room called "Lost to Sight", at three o'clock on Friday afternoon. Major Benjamin Flint has kindly consented to take the chair. At exactly that hour the Padre will be taking the chair at the Institute for me. I know what I shall do. I shall send a special invitation to Elizabeth to sit on the platform at my lecture, and I shall send another note to her two hours later as if I had only just received hers, to say that as I am lecturing myself that afternoon at the Institute, I much regret that, etc. Then she can't say I haven't asked her.'

'And when they come back from their drive this afternoon, she and Major Benjy,' cried Georgie, 'they'll see the High Street placarded with your notices. I've never been so excited before except when you came home.'

The tension next day grew very pleasant. Elizabeth, hearing that Lucia had taken the Institute, did her best to deprive her of an audience, and wrote personal notes not only to her friends of the immediate circle, but to chemists and grocers and auctioneers and butchers to invite them to the garden-room at Mallards at three o'clock on the day of battle in order to hear a *true* (underlined) account of her adventure. Lucia's reply to that was to make a personal canvass of all the shops, pay all her bills, and tell everyone that in the interval between the two sections of her lecture, tea would be provided gratis for the audience. She delayed this manoeuvre till Friday morning, so that there could scarcely be a counter-attack.

That same morning, the Padre, feeling that he must do his best to restore peace after the engagement that was now imminent, dashed off two notes to Lucia and Elizabeth, saying that a few friends (this was a lie because he had thought of it himself) had suggested to him how suitable it would be that he should hold a short service of thanksgiving for their escape from the perils of the sea and of cod-fisheries. He proposed therefore that this service should take place directly after the baptisms on Sunday afternoon. It would be quite short, a few prayers, the general thanksgiving, a hymn ('Fierce raged the tempest o'er the deep'), and a few words from himself. He hoped the two ladies would sit together in the front pew which had been occupied at the memorial service by the chief mourners. Both of them were charmed with the idea, for neither dared refuse for fear of putting herself in the wrong. So after about three-forty-five on Sunday afternoon (and it was already two-forty-five on Friday afternoon) there must be peace, for who could go on after that joint thanksgiving?

By three o'clock on Friday there was not a seat to be had at the Institute, and many people were standing. At the same hour every seat was to be had at the garden-room, for nobody was sitting down in any of them. At half past three Lucia was getting rather mixed about the latitude and longitude of the Gallagher Bank, and the map had fallen down. At half past three Elizabeth and Major Benjy were alone in the garden-room. It would be fatiguing for her, he said, to read again the lecture she had read him yesterday, and he wouldn't allow her to do it. Every word was already branded on his memory. So they seated themselves comfortably by the fire and Elizabeth began to talk of the loneliness of loneliness and of affinities. At half past four Lucia's audience, having eaten their sumptuous tea, had ebbed away, leaving only Irene, Georgie, Mr and Mrs Wyse, and Mr and Mrs Padre to listen to the second half of the lecture. At half past four in the garden-room Elizabeth and Major Benjy were engaged to be married. There was no reason for (in fact every reason against) a long engagement, and the banns would be put up in church next Sunday morning.

'So they'll all know about it, Benjino mio,' said Elizabeth, 'when we have our little thanksgiving service on Sunday afternoon, and I shall ask all our friends, Lucia included, to a cosy lunch on Monday to celebrate our engagement. You must send me across some of your best bottles of wine, dear.'

'As if you didn't know that all my cellar was at your disposal,' said he.

Elizabeth jumped up and clapped her hands.

'Oh, I've got such a lovely idea for that lunch,' she said. 'Don't ask me about it, for I shan't tell you. A splendid surprise for everybody, especially Lulu.'

Elizabeth was slightly chagrined next day, when she offered to read her lecture on practically any afternoon to the inmates of the workhouse, to find that Lucia had already asked all those who were not bedridden or deaf to tea at Grebe that very day, and hear an abridged form of what she had read at the Institute: an hour was considered enough, since perhaps some of them would find the excitement and the strain of a longer intellectual effort too much for them. But this chagrin was altogether wiped from her mind when on Sunday morning at the end of the second lesson the Padre published banns of marriage. An irrepressible buzz of conversation like a sudden irruption of bluebottle flies filled the church, and Lucia, who was sitting behind the choir and assisting the altos, said 'I thought so' in an audible voice. Elizabeth was assisting the trebles on the cantoris side, and had she not been a perfect lady, and the scene a sacred edifice, she might have been tempted to put out her tongue or make a face in the direction of the decani altos. Then in the afternoon came the service of thanksgiving, and the two heroines were observed to give each other a stage kiss. Diva, who sat in the pew immediately behind them, was certain that actual contact was not established. They resumed their seats, slightly apart.

As was only to be expected, notes of congratulation and acceptance to the lunch on Monday poured in upon the young couple. All the intimate circle of Tilling was there, the sideboard groaned with Major Benjy's most expensive wines, and everyone felt that the hatchet which had done so much interesting chopping in the past was buried, for never had two folk been so cordial to each other as were Lucia and Elizabeth.

They took their places at the table. Though it was only lunch there were menu cards, and written on them as the first item of the banquet was 'Lobster *à la Riseholme*'.

Georgie saw it first, though his claim was passionately disputed by Diva, but everybody else, except Lucia, saw it in a second or two and the gay talk dropped dead. What could have happened? Had Lucia, one day on the Gallagher Banks, given their hostess the secret which she had so firmly withheld? Somehow it seemed scarcely credible. The eyes of the guests, pair by pair, grew absorbed in meditation, for all were beginning to recall a mystery that had baffled them. The presence of Elizabeth in Lucia's kitchen when the flood poured in had never been fathomed, but surely. ... A slight catalepsy seized the party, and all eyes were turned on Lucia who now for the first time looked at the menu. If she had given the recipe to Elizabeth, she would surely say something about it.

Lucia read the menu and slightly moistened her lips. She directed on Elizabeth a long penetrating gaze that mutely questioned her. Then the character of that look altered. There was no reproach in it, only comprehension and unfathomable contempt.

The ghastly silence continued as the lobster was handed round. It came to Lucia first. She tasted it and found that it was exactly right. She laid down her fork, and grubbed up the imperfectly buried hatchet.

'Are you sure you copied the recipe out quite correctly, Elizabetha mia?' she asked. 'You must pop into my kitchen some afternoon when you are going for your walk – never mind if I am in or not – and look at it again. And if my cook is out too, you will find the recipe in a book on the kitchen-shelf. But you know that, don't you?'

'Thank you, dear,' said Elizabeth. 'Sweet of you.'

Then everybody began to talk in a great hurry.

THE STORY OF PENGUIN CLASSICS

Before 1946 ...'Classics' are mainly the domain of academics and students, without readable editions for everyone else. This all changes when a little-known classicist, E. V. Rieu, presents Penguin founder Allen Lane with the translation of Homer's *Odyssey* that he has been working on and reading to his wife Nelly in his spare time.

1946 *The Odyssey* becomes the first Penguin Classic published, and promptly sells three million copies. Suddenly, classic books are no longer for the privileged few.

1950s Rieu, now series editor, turns to professional writers for the best modern, readable translations, including Dorothy L. Sayers's *Inferno* and Robert Graves's *The Twelve Caesars*, which revives the salacious original.

1960s The Classics are given the distinctive black jackets that have remained a constant throughout the series's various looks. Rieu retires in 1964, hailing the Penguin Classics list as 'the greatest educative force of the 20th century'.

1970s A new generation of translators arrives to swell the Penguin Classics ranks, and the list grows to encompass more philosophy, religion, science, history and politics.

1980s The Penguin American Library joins the Classics stable, with titles such as *The Last of the Mohicans* safeguarded. Penguin Classics now offers the most comprehensive library of world literature available.

1990s The launch of Penguin Audiobooks brings the classics to a listening audience for the first time, and in 1999 the launch of the Penguin Classics website takes them online to a larger global readership than ever before.

The 21st Century Penguin Classics are rejacketed for the first time in nearly twenty years. This world famous series now consists of more than 1300 titles, making the widest range of the best books ever written available to millions – and constantly redefining the meaning of what makes a 'classic'.

The Odyssey continues ...

The best books ever written

PENGUIN ✦ CLASSICS

SINCE 1946

Find out more at www.penguinclassics.com